HELD UP

CHRISTOPHER RADMANN
HELD UP

headline
review

First published in 2012 by HEADLINE REVIEW
An imprint of HEADLINE PUBLISHING GROUP

1

Cataloguing in Publication Data is available from the British Library

ISBN 978 0 7553 8919 3 (Hardback)
ISBN 978 0 7553 8920 9 (Trade paperback)

Typeset in Hoefler by Avon DataSet Ltd,
Bidford-on-Avon, Warwickshire

Printed in Great Britain by Clays Ltd, St Ives plc

Headline's policy is to use papers that are natural, renewable and
recyclable products and made from wood grown in sustainable forests.
The logging and manufacturing processes are expected to conform
to the environmental regulations of the country of origin.

HEADLINE PUBLISHING GROUP
An Hachette UK Company
338 Euston Road
London NW1 3BH

www.headline.co.uk
www.hachette.co.uk

For Lesley, Michael, Helena and my parents,
Pamela, Helmut, Betty and Hugh.

And for South Africans, who live it.

It is always yesterday in South Africa.

Christopher Hope, *White Boy Running*

Across valleys of space and time we strain ourselves
to catch the pale smoke of each other's signals.

J.M. Coetzee, *In the Heart of the Country*

The term 'Coloured' is used in its official South African sense to classify a person of mixed race, specifically black and white.

1 second

ELD UP. PAUL VAN NIEKERK is being held up.

He is sitting in his new baby, his bright shining-white 318i BMW, at the traffic lights, trapped in a queue of cars. Now this.

There is a gun. In South Africa there is always a gun. Paul does not have time even to wince as the hand tightens on the trigger.

From the BMW dealership in Midrand outside Johannesburg, Paul has cruised with perfect climate control into this. The snub-nosed gun is right beside his head. The black barrel gleams in the sunlight and its round mouth gapes with obscene promise as it taps once on the glass. There it is: nightmare horror on the other side of his closed window. For who, in South Africa, in their right mind, drives with an open window? And now there seems to be no air, and Paul is suffocating in his own surprise. And his lap is suddenly warm and moist.

Paul tries to think. He is paralysed, yet trying to think. His blood beats like a drum, pounding through his head. He can barely hear. He can barely breathe.

Through the shimmering exhaust fumes, through the

clench of his fingers on the steering wheel, through the split second of the urgent tap right in front of his nose as he stares at the window, he thinks: I am being held up. I am stopped. If I move I might die. If I don't move I shall die.

The moment has a profound depth. Paul knows with palpable certainty that he will not even flinch as the gun explodes the window and shatters his face. In a burst of blood and faster than sound, his last thought will be teeth and brains, a blossoming pearl of lead. The world will implode. Anything has become possible. Anything is good or bad. He is stuck, thinking.

The gun gestures downwards. *Maak oop*. Open the window. The blunt command comes from outside.

Paul tries to obey, but his hands, out on a limb, are numb. They have become part of the steering wheel, fused with the expensive leather. The final tap against the glass is decisive.

Paul's hand presses the button. Nothing happens. Paul's eyes swivel from the hand and the gun, from death to the button on the door handle. His fingers, far away on some holiday perhaps, miraculously make more certain contact and the window purrs past his nose.

He cannot blink. The transparent curtain unveils the heat and the stink of outside. With dramatic grace, it unpeels the horror.

Even the window is afraid, thinks Paul dumbly as it retreats into the metal snugness of the door. He can't stop staring at the slit through which the window has disappeared. The dark divide seduces his eyes. And, of course, you don't look at them. These wild Africans. With their guns – their beloved AK47s and ready revolvers.

Am I racist? The glimmer of a question, that hard-wired thought, flickers through his marvellously intact brain. Paul almost feels the thought bounce off the sides of his skull. The barrel touches his temple.

It is so gentle.

Hande agter jou kop! The voice is urgent, but not aggressive. Hands behind your head! *Stadig!* Slowly!

I am being held up. Paul still cannot move. He has read about this, this . . . *stasis* of fear, a profound paralysis induced by terror. But is he terrified? Is he paralysed by fear?

For too long now he has been held up within his own white skin. Talk about stasis. How can he, a white man, act decisively when in this country a brotherhood of white men has acted so decisively? How can he take charge when his race has dominated for so long? Dominated so insidiously, so destructively. Why, looking in the mirror, he should probably shoot himself. So this stasis is nothing new. His mind jars.

For how long has he been forced to sacrifice the name of action for the sake of principle?

And now the gun. The gun at his head.

In the seconds split by terror, fractured by fear, Paul feels another gun.

This time there are supposed to be guns. It is the army. The exclusive privilege of every white South African male. His mind is conscripted by the past as his flame-haired corporal – *Korporaal!* – screams at him. He screams. Yes, it is not too effeminate a term. He screams in Paul's face. There comes wet Afrikaans spit and abuse, as Paul is a conscientious objector. He is a rare breed, an endangered species. Possibly about to be culled.

A paradox. A man unmanned.

Carefully, conscientiously, he has objected to his body being called up to serve the system. He has registered his distress, again not too effeminate a term. His distress at having to learn to bear arms against a sea of troubles. How can he shoot? How can he hold up a gun in the name of the National Party? How can he, by such impossible actions, help to secure another strut in the architecture of apartheid?

And so Korporaal Krause screams in his face. *Fokken poes*, the man screams.

Paul stands to attention, rigid. He was ready for this.

To be called a fucking cunt in Afrikaans. To be emasculated in the language of apartheid, with its sharp consonants and crushed vowels. He, a man, standing up for what he believes to be right, is called a cunt. Moral rectitude is debased in sexualised, reproductive and female terms. When did conscience become cunt-sense? Paul almost grimaces, it is so ridiculous.

Korporaal Krause must sense his desperate amusement.

For here comes the gun. Underpinning the verbal abuse comes the cold metal, an R4 assault rifle.

Is it loaded?

The rest of Paul's platoon stand rigid. Forty-five men. Holding their breath. They know Paul. Paul, the man who with two other men in Bravo Kompanie has started basic training with a broom. Going through all the manoeuvres on the parade ground holding a stupid broom. He is not a bad man, just a stupid man with a stupid *blerrie* broom. They want to laugh. They do laugh at the incongruous sight. They laugh at his humiliation and laugh to keep their own humiliation at bay. They laugh too because they know that they could not do what he does. Skitter van Niekerk. Rifleman van Niekerk. That is his ironic rank in this perverted system.

The flecks of spit feel cold on his face. Korporaal Krause is not as tall as Paul. The Afrikaner has to tilt his head and stand on tiptoe to face up to him. The rifle comes snaking up under his chin. Korporaal Krause's hands brush his chest as he holds the assault rifle, and its delicate tip touches Paul under his chin on the soft skin, so recently shaved at 5.20 a.m.

Paul swallows, a reflex action to the searching kiss of the R4.

This blond Afrikaner will not shoot. Paul has heard of insane officers, mad majors. But this *korporaal*'s actions are calculated. He is insulted. Paul senses the man's outrage.

Maybe he will shoot?

Ek vra nie weer nie, the *korporaal* whispers.

The touch of the rifle becomes an uncomfortable lump in his throat. Paul cannot swallow.

And then Paul knows that maybe this man will shoot. Make an example of him. And his wry self-righteousness yields to the immediate threat. His arms go lame, his legs suddenly limp. He sinks on to the thorn of the rifle, pinned upright by the spike of hard metal.

This stasis of metal. This shock of uncertainty. Stuck in his white liberal skin.

Paralysis.

But is he paralysed?

And now he is being held up once again. This time, the stuff of urban legend. Yet another dinner-party-conversation set piece. And this very scene he has visualised a hundred times. A hundred thousand times. His car or his wife's car. The gun.

The agonised and protracted wince before the bullets. There were always bullets.

They took the car and they shot you.

They didn't take the car and they shot you.

You cooperated and they shot you.

You tried to stop them. They shot you.

Pumped lead into your soft white head. Blasted your brains out, so you dropped dead.

They held you up – then they dropped you.

Bang.

He wonders if you ever hear the sound. He wonders if a word like bang can express the death that smashes from the perfectly round metal mouth? The mouth that now kisses his temple.

Ek vra nie weer nie. I won't ask again, said quietly, almost whispered. Is his assailant afraid that he might be overheard? So different from the spitting screams of Korporaal Krause. No point to prove. Nothing conscientious about this, and highly objectionable. Here in the middle of the midday traffic. Surrounded by gleaming cars, bright windows that burn with the sun and blinding disinterest. Uninterest.

Who would give a damn? Who could? Try to help and you end up dead. Bloody fool.

Paul's hands find their way to the back of his head. One clasps the other with rough relief. Aren't your hands supposed to sweat?

Another black arm snakes into the car, the handle clicks and the door springs open with appalling enthusiasm. The intruding hand jerks. *Uit. Klim uit.* Get out. *Nou!*

This is it. Paul knows that he cannot move. He will be shot

where he sits. The blood that pounds through his body will gush into the soft leather of the seat like a sigh, seeping through the bullet-torn perforations. The bullets will have ripped both him and the car seat to shreds. He and the seat: seamless, in a scarlet pool, crimson. Yes, the accusation: crimson – a bloody crime. His body screams out against the crime, committed in warm blood.

Has he gone mad? The memories, the fear, and now the warm, wet crotch. Just like the army. Is this a war?

The free hand, the unencumbered black hand, grips a chunk of his hair and rips. Paul is half pulled from the car before the strands tear free from his scalp. For one second he comes face to face with the black man. So ordinary. The shining skin, the flat nose and thick lips. The hair is short, kempt. The face is impassive, like a wooden mask. It is beautifully polished, any one of a million, million African statues: sculpted faces that scrutinise tourists with dark disdain beneath an impossibly blue sky. Black heat that almost sings. Paul feels blinded.

But their eyes meet.

Paul slithers unheroically out of the side of the car. It does not happen in slow motion. No. It is quick and sudden. He is simply born, yielded up by the uterine car. His seat belt zithers loose; it is a limp umbilical cord. And he is a foetal man, half coiled, half kneeling on the hot road. A pink prawn.

He is kicked aside. A rib snaps with a wheeze and he rolls to one side. The car door slams, the engine roars.

Hissing tyres, and gravel flicks at his head from the side of the road as the car jumps the queue. There is a brutalised engine, diminuendo. Gone.

That's that.

Gone.

Half a dozen cars pant with fear and relief.

Now worms. White, wormlike hands, helping hands, emerge from the surrounding cars. Brown hands too. This is the new South Africa. Brown hands help white. Heels scrape on the tarmac and shuffle closer. Voices shimmer in the midday heat. *Ag shame. You orlraait? Hau, this is not good. Fooi tog. Kaffir. Die nuwe Suid Afrika. Ag shame, man. The new South Africa! You orlraait? Hau, man.* Particular and political expressions of sympathy and concern – safe from the recent past. Unearthed. The rock has rolled and there seem to be worms. Possibly delirious, Paul is helped to his feet.

Eyes flinch in case they missed the shot. But he is whole, although there is blood dripping from his scalp. A few nasty rivulets run down the side of his face. Really dark, more purple than red. Weird. Voices murmur into cell phones. *Yebo, yes, ja. Hijacking. On-ramp to N1. Midrand. Flying squad. N1. One man. Black – ja, sorry man, but that's a fact. True. Gone. Buggered off with the oke's BM. White – the car. Him also. White. No. Not shot. You aren't shot, hey? No, he isn't. White. Blood – from his head, man. But not shot.*

Paul stands and stares. Cars are already on the move. Wheels susurrating past. Mesmerising black circles rotating the road. Paul watches them dig into the tarmac and send it sliding behind them. That is how it seems. He is dizzy. He can't really hear much. The cars seem now to be tiptoeing. Almost embarrassed. Tiptoeing off stage into the wings – flying off.

Side windows are sealed. They shine. The harsh sun and the merciless blue of the highveld sky. Sealed windows. They – we – are meals on wheels, Paul blinks. Mobile lunch boxes. Metal picnic hampers. Takeaways for those who starve, who do drugs, violence, adventure. Who knows in South Africa?

And then he realises that his baby girl is still in the car.

What makes him remember?

What made him forget?

1 minute

H IS GUTS FALL THROUGH A cavern in his body in a whispering instant. His baby girl, Chantal, is still in the car. She is now a whole world away and moving fast.

He wants to run. He must run after her. The impulse is ripping his intestines. They are caught in the slammed car door and being driven off at an impossible speed. Paul van Niekerk is disembowelled by the horizon.

He staggers towards the robots that flash green-orange-red. He feels like an astronaut on some strange moon. His head balloons like a glassy bubble as he tries to shout her name, her soft name. His daughter, his beloved daughter.

How long did they wait for her? And now she is gone in an instant. Just like that.

Their little longed-for miracle. Now miraculously vanished.

Almost as miraculously as when she first appeared from out of her mother's body. The first time he held her up to her mother. A water birth; he was there. After all the medical attention, they wanted a natural birth. What could be more natural than water? Chantal was born to the world in soft water and held up to her mother by his very own hands, now suddenly a father.

They wept as she was delivered to them. The archaic phrasing, delivered of a child. Come from somewhere else, from heaven. A deliverance.

Claire lying back in the raised bath at the Marymount Hospital, Johannesburg, which specialised in water births. As natural as possible. No more test tubes, no more screenings and charts and sperm counts and statistics and injections. No, their fears had become warm flesh. Chantal had taken root. She was alive.

Mother and daughter doing well.

Claire lying back exhausted. Somewhat hoarse. Giving voice before giving birth. Paul was amazed at how vocal and primal the entire experience had been.

He was used to Claire crying out during their lovemaking. She was rather carefree when it came to expressing her passion. But these grunts and gurnings and gasps had been of a different order. And order was the order of the day.

He was ordered here, there and everywhere. The midwives kept him busy. He was a mere man, an appendage. Moderately useful (certainly nine months ago), but an appendage none-theless. He was instructed, Here, help fill the birthing pool. Run the taps. Watch the cold water. Is it warm enough? Check. There is the thermometer in the pool. What does it say? Quick. Now rub her back.

Paul was quick. Paul rubbed her back.

Rubbed his wife's back as the water filled the pool – actually, more of a bath. Rubbed his wife's bare back as she crouched with her backside in the air to slow it all down. But Chantal was in a hurry. Did not want to be slowed down. After waiting and waiting to be brought into existence for all those years, nothing was stopping her now.

Nothing will stop her now, Claire managed to smile at him from somewhere beneath her pain. And Paul, far away, on the other side of the world, stuck in his lumpen gender, beamed and rubbed for all he was worth.

He wanted to laugh out loud. His pregnant wife was naked, with her bare bottom in the air, panting and heaving and trying not to crawl over the bed and up the wall. He rubbed her back and murmured sweet nothings. His deep voice strove to be hushed and low in this most female of spaces.

Then the uniformed midwives nodded and he brought his wife from the little bed on the one side of that cosy room to the raised bath several shuddering metres away. They made it, he and Claire, together, across the aisle of space and time. Claire walking as though on shattered glass, as though she might actually levitate out of the bulging pain that dragged at her belly, below her belly, out of her utmost, innermost self. And Paul supported her, stalwart at her side, easing her over every centimetre, his resonant voice, now soft, urging her on. Whispering her over the final millimetres as she began to panic.

Was this the right thing? Could she do this? She couldn't do this. Paul!

Darling. His anxious eyes. His firm arm, helping her.

Darling, you can do this.

Keeping his voice sure and steady as she wavered. God, who wouldn't waver? Paul supporting her in amazement at the power of the here and now. His blonde, beautiful wife caught up in the biology of the moment. Ancient, but here, as old as the hills, but now. All-consuming. Their entire lives lifted up to this moment, now, as Claire panted through the pain.

She clambered, a pink ape-woman, into the deep bath that was raised up to bring her to their level. But she had found her own level. A grateful flick of her eyes that caught at his heart, then she was puffing and panting again, disappearing to some new, primitive plateau. Claire was digging through geological layers of pain and flesh to emerge triumphant with her treasure, their treasure, the flesh of their flesh.

He could only watch.

They gave him a net, a little scoop. He felt like a child on some strange seashore. Whilst the tides of Claire's contractions ebbed and flowed, grunted and groaned, he played safely on the shores of existence, scooping up little bits of past meals. There had been no time for an enema. Their child was in a rush to be born. Just as Claire, it would turn out, had pushed her way quickly into the world.

Mid-scoop, Claire reached out and grasped his arm. Don't let me go, she said. Don't ever let me go.

He had left the scoop and held her arm. He did not let her go. He held on for dear life, for his dear wife. But the contractions had pulled her loose. She wavered and slipped. She was gone into herself, into her pain. Paul lost her to the tides of pain that pulled her away, that made her eyes unseeing and her ears deaf to all but her own panting and her screams. She groaned and shuddered from a different world.

Chantal crowned.

Paul saw a piece of his daughter for the first time. A sliver of white hair amidst the black as Claire gaped wide.

When they said, Push, it is time to push, Claire did not hear them. Then the moment passed, before it returned with redoubled intensity. This time, Claire pushed. With an almighty heave and a tearing gasp, Chantal was born. From an impossible mound in the middle of his wife, a wondrous midden of uterus and guts and amniotic fluid and blood and flesh, there slid out into the oily water their own pink prawn. The love of their life.

There were stunned tears. The adrenalin burst and the shock of relief sank deep. Chantal's first sound, a wavering, watery cry, amidst their crying. Then Paul was offered the surgical scissors and he cut the tough cord, forever freeing Chantal. Through the pain, through the gasping storm and through the water she had come.

Now she is gone.

Nine months with them, now their baby is gone. Nine months inside Claire, nine months in the wide world with her mother and father, now she is gone.

He tries to shout her name, but he chokes. He rolls in the hot sun and spins through the cars that move away. Chantal has been ripped free. Some other cord has been cut. His mind tears. The afterbirth, it seems, drags from his scalp. He clutches at his torn hair and he gasps. He moans. He seems to beat at his head. As though to beat the thought of his stolen daughter back in. Birth in reverse. His head is bursting, but it is empty. He hits himself. There is no one else to hit.

A large Afrikaans man restrains him. His meaty hand catches Paul on the shoulder. *Wag, my seun.* Wait, my son. The hand is gentle. The beard moves again in a fatherly fashion. It's Paul Kruger. Straight from the history textbooks. The beard moves and Paul hears sounds. The police, they'll be here soon. The bearded man's great hands grasp his arm, restrain him. He must not beat in his own head. The man leads Paul by the arm back towards his *bakkie*.

Most of the other cars have slunk away.

There is one black woman yammering into her cell phone, her car pulled off at the side of the road. Another, older woman, her car also dislocated from the streaming traffic, stands anxiously by.

She comes over to them, shaking her head. She's in shock, the older woman nods in concern at the cell-phone woman.

Paul struggles to make the connection. He feels as though he is still running down the highway. He feels as though he might still tear through time and pull Chantal back from the brink. Yet he has just been unravelled, like a woman. Never before has he felt what it must be like to be a woman, the world dropping from his insides, pulled inside out. Not thrusting, but feeling, giving, having to give.

That black lady's been hijacked before, says the woman. This has sent her a bit *mal*. She looks at Paul. You all right? Her eyes appraise him.

He will be better when the *blerrie* police get here, if they ever do, says the Afrikaans man. Come, he leads Paul to the driver's seat of his *bakkie*. I've got a *dop* for you.

Paul stands blankly, holding his stomach. Can he ever sit in a car again? The man guides him into the seat. Paul sinks into the cockpit of despair.

The man reaches past him, down the side of the driver's seat, and pulls out a small flask. He grins as he unscrews the cap. Just a *doppie*, he offers Paul the silver flask. I sometimes have just a *klein doppie*. Mostly to survive the *kaffir* taxis. It's my own *witblits* – my own white lightning home brew.

Paul reaches out to the flask. It is like a baby's bottle. His hands shake uncontrollably.

The man pretends not to notice. He takes Paul's fingers and closes them around the little cylinder. Then he thinks better of that idea and raises the flask to Paul's lips himself.

It'll do you good, he says. *Gee jou 'n bietjie krag*. Put some fire back in your belly.

Paul chokes as the liquid flames sear his throat. The man chuckles. That's the stuff. *Kolskoot*. One more *dop*. Paul splutters again. His intestines twang off the edge of the world and leap back inside his body. They seem to snap back audibly.

Does she want a *dop*? The man gestures to the woman still sobbing into her phone. He seems to have taken on the role of parish priest, offering an impromptu communion.

I'll check. The older woman totters off on high heels.

They wait.

Paul still shakes. He can't stop. Stress, the beard jerks in the direction of Paul's fluttering hands. I had it in the army. On the border. When I shot my first *terroris*. He is trying to make conversation; it is kindly meant. Just after I shot the *bliksem* . . .

Paul's stomach writhes and he throws up over the man's steering wheel and dashboard.

What made him forget?

1 hour

HIS WIFE DOES NOT TAKE it well. How can she? Her daughter – their daughter – has been taken. Well, what can she say?

The police car drops him off at Claire's work. A plush place, a house in Morningside. She works for an educational NGO. Running Saturday-morning classes for township children. Trying to give them something more than they have got: a future. The black parents she meets are desperate. The township schools are no good. The kind legacy of apartheid. The parents' hunger, their desire to establish a future for their children, is truly humbling.

She is not expecting him. She has no clue. She is hard at work somewhere in the house.

He gets out on the pavement and thanks Sergeants Dhlamini and Rapele.

The statement at the Midrand Police Station took an age. Rank with a heady eau de cologne of sweat, piss and puke, he dictated a clear statement, and watched in disbelief as the duty sergeant chiselled each word on to the form. Three times his voice, still rich and resonant, had to make clear that his name is Paul Owen van Niekerk. Eventually he offered to fill in the relevant sections himself. No, the sergeant carefully and unhurriedly explained to Paul Owan, *hau*, sorry, Owen van Niekerk, that that was his job. The sergeant formulated another word and seemed to step back from his creation with genuine pride. Paul felt like ripping the Bic pen from his hand and screaming.

Each second that slipped by took Chantal Claire van Niekerk further and further into South African obscurity. What if she were abandoned at the side of a dangerous road? Thrown from the car – his mind jarred there, fortunately. And she would need her bottle. She would need a nappy change. She has been chuckling recently and is on the verge of saying Dada. She might be crying.

Occupation? The sergeant's pen quivered.

Paul stared at him. Chantal . . .

Professional? Business? Self-employed? the sergeant started to ask.

Teacher, Paul said, then shook his head. That was last year.

Advertising, he said. Copywriter, with BB&P. Badenhorst, Brown and Patel. In Sandton.

BB&P? the sergeant repeated.

Paul leant against the counter as his world tilted and threatened to tip him off its edge.

Now, the two kindly policemen reverse their car and Paul presses the intercom buzzer at the imposing security gate with its crown of razor wire.

The early-afternoon sun throbs on his scalp. There is a lawnmower meditating somewhere, humming a gentle *aum*. He can almost smell the incense of freshly mown grass: rich, sweaty sweet, essentially green. He coughs drily. A voice crackles beneath his thumb. Hello?

It's Paul.

A cheery *howzit*, metallic. His wife's boss, also called Claire. The electric gates crank open. The brick driveway shimmers redly all the way up to the front door. The windows regard him as windows always tend to: impassively.

Behind him, the police car saunters off to a world of crime. The two policemen wave.

Paul has to think, consciously think how to move his feet, to lean forward, to move. An inertia, something more terrible than fear or horror, holds him back. He carries something so utterly dreadful to his wife. What could be worse? Our child is dead? That is at least decisive and final. But, our child is gone . . . I know not where . . . And worse still. I let her go. I did not fight for her life. There was a gun. I opened the window. I was dragged from the car. It drove off. I never even called goodbye, my little pet. I never thought about her until she was gone. Now she is gone. And I place this news at your feet. I sink you in it up to the knees. Our daughter ripped from the loins of our love. What is happening to her right now? In this land of ours. Our rainbow nation. Our tiny pot of golden joy.

The front door opens. Claire the boss calls out. Come on, man. I have to close the gate! Behind her is Claire, his wife.

She steps past Claire. My God, can she know? Can a mother know? She runs down the redbrick path.

It is Paul who stalls. He cannot move forward, only down. His legs buckle and he sits slowly on the steaming drive, the hot bricks biting through his damp trousers. The gate cannot close.

Claire stops before she gets to him. Cautious. A mother's instinct. Her hand flutters to her face, her other reaches out to him. Past him.

Chantal!

Their daughter's name is a bleat. He almost does not recognise it. His wife barks again, like some wild deer.

His voice is speaking. He feels it in his throat somewhere. Words, masculine and guttural. There is a rumble. She is shaking his head. Her icy hands clutch his face and she shakes him. Chantal. Chantal. Chantal. Hysterically.

Like the time she locked Chantal in the car. Such a simple mistake when you are forever having to fiddle with locks.

Always such a palaver, this locking and unlocking and relocking in South Africa. Keeping things safe. The few who have, keeping things safe from the many who have not. And so this rhythm asserts itself. Security gates across gated complexes that are buzzed back, often by guards or by remote control, beeped from the car. The unlocking of car doors to get out, the relocking of the car. The unlocking of security gates across front doors. The unlocking of front doors and quick rush to the panel to disarm the alarm. Then the locking of both sets of doors, just to be double safe and secure. Unlock and relock. Unlock and relock.

And so it was with Claire's old Honda Ballade that she unthinkingly locked by depressing the little knob then slamming the door shut with Chantal and the keys inside. Force of habit. The usual, safe rhythm and ritual now a shocking aberration.

Paul was not there. He was taking an afternoon football practice. And there was Claire standing with all Chantal's things, but no Chantal. The tiny baby trapped in the car.

No matter how she beat at the door, how she tugged at the metal, the car remained closed. Claire was frantic that Chantal would begin to scream. That she would see that this was no game and would stop gurgling to herself and jerking her little legs in that happy spasmodic way. The sun was beating down and the car was already beginning to get hot.

Claire hurried inside and called the breakdown people. They were on the road, the operator said. It would be a while. My baby, Claire gasped, my baby. They would be there quick as they could, the operator said.

No one else in their townhouse complex was at home. All out, out earning a living. But there was the guard. The black, uniformed man at the gate. Gideon. Claire ran up to Gideon. He was startled. Expected trouble to come from without, not within. He looked at his gate; he looked at this desperate white woman who was clutching at a pain in her belly, dancing before him.

He came quickly. There they stood, side by side, peering in the obtuse, hard window at the baby girl in pink who was getting red now. Red from the heat and from crying.

Again Claire beat her fists against the tough glass. Confounded by metal and glass. Her baby a reddening goldfish. Her little mouth opening and closing.

A coat hanger, madam, a metal one, the guard suggested, tugging at his ear.

Of course, Claire ran back inside. Where was the breakdown service? Where was a metal coat hanger?

She shoved the only one in the house at the guard. Then she watched the black man try to break into her car.

He wasn't very good at it.

Claire watched him try to get the prong right, a long looping arm made by unwinding the hanger. Then he had to attempt to prise the car door open a fraction, just a few millimetres. It did not budge. Claire ran through the house again to their back garden to get a spade.

They rammed it in at the top of the car door, scraping the paint, digging for treasure. But then the metal arm of the coat hanger loop kept slipping off the little knob that locked the door. And all the while the keys dangled jauntily inside.

The car was becoming hot to the touch; Chantal would soon be roasting. Could they just bend the door back? Break off the door?

It was too strong, too secure.

Where were the breakdown people?

In the end Gideon used a hammer that Claire had found. They chose the front window on the passenger side, as far away from Chantal as possible. The hammer bounced off the glass. Were they cursed? This impregnable metal and glass, rubber and hardened plastic.

Eventually it shattered, spraying Chantal with a benediction of crisp glass, not too sharp because it was made not to shatter into sharp pieces. Gideon carefully inserted his arm, popped the little knob and opened the door, delivering Chantal safely to her mother, who was too stunned to weep.

She could only stagger inside, leaving the black man standing over a suspicious scene with a hammer in his hand and a spade at his feet.

But this, this here, this now is no simple mistake.

And there is no Gideon, and no happy ending.

No black man in uniform has helped them here.

No.

Oh no.

It is a very different black man who has had a hand in this.

Is it at all like the time Claire locked Chantal in the car? What is wrong with him?

Paul stares up at Claire. His hands try to find hers. He can't seem to see properly.

Then she slaps him. His face jolts to the garden. His ears sting and ring and the side of his neck burns. The lawn-mower steadies itself and renews its peaceful incantation of suburban bliss.

She falls to her knees and finally his body snaps into gear. His tongue comes unstuck. Calmly, with dreadful lucidity, he tells her.

Has she registered the information? Has Claire understood? There is no pause before she speaks.

When did you realise Chantal was in the car.

It is not a question. No.

So, when did you realise.

He cannot say.

He wants her to rant and rave. He could deal with that. Hold her. Hug her. Maybe slap her as she slapped him. They would be together, dancing their way into their news, or maybe clutching at each other like swimmers in this blinding murk. Claire loves to dance. She is an excellent swimmer. Surely they can do this together?

That bloody car. A new BMW. What did you expect? That bloody car.

Unlike him, she does not splutter vomit all over the sizzling bricks. No strings of saliva glisten from her lips. Her lips are red and tight. Her face is firm.

It is Claire, the boss, who goes to her. Puts a hand on her shoulder. Helps her up.

The boss turns to him.

Jesus, she says, seeing Paul's head for the first time. The torn furrow at the side of his scalp, black with dried blood. Jesus.

Paul's hand reaches for his beaten rib. Yes. Jesus. Gentle Jesus, meek and mild. Suffer the little children. My little child . . . our little Chantal.

Chantal. Chantal. Chantal. His wife chants.

Jesus, he thinks dumbly.

11 hours

SIX O'CLOCK COMES AND GOES on that particular day, that first afternoon-evening-night without Chantal.

It is bath time. At least, it should be. Claire is beside herself with fear and anxiety. The contours of her life threaten to collapse.

She stops pacing. She can wring her hands no longer.

Give me something to do, she demands of Paul.

Tea? he responds. Tea? Coffee? A hug?

Claire takes a deep breath. She tries to take stock. Then she falters.

She could be crying, Claire cries out. Our baby girl could be crying. Who will go to her? She needs her bath. It's six o'clock. She needs her bath.

Paul goes to Claire, but she has turned and run. Upstairs, there is the familiar sound of water splashing into the bath at the familiar time. Paul stands transfixed.

The late-afternoon sun streams through the dining room window. Dust motes dance in and out of the golden glow. Drifting. A patch on the yellow-wood table shines with silver fire. The gentleness of the everyday setting cuts him to the quick. Here it all is. Yet she is not.

Safe and sound. Yet she is not.

It must be like this when your child dies.

But it cannot be. Chantal must be alive. Her ghost does not haunt the family hearth. Everything is here in its proper place. Yet she is not.

She is missing. She is out there.

Paul turns to the front door. There it stands, dumbly. Stupidly closed. Beyond it, the security door, slam-lock safe and metallically secure. Then the bricked driveway that runs to the road that snakes through the townhouse complex to the towering electric gates beside the guardhouse. There, the black men in uniforms keep out the black men without uniforms. Keeping in the white folk, and the odd rich Indian as well as Grace and Happy Mabuza, the Zulu sisters who live next door, a pair of fat spinsters, podiatrist and dentist. Foot and Mouth.

Paul's mouth twists at the familiar joke. Then beyond the gates with their razor spikes and electric wire, the rest of Midrand. Snug townhouses pooled together and moated by brick and barbed wire. Little bastions of separate development set against the veld and the blue, blue sky. Paul feels the grass wave in a ripple of midsummer heat. The eternal veld cut to ribbons by the busy roads that lead to the N1.

One way Pretoria, the other Joburg. Soon to meet in Midrand.

The N1. The concrete highway. Blinding white and a-dazzle with cars, trucks, motorbikes, *bakkies*, taxis and somewhere, recently, a white BMW driven by a black man with Chantal stuck in the back. Asleep and silent. Abandoned by her stupid fucking father.

Paul's head rings as he smites his brow. He wishes he could punch himself properly, but he can't. His fists dance before his eyes, clenched. The ripped hair on the side of his head stings, and he sways in a flurry of salt-and-pepper dust motes, bathed in the golden light of the low sun.

Chantal swims before him, her head resting against the side of her car seat, a Farley's rusk damp and gnawed but now forgotten in her chubby hand. A dark shape hunches over the steering wheel – or leans back, arm around the passenger-seat headrest, casually manoeuvring with one hand, changing lanes with a proprietorial flick of his wrist. He has got away. There are no sirens. When does he glance in the rear-view mirror and see the sleeping bundle of joy? What does that unknown black man do then?

Paul feels drunk. He could do with a drink.

Upstairs is quiet.

He does not want to think about that driver. He cannot stop thinking. He is not much of a drinking man but he really could do with a drink.

He cannot taste the *witblits* that the bearded man gave him earlier that day. And it did not settle his nerves. He cannot recall the kindly face. There is just the man's voice and his beard, his big beard. What a tangle of hair. Why would a man in this day and age grow a beard? Goatees are in vogue, but a full face of hair? It is almost primitive. Then the flying squad officers arrived, the crawling squad, the limping squad, in a blaze of sirens. But everyone was gone. Chantal was long gone. Only the black woman and Paul Kruger and his beard remained with the man with the torn head, the daughterless father.

They stood together in the baking heat. Thank God, said the kind black lady at the last peep of the siren.

The two cops eased themselves out of their car, which hunched, suddenly silent, at the side of the road. Paul wanted to run up to them gesticulating wildly. He wanted to turn from them in a parody of despair. He thought, simultaneously, that he might accuse them, point a trembling finger at them. Where had they been? Why had they come only now, an hour too late? And you call yourselves the *flying* squad?

Instead, he told them what had happened. His trembling voice was shored up by the sturdy tones of Paul Kruger and by the black woman's precise observations. This is what happened. This is how that man, Paul van Niekerk, was hijacked and his daughter stolen. The cops nodded, took notes. The little trio came to the end of their story. That was that. Chantal was gone. About an hour ago, for Christ's sake.

The cops, their faces a blur, seemed to absorb Paul's words like khaki sponges. One returned to the car and murmured into the radio. The other one looked at the three of them.

This is serious. He spoke suddenly. *Ja*, this is serious, man. Vehicle hijackings, they happen all the time, all the time. He rubbed his pencil against his cheek, facing up to the facts. But a child in the car, that is a problem. That is a *moerse* problem.

They stood there.

Then things started to move. The cop in the car emerged, his radio crackled and coughed behind him. He strode up to them. We have broadcast your registration number to all units, he quantified. They have the details – heading west on the N1, about an hour ago. Black driver, white baby, Chantal Claire van Niekerk. We have your contact details, but we shall take you to Midrand Police Station. There are some forms to fill in. That will help us.

And so he left Paul Kruger and the helpful black woman. He never remembered asking their names. Like his daughter, he was driven off in a car. He was delivered to the police station and made to give his details again, all over again. Then he was told that he could do nothing, must do nothing. He was instructed not to alert the press. He must wait. There might be a ransom call, they might find the car, they might recover Chantal. The possibilities were reeled off. One by one they reinforced that he must do nothing. He must sit tight. And then, like a child, he was delivered by another car to his wife's work, into her unsuspecting arms.

His mouth turns dry. He could do with a drink. He urgently needs a drink.

Paul glances towards the small bar area in the *lapa* outside. On the other side of the tiny pool. He looks back to the stairs behind him. He almost has to shake himself, pinch himself. There is no chortle of slippery limbs or happy endearments. No cooing or gentle jokes about the elephantine wrinkles on their daughter's legs, their little pink elephant. Their chubby pork chop. He should be up there washing her hair.

Paul pauses.

It is too quiet.

He bounds up the stairs, two at a time.

Claire is not in the bathroom. Chantal's little plastic bath, perched over theirs, is dripping with warm opalescent bubbles.

Paul charges into their bedroom. A towel with a damp

imprint on their bed. Cream, oil and a disposable nappy waiting. The nappy is a strange, soft, empty pelvis. Plumped open and wide with a gap for the missing body and lost legs.

Is this an omen? The empty nappy. Like Claire's empty womb.

He is dragged back to a time, a dark time, when the universe seemed hollow and despairing and populated by other people's darling children. And they had no prospect of a child of their own.

They seemed to spend their lives hearing about fecund friends. How often did they write endearments in ghastly cards adorned with all manner of cute and fluffy mayhem, congratulated their friends on yet another baby.

Whilst their own lives were screwed to some strange sticking place. First the waiting. Waiting for a child and wanting a child. Then the worry as the months slid past and no child came.

And it was the new South Africa. It was the birth of a new nation, a birth that everybody could celebrate proudly. For everybody had had a hand in this miraculous birth, so longed for. So late in coming. Another deliverance. And Paul and Claire van Niekerk longed so specifically for their own child. They ached for a child amidst all these wonderful beginnings.

Then their worry intensified.

Then came the doctors' visits. Then the tests and smears. Claire was given the all-clear.

He was the one.

It was all down to him.

Holding hands as they received the news.

The reassuring squeeze as Claire held his hand and he rolled with the blow to his manhood and his marriage.

It was he. Betraying their bodies. Unable to assert himself in the simplest of ways.

But there was treatment.

There was no blockage in his tubes, and no varicocele – no enlarged vein on his testes that would raise the temperature and render him infertile. No, it seemed that it was something to do with his pituitary gland. He fell into a minute proportion of men, one or two per cent, the specialist beamed the news like it was something special. As opposed to identifying him as the man in the marriage who had something wrong with his head that was preventing them from experiencing the profound bliss of parenthood. That his brain had somehow hijacked his balls. More of a fucking pacifist than he ever suspected.

Shocked to the core.

He felt like thumping his head. Beating up his own head, giving the goddam pituitary gland something to think about.

It was Claire who held his arm.

It was she who said, be logical, think about it. At least there is a cause. And then she echoed the ebullient doctor. At least we do not fall into the forty to fifty per cent of couples where there is no identifiable cause. And whilst she smiled at the specialist and listened to the proposed treatment of a series of injections over the next half a year, Paul could only hear the mad echoes: it is the cause, it is the cause, my soul, juddering from his set texts.

Be logical, said his wife, the dancer, the swimmer.

He stares at the hollow nappy. Deep down he feels again

the sense that he has hollow balls. He is tall, yet he is called Paul, meaning small. He is a man, yet he does not have the fucking balls. His hands shake again. He is drowning.

Claire, he calls out at last. He flounders into her reply as he rounds the corner of Chantal's pink room.

It is a ghastly, muffled sob.

Claire has clambered into Chantal's cot. Face down, she weeps into the tiny mattress. Paul freezes beside the door, almost stumbling against his own momentum, which suddenly seems impetuous. Impulsive. His wife's grief is so orderly. The bath, the bed and now the cot. At six o'clock.

Paul wants to reach out and touch her.

But like Chantal, she seems a world away. Lost in the tiny cot and the coiled spasm of her private grief.

Paul hovers in the door. God. He really could do with a drink.

Paul stands in the living room. He gulps down a whisky. The light has left the yellow-wood table. In the growing gloom he finds himself staring at the wooden giraffe. Superior and supercilious, it stares back. His eyes travel down its long neck and legs. Gathered round it, he notices with a start, the carved heads. Black faces. On a low ledge, a series of black heads, the usual objets d'Africa, preserve a stony silence. He has never noticed their malevolence before. Their eyes, or the dark holes where they would have eyes, regard his knees or his groin for they are situated at that height. It cannot be the whisky. He has had but one slug. He wants to cry out. How dare they? Here in his home. At his very hearth and in his home. With trembling hands he approaches them. One by one he turns the dreadful dark faces towards the wall. Like bad schoolchildren. Evil little homunculi. Please, not in his home. Not in their secure complex. He pours another whisky and stumbles outside.

There is a violent sunset.

Paul wanders around their tiny garden. At his head, the heavenly mayhem. At his feet, the bloody sky is reflected in the swimming pool. A world of spectacular brutality. And all the time he feels his cell phone in his pocket, waiting for the call. Waiting to hear the news.

Paul sips a whisky and scoops a flotilla of drowning insects from the pool with his free hand. It is usually Claire's habit, he knows, part of her compulsion for order and rectitude, but tonight he feels that this act of kindness might trigger some reciprocal response in the universe. Every beetle, bee, ant, butterfly, fly and now moth might add up to Chantal in some strange heavenly reckoning. Most of the insects struggle gamely in the searing fire of the sunset pool. They beat and whir, then cling with brave legs as he hoists them to safety. He does not use the net. No, his immediate helping hand is better. He splashes the ones in the middle of the pool towards the far side. A few have given up the fight. They hang in the water, little foetuses from another world, bent and coiled around their scaly suffering, their overwhelming loss. He scoops them out too, breathes on them, tries to resuscitate them. Amazingly, a few do stumble to life, do suddenly lurch back into drunken momentum across the bricks that still pulse with the warmth of the day. The sun that warmed the bricks shone on him that day. Shone from a great height on all that happened that day.

He cannot believe all that might happen in a day. A mere day. A lifetime of a day. Paul blinks.

The sky is now the colour of his whisky. He has the satisfying sensation that he is drinking the sunset. He has become God. The world is his. Part of him thinks that there must be a slogan in there somewhere, but he does not hold on to the thought. Instead he enjoys the billowing sense of the alcohol and the benign bending and scooping, bending and scooping of insects from the whisky pool.

When it is dark, he switches to brandy and Coke. Around him, the lights of other lives signal supper and living rooms and television. Through open windows stream the sounds and scents of a small cross-section of Midrand. Garlic, the smells of garlic and seared meat waft like ghosts across the garden. And those aromas are tinged with bacon and eggs. He smiles into his drink. Surely Happy and Grace are not having bacon and eggs for supper? He thinks that he could have bacon and eggs for supper. He feels intensely alone in his tiny garden with the black pit of the pool at his feet. He marches unsteadily inside.

Claire, he calls.

Claire. His voice stumbles thickly over the monosyllable of her name. For a moment he wonders whether he has called *Clear* or *Klaar* or *Claire* in the darkness of their home. His voice feels furred.

It is clear that Claire is still upstairs. Paul ambles towards the kitchen and almost trips over Claire's foot.

God, he says. He wipes some drink from his hand.

In the blackness she is seated beside the phone. In fact she cradles the phone in her lap. It is a little plastic baby held gently, still trailing a coiled umbilical cord. Her delicate hands hold the phone so that it does not slip and wake up. But surely they want to jolt it awake. Surely they want to shake it, want it to cry out with the jangling news of Chantal's discovery. Surely.

Paul stands before her, over her.

He feels her move. She looks up at his black shape born out of the surrounding darkness.

She reaches out a hand and touches his side. Her hand slides partly around his waist and she draws him closer. She leans forward and presses her cheek against his thigh.

Paul feels her inhale to say something, but she says nothing.

Then her voice does come. Talk to me, she says, small and clear.

Paul braces himself. He tightens his grip on the squat glass.

I have been doing the pool, he says. I know you like to . . . His voice trails off. Her face is warm against his leg.

I don't mind, she says. Just talk to me.

There was an incredible sunset. His voice is off-kilter, then settles into its deeper rhythm. She has always loved his voice, he knows that. Yes, he is a tall man, more or less good-looking, he knows, but it is his voice, the rich, resonant promise of his voice, that won her heart. Won him the first prize of a beautiful wife. Petite to his height. Blonde to his brown. Neat and nice to his more casual, not-quite-tucked-in self.

A *helluva* sunset. Suddenly he finds that he has no more words to add to that scene of silent, celestial blood. He stands there, lost for words. He leans against his wife's warmth.

He begins again. There were lots of insects in the pool. A pair of dragonflies. Brilliant blue. He tries not to let the effort of each description drag at the buoyancy of his voice. No ladybirds, though. Not a single ladybird. They must have all flown away home. He stops close to the edge of that particular cliff. Then, gamely, he describes a bumble bee in its striped felt jacket and pollen jodhpurs.

She chuckles. He thinks she chuckles. The sound is low and deep. Jodhpurs. The ridiculous word, jodhpurs. Urgent yet satisfied. Jodh-purrs. Why might Jodh purr? Who the hell is Jodh?

She is chuckling soundlessly. She grips his leg. He steadies his glass, then quickly drains it. She isn't crying?

I am starving, his voice announces. Are you hungry? I thought I might make some bacon and eggs. I think Happy and Grace are having bacon and eggs and suddenly I wanted some bacon and eggs.

At first he thinks she might be shocked by his urgent appetite. But then, it is well after eight o'clock. They usually sit down to eat at eight o'clock.

She holds on to him in the darkness. She takes a deep breath.

Let me make them for you, she says.

Let's make them together.

Okay.

You sure?

Yes. She lets go and stands up. The phone crashes off her lap and she gasps.

In the dark, Paul scoops up the mess of receiver, appliance and the ridiculous cord that always knots itself in a stupid tangle. He returns the receiver with a snug click to its cradle and tries not to think about cords and cradles. He needs another drink before any midnight breakfasts.

Within eight hours, within four hundred and eighty minutes

of their daughter's disappearance, they cook together. Like man and wife. Like a single couple. Like lovers.

She cannot talk about Chantal. She cannot say much at all.

So in the kitchen, it is a strangely companionable silence that they share. Paul finds himself sipping another brandy and Coke, offering her a drink yet again and being refused yet again. Claire does drink, but then she likes to have more than one. Paul likes to watch her drink. Sip her cool Chenin Blanc and gently slip into her more loquacious, comfortable self. It is as though with each sip she is shedding something. Stripping. She begins to be revealed. So many layers to his wife. Her cool exterior is stripped back and a hotter, more libidinous self is liberated. Her Chenin Blanc is like her lovemaking . . . but the beeping of the microwave intrudes.

Claire defrosts some bacon in the humming microwave. Paul slices two tomatoes. And an onion. His eyes weep but he feels dry-eyed. Claire, he glances furtively at her, looks remarkably composed. It is like charades. Let us see who can act out being composed. The whisky burns his stomach. The pair of tomatoes seem to wince then bleed. The onion winks then weeps.

Claire opens the fridge and it is then that she makes the dreadful discovery that they have no eggs. No eggs at all! She steps back, her lower lip trembling. How could that be? How could she have forgotten?

I could pop next door, ask Grace and Happy, Paul offers neither too casually nor too sincerely. He tries to speak Clairely. Clearly.

Claire shakes her head.

Will she burst into tears?

I'll go, she says fiercely. Then more lamely, I'll go.

Paul lets her go. He waits for the clank of the key in the security door, then somnambulates himself towards another brandy and Coke. It is the last of the Coke, it seems. In the fridge, the empty egg box swims past Paul's eyes and he clutches at it and takes it out. He remembers using the last three eggs when he made Chantal and himself some scrambled egg on Saturday morning. His fingers wave in front of his eyes. Two days ago, or three if you count today. Three fingers waggle sadly at him and the egg box broods.

Suddenly he has to sit down. He does so on the kitchen floor. He is overwhelmed by an egg box. Tears do flow now. They stream freely from his eyes. He does not sob. His rib aches intensely and his stomach still cramps from the ghastly vomiting and vomiting in that man's *bakkie*.

The egg box swims before him. He looks through his tears and stupidly finds himself trying to read the copy on the box. Sunshine Farm Eggs. Free range and extra large. The folksy slogan in honest imitation handwriting: *Start every day the Sunshine way!!!* Simple, he thinks. And rammed home with three exclamation marks. His new, copywriting self smirks idiotically. Then he burps and wonders if Chicken Little would agree. Or Old Mother Goose? And then it is one drunken slip back into the old ways. The fey, whimsical mode of the English teacher.

Yes, his mind wanders off along avenues opened up by alcohol as he weighs the egg box in the palm of his hand. How does all the writing in the world prepare you for this? He hopes Claire comes back soon, to save him from himself. His mind slips and slides. What is the loss of an Ophelia or a Cordelia or even a Jessica to him? He reaches for his glass. Or a neat sonnet about the marriage of true minds? Come on, Claire.

He addresses the egg box in his most resonant voice, raising it up in pathetic mockery. Alas, poor egg box, I knew her well, he intones. He stares foolishly at it. Then changes tack. With faux severity he scolds it. About suffering, the old masters, he employs his most emphatic tone, were never wrong. *Never*, he repeats aggressively. The egg box does not flinch. Maybe that is it, he thinks with obtuse profundity as the microwave beeps again. Maybe Auden was on the right track with his poem about Bruegel's Icarus. Shit happens somewhere out there in the corners of other people's lives and the world goes on and an egg box outlives your daughter.

For a moment he cannot believe he has just thought that. That he has dared to think that. Stupid. He knows it is the alcohol. He blames the alcohol. He smashes the glass from him and staggers to his feet. He is going to be sick again. Where is Claire?

Claire returns as he emerges from the little downstairs loo, wiping his lips. He sees her and has to rush back in and retch drily for another rib-tearing spasm.

Eventually he trusts himself to return. He is resolved to weather the storms of egg and bacon that gust from the kitchen. As he enters, Claire is coming out with two plates swimming with food. He gulps.

Bring the tomato sauce and Aromat, she says.

He brings the tomato sauce and Aromat to the table and sits down. She is cutting into her egg and the gush of yellow yolk is an almost physical sensation. She squirts tomato sauce into the carnage and sprinkles Aromat over the entire scene.

Given her fastidious nature, he is always amazed at how she eats. The spices, the large portions, the bleeding steaks. She glances up at him and points to his knife and fork.

Put that stupid egg box in the recycling, she says, and eat your food.

He pads back to the kitchen obediently, noticing the fragments of glass in a neat pile on the kitchen counter on top of a square of paper kitchen towel. He returns.

He picks up his knife and fork then puts them down defeated. Claire crunches into her crispy bacon. She lets out a few words as she chews.

I didn't mention, she munches, what happened today. I mean, to Happy and Grace.

He nods. She does not seem to be noticing that he cannot eat.

She bites some toast loudly. I still don't think we should say anything just yet. To our families.

He nods. That's what they decided earlier. Their bosses both know. Have been very understanding. But to spread the news begins to make the situation seem more real. Will underscore and reinforce and emphasise the terrifying absence in their life. Will fling the loss of Chantal across the world.

Yes, he says. You are right.

She reaches across the table and touches him on the hand. Your eggs are getting cold, she says.

I can't, he confesses.

Do you mind? She points her fork and he shakes his head. She scoops one of the eggs on to her plate and the bloody tomato sauce appears again. Paul watches her closely and she knows it. She tucks a stray strand of blonde hair behind her

ear. Her bobbed hair shimmers as sh
rhythmically and her dainty hands con
mouth with fastidious . . . he searches for
ferocity, that's it.

Her grey-green eyes flicker once or twice in
he is not sure if she bridles under his gaze. Pau.   .r
another drink, which she refuses with a gesture at her ..kfast
plate. But why not have another of whatever you're drinking,
she says. She continues to eat.

It is too quiet in the house. They both realise that simultaneously. The silence is not the full, happy-bellied silence that
Chantal's slumber upstairs would represent. No, it is an
oppressive hollowness above them. It is the terrible distance
between them and their daughter. That distance expresses
itself in the silence that stretches in all directions. Even Claire's
chewing merely emphasises that absence of baby-sound.

Claire, he finds his mind jarring. Claire.

She has stopped chewing.

He could not begin to pretend to chew.

She has forced the pretence one step further. But now she
falters. She looks as though she has just been punched in
the stomach. She must have a mouthful of dry toast lodged
in her throat.

A prickle of sweat breaks out on Paul's brow. He is watching
again the poor creatures writhe in their last spasms of life. But
now Claire is coiled up inside herself. Claire is drowning and
she has just realised it. Claire the erstwhile champion swimmer
is drowning like a blonde dragonfly.

He knows that she looks back on her adolescence with
undiluted horror. All that swimming. All that training. The

urs and hours – months, even years, when added up in a terrible calculation – spent in a vast rectangle of anaemic blue. Her skin, she said, was never free from the stench of chlorine. Despite the tight seal of her swimming cap, her hair was brittle. She was crowned by success and the stink of a childhood spent swimming. Pounding up and down the lanes, marked in black along the bottom of the pool, and the floating barriers that shredded the waves and trapped their watery traffic. Up and down. Hermetically sealed into her goggles, nose plug, ear plugs, swimming cap and costume. Not to mention a punishing schedule that had her in Joburg by 5.45 a.m. Starting her day even earlier in her mother's car – before the shock of cold water. Then up and down, up and down. Butterfly, backstroke, breaststroke, front crawl. The individual medley. That sounded mellifluous, almost musical. Individual medley. Yet Claire told Paul that it did not disguise the brutal fact that she, they, punished her body. And that she enjoyed every minute of it. Even after the Terrible Thing That Happened when she was fifteen – or perhaps because of it. The power, the control. The way her lithe form sliced through the water sending a perfect V behind her as her muscles rippled and sang in complete harmony. A performing aquatic poodle. A young girl buoyed up by success and pliant liquid.

But now she is drowning. The look of intense surprise as she finds herself out of her depth. A completely different pool demanding a wildly different skill set. Plunged into shock and horror and fear, she is drowning. She is stunned. He sees the violent meekness with which she succumbs. Paul watches her as she puts down her knife and her fork. As though, unencumbered, she might be able to float above this. But she continues to sink. Her jaw is rigid, her mouth filled with food that she can neither swallow nor spit out. There are no lanes, no markings in a pool, no shrill whistles from the coaching staff to guide her, to help her swim better, swim faster. Swim at all. No butterfly stroke for this drowning dragonfly.

Paul stretches out a hand. His warm hand touches her arm. It is freezing with thin sweat.

She grabs his hand, aware at last of a lifeline. She lets him draw her closer towards him. Her locked jaws prohibit sound. Then she shakes her head and is quietly sick on to her plate. He leaps to her rescue but she shakes her head and is sick again. Her trim body shudders. If you can vomit neatly, Claire vomits neatly. Paul stands beside her. And her spasms turn to sobs and she is weeping and at last she allows him to hold her. To sink with her in his arms to the floor and to come to rest against the leg of the table. They drown together. Her arms are clasped around his neck and she weeps in time to his tears, to his heaving chest. This is no individual medley now; it is a duet of grief.

They are together for a long time.

Sobbing and shuddering, faces wet with tears. Wiping their faces and holding on for dear life to the only body left to them.

At last they are silent, aching and sore, quiet at the bottom of the pool.

Then, as if on terrible cue, the telephone rings. The sound is calamitous in the yellow air.

Their faces leap towards each other, jumping in fearful hope. Their lives instantly whittle down to this single point: the telephone, the sound that comes jangling from afar.

Absurdly, they hesitate.

Then Claire attacks the phone in a single lithe movement. The receiver almost fumbles from her grasp and she gasps her greeting.

Claire van Niekerk. She gazes far away into the dark world out there.

She is instantly crestfallen. Lucky, she says. Hello, Lucky. Her eyes flick despair at Paul. No, not at all, she says. Of course. There is a pause. Do you really think so? I would never have believed that. She plays a dreadful game of conversational give-and-take, rolling her eyes at Paul.

Lucky must sense that something is amiss. That someone is missing. Surely. She blathers on. Okay, Claire nods, her voice tight as can be. Yes. Are we still on for Saturday afternoon? She mimes despair at Paul, who stares transfixed. Let me check with Paul, she says.

She brings the phone to her chest. Surely Lucky can hear the thumping-thumping pain and grief. The almighty strain on their hearts.

Claire and Paul stare at each other. There is no way that they can socialise on Saturday afternoon. No way at all. They shake their heads together. Or they want to shake their heads together. But they cannot.

Claire raises the receiver and whispers down the line.

What can we bring? She offers, close to tears. She fiddles desperately with her fringe. Okay, my three-bean salad. Are you sure? She stares in horror at Paul.

Paul slumps back. So this is what reality sounds like. Never mind Chantal, let's all organise *bring-and-braais* and three-bean salads for Saturday. What will they say on Saturday? What can they possibly eat?

Claire puts down the phone. Lucky, she says redundantly. Saturday at three. I wanted to say no, but I couldn't.

Paul nods. She would have asked why, he says. You would have had to tell her. You had no choice.

I had no choice, Claire says, and Paul nods.

Claire looks at the phone nestled in its cradle and trailing its coil of cable. Paul tries to speak, tries to tell her to come to his arms.

Then, like a baby, Claire drags herself away from the phone and crawls to Paul's arms. They lie together, children together, cradling the empty space between them, together.

They cannot think of Saturday. Today has banished all Saturdays. The future has been made redundant.

They have been cast adrift on the shore of the present. Worms on the hook of a terrible now. Paul cannot stop thinking of the insects he lifted from the pool. He and Claire lie like insects clutching at the terrible, nauseating enormity of it. Clasping the very thing that drowns them.

After a long time, the smell from Claire's plate forces them to move. They unwrap themselves gingerly. The hard block of their baby's absence has not softened. Will they go mad?

Claire helps Paul to his feet. He has further to travel, it seems.

She bears the plate of cold sick to the kitchen.

Paul manages to locate his legs and he slowly clears the table. Then he finds himself in front of the fridge. He gets another drink. A leftover Windhoek from some *braai* or other. He does not care if it makes him sick again. He feels sick to the soles of his feet anyway. Claire pokes something in the sink.

Paul opens the back door and almost falls into the garden. He takes the can to the edge of the pool and then cracks open the beer. His hands must have been shaking as it sprays a shot of foam into the black water. Shit, he says for no apparent reason. He is not one of those South African men who weigh beer and blood in balanced scales. Shit. His voice cracks in the back garden and then comes peeling softly back at him off the bricked sides and satellite dishes of the other houses.

Street lights glow with fuzzy yellow halos around him. A car drives past on the main road nearby, slows at the four-way stop, falters briefly, but keeps moving.

He sips his beer and glances up. Despite the light pollution, the African sky vaults hugely above him. Stars gleam and twinkle. Orion's belt and Orion of course. The Southern Cross with its two pointer stars. The Seven Sisters. Sirius the dog star. They're all there in the right places, pointing to the right places.

His daughter is in the wrong place. He wishes with his aching, aching rib that he could reach up and over to where she must be and scoop her little soul into his tender hands. God. If he could pray, he would. His sister would, he knows that.

Finally, his neck hurting, he looks down on to the flat water of the pool and drinks his beer.

Claire comes and sits beside him. Her knees are tucked up under her chin and she stares at the pool. They do not speak. They do not need to speak.

The sky swivels slowly. Lights wink out and Midrand settles down for the night. Claire has switched off the kitchen light deeper in the house, and a greater weight of darkness has come to rest on the garden. Their bedroom curtains shift slightly in the wafting air and then the house is still. Paul gets another leftover can from the *lapa* fridge – an Archer's cider this time. He sits on the bricks, still vaguely warm from the heat of the day, and removes his shoes. His feet dangle in the pool and he drinks the cold cider sip by sip. Claire does not want anything.

Paul stares into the pool.

Chantal and Claire. Claire and Chantal. Himself. A cameo of South African life. But that has changed. He has the oppressive feeling that they are living an opaque newspaper headline or becoming a meaningless national statistic. Well, so much for statistics. He is also aware that there has been talk of a moratorium on crime reporting, to boost morale in the Rainbow Nation. He tries to shake his head. Hide the clouds and the rain, and where is your rainbow? Surely you have to bow to the rain, at least acknowledge it, in this new nation, this new sunny South Africa.

With each mouthful of fermented apples and fizz, he feels a strange welling up. It is not phlegm or bile or half-digested alcohol. There is a different kind of pressure. It seeps up from the pool, from the stars on its reflected surface. It presses down from their bedroom window and wells up within him. He wonders if he truly knows himself. Who is this man who sits with his feet in the pool whilst his wife huddles by his side? Why this parody: man and booze? Does he really wish to relive that day so that he might grip the hijacker by the throat and scream and throttle him? Does he tremble with fear or with impotent rage? There are glimpses.

Bed, says Claire.

Shall we go to bed?

Paul winces. To the bed where they tried again and again to make Chantal.

He places a large arm around Claire.

You go up, he says.

Darling? She looks up from her knees, her face pointed like a pixie.

I'll be up in a while, he says, waving the can, a handy prop. His toes squirm in the black water.

Claire kisses him on the cheek. I'm sorry I slapped you, she whispers to the very cheek she slapped just a few hours before.

Paul chuckles. He makes a sound like a chuckle and kisses her and Claire wanders inside, lost and alone.

Then Paul raises a limp hand and uselessly thumps that very cheek again and again. If only by beating up his body he could bring back Chantal. He hits the side of his head, which feels like one of those obtuse wooden statues.

It seems as though he could cry again. But he cannot.

The night sky wheels slowly above him. It is getting cold.

He tries to stand up.

When he knocks against a series of crushed cans, sending three into the pool, he realises that it must be late. In many ways it is too late, but he knows that he must. He is on his feet, pulling socks and then shoes over the sticky-wet skin and yanking at his laces. Like a man, he marches inside, but then pauses, decides to tiptoe. A pen, a scrap of paper, a terse message left on the kitchen counter. She will think he is crazy. But he has to.

He did that. Now he must do this.

Crazy.

He moves. Swift and silent and almost sober.

So.

So, the message left on the counter. Claire's car keys whisked off the hook marked Honda Ballade. Cell phone secure in his pocket. Front door silently unlocked. Security door negotiated then both locked behind him. Horrible wince as he beeps open the ghostly white Honda with the scar in the paintwork. Sinks by painful degrees – bloody, bloody rib – into the cool leather and suddenly realises that another steering wheel confronts him. Slow breath – not too deep. Another slow breath. Adjusts the seat for his long legs. Hopefully he has not drunk too much. Can you be drunk without drinking too much? He has drunk too much. Ignition, reverse slowly then forwards up to the main gates and a pause for Gideon – is it always Gideon? – to open the gates. They clatter open – the usual thought: thank God we don't live next door to the gates – and the Ballade sings out of the complex. It is a confounding aria.

Does one ever truly know oneself? He drives the very route that he and Chantal took but ten hours ago. He was Mr Casual. Mr Easy. The Big Easy, just like Ernie Els. Who then is this dark and dangerous man who grips the steering wheel of Claire's car and sends this ton of metal careering wildly towards the on ramp of the N1? Who is it that speeds up past *the site*, and accelerates through the orange light, savagely bending the little car to his will and the tugging curve of the road? Who is it, and why does this man torture the 1,600 engine so that it screams past a flurry of tail lights and bashful headlights and guns towards the N1–N3 junction?

Alexandra or Soweto? The two big townships. One northeast, one south-west of Joburg. Which way shall he go?

Who decides to take the N3 Eastern Bypass towards Alex? The Honda throbs down the highway, and after a sweaty few minutes, Alex appears on his right-hand side. She is a sprawl of lights, but also great bowels of darkness in which tens of thousands upon tens of thousands of men, women and children eke out an existence. Apparently, that is the case. Before, he has simply driven past it. Half city, half informal settlement – or squatter camp in the common parlance. It is a township. Always adrift of what used to be a white town.

He suddenly slows down.

What if Chantal had been hurled from the car? If the hijacker had slowed down before entering Alex, maybe he turned and, with a quick hand, unclipped her from her car seat, gripped an arm, tugged her on to his lap before flinging her like a *stompie*, a cigarette butt, from his window.

He slows right down and scans both sides of the road for his baby daughter. The road is hard and new, and is flung up rather quickly by the headlights. He slows down even further and unwinds the window. He drives with his head lolling in the midnight air, still warm and sticky. He starts to smell the smoke of the township.

Chantal's mangled body, her fluffy head, appears in the beam of his headlights. Before he can cry out, she becomes the tangled beige fur of a dead dog, horribly splayed and twisted. Shaken, he picks up speed. The stranger at the wheel of the car begins to feel more uncomfortably like himself. His breath catches in his throat.

He takes the Alex exit. With his lights still on bright, he swings towards the unknown township. He is overtaken by two Hi Ace taxis. They career past him, spurting luminous dust. He follows them, whilst still scanning both sides of the road. Lots of litter, but no daughter.

The road twists and turns. There are suddenly shacks. And people. A man walking off into darkness. A woman at the side of the road. He passes someone in running gear, jogging with glowing heels – a strange black Hermes. There are more shacks as well as little houses with fenced front gardens. He drives past a deserted café, a petrol station, a KFC and a *drankwinkel* ablaze with neon light. The taxis disappear at turn-offs. He tries to keep on straight. But then a junction forces him to make a left turn, then a right. The car has become a little aimless now.

He still scans the side of the road, but it is the tangled cluster and clutter of neat homes and shanty town that starts to overwhelm him. Starts to crowd around him. The shadows cannot hide the squalor. The cans and the plastic bags. He is astounded at the sheer number of plastic bags that drift and are scarecrowed against every fence and pole that he sees. A sea of waste that is flung up by his lights. And dogs. Their dark shapes and gleaming eyes. God almighty, he hears his voice say. God almighty.

Several people swim out of the yellow pool of a street light ahead of him. They turn to face the car. He slows down and a man, a drunk, lurches out of the darkness against the side of the Honda. Paul tears at the wheel. The car spins to the left and Paul sees the man stagger off, back into oblivion. Terra incognita. Terror incognita.

He has to stop the car. A panic wells up all around him. He knows that he must keep moving. It is only the thought of his baby girl alone in this place that keeps him perversely sane.

If she is here, he must keep looking. There is a chance. Statistically. Surely statistics can also work in your favour?

He struggles for a moment to find first gear. The car jumps skittishly. It too seems nervous. The rough road grinds at its wheels and Paul has to steer clear of potholes and *dongas*. Whatever rage had carried him this far has now evaporated. Paul feels small and alone. He cannot imagine what it must be like for Chantal.

Yes, she is nine months old. Yes, wherever she is she must surely have dropped off to sleep. But if she is here? Here!

For an hour he negotiates the squalid, unquiet darkness and some of the strangely sectioned neighbourhoods. The fall and sprawl of Alex. Every few minutes he feels that he might be lost irretrievably. His eyes feel as though they are bulging out on stalks and the torture of the day grinds his nerves. Twice he forces himself to stop, to open the door and to stand on one hesitant foot, listening. Once it is quiet, once there is a knot of voices in a back street seemingly arguing. Men shout and a woman or a boy screams like a pig. He jumps back into the car as though bitten. He begins to sweat. He fights away the obvious echoes of E. M. Forster's Marabar Caves and Conrad's heart of darkness, here, reverberating all around him. Literally, he wipes his brow. What would Dante make of this place? Or Dickens? Or Milton? Or Marlowe? But he has left his set texts and examination courses behind him. He is off the neat, prescribed page. He is in Alexandra. How might one make sense of Alexandra?

He kicks the car into gear and drives some more. He feels vulnerable as well as hermetically sealed in the glowing white Honda Ballade. Ridiculously, he could be in a game reserve, he thinks. On safari in a wild land. And all this on his doorstep. This, this is Africa. But where he lives is somewhere else. Yes, he is Ernie Els, Ernie Elsewhere living in an oasis – no, a fortress – in a foreign land. He thinks of Claire and begins to turn back towards home. He knows that he has no idea where home is. The roads are barely signposted. Part of him, most of him, does not want to abandon Chantal, and he forces himself to think logically, to think that she could be anywhere, absolutely anywhere, not just alone in Alex.

Somehow the little car picks its way back to a main road and from there out on to the highway. In a remarkably short space of time he is on a first-world strip of tarmac that bears him back to civilisation. Conrad would be proud of him. He feels empty and dry. *Mistah Kurtz, he dead* stupidly beats in his head, but he is too overwhelmed to care. He slides away from Chantal and the dead dog and all that darkness. He drives the little white car gently, even tenderly, back to Midrand.

He arrives home and parks the Honda. Back through the security door and the front door. The house is quiet. He returns Claire's keys to her labelled peg, so specific and precise, and sees that his note is exactly where he left it. He shoves it in his pocket and sinks into an armchair, letting the quiet, familiar smell of the house wash over him.

His hands eventually stop twitching. He swears he can breathe the scent of Chantal as though she were in the room with him, cuddled up on his chest. He tries just to inhale. To breathe her in, not out. And the warmth of her burns and burns in his chest.

1 day

PAUL KNOWS THAT HE HAS not slept a wink, and yet he awakes with a start, clutching at his chest. She is not there.

For a moment he thinks he has hallucinated the entire expedition into Alex, but his hand locates the crumpled note in his pocket. He takes it out and reads it in the bright light of another summer's day. He shakes his head and shoves it back.

He is aware of Claire's hair dryer as soon as it stops. What time? It is seven o'clock. Right on time.

Both of them have been given the day off. What is Claire up to?

He does not have to muse much longer. His wife walks steadily down the stairs. He sees her appear, high-heeled feet first, legs, hips, and there she stands before him, looking as though she is off to work.

Claire is impossibly neat and trim. Her figure, a little fuller after Chantal, was quickly beaten back into shape. She almost wore out the rowing machine upstairs. Rowing for all she was worth across the same tiny ocean of beige carpet. To and fro, to and fro. With a faraway look in her eyes.

Her face with its clear lines of jaw and nose holds his gaze confidently. Her eyes are beautifully framed by mascara, her lips shine redly. She stands above him, a picture of professional femininity. So cool and crisp. He smiles up at her. He feels the need to hold her, to cup his hands over her breasts and reassure himself that they are warm and pliant beneath her collared shirt, so beautifully ironed and straight.

As though sensing his impulse, Claire bends down to him. Her perfect nails trail over his cheek, rasping gently against the stubble. He stares straight at her cleavage.

Darling, he says thickly. His tongue seems swollen.

Paul, she replies brightly. Then, more tenderly, Darling. I waited for you. You know I hate to go to sleep alone.

Paul holds her hand against his cheek. It is so small and soft. And he does not have to wonder whether her nails are freshly lacquered or whether they match her lipstick. He holds her hand. He does not want to say, I ran away. Not only did I go looking for our beloved daughter, a tender needle in a haystack, but I ran away from our chewing and spewing, from the drowning insects and empty egg boxes and my infinite limitations as a father and a husband and a man. I had to escape normality under such extraordinary circumstances. I am not as strong as you are. You are made of sterner stuff. Remember, I am the man with the faulty head that almost cost us Chantal. Your body runs as smooth as clockwork. My cheeks need to be shaved just as my stupid body had to be injected all those times. For all those months and months. And after half a year, the wait, then nothing. Then the repeated course of injections to get my fucking system going. Whereas your periods came and went in perfect red splashes. First the twinge of ovulation pain, a pang of potential. Then the slightly raised temperature. Then expectation. Then nothing bar a general irritability and the blood marking the end of another cycle of despair. And so on, and so on. And all the while you waited for me to catch up. To be kick-started. As you ached for a child. Remember how you ached for a child? How you kept yourself trim? How you kept yourself in perfect shape, ready to receive me? Ready to respond to me the moment I could fulfil my function, my basic calling as a man? Remember how our lovemaking was never free from fear? There was love, yes. But there was also the making. Always the making. We were fearfully making, attempting to make. Making love, but also using our love, engineering our love to make a child. Remember those times? How brave you were. There must have been moments when the bitterness almost broke through? When you were not spared another bitter period spot-on time and there was no Chantal? But you never said a word. There was no reproach. No accusation. No crime. Just the usual crimson blood.

But you must have put on a brave face. Along with your make-up. A perfect face. What can I know, a mere man, of all that flowed beneath those menstrual tides and L'Oréal make-up? As I strained and heaved and you waited to receive me, waited for my tardy sperm as all around us the new South Africa was being born and all our friends were giving riotous birth. All except for Lucky and Sunny. Thank God for Lucky and Sunny, even though their dogs and house and new garden are their children and that is fine as far as they are concerned. That is their strange choice.

But we were of an age. Our country and us. It had to happen.

He looks up at his perfect wife and does not want to say, I

am not as strong as you are. I had to run away from all that you are – just for a few hours. That's all. But do stroke my cheek. Please, darling, do stroke my cheek.

He rubs his cheek against her smooth hand.

I'm sorry, he says more distinctly. You know, he begins, then stops.

Claire turns her body and perches on his lap. She is light, almost like a child. As though from another world, he feels himself stirring strangely beneath her.

I suppose sitting here was like a vigil, he says. Another kind of vigil. Back to waiting, just waiting. Hoping and waiting. I'm sorry, I didn't really think about you.

She looks into his face.

We will get through this together, she says. Her statement of simple fact astounds him.

Get through this? Paul finds himself repeating.

What is this? His mind locks on to the thought. What is this? He has no term in his vocabulary for *this*. *This* cannot be named, surely? *This* state, *this* limbo, *this* hollow but over-whelmed feeling. Can it be got through? Crossed or traversed like a river or a region? All that is required is their own Great Trek?

The full force of Alexandra drags at his gut. Terra incognita. How do you cross an escarpment of fear and horror.

Paul makes a moaning sound. Together, he says, I can only really think of *together*. He draws her closer. You and me, we're strong enough, together? He does not know why he frames it as a question when he knows it as a declarative fact. *Eendragt maakt macht* as the Union had it. *Unity is strength* used to be the watchword of the day. Was stamped on all the coins. Unity in the Union of South Africa. He realises that he dare not go on to explore that premise any further. Like too many captions and slogans and mottos and brand names. Just advertising. Mere politics.

Instead, he clasps her closer to him. For a moment he believes that she will rest her head on his broad chest, that he will stroke her as she lies there, the top of her head fitting perfectly under his chin. That his deep voice will resonate through her and that he might gently remove those terribly formal clothes, unstrap her, release her. And that they might be together in the most urgent and immediate way. Together, comforting each other, making their way through this. Making love, creating tenderness where the world has been less than tender.

Claire adjusts her arm. He does not think that she is struggling, even though her blouse must surely crease. Her shoulder digs into his side and softly elicits the most exquisite pain from his broken rib.

His cry causes her to push away, which sends yet another stab right through his chest.

Paul, she says.

God, his eyes are closed. God, my rib, sorry.

When he opens his eyes and wipes away the tears that have sprung there, she is on her feet.

Have you taken the Disprins? She seems cross. Almost petulant. I'll get you the Disprins.

Claire, he says, but she has gone to the kitchen.

She returns, rotating a glass so that the tablets dissolve in a merry fizz.

Claire, he says again, taking the glass and swallowing

quickly. He holds on to the glass as she tries to take it. Claire, we need to talk about my baby.

Your baby? she says very quickly. She's my baby. Too.

Habit, stupid habit, he knows. From the song. You are my sunshine, my only sunshine . . . sung so often to Chantal. Our baby, he corrects himself.

Her eyes flutter behind their feathered mascara.

He tries again. What, he says, what if we just don't hear? Or what if the news is bad?

Claire lets go of the glass so that it jerks back towards him.

No, she shakes her head so that her blonde bob ripples. No, she repeats emphatically. That is why we shall go to the *braai* on Saturday. We must be ready for Chantal to return. I have thought about it all night. We cannot go mad. We must be normal.

Paul feels the glass, round and hard and normal in his hand. Claire, he begins, but she cuts him short.

Don't you agree? Chantal cannot come home to chaos. We must be ready. Chantal will come home. Chantal will come home.

For a terrible second Paul thinks that Claire is going to run screaming into the walls of their home. That she will brain herself screaming, Chantal will come home, Chantal will come home in a desperate female mantra, the precise emotional chaos that she wants to avoid. But his wife is made of sterner stuff. Up and down, up and down. She is more used to patrolling the barriers of ordinary life. That's what kept her sane in the past, after that other Terrible Thing. And even now she dives in, swimming with quick, elegant strokes. Reach and pull, reaching into the dull water above her head and pulling it past in a shimmer of ripples and powerful swirls. Her head is steady, her mouth is a neat O and her feet churn the liquid into a bubbling blur. She can swim all right.

Don't just sit there, she says. Get ready. We have to get ready. Not a moment to lose.

Her backstroke is sublime: she is able to reach far behind her with a rhythmical elegance that cuts through the water and quite takes the breath away.

He stares after her as she turns, a neat tumble-turn filled with explosive energy, and straightens the curtains. She is off and away with quick strokes. God, she can swim. Then she gets the keys and unlocks the back doors, throwing them open to the greenness and the fresh air and the shafts of brilliant sunshine. Another perfect day. This could be a television commercial.

You might want to shave, she says as she swims past en route to the kitchen. The coffee machine starts bubbling and he identifies the deft chop of a grapefruit being split in two. He cannot move. He sits and weeps and doesn't care that his tears trickle through his stubble and dribble down into his sweaty shirt. He is drowning.

When Claire comes into the dining room with their equal halves of pink grapefruit and her seventy-five grams of Kellogg's All-Bran, he gives his face a quick wipe and clambers upstairs to the bathroom.

But he does find the strokes of the triple-bladed razor soothing. He is saved to some extent by the ritual of water and foam and the smooth, sweeping, familiar motions that clear such definite channels across his cheeks. He avoids his eyes, and like his wife, he now tries to keep moving. Shower, as hot as he can bear it, an aggressive lathering despite the wincing of his side, then the immediate comfort of a fluffy towel.

He smacks his aftershave antiseptically all over his cheeks before he goes to the built-in cupboards. Then he sees that Claire has set out his clothes on the bed – that, seemingly, he lies on his side of the bed like a neat cardboard cut-out: smart chinos, beige, and a boldly striped collared shirt. Demure socks and belt, his brown leather shoes at the foot of the bed. Mercifully, no tie. For a long time Paul stands naked before the bed looking down at his multicoloured shadow, which stretches before him, which seems to have dived on to the bed ahead of him. The bed is a pool; he is beaten by a shadow.

He wonders what Claire would do if he wandered down-stairs and had breakfast in the buff, *kaalgat*. He could eat his squirting grapefruit with impunity and not give a damn about the sheet-sized napkins. He could smear Marmite to his heart's content and crunch his toast with reckless abandon. He thinks back to a Valentine's meal that he prepared for the two of them, and which he ate in the nude save for a red bow tie and a heart with an arrow through it that he had emblazoned on his chest with the aid of one of Claire's deepest-reddest lipsticks. They were carefree then. Both teachers at the same school. Busy terms and long holidays. So much to do and see and feel.

Then Claire left teaching. Went to work for an educational NGO: the Jabulani Ladder in Joburg. Still in education, but one step removed from all those children. Paul recalls before that change in career the tears at home in the evening. Claire crying, her red pen in her hand, tears trickling on to her marking. Staining the marking. Making the ink run. How could she face another class of lively children when all they wanted was a child of their own? Every glowing face was a ghastly reminder. Every tick or cross she made in their books was a red smear on a sanitary pad. Another mark against their future. Whilst they waited for the medication to take effect, she had to do something. So the administrative nature of the job at the Jabulani Ladder appealed. Trips into townships, no problem. Ordering Cuisenaire rods and other equipment, a doddle. It was a bit like playing house. Getting things ready, ready for their own child.

Paul knew that just as her body was waiting, so too was Claire's mind. So logical. So clear.

But for him the pressure mounted. Not only yet another busy school term, but also his sperm. An entirely natural fixation with what went on below his belt, and now, with the injections, what went on inside his head. The tiny pituitary gland, which, it seemed, controlled so much. Which determined whether they would have a living, breathing child. Or not.

Now it was Paul's turn to stop marking essays on *Hamlet* and his cerebral delaying, his verbal antics and excoriating bitterness, and to stare at his stiff red pen before sinking his head in his hands.

Or to stand and stare at himself in the bedroom mirror. A naked man. Ostensibly a man. But waiting for the drugs to kick-start his manhood.

Those were dark days.

He shakes himself. What should he wear now, on this darkest of days?

He walks naked to the top of the stairs. He stops, scratches himself reflectively then goes back to the flat-pack man floating on the bed.

Claire is pouring her second mug of coffee when he appears at last. She holds up his napkin to him as he lowers himself into the chair opposite her.

Your torn jeans and Two Oceans Marathon T-shirt? She watches him over her steaming mug.

That okay? Paul scoops a segment of grapefruit that has been pre-cut for him. Even so, he manages to shoot himself on the chin with a burst of juice. He sends his tongue out to lick it off. He thinks about commenting on the ubiquitous nature of citrus juice but keeps his mouth shut. The second and third scoops are more successful.

I have been thinking. She offers the words in a particular tone that causes a tightening in his belly. Usually that four-word sentence presages a bout of DIY. In the heady glow of the early days of marriage he was prepared to surrender his sanity on the torture rack of DIY. Lately, he has been more circumspect, more inclined to explore VISA than DIY.

Pauls nods encouragingly though his eyes are wary.

But don't get how you get.

Her hedging makes him all the more anxious.

Yes? he says cautiously, shoving the remainder of the grapefruit into his mouth and brushing a hand across his lips and chin.

I think we should get a gun. For you and for me.

Two guns? His tart riposte comes too quickly.

She is in deadly earnest.

But we have discussed this to death. He is aware that he is jabbing the spoon at her. The statistics tell us that more people are killed in their homes with their own guns than . . .

Fuck the statistics, she cuts him short. Statistics might

help an ad campaign but where is our daughter? Statistics did nothing to help Chantal. Our baby, she continues, but he is only vaguely aware of what she is saying with such controlled violence. He is shocked by her use of the expletive. But Claire does swear. Sometimes magnificently. Again, the pristine exterior and the more libidinous inner self. Now she desires a gun.

If we had a gun, she looks levelly at him. If, yesterday, you had had a gun . . .

Claire!

He feels as though another rib has snapped.

Claire, you can't be serious?

But I am. She keeps cool.

Claire, his voice comes out strangely. I was there.

Yes, she says, there without a gun, without any means of saving our daughter.

At last, he looks stupidly at her, at last she is out in the open and her true thoughts uncovered. No make-up now. If only she had said what she thought when she hit him yesterday, kept hitting him all day with her little fists that could not batter fate or make a mark on the new South Africa. He would happily have helped to vent her impotent fury. But to attack him with this? Here, now, in front of the grapefruit?

When she never, ever said anything about his infertility. Not once. Now this.

For what else is a gun? A fucking gun?

Do you think I just sat there and let the bastard take Chantal? He half stands out of his chair.

Didn't you? Her face has gone very white. Did you beg him for Chantal – to let you get her out of the car? Did you use your strength? I mean, how big was he? Did you use your common sense?

Common sense? Paul feels delirious. The chair flips back behind him and smacks the floor. Common sense? You have no idea. There I was . . .

With Chantal . . .

Yes, with Chantal, I am perfectly bloody aware that I was with Chantal! He is shouting now.

She does not back down. She is unrelenting. She has dived in with brutal expertise.

He does not pull back either.

And suddenly there was this bloody great gun right up my nose and this mad black guy and . . .

But if you were used to guns? If we had guns? If you had some training?

Training? He tries not to splutter. I'm talking about real fucking life. He is leaning on the table, astounded by her. What would you have done? What the bloody hell would *you* have done?

She has not moved. Her coolness incenses him.

But I wouldn't have been there, she points out patiently. I drive a Honda Ballade, not a brand-new BM bloody W. He wouldn't have noticed me.

For a fraction of a second he thinks he could actually hit her. Impossible, but briefly true. He shudders.

His voice throbs at his larynx, but he bites it back and nearly chokes. Then he shakes his head at her and is out of the back door in a few giant strides. Out from under her surgical stare and the forensic intensity of those abrupt few seconds.

He cannot comprehend her response. Grief, yes, shock, of

course, even some resentment, but to take it out on him like this? He marches around the garden, seething in the brilliant sunshine.

Training. Basic training in the army. So it comes again to this. If he had simply said yes in the army. In fact, just not said no, not said anything. The implication is that he would have been trained in the handling of weapons. That he would have gained something, not lost an essential part of himself. Is that what she meant? That he would have been more of a man. That he would have had the balls to get a gun. But he was a fucking pacifist. In more ways than one. Does it all come down to this?

Who is she? He almost punches the wall that separates their property from that of Grace and Happy. Then he leans against it, pits his weight against it. But then he is off again, moving, having to move.

Who is this woman with her perfect hair and lacerating talons? His long legs stride to and fro and he thumps a right fist into a left hand.

Who is this woman with whom he has lived and slept and eaten these past seven years? They have had their differences, certainly, but nothing like this. She wanted children slightly sooner than he did. That caused a few stirs. His legs eat up the garden, to and fro, to and fro. But nothing like this.

He remembers the hours and hours and hours of discussion concerning the pros and cons of a junior Claire or a little Paul. But when you teach teenagers you tend not to see the cutesy baby phase but rather move fast forward to acne aggro and gangling confusion. The hormones: the budding breasts and the awful sprouting sex drives. Now he does lean against the wall, the sun sternly at his back and on his shoulders.

And then, when they had decided that of course they wanted a child, that's when it got difficult. The heady expectation. The excitement. The sex not just for pleasure. Rather the true sense of consummating their marriage. Mating, in all its primitive senses, but also as a consummation of their love.

Then nothing.

Before then, he could happily, he feels shocked to admit, quite happily have continued his life sans Chantal.

Before then, well before then, yes, he was the one who wore the condom. The one who almost religiously would stop their passionate entwining to roll on the prophylactic whilst his wife was hotly groping for his love. And yes, he was the one who always provided the cool logic when the subject came up for discussion.

But then it all changed when they both wanted a child and it was he who could not provide them with a child.

And the tormenting sense that maybe for those several years when he filled condom after condom, that those were golden chances that went to waste. Mr Willy Wonka's golden tickets chucked in the bin. Time after time.

Claire never said, I told you so.

She never reproached him for all those times when he stopped them. When remarkably, he would withdraw from her and sheathe himself. Or physically lift her lithe form from him, from where she was so enthusiastically impaled. Then with due caution and concern, he would open the box, rip another little square and roll on the rubber the right way round. Big mistake.

But Claire never looked back and said, Big mistake, my boy. We might have been pregnant many times over. And he loved her for the way she said 'we'. Her benevolent use of the third person plural, the inclusive pronoun. Part of the teacher in him gave her full marks. So, yes, whilst it was her womb that waited so anxiously, that longed monthly in near terror for the sacred signs, she never said 'I'. Only 'we'. Should we become pregnant . . . If only we could get pregnant . . . I am sure, darling, that we shall manage to fall pregnant . . .

. They were in this together, as she said. Dancing, swimming through this together.

And then finally, finally, Claire did become pregnant! They were pregnant: with child! And after a paranoid age, Chantal miraculously appeared! They were in this together. Together at last, the three of them. Despite all of his stupid body's attempts to thwart her existence. And he was head over heels in love with her. With both of them. Who would want it any other way? Such a profound sense of fulfilment. And so simple.

But now the complexity tears at his insides. How could he have done anything to save Chantal? Could he have done anything to save her? His head makes an insistent thumping sound against the concrete panels of the wall. He ignores the tight feeling of the deep scab on the side of his head.

Despite the abject terror of that time, those few ghastly seconds, he would give anything to go back and relive what happened yesterday. He would happily take a bullet if it meant keeping Chantal.

Claire is right in some respects, his head concedes against the unyielding concrete fact. If he had just been aware of their baby. And, if he were brutally honest, as Claire seems quite capable of being now, he was rather taken by the whole BMW experience. It was his gift to himself from part of his pension payout when he left teaching. It announced his arrival in the real world where men earn and punch their weight. This was going to be the new Paul. He meant business. Anyone could see that as he drove up beside them. He had traded in his old car with his new little girl. He and Chantal had driven together to do the exchange. And Claire was neurotic that he made sure that the advanced safety features of the BM were suitable for Chantal. That it wasn't just some perverse sense of male display. He was being a responsible daddy too. In fact, he had been the one to advertise those very features of the car. His persuasive powers came into full play. All the side impact protection, advanced suspension and superior handling under difficult conditions. He finds himself barking with laughter. Difficult conditions. How does he drive through this? What German automotive engineering can get him safely to the other side of this? What Vorsprung Durch Technik? Talk about terra incognita.

And there they were, he and his daughter, on their way to show mommy. Chantal asleep in the back of the BM. The indulgence of a sticky Farley's rusk against the perfumed heaven of brand-new black leather seats. His first new car – ever. Only thirty-seven kilometres on the clock and Chantal's peaceful slumber already ample testimony to the superior qualities of the car, its beautiful suspension. And he, big daddy, the main man at the helm of this cruising ship with its white fins and gleaming bonnet. And the variable climate control, the air-conditioning that so neatly and instantly took the sting out of the late-January heat. The powerful acceleration, smooth, like a spaceship, and the brakes, pure velvet. The salesman – Govinder Naidoo, call me Go, me, the only Naidoo who will never *naai* you! – had treated him like a god. Had become his new best friend, it had seemed. Go had been so careful to ensure that Chantal's seat was properly secured. He fussed and he joked and he waved his fingers across Chantal's nose whilst running an expert eye over the straps and buckles and belts. Of course, Paul had let Go know that he was a daddy and that the car represented a step up in his automotive and parental responsibilities. Go had put a firm arm around his shoulder and playfully cocked a finger with his free hand. Paul, he had said with a most disarming smile as his trigger finger snapped in jest, I shall shoot myself if I don't get you the best deal for this set of wheels. And later he had said, before they finally left, that the name Chantal reminded him of Shanti – peace. Did she have a nickname? he smiled. I give you the car for the best price and the name Shanti. A BMW 318i and peace be with you!

Fifteen minutes later all were gone. Paul wonders briefly what Go would say. He did not have the heart or the stomach even to think about telling him. No doubt the insurers would soon be in touch about the bridging insurance. Paul feels the present moment leap forward into future like a half-built arch. The facts speak for themselves and a world of police reports and insurance claims and telephone calls will conspire to underpin with concrete struts the certain fact that Chantal is gone. And he stands leaning against a neighbour's wall, seeking solace from grey stone, feeling for the comfort that his own wife cannot provide. Maybe will not provide. He feels dizzy. He wishes the wall would hold still. He wishes the merciless sky could be packed away like an old blue rug after a bad picnic.

Stop all the clocks, yes, and pack away the sun. He stands there for a long time, a tall, leaning man.

What makes Claire so hard to fathom?

He flicks through a mental slideshow of their marriage and before that. Bits and pieces, glimpses of each other before they were together. Fragments – moments that they reported to each other with humour, pieces of the past dredged up, secrets shared. Amidst the usual dross of family friends they might have fancied or lavatorial embarrassments or someone who offered them drugs, there is one event.

One significant event. The Terrible Thing. Paul grimaces at the sharp rectangle of the pool as he remembers from long ago what Claire had said. Just before they were married, just before her father drove up from Port Elizabeth to give her away. They were talking about swimming. Paul had traced a finger along her naked shoulders, seeming to draw the outline of her strong, supple muscles, and they had got on to swimming, the training required, the discipline demanded. How Claire had finally forsaken such a life.

Paul stroked her and made a clumsy joke about breaststroke and backstroke and front crawl. Claire had gone from warm and passionate to suddenly sombre, as though she had been plunged into an icy pool. No, she had said, stop.

But it was that stage in a relationship in which you share, you have to share yourself. Where you more clearly blur your boundaries and lay open the emotional territory that comes with being with you. With Claire, it was not so simple. The site of herself came with warnings, and cul de sacs, he could see that now. Clear signs that might have read Beware: Electrified Fencing or Beware of the Dog – *Pasop vir die Hond*.

She could be decidedly categorical. Black was black, and white was white, not an easy thing in the last days of Apartheid South Africa. And this was personal.

She, Claire said, had injured herself at an afternoon swimming session at school. A different warm-up routine and some new stupid teacher. Training for the school team, not with the Joburg 'professionals'. Her best friend's mum offered to take her home early. Nothing too serious, a strained shoulder, and Mrs Green dropped her off at home on that afternoon in 1982. When Claire was fifteen.

And there was her father, early fifties and naked as the day he was born. As Claire came around the side of the house after letting herself through the locked door in the high wall, there was her naked father sitting on the side of the pool with his naked secretary. Miss Robinson, who always had peppermints in her desk drawer and who lately, when they visited the office, had chatted to Claire about nail polish and boyfriends. And there she was kissing her father at the side of the pool with her nipples like large pink peppermints all puckered up and her hand groping her father like a gearstick and looking like she was in the driving seat and wanting to go faster. Before Claire's stunned eyes, they slipped into the screaming blue water without so much as a splash and in perfect profile, oblivious to her shocked presence, her father's personal assistant got very personal. Claire forgot that she was standing there, her school bag on her good shoulder, her injured arm tucked into her dress, which supported it like a sling or a broken wing.

All she could see and hear was the loud blue splashing, the shocking pink intimacy. She never moved. Not even when

Miss Robinson threw her head back and shrieked like she was on fire and when her father threw Miss Robinson against the side of the pool with a great splash and grabbed her from behind and Miss Robinson, gasping, looked up and saw the angel with the broken wing just standing there and turned and hissed at her father, who also looked up and saw his daughter with a strange twisted face, her mouth open and her howl echoing silently across the garden, through the bordering trees and deep within his thrashing heart.

Claire did not faint. She did not move. She watched as the pair scrambled from the pool and clutched at scattered clothes and covered themselves and scuttled past her like refugees or guilty crabs. Watched how her father stubbed his big toe on an uneven brick right in front of her and did not even shout and swear but dripped blood and pool water all the way into the house.

Claire never said a thing to her mother or to her father. Not a thing to anyone about that afternoon. She threw herself once more into her swimming, into the bleaching, sterile water, her mind and body sealed with cap, goggles, plugs and swimming costume. And the memories were drowned in the swish of soothing water and were banished from the certain lines that she patrolled up and down, up and down until her arms and legs were limp and she could barely breathe. Fierce and pathetic and alone, she swam and swam. Claire, barely coming up for air. Claire, a little water baby. Crying in the serenity of water where no one would hear a sound and her sobs were silenced in soft bubbles. And if she swam fast enough, she had no breath even to weep, only to gasp.

How many miles did she swim?

How many hours did she spend suspended in liquid silence?

Of course, she could never swim fast enough and she had to surface if only to gasp.

If only to gasp.

Paul surfaces abruptly.

Is Claire gasping?

He is not sure if he hears her call the first time. Claire has to come into the garden.

Paul, her voice is an urgent gasp. Paul.

He springs back from the wall and nearly falls. He has not heard the phone. Have they called? They haven't phoned his cell.

The police, she says. Detectives. In the lounge. She holds the door open for him as he wipes his brow. And so he ducks in out of the sun.

The news when they get it is shocking.

Two plain-clothes detectives from some special branch of the police are seated before them. It is still less than one day since Chantal vanished.

The two men, one white and very Afrikaans, the other Coloured and softly spoken, sit on the edge of their sofa, like a married couple. They do not look comfortable. These are men of action. Their bodies strain against their clothes, their open-necked shirts and neat trousers. They have holsters. Dark brown and shiny, each bulging with the handle of a gun. They stand up and introduce themselves. Detective Smit and Detective de Jager. They sit down again. They glance around the room. Claire coughs.

This is a *blerrie* nightmare for you. Smit's, the white man's, voice is rough. A growl. His companion nods sympathetically. There is a pause.

Paul tries to concentrate on the men. He tries to fit them into their incongruous surroundings. But the sideboard, the showcase, the coffee table, the carpet with its stain from Chantal's recent illness still faintly discernible, the myriad pictures of their smiling family, the back door and the garden make it impossible. The detectives seem to be shop-window mannequins. Decidedly unreal. Emissaries from another universe.

Paul struggles to hear what they are saying. Their presence is disconcerting. He wonders what Claire is making of their guns. He cannot bring himself to look at her.

A gang, the Coloured man, de Jager, is saying. There seems to be a particular gang. A gang that specialises in the stealing of cars.

Smit rumbles in. Specialises in cars carrying children. Often babies. Just now, now-now, there have been several such incidents. A single attacker, always at an on ramp to a highway. Driver pulled out, as Mr van Niekerk must know, or shot. And the child strapped in and trapped like a sitting duck. And off they go. Gone. He gestures hopelessly.

Paul watches the man's muscular hands, notices the veins bulging in his wrists, wrists that seem strangely delicate. One hand pauses to brush the holster. Paul breaks into a light sweat. He glances across at Claire. Like the men, she is perched on the edge of her seat. She seems carved out of pale stone.

Now de Jager is speaking. They head into Soweto, it seems.

Soweto! Paul starts and almost thumps his head. Soweto, not Alex!

De Jager continues. From the East Rand and the West. From the northern suburbs as well as from south of Johannesburg. The cars are not being found. At least, not yet. The gang seems even to have found some way of disabling those vehicles fitted with GPS. So the cars cannot be tracked, they have to be honest. And neither are the children. The babies. Eleven such incidents in the past month. Three weeks, in point of fact.

What point? What fact? Paul wants to cry out. There is only one fact. And he cannot point to it as she is not there. That is the horrific point on which they must live, on which their soft-bellied lives must spin. He stands up, choking. They look at him sympathetically, these strange men with their terrible guns. Paul tries not to do anything silly.

Would you like something to drink? he asks. He pauses awkwardly. Some tea?

Coffee they reply, kindly. A nice cup of coffee. Black. The sweeter the better.

Let us go to the kitchen together, de Jager says softly. Let us go to the kettle and pour in the water and switch it on. Let us gently remove the mugs from the dishwasher and get the spoons from their funny ceramic holder in the shape of Table Mountain.

I collect teaspoons, de Jager says with a smile. It drives my wife *mal*, I swear it does. She says I waste my bucks and then she has to get the maid to clean the *blerrie* things with Brasso once a month. Teaspoons from Oudsthoorn and Knysna, from Durban and the Kruger Park. Even one from Benoni, can you believe. The Jewel of the East Rand. He chuckles. But his wife doesn't get it at all.

Paul glances across at Claire. Here they are in their kitchen hearing a man talking about teaspoons when he should be telling them where their daughter is. In point of fact. The kettle boils with a soft roar and clicks off.

Claire does not seem to mind. She picks up one of their teaspoons. For a moment Paul thinks that she is going to give it to the man who collects them. First a daughter, and now a teaspoon. Paul feels the kitchen tilt slightly and he braces himself against the oak surface of the counter.

A teaspoon is not just a teaspoon, Claire says brightly. She stirs the air in front of her. Then holds out the spoon to emphasise her point. Paul finds himself watching the tiny ladle of empty air in the spoon. It cannot spill, he thinks ridiculously. It cannot spill.

De Jager smiles broadly and slaps one hand into the other. *Kolskoot*, he says. Exactly.

We weren't born with silver spoons in our mouths, Claire says.

It's a – the detective grasps for the *Engelse woord* – reminder. He does not seem to have heard her.

We have worked for everything we have. Claire passes the spoon to Paul. He almost drops it. It feels icy hot: freezing, burning.

The detective nods. You've got to earn it. The places you've been, the things you've seen. That's why even when Karel here gave me one from Windhoek, I *dirrint* add it to my collection. I never visited Windhoek.

But you could go, Claire points out. If you wanted to, you could go. We can't. Not now. We can't.

De Jager catches the glance of his companion, Karel.

'Strue, he admits. *Ja*, I s'pose 'strue. He seems embarrassed. It's difficult to know if he is blushing.

The clock on the microwave shows 10.01.

They troop back to the lounge and sit, peering at each other from behind the mists of steam rising from the mugs.

So, *howzit* going? the detective named Karel asks them.

How do the hijackers know? Paul finds himself asking. Slurping his coffee and asking.

Who knows, de Jager shakes his head. But somehow the *blikskottels* do. It's like a sick sense.

Paul turns the corrupted phrase over in his mind. Sick sense? He decides that he couldn't agree more, but he doesn't say so. De Jager is talking about what next. It is unlikely that there will be any ransom calls. But there might be some cursory press interest. Though they doubt it. This is not America or England. And it's been a while since the disappearance of all those Gert van Rooyen children. All those little girls abducted. How many were there? Five or six? All that was left behind was their shining faces in photographs. Faces in newspapers, on posters in shop windows, even on cartons of milk if he remembers correctly. But that was the old South Africa, when things were different. Such crimes were significant. Now? Well now it's getting worse. It's a sad South African fact. Life is just too damn cheap here.

Claire puts down her mug. She has to stretch right up to de Jager to set it down on the small circular coaster. Paul clenches his fists and feels dizzy.

What are you going to do? Claire enquires coolly.

The men set down their mugs too. At last. Business.

They speak purposefully, with manful intent and many gruff

colloquialisms. Paul finds himself feeling strangely effeminate in his fashionably torn denims, and even his T-shirt seems to broadcast silly bravado: look, I ran a marathon in Cape Town years ago. My wife was a top-class swimmer and I ran a little marathon.

They have contacted and interviewed witnesses. That's what they spent most of last night doing. They are trying to get an identikit together to see if it matches the hijackers, the abductors of the other children. Did Mr van Niekerk get a good look at the man? the Afrikaner asks.

Paul nods.

Then they will need him to come to the Joburg Police Station.

De Jager continues. They have alerted the various police departments in and around Soweto, as well as border controls. They will get colleagues to speak to contacts at the garages that are slightly *skelm*, garages and dealers that might be acting as fences for the stolen cars. If there is the smell of *verneukery*, they will find it. Something, *enige iets*, must come up. Will come up.

But what are they doing to my baby? Claire interrupts them with a sudden cry. Why have they done this?

De Jager glances at Paul, almost seeking approval to hand over the bloody package. Paul cannot move, cannot think. The white detective watches him intently. The Coloured man speaks gently to Claire.

The truth, Mrs van Niekerk, is not nice. It could be a number of things. Like people trafficking, *jy weet*, slavery and sex, that sort of thing. It's not a *gewone* kidnapping like they are getting in South America with ridiculous ransoms and *sulke goed*. No.

Or it could be *muti*, the Afrikaans detective says flatly. Children taken for their body parts. With AIDS getting as bad as it is, there is a demand for strong medicines. They have heard about some *sangomas*, some *skelm* witch doctors, who offer powerful *muti* – medicine made from the hands and hearts and other pieces, which do not just come from monkeys and baboons, it seems. They are looking into this.

Paul feels the world of Midrand spin on its axis and slide headlong into turmoil. He feels Alexandra jump closer, like the savage male baboon they once encountered at the Cape Point nature reserve when they had a picnic, years and years ago, and the troop came to steal their sandwiches. The barking and the teeth. The deep-set eyes flashing, wild and terrible, and they all screamed to his mother's friend to let go of the stupid bag with the bread rolls because they were just stupid bread rolls. She did. No one was hurt. All they lost was a bag of bread rolls. Now? Here?

Paul glances at Claire. Her face is white. Opposite the Coloured detective, Paul thinks stupidly how incongruous she seems. These tough men, this Coloured man in their home. Africa, even South Africa, is dark and unfathomable. Here they are, two whiteys. He hears the chant, the savage, spiteful chant, the freedom fighters' song: *one settler, one bullet; one settler, one bullet*. They are still settlers in this beautiful, savage land, in this crying, wailing, beloved country. His mother is a second-generation South African, though his father has a long Afrikaner heritage. Claire was a Marais, a French Huguenot. She can trace her family back to a certain Claude Guillaume Marais who arrived in 1820 with not much to his name, but a hunger to succeed. And succeed he did.

Claire clenches her teaspoon like some small silver support.

We are very sorry, the detectives say. Their eyes mean it too. They lean forward on the edge of their seats and mention psychological help and two support groups. In case they cannot sleep, or whatever. Everyone is affected differently, the detectives tell them. Paul nods and knows that he can detect the shiny fecal smell of their leather holsters. They could have left them in the car, surely? Why bring them into his home?

The detectives give them some numbers to call if they need to. They shake them by the hands and shake their heads. They hope to be in touch. But, there is a but.

But you know what it's like, says the Coloured detective.

This is South Africa, the Afrikaans detective says.

Paul and Claire stare. Yes, this is South Africa. Paul feels as though he is going mad. Where do they think they are?

The new South Africa, the Coloured detective says. It's not how it used to be. The police, the courts, *alles, jy weet*.

They don't *weet*. What *alles*? What everything?

The detectives look at them. Maybe sternly, maybe sadly.

Paul shifts his feet.

Well, from here we gotta go to a murder; in fact two, the Coloured detective says.

Ja, the Afrikaner nods. Then there's a burglary that went wrong and a family that got killed in their beds. That was after . . .

You get the picture, the Coloured detective tries to be kindly. There's a lot of stuff happening, but with the moratorium on crime reporting – the police not releasing crime statistics so that things look better, *jy weet* – the general public doesn't really have a clue, not a *blerrie* clue.

They look at the van Niekerks with pity. Paul feels their tough pity, poking through the eyes of these hard men. It seems as though they do not hold out much hope. Missing babies will be swamped by tides of other crimes. Yet more crimes. Crime all the time.

Claire speaks. He cannot make out what she says.

We made time to come and see you, the Coloured detective says.

For what it's worth, the Afrikaner says.

And then they are gone.

All that remains are the reverberations of their sympathetic voices, their empty mugs and that lingering stench of well-oiled metal and leather.

Paul stares at the coffee table whilst Claire remains at the door.

The detectives have gone out into the world.

Then she locks them in with their horror and pain.

Paul feels her cold hand on his arm. Is this sympathy? An apology? He turns to her and does not want to think or feel. There is too much to think and feel. They cling to each other, desperately hold on to each other.

We must let the family know now, Claire finally says from against his chest. He thinks he has not heard her muffled voice. The last thing in the world he wants to do at that moment is talk to his family, to pin down in intractable words the fact of Chantal's abduction.

God, he says, must we? Now?

Claire is firm in his arms. He feels her nod against his tender rib.

You first, he says.

Claire lets go. Mom'll be at work, she says. We could drive to Benoni first then go to Mom. I don't think we can just phone them.

Paul is not too sure. He no longer feels certain about anything. He thinks back to his midnight excursion to Alexandra. Was that him? And then this morning: smart casual or torn denim? He thinks it might be easier not to resist his strong, pale wife. He draws strength from her composure.

Okay, he says, nodding. *Ja*. That makes sense.

The exact opposite of when they told the universe that Claire was pregnant – shortly after the Rugby World Cup final in 1995, when they were the champions of the world. After they had made absolutely sure that Paul's sperm had taken root, that their child was beginning to grow, was in fact the size of more than just a pip or a seed, was actually as big as a thumbnail. Claire beaming. Paul as proud as the proverbial Punch. Claire had wanted to keep it quiet for a bit longer. But how could they? After so long. Such agony.

Never had they felt closer as this child-to-be cemented their love. The miracle of modern medicine, and Paul could look at his body again with some sense of self-respect. That he could feel himself held by his wife, held up with no sense of shame. Sex became again something to celebrate. A pairing of equals, a flowering of their love that was soon to bear fruit. The joy of those early days as Chantal began softly to burgeon. The tender swelling of Claire's body as all by itself it knew wonderfully what to do. Literally, the glow stoked by her inner little firefly, a will o' the womb finally come to light up their lives. Claire's face filled out with more than pride and maternal joy; her breasts ripened and her stomach flourished plumply in a welling up of life. She would hold Paul to her softening flesh, as though never to let him go. And he would stay inside her, as close as he could be to her, a very part of her and as near as he could possibly be to the child who had finally swum from his loins after being held up for so, so long.

No wonder such a fuss was made.

No wonder they were the toast of the town. Several towns!

The drive from Joburg to Benoni is uneventful. They leave Joburg, City of Gold, and for half an hour venture east along the R22 towards his past, the town in which he grew up. They pass bright man-made lakes glittering in the late-morning sun, and on the horizon are the remnants of mine dumps, great hills left over from the gold mines. Like soiled innards, the used, exploited guts of the earth lie bleaching in the sun.

Paul remembers one of those childhood excursions that was meant to be great fun, hiking with his brother and father around one of the biggest of the dumps on the outskirts of Benoni. On a different continent, that great mound might be called Mont Blanc or the Matterhorn. Admittedly, the scale is somewhat different, but it looms still in his child's eyes as a blinding white Uluru, a monument stark with a fine white silt and populated almost impossibly by eucalyptus trees and wattles and lethal pampas grass and heavy, silvery rocks and stones. He feels small and fidgety, as the Benoni turn-off approaches. He remembers the abandoned mine shaft to one side of the dump. It was fenced off with rusted barbed wire, reddish like dried blood, but Paul's father easily found a way through. He took them through the wire strands and on to the concrete section, right to where the square shaft yawned so darkly and filthily. Paul's stomach still clenches as he remembers how his father stepped closer and closer to certain death. His father threw something down the shaft, rocks, Paul thinks, and their echoing crash and bouncing *boum, boum, boum* still haunts him. They never heard the rocks hit the bottom. At least a hundred metres down, his father reckoned with a cheerful grin. And John, Paul's younger brother, delighted at his older brother's distress, threw some stones down too. And there were bats. Yes, he remembers the bats being startled into the hot morning sky.

Now, as they pass that mine dump, it is being slowly reclaimed. The sand reused and the rocks crushed for building materials, he assumes. It is a Herculean task. The dismantling of Mont Blanc. Some part of him is relieved. Hopefully no other little boys will spend months and months jerking awake with a twitching leg as they drop off to sleep down the gaping shaft.

Pauls turns off the highway.

He does his best again not to think of the same trip they made an impossible nine months ago. When they took Chantal to his parents for the first time. That was April, late summer of 1996. He would rather think about mine shafts than that.

Five minutes later they turn into the street leading to his childhood home. It stands opposite the Bunny Park, in Rynfield. Again Paul has to flinch away the thoughts of Chantal's excitement in that half a square mile of childhood adventure.

Claire phones his parents from her cell and tells them that they are about to arrive for an impromptu visit: could they open the electric gates? His mother's excitement is audible in the car and Paul's throat goes dry.

It's not just the news.

News. For a moment he wonders at the word, with its freshly minted quality so beloved of copywriters. What can such a bright word, with its playful rhyming hint of a little kitten's sound, convey on a daily basis: war, famine, Rwandan genocide, the weather, the dollar-pound-rand exchange rate and Chantal's disappearance? News?

And then he also wonders, will they be angry that they haven't been told already? Now that it's twenty-four hours on. One whole day deeper into the nightmare. Falling further and further into the blackness. Time lost. Chantal is gone. The past and the future plummeting into the chasm of loss. Chantal is gone. She may be alive. The little girl that is . . . was . . . is our daughter.

He has negotiated the electric security gates with their fringe of razor wire and has guided the Honda up the leafy drive. His mother is coming out to greet them; they have arrived.

Mrs van Niekerk is small, bright and chic. She is ever so upbeat, Paul steels himself, with a terrible habit of greeting every utterance with an Anglophile Super! or You don't say? Probably to compensate for the fact that she slipped from being a Kingsley-Ward to a van Niekerk when she married.

My darlings, she springs towards them, her eyes already greedily searching the back seat of the car.

It is Claire who gets to his mother first. Claire who holds her and tries to keep her on her feet as the news overwhelms her. They guide her up the steps to the front door. Johan, Paul's father, meets them there, wiping his hands from some project in the back garden. His moustache pouts and his manly greeting dies in his throat.

So they tell Paul's parents.

We hoped Chantal would be back. We didn't want to put you through what we were ... are ... going through. We wanted to spare you, to save you the agony. But now it's worse. Yes. We know. No sorrow shared, no sorrow halved. It's doubled now.

A million times worse.

An infinite factor of pain.

How can you measure loss?

Paul finds himself philosophising through his mother's hysteria. He can only hold her tighter and tighter as his solitary father curses and swears at the plants in the garden and his mother sobs soundlessly into his chest. Claire moves to embrace them both: mother and son. Grandmother and father. And still his own father, Chantal's grandpa, rants and raves in the lush green garden.

Yes, his mother nods through her tears, they will tell Rachel, Paul's older sister. She is away on business. They will let her know. They leave his parents, one rocking alone inside the family house, the other lost in a belligerent march around the bottom of the garden.

Claire's mother is no better. After another forty-minute trip, this time up the R21 past Kempton Park and towards Pretoria, they stand in her kitchen in Monument Park with the sun gleaming over the tiny Voortrekker Monument in the distance.

She has lost before. Her husband left without a word and lives with his once-upon-a-time secretary in Port Elizabeth. Claire's mother sits stoically poised, only her mouth breaking the supreme control needed to be exerted over the chaos of chance and loss. She has twin grandsons – but they absconded with their father, Claire's brother, and his wife, to Cape Town, 1,600 kilometres away. She could bear that, barely. But now Chantal, her daughter's daughter, the link in the female line, is gone. Some black man. With Chantal.

Ages ago, Claire's family moved up to Rhodesia and farmed there. Then they left Rhodesia – Zimbabwe – because of the terrorists that lurked in the bush, threatening hearth and home. Now here, in the new South Africa, the Rainbow Nation, comes the terror. The Rainbow Nation, she laughs bitterly. Yes, seven shades of black and a pot of pain at the end of the rainbow. She, too, holds her daughter. Is held by her daughter. But she cannot weep. Her bitterness is overwhelming.

They phone Claire's brother. Then they wait until much later, until they are home, to phone Paul's brother in Sydney. His girls are safe and sound – already their Australian accents are thick and deliciously twangy. They answer the phone sleepily; it is the early morning of the following day. Yesterday they went to a birthday pah-tee. Their little friend, Mah-lee. Celebrating in the pah-k on the swings and roundabouts. The little girls chortle their happy news.

That's nice, Paul says. Where's your daddy? Can we speak to him?

Then comes their news, sounding very old by now.

John is shocked. They can feel him hug his little girls closer to him and he struggles to articulate his commiseration. Paul shakes, feels sick about spreading bad news. Sick about talking about his daughter as though she weren't there. Confirming that she is not there.

But Paul senses John's perverse relief. The insidious vindication. That is why they are in Australia. Why aren't you in Australia too? Nice, civilised, safe Australia. Great white sharks, taipans, funnel-web spiders, redback spiders, box jellyfish, riptides and red deserts, but nothing dangerous like in South Africa. Nothing to terrorise you. No one to steal your flesh and blood from under your nose, from the back seat of your car. Thank God they are in fair, advanced Australia.

They hang up feeling empty and alone. John was in tears. His girls whimpering in the background because Daddy was crying.

Paul and Claire cannot cry.

Will it get any easier? Paul wonders.

He reacts violently to the unbidden thought. Even to ask that suggests submission! How can they give up hope? Chantal is out there. His baby girl. She must be found. They must find her. He will find her.

At that precise point the buzzer grates on their raw nerves and Paul's father arrives. He apologises that it is so late. He wants to speak to Paul alone, but relents when he catches Claire's eye. He sits awkwardly on the sofa, flanked by Paul and Claire in the soft chairs. He hesitates, swallowing hard lumps in his throat.

He produces a rank-smelling oilcloth, and after a pause and another swallow, then a cough, he unwraps a gun. Paul recoils. Not another gun in their house, their home.

It is Claire who reaches forward to take it from her father-in-law's lap. The old cloth lies empty on his thighs, like a soiled nappy.

Claire stares at her white hands and red nails and the

monster they enclose. The thing is heavy. The weight of the world. She stares at it.

Her arms begin to rock the gun. She cradles it. The weight. The dull sheen. The delicate tiny trigger. The death it carries in its pregnant little chamber. It slips from her hand but her other catches it. Easily. Maybe even eagerly. The gun coils into her palm, the trigger ring slides gently over her finger and there – it points at Paul.

Claire, he murmurs. Claire. A vein is about to burst from the side of his head and spray the scene with bright blood. He can feel it.

Do you remember? His father is speaking. To him. Do you remember when you were young, about seven or eight? I'd take you and John to the shooting range on that farm. You would play with the cows and watch the pigs whilst . . .

Whilst Dad fired away, usually with about three other men. Fired off their guns at targets fifty? twenty? metres away. One man always had life-sized silhouettes of real people. He would blast holes into them for the entire afternoon. Paul remembers the row of middle-aged men with their shorts and long socks, their hairy legs and muscular arms, their Martian ear muffs and their brutally comic intentness – the way they peered and squinted and frowned down the black barrels and spurted bursts of sound at the targets for hours on end. Then, when the shredded targets were periodically changed and the manly voices rang in their ears, their little ears still singing from the bang bang bangs, he and John would be allowed on the range – to scale the earthen ramp at the far end and to dig in the dirt for leaden pearls and the occasional gleam of a copper-topped bullet, still whole and beautiful in the soft sand.

When they got home, Dad would melt them like dirty hailstones in an old saucepan over a simple gas flame. And they would pour out the steaming lead into paper cones, making dull pyramids that gleamed if you scratched them. The bullets were toys, entertainment. They were things you collected and admired. Paul remembers looking down the range, from the shelter back to where they stood on the mound with the concrete wall rising above them, and thinking about how, a few seconds ago, the air around them had been whizzing with lead, flung so fast that you could not see it. How the still air carried lines of certain death but a moment ago. The thought of it was fascinating back then. It did not trouble him back then.

Dad, he says. I've got to go to the loo.

He sits alone on the cold seat cover. His head throbs.

He knows that his father is telling Claire that it's a .38 Special. Packs a punch. Means business. Not the most accurate over fifty metres but if someone comes at you from close, boy, he better watch out. You can even get soft-topped blunt slugs. They'll knock a man down. They'll stop him. In his tracks. Just like Uncle Pat did years ago when they had an intruder in their kitchen. Told the black to stop. Told him not to move. Screamed to his wife to call the flying squad. Then the *kaffir* moved. The silly bugger came at him despite the .38 Special and Uncle Pat had no option. Shot him dead. Just like that. In his kitchen with his wife on the phone to the cops. Sometimes that's the only way. Can't bugger around with some of these savages. The idiocy of it all. You tell them, but . . .

Paul splashes cold water over his face and wipes his forehead with a crisp towel. He knows what Claire thinks about the gun.

But he wonders if she could ever curl a finger around the sickle moon of the trigger. Then gently squeeze it so that the heavens shatter and a pellet of soft metal is smashed into another living being. He wonders if she could pull the trigger.

Claire has already promised his father that they will keep it safe. That they know that the first thing burglars do is check under the mattress or in the bedside cabinets for guns. And then they might hold you up as you come home. And rape wives and daughters. That sort of thing. Paul's father recommends the bathroom, amongst the toiletries. They're not usually interested in cleaning things, he says sarcastically. Just breaking and messing up things. He has seen it all his life. Still bitterly going on about the *kaffirs*, he leaves them. Paul finds it impossible to avoid his father's reproachful glance. His son, a conscientious objector.

1 week

HOW LITTLE AND HOW MUCH can change in a week.

A week without his daughter.

Paul finds himself living a parody of a life. A parody of grief.

Work resumes. Work must resume. Work is another four-letter imperative – and one for which he is strangely grateful.

It was Claire who first said that they should get back to work. She was right. They had to.

But it was really Lucky and Sunny who were to blame. Or to thank.

As soon as their friends were SMS-ed the news, they phoned.

It was Lucky who spoke to Claire. Sunny was too upset, she said. Would have cried on the phone. So whilst the women spoke in low, sombre tones, the two men haunted the background, prowling the limits of their white South African impotence.

And after Claire had told the tale of Chantal's abduction, skilfully eliding Paul's inability to save his daughter, Lucky mentioned the *braai*.

For your own sakes, she had said, her Indian accent soft and tender. You know. It's more than just a *braai*.

And Claire had listened to their Indian friend define an essentially Afrikaner, essentially South African experience. We shall be there for you, Lucky said. For you to *kom kuier*. She had to invoke the Afrikaans again. How else to explain the togetherness, the ritualistic, stately procession of a *braai*? The sense of communion. The bringing and the sharing. The sacrificing of animals on the fire and pouring of libations. The smoky incense under the great cathedral of the African sky. The amused confessions and paeans of laughter, guttural and half pissed, as the world that could not be set right was set right. *Kom kuier*, she said. We shall be there for you. Your friends will all be there for you. You must come. We shall not let you not come. We shall come and fetch you.

And Claire and Paul had nodded and had hesitated again and then had said yes. Glancing around the silent townhouse, looking into each other's eyes, they had said yes, they would come, they felt that they would have to come. Claire had been right.

And Lucky had quickly put the phone down – but they had heard the strained voice of Sunny and the whining of his dogs, gruff yet oddly piercing.

But the *braai* was Saturday. Days away.

Today is today.

Both he and Claire are desperate.

If they remain in the townhouse locked up with their despair, they will go mad. They can do nothing but wait. Wait and pace and weep and wonder. This is not America or England. No news crews. No public pleas. Life goes on along the South African highway of crime and pain. A rape every fifteen seconds, God knows how many shootings and stabbings every hour and . . . God knows.

Paul and Claire know that they must get out. To be ready for Chantal's return they must face the world, otherwise they will go mad. So it is back to work they go, feeling very odd. As though they have turned up at a wedding dressed for a funeral. Their hearts squirm in clothes that feel suddenly strange.

The partners at BB&P have been incredibly understanding. Paul is the new kid on the block, he and a youngish black woman called Thandi who has worked in London and is terribly sophisticated. There has been no pressure for him to resume the good start that he made to his new job. But Paul is suddenly, nervously desperate to head back into the glass towers of Sandton. For a few hours he can make little castles, little pies in skies with clever words.

His creative director, Nolene Claasens, wants her team to come up with a series of slogans, a new campaign, for Durex. There is a rumour that that account will be up for grabs and that they might be able to wrest it away from the giant McCann Erickson. Instead of the awkward emotion that the dreaded *braai* at the weekend will entail, he spends the second day after Chantal's disappearance desperately bandying lewd puns about. Each hour kept busy is another hour in which he clings to some semblance of sanity. Swimming not drowning. Claire would be most proud of him.

They try to come up with a new angle, a new unique selling point for the little rubbers. It's like being at school again, Paul thinks. Treading a fine line between smut and humour. He knows that Nolene and Thandi are probably doing their best to help him 'to cope', and that he is also probably a bit too keen to throw himself into the creative fray with his deep laughter and the manic snapping of his fingers. But it feels good. So much better than the tightrope he has been treading for the past forty hours with the abyss of his daughter and his wife and the future and the present and the past all gaping like a mine shaft below him.

No mistakes with our rubbers, Thandi grins widely. Her mouth could compete with any American film star for dramatic impact. Her hair, however, is very African: long and braided, brightly beaded – a very colourful statement. Look at me, it says. European, but African. Maybe even American. Pigeon-hole me if you dare.

Nolene smiles at Thandi's attempt but shakes her head. Too European, she says. We have to seduce the black market.

Of course, Thandi concedes. She flicks a pencil through her long fingers.

But there's a natural reluctance, isn't there? Paul asks.

Sex or condoms? Nolene says.

Paul almost blushes. You know, he says. I thought African men don't like wearing condoms.

You're an African man, Thandi's smooth, fairly posh voice purrs. What do you like on the condom score?

Paul is stung, and rightly so. Touché, he says.

Touché? Thandi glances at Nolene. A hit, a palpable hit? A score?

It takes a while for the elegant black woman and her Coloured boss to stop laughing. Paul feels as though a yeti, a large white oaf, has just crawled out from under his skin.

He holds up his hands. Okay, he concedes again, okay. I just thought with AIDS the way it is, and a perceived reluctance amongst black men – aren't the press always bleating on about that? – that we might have to change tack a little.

Different tack, same tackle? Thandi asks blandly.

Don't, Nolene warns. Paul has a point.

He does? Let's see it. Thandi is unrelenting and Paul suddenly feels giddy. He wouldn't mind leaping up on the little table over which they sit crouched and dancing an exuberant jig. This is better than drowning. Better by far than desperately hoping and hoping with his guts screwed in impossible knots. But most of him knows that silly distractions like this are fleeting. A brief respite, before the torture recommences. In fact the torture is still happening, though just now it seems to be next door, in a different room, just a little way off. He is ludicrously grateful for small mercies, and terrified at the same time.

Paul is correct, Nolene says, choosing her words more carefully. This campaign has to be fresh, has to strike a chord with the biggest market. In fact, given current prejudices, we have to create a need to wear the silly little things. Build an entirely different brand.

They sit musing. Doodling. Muttering.

Why would our Township Man, if we can call him that, want to wear a condom? Thandi's pencil twirls through a succession of fingers.

Safety? Nolene doesn't sound convinced. Lifesavers?

Nope, Thandi affirms.

Heightened pleasure? Nolene glances at Paul.

Don't think so. Thandi's pencil twirls and twirls. Despite her elegant coiffure and Notting Hill facade, her nails are bitten to the quick. They perch oddly on the end of her long, delicate fingers.

We can't get all altruistic; we'll sound like some AIDS awareness campaign. Thandi's pencil jabs at both of them.

Fashion, says Paul. Fashion accessory. Dressed to impress, you know, don't go on a date without one. Without a whole packet.

DJs and Durex? Thandi sounds disbelieving. How many township men . . .

No, I'm thinking more of the younger scene. Rappers, *kwaito*, hip hop, music video, the cool *okes* helping out some younger dude by giving him a couple of Durex, fun ones. Ribbed, strawberry-flavoured. I wonder if you can get mango? That would . . .

Man come, mango. Not much of a slogan. Thandi's laugh is low and dirty. Her teeth gleam in her impossible mouth.

Paul is right, Nolene defends him. It's got to be a youthful campaign. Build a market. Distance ourselves from the clever-clever approach that McCann have always used – that might excite about one per cent of the population.

What do you think? I'm just some white guy.

Thandi looks at him thoughtfully. Yes, she says. I suppose I am the black person in this little triumvirate, and I have had my fair share of sexual encounters both home and abroad, of various shapes and sizes. I used to live in Soweto, that's true. Her pencil stops moving as she stares through Paul.

They don't interrupt. They watch her.

Soweto boys. Thandi stops abruptly. She laughs. You'll

have to make a damn good job of emphasising the fashion–brotherhood link. But where are the women in all this? Passively waiting? I don't think so.

And so the morning continues. Although they have yet to consult Art and Design, they want to push for a campaign that features sophisticated young black adults having a good time, built around the slogan 'Dress to impress with Durex'. The ad, they think, should be black and white and should portray smart urban men and women, three couples – different races – with three Durex condoms underscoring the party scene. Thandi suggests provocatively angled palm trees and stone columns. Some phallocentric shit, she says, to load the scene with subliminal testosterone – and for oestrogen, maybe some inviting doorways, arches or porticos?

It seems good: viable, simple and sexy.

They nip out to lunch at a nearby café. Paul knows that he is being taken out to lunch to help him, but he still feels flattered by the attention of the two women, both several years younger than he. They sip sparkling mineral water, nicely chilled, and munch wholewheat rolls and Greek salads, sitting al fresco under an awning that keeps the brutal January sun at bay. The square is filled with lunchtime shoppers. They are busily and purposefully affluent. Cell phones murmur and people stroll past talking to the airwaves. Paul sits back, soaking in the exquisite ordinariness of the scene. This is life – brisk and businesslike. A far cry from the many bored and nervy adolescents that used to populate his classroom. Oh, to be alive and bathed in such a sense of purpose. Washed bright and shiny as a new tie pin, a pair of solid cufflinks. It is almost as if tears prick his eyes, so sharply and so keenly he watches the scene. Lives the scene.

How are you coping? Nolene's voice filters into his ears. Paul is loath to tear his eyes from the swirling hypnosis.

He mumbles a non-committal response. But the tension wells up in him. The shininess of Sandton Square fades and he can hear the screams coming from that room next door. As if he could ever break free.

What did I just say? He turns to them.

You weren't exactly distinct. Thandi's eyes scan him over the top of her drink.

I don't know what I would do. Nolene's face is pale.

She is a beautiful Coloured, Paul thinks, then is ashamed of the thought. He likes her vaguely *Kaapse* accent. Her cheekbones are unusually high; her striking eyes, light green or light blue, he can't be sure, are wide with concern.

I have a nephew, says Nolene. Almost two years old. I don't know how I would cope if he was abducted. And he's just my nephew. She places a cool hand briefly on Paul's arm.

Paul shrugs. He smiles his appreciation, but doesn't trust himself to speak just yet. He puts down his fork.

I drove into Alexandra on Monday night, he finds himself telling them. Looking for Chantal. I felt like I had to do something. We don't have a gun. At least we didn't, until last night. My father gave us his gun. So now we have one. His voice feels tight, like it does not fit him any more. He is not sure if the two women have heard him.

How did they know? Thandi looks at Paul fixedly.

How did they know? he repeats, confused. It was all so quick. At the on ramp, me, no gun, Chantal, then it was all over. He had already told Johan Badenhorst – the first B in BB&P – all about it when he had phoned that terrible afternoon. And then he had phoned in again the following day after they had seen the police – and he had gone in to help with the police identikit.

So let me get this straight. This is a gang that seems to specialise in car- and child-jackings. Thandi's voice is clear and logical. There is a lone man, who just happens to target expensive and rather brand-new cars with a child in them and he just happens to be at your on ramp? Lucky strike? Coincidence? You told Johan that this was the eleventh in three weeks.

Ja, but not at the same on ramp.

Okay, maybe not at the *same* on ramp, Thandi emphasises slowly.

Paul looks at Thandi as though he has never seen a human mouth move. How did they know? she repeats. How did they know?

He can't tell whether he thinks it, or whether Thandi tells him. Her mouth has stopped moving. Yet he hears her voice: How did they know? And then he knows. As he puts his knife down on the solid wooden table and as he folds his crisp, starched napkin, he knows the fact as crisply and as solidly as the white napkin, the dark wooden tabletop and the shining, shining silver knife. He knows.

He lifts his face to the two women. He clears his throat. When his voice speaks, it is thrilling. And impeccably sincere.

If I begged you for your help to get Chantal back, right here, right now, would you help me?

Thandi sips her sparkling water. Nolene regards him palely.

Are you okay? Nolene leans forward. Your face has gone white, man.

Very white. Thandi's comment could be a barb. Could be a simple statement of fact. Could be commiseration.

If I begged you for your help . . . Paul starts to repeat what he just said. Did they not hear what he just said? Did his voice not just speak those very words?

Ja, Nolene says simply. *Ja*, man. Of course.

Paul reaches for his wallet. The time for thinking and wondering and agonising and fishing insects out of pools and driving around like a maniac and Greek salads is over.

This, he says, is what I need you to do.

And, here is the wonder, Nolene does it.

Standing back, sitting behind his voice, which speaks with soft urgency, Paul stares at her in grateful amazement.

Okay, she says, *ja, ja*, okay. She pauses, asks a sensible question, and nods. Of course. I get it. But we don't want any trouble, she adds, her eyes open wider than ever. No trouble. Please.

Paul finds himself nodding sagely. Yet he is aware of Thandi's silent scepticism. Is she scornful? Incredulous? Cynical? Realistic? He doesn't care. He knows.

He gets Nolene to make a call from her cell phone.

The conversation proceeds swiftly. They are lucky.

Then they make another call. Trickier this time. Nolene speaks tersely into the phone. Then Paul is put on to speak. He feels his voice fathom new sonorous depths. It's a weapon too. So much simpler than a gun. The third call, after Nolene completes the conversation, is also a success.

But there is one more call to make. One more arm to twist with his splendid voice.

Sunny. His best friend from school, all that time ago.

Benoni High, standard six. Johnny Raine, forever known as Sunny.

Sunny answers his cell phone before the second ring.

Ja, Lucky told him the news. Shocking.

Sunny seems matter-of-fact. Almost gruff. How quickly the word gets around. There is no time to think.

A favour? Paul does not need to ask. Of course, anything.

Ja, he knows anything is a *moerse* big thing.

Ja, he is alone. He's in the garden. Just the finishing touches. Are they sure about the *braai*? If they want to . . . Okay, well that's fine, then.

Paul tells the phone against his ear his plan.

Sunny's phone speaks with Paul's voice. Paul's voice says that he has a plan.

Paul listens to the silence of Sunny hearing his plan.

Sunny is stunned.

Paul repeats his request.

You must be mad. His phone crackles with Sunny's surprise. Are you fucking serious? You're not fucking serious?

Syllable by syllable, as Nolene shuffles in the background, Paul indicates to Sunny that he – is – fuck – ing – ser – i – ous.

Shit, says Sunny.

Yes or no? Paul asks. And you cannot tell a soul. Not Lucky. Not Claire.

Paul's phone is a silent slab. Quiet as the grave. Nolene tries to look away. Paul is transfixed.

Maybe it is pity that causes Paul to add an escape clause. I'll understand if you can't or won't.

Will their friendship turn on can't or won't?

Paul's phone murmurs Sunny's reply.

Paul tries not to grin or to punch the air. Now they just need to get to a bank. Standard Bank. He feels as though he is a standard-bearer himself, a Roman centurion. He doesn't allow himself to think of Claire. Until he remembers the gun. He needs the gun. He almost laughs at himself, but they withdraw most of his savings and he secures a personal loan there and then. R100,000. R100,000 in blue banknotes, featuring a thoughtful buffalo on each and every one. They put the money – it's heavy, surprisingly heavy – into a simple plastic bag, one from Woolworths that Nolene happens to have with her. Thandi asks no questions. She has gone back to the office to talk to Art and Design and to say that Nolene and Paul might be a little delayed. Something has held them up.

Paul does not ask Nolene if she wants to change her mind. He is so clear in his own expectations as they drive up the M1 north in Paul's hire car, a white Toyota Corolla. Nolene directs him to her sister's house in Buccleugh.

They pull up to a set of spindly gates, held together by a padlock and chain. Then a large dog comes bounding around the side of the house. A Rhodesian Ridgeback, all barks and grinning mouth, and a hyperactive tail.

Nolene's younger sister, an even paler copy of her, emerges and shushes the dog. She peers down the road, either side of them, then unlocks the gate. The dog barks one last time before lapsing into an idiotic grin, jokingly accentuated by its too-long pink tongue cascading over its teeth.

Friendly chap, Paul says by way of greeting as they get out of the car.

Too friendly, stupid *brak*. Nolene's sister's voice is clipped and tight. Come in, she says after a pause. Her accent is definitely *Kaaps*. They follow her trim figure. Her hands are tightly folded over her narrow chest.

The house is dark and cool after the brilliant heat.

Shoo! Nolene's sister uses a sharp foot to keep the dog at bay. It grins stupidly and remains on the other side of the security gate like a jovial burglar.

They stand in the small, tidy entrance hall. There is the faint sound of a hymn playing – something that sounds religious, coming from the kitchen.

This is Paul, Nolene says. Paul, Erica.

Paul leans forward and shakes Erica's hand.

I am sorry, Erica says.

Paul looks at her, possibly in disbelief. You, he says, you . . . no, I am sorry.

To lose a child and not know, Erica's eyes keep to the neat beige carpet.

I am hoping, Paul tries to sound optimistic. He tries to sound as though his heart is not going to leap out of his mouth and go pulsating across the neat, perfectly hoovered carpet.

Into his field of vision comes a small boy. A toddler holding on to his bottle and obviously keen to find his mother.

Erica looks up at Paul for the first time. Anton, she says. This is my Anton. He's eighteen months old.

Double Chantal's age.

Hello, Anton. Paul bends all the way down to crouch before the creamy-faced child. His soft skin glows against his denim shorts and blue shirt. His feet are encased in multicoloured little sandals. The dog huffs and puffs with excitement at the sight or scent of the child. The child waddles over to his mother and clasps her knee.

He won't be in the car. Erica makes a statement.

Of course not, Nolene says as Paul shakes his head.

Paul looks at Erica, but she looks only at her child.

And the doll? Nolene gently asks of her sister. In the back bedroom, says Erica, and hoists Anton to her bosom and holds him tightly. Let's be quick, she says, before Sollie gets home. He definitely won't understand.

Nolene fetches a large doll as Paul stands before Erica and Anton. He reaches out a hand to stroke Anton's hair, but the child squawks through his bottle and turns his face over his mother's shoulder. Erica holds him very tightly. Paul might almost feel bad. What would Claire think? Claire, who thinks too clearly.

They make their way to the car. Erica insists on securing the child's car seat firmly in place herself. She yanks at the seat belts and assorted straps.

Done? asks Nolene.

Her sister nods and eases Anton into the car. She moves quickly around to the other door and slips in beside him. Paul drives to the gate as Nolene scans the road and then fiddles with the pendulous padlock. Nolene shouts the dog back and the gates grate open. They drive through. A scrape and clang and clanking sound later, Nolene jumps in beside him and they are off.

It is early afternoon and the roads are busy.

Paul squints through the mirages that conjure pools of phantom water on the road ahead. Stop signs surface like giant lollipops. Cars dissolve in the distance or materialise out of the heat. It is building up for a storm. Paul can sense the electric stillness in the highveld air. It is too hot, too still to continue.

A trickle of sweat tickles his spine. The air-con does not work so well in the hire car. Another inconvenience in life's little catalogue of irritations.

They preserve a tense silence all the way to Paul's Midrand townhouse. More gates creak aside and they arrive. Claire's Honda is not there.

I won't be long. Paul leaps out of the car. Nolene and Erica open their doors too before the air inside the car can thicken and solidify with heat. Anton sucks quietly at his second bottle. The air feels sticky. There will be an afternoon thunderstorm. Typical midsummer mayhem.

Paul fiddles with the security gate then the lock on the front door. It is odd driving home so early in the day. The horrible jarring sense of what happened two afternoons ago, when he and Claire drove home in the afternoon heat without their baby girl, catches on his nerves.

He knows that Claire is out. He can't remember what she said. Where she said she would be. Typical, he thinks what she would think. This morning, her voice spoke, and his ears did not hear. The door whispers open and he is inside. It is cooler inside.

It is only when he retrieves the heavy gun, swaddled in that filthy cloth, from the oven and the box of bullets from the basket of cleaning goods beside the upstairs loo that he begins to shake. Nerves? Anticipation? Or is it simply fear? He can barely lift the revolver. He remembers the starter at school athletics raising the gun, the strident call: on your marks, get set, then the pause. That long pause before the bang unleashed the athletes, all pumping limbs and nervous energy and exuberance. He used to love the thrill of masculine competition. His long legs, the chance of a school record, his proud parents. The chants of the competing houses cram his ears and he has to sit down. He is shouted down by those sports day war cries. *Shawazzawaka!* he hears, oddly. *Shawazzawaka!* And the catechistic cry of *Wa! Wa! Wa! Who are? Who are? Who are we?* And the answering *We are! We are! Can't you see?* He sits on the side of the bath, trying his best to hold fast the terrible weight of the .38 Special and staring dumbly at Chantal's bath, propped to one side behind the bathroom door. That sets him straight all right. That is why he gets up and, standing, loads the revolver with five bullets so sleek that they are almost soft to the touch. Five more slip into the right pocket of his trousers and sink gently down into the depths against his thigh. They're almost ticklish. He hides the cloth and the box of bullets behind Chantal's bath. The war cries have subsided. There is purpose and symmetry once again in the world. It is just the blood thundering in his head that makes him feel sick. He wraps the gun in one of Chantal's disposable nappies, the very one left yearning on her changing mat by Claire not even forty-eight hours ago. The darkest blanket that he can find is brown and too light. He takes his navy-blue dressing gown instead.

Then, as a bereft father and a man with a gun and ten chances to kill or be killed, Paul leaves the house, dutifully locking up behind him. He eases his long body into the modest car. Nolene and Erica close their doors. Anton has fallen asleep. They make their way out of the complex.

Simple.

In some ways the gun seems to be driving him. It hides in the compartment beside the driver's door but he feels it thrusting forwards, eager for the hunt. The bullets roll heavily against his thigh. He senses their explosive power, still dormant, but potent nonetheless. Nestling close to his genitals is enough explosive power to kill many men. He feels his penis shrivel and his belly tighten.

They travel the short stretch to the business park. To the BMW dealership. To meet with Go Naidoo. The only Naidoo who will ever *naai* you. Paul smiles through his gritted teeth and Nolene clutches the Woolworths bag full of dreaming blue buffalo. The light takes on a richer tone – something to do with the gathering thunderclouds. The sky to the east is turning dark and ugly, whilst in the west the sun shines with its usual brilliance. There is no refreshing wind yet. Usually Paul would savour the build-up, the intake of breath before the heavens crack. As a child he used to love the sense of occasion. There was something heady and exciting about the drama soon to unfold. Maybe it was the contrast between the dry heat and the sudden rain. Blue heavens then the big fat raindrops, the belly of the black sky split by stabs of lightning. Often a cooling wind, then the crash of thunder and spears of rain. Clear lines of silver slanting into the earth – then the roads and gardens would be awash. And all the while Paul and John and Rachel felt cosy and warm inside or on the veranda, watching the drama from the wings.

But now he drives, his mouth dry and throat tickling with an irritating need to cough.

It's only when he approaches the side road before the dealership that he turns to face Nolene.

Thanks, he says. His voice sounds vibrant.

Nolene shakes her head. I keep thinking of Anton, she says

with a jerk of her head. I don't know what I'd do.

Paul hops out of the car and goes around to help Erica with Anton and his chair. Erica has deftly extracted her son from the car seat. He lies on her shoulder still fast asleep.

I'll get the seat, Paul says, and Erica nods. Her eyes are stretched wide and her face is gaunt. Flowers of dark sweat have bloomed under her arms.

Nolene takes the money out of the bag and inserts it into a section of her handbag. It's going to rain, she says.

Erica squints at the sky.

Okay, Paul says. You know what . . .

We know, Nolene and Erica, two stern sisters, do not want to delay. Their appointment is for 2.15 p.m. It is 2.15 p.m.

See you soon, Paul says, and watches them walk carefully along the pavement, then around the corner that takes them straight to the glass and stainless-steel heaven that is Midrand BMW.

He can only imagine what happens next. He seems to be spending his life imagining what happens next.

The clouds gather and the light grows almost yellowy.

He glances up and down the road. A street vendor on the corner, selling coat hangers. Two men walking away in the distance. Cars and houses. A pigeon is cooing monomaniacally – it sounds more like a full-throated growl – in the garden beside him. Its *koer-koer, koer-koer* is broadcast belligerently to the world.

Paul is aware of the vendor staring. Could he be a lookout? A gust of wind blows dust around his ankles. It subsides. Then it returns stronger.

Paul climbs quickly into the car. He turns and heads to the

crossroads. The vendor shuffles forward. Paul tries not to flinch at his approach. It is only wooden coat hangers. Twenty rand for four. He is about to drive through the four-way stop when the vendor taps on his window. Paul stalls the car. The vendor keeps tapping.

Paul finally glances up. The battered face is kindly. *Baas*, the man's lips move and reveal a startling array of gaps, thick spaces where there might have been teeth. The window seems to wind down all by itself.

The vendor's voice is clearer now, his lisp more pronounced. *Baath*, he says. *Twintag rand vir die vier*. Behind the man's shoulder is the road to Midrand BMW. Paul cannot stay there. He cannot be seen. And yet he finds himself handing over R20 and becoming the new owner of four wooden coat hangers. The man makes a gesture of subservient gratitude. Behind him, another man comes shuffling. Paul finds first gear and skids over the crossroads. The first plump drops of rain belly-flop on to the windscreen.

Half a kilometre down the road, Paul turns into a driveway, turns the car around and parks against the kerb. Timing is everything. At least, he thinks it is. He must be facing the way they will be coming. He keeps the car switched on so that the windscreen wipers can stoically smooth the heavy splashes and dusty smears out of his line of sight. The rain drums heavily above him on the tin roof. Paul keeps checking the rear-view mirror. A woman looms into view, trundles past, her child wrapped in a blanket on her back. It will get soaked. Paul switches the wipers on to their fastest speed. Lightning sizzles all around him and simultaneously a wall of sound smashes abruptly. He is that close to the centre of the storm. The wipers cut and tear, cut and tear a diminishing view of the hurrying woman. The rain pours and pours. The road is awash. Another car sloshes by trailing a wake of foam. Paul shivers. The temperature has suddenly dipped. Cold country with a hot sun, his father's usual phrase automatically sounds in his head. Another flash of lightning and instantaneous thunderclap. Paul's hands slowly unclench as he watches. The woman has finally taken shelter under a tree. But then he knows that that is the last place you should stop during a thunderstorm. Her child . . . The woman adjusts the blanket and sways on, running in slow motion. Paul feels the impulse to help her, but he must remain exactly where he is. It can't be long now.

He does not look down at the gun or fiddle with the five bullets in his pocket. The dressing gown lies pooled on the back seat, obscuring the large doll from his view. He reflects on how dolls, with their bright, lifeless eyes and plastic clasping appeal to the living, have always given him the creeps. He is glad that it is covered. But its very presence seems to mock Chantal's absence. She should be in the back of the car, not some haunting substitute. For the umpteenth time he wonders if she can hear the same thunder and rain. There might be only a few seconds' delay for her. He trusts that she is warm and dry, and that she is fed and not crying and . . . The list extends itself into an anguish of parental infinity.

Paul's phone rings.

Sunny.

Paul's voice leaps at the phone.

Sunny is sorry. He can't. There is no way that he can. He has thought about it. No way.

Sunny, Paul is shouting. Sunny? What?

Can't. No way. No way. It's madness. He would have come, but he fears that Paul is not right. This is crazy. That's why he is calling. Safer. Does Paul know what he means?

Sunny!

Paul, listen, don't. Whatever you do, don't . . .

But Paul hangs up before Sunny can spell out just why this is a bad idea. Before the worm of doubt can twist in his own belly courtesy of his best friend. After all this time, so many favours. Now this.

Paul gasps. He clutches his throat where his nerves choke in a goitre of doubt. But then no. A fierce no. A no that Paul strikes against the dashboard. No. He must. He must, yes. Just as he had to go in to the doctor's three times a week for six months, and then repeat the entire process a few months later, so now he must once again be brave. Otherwise he shall be undone.

He will have to go it alone.

That is that.

Fuck Sunny.

But he knows that if the roles were reversed, Sunny would be saying fuck Paul. Simple. Sensible. He was silly to ask in the first place. Poor Sunny. He should phone him.

Say to Sunny, it will be okay, just as they say in the movies.

Paul shivers in the car. The windscreen wipers seem to work in tandem admonishment, waving stern black fingers of denial at the scene playing out in front of him. No, no. No, no, they go. Not so. Not so.

The rain has lessened; he can slow the wipers to a calmer setting. Now they creak and glide over the screen and draw back the curtain of water to reveal the approach of a bright red BMW. There is no time now to phone Sunny. He must do it alone.

Paul flashes his lights once, and an answering glimmer comes. The sleek car cuts across the road and draws up in front of him. It is still raining steadily as Erica and Nolene emerge. Paul leaps out to greet them.

It worked? he yells at Nolene.

She is out of the car. She opens the rear door and retrieves the original car seat. Erica is already opening the back door of the hire car. The old seat is resecured and Anton ensconced. Paul grabs the dressing gown and the hideous doll. It is as heavy as a baby, and looks the part, woollen hat, breast-fixated cherub mouth and all. It probably wets itself. Paul carries it over to the BMW.

Nolene holds open the rear door, squinting at the rain. Her blouse is soaked.

He threw in a Babycare de luxe car seat, says Nolene. That clinched it.

It was Go Naidoo? Paul shoves the doll securely into the seat and attempts to strap it in.

Oh yes, unmistakably. Nolene nods.

And you told him . . .

Told him that we were heading into Joburg to take Erica back home to Sandton. That we were going to take the highway to avoid any waterlogged side roads in the rain. In fact, he suggested it.

Paul's hands shake and he fights with the complicated straps. The doll looks dumbly over his shoulder. He can do this. He can do this.

Paul gets the gun, still wrapped in the snug nappy, and hands over the car keys to Erica.

Thank you, he says simply.

Anton starts whimpering. Erica takes the keys. Good luck, she says, and climbs into the driver's seat. Nolene stands in the rain, her hand on the open passenger door, letting rain into the car.

You sure? she asks.

Paul waves her away and tries to smile. His mouth will not move.

Come on, man, Erica's voice snaps.

Nolene nods at Paul and ducks into the car.

Erica drives off in Paul's hire car.

Paul stumbles with the gun-laden nappy to the driver's seat of the new BMW. He looks at the dark dressing gown in his hands. Plans have changed. He shoves it across on to the front passenger seat.

He was going to lie, hidden on the floor, his bended knees bridging the ridge between the seats. His back would have been lodged against the door, so that he was half reclined against that back door, behind the passenger seat. He would have created no telltale silhouette; he would have been a stowaway in Nolene's brand-new car, secured by the large deposit paid for with his money.

The doll purses its lips at the ceiling.

Sunny would have driven them to the on ramp, to the hijacker. But now his plans have changed.

Dripping, he jumps into the driver's seat.

He removes the gun from the nappy. It's loaded and ready. The spare bullets still tickle his thigh.

Go, he says to himself. Go now.

He must not let himself think. He must only act.

He jolts the car. He swears. He finds first gear. Then he stops the indicator and locates the windscreen wipers. They are barely required now. The rain has become a light drizzle and there is the promise of yet more sunshine. The storm is moving on. Paul holds the gun tightly, but then places it between his legs; the metal warms quickly against his skin. He shakes uncontrollably.

Paul drives. Despite the sophisticated suspension, he feels every ridge and jolt in the road. He does not put on his seat belt. He cannot put on his seat belt. He remembers being lulled as he lay on the back seat of his father's VW Kombi in the early hours of a holiday morning. Setting off on a trip, on holiday. Wrapped up warmly in a mohair blanket when they set forth to the Kruger Park, or Balito Bay or the Cape. Then it was a childish pleasure. No seat belts required back then in the mid-seventies. Just a family and a destination, leaving early in the dark to avoid the traffic of the holiday exodus. The juxtaposition between then and now is physically painful. The gun waits heavily between his legs. Paul takes a deep breath.

Almost there, he indicates softly to himself. He seems to be talking out of the corner of his mouth. The traffic is now stop-start. Paul half lurches without the seat belt as the car accelerates, stops, accelerates. A few more turns, then this is it.

He has joined the queue to the N1 on ramp. This was where, just over forty-eight hours before, forty-eight lifetimes ago, he and Chantal had waited, ready to drive to Mom's work, ready to show off his – their – new car.

Now, two days later, in another BMW, he nudges forward.

Then he does the unthinkable. He presses a button and the driver's window slides from his sight. Wilfully, intentionally, he exposes himself to the air outside. To whatever might come from the outside. There is no Sunny; he must do it alone.

Not many vendors; the rain must have chased them away.

He moves forward again.

Go slowly, Paul says to himself. He tries not to think. Not to think.

I must go with the flow, his voice sounds brittle.

And here comes one.

Paul stiffens in his seat. He dare not think.

Videos. The man is just selling videos. Paul shakes his head at the figure outside and a shadow passes by the window. Paul senses rather than sees him. He pushes the car into first, then brakes. He is about twenty cars away from the robots. He grits his teeth. He feels the weight of his life coming to rest on the thinnest sliver of hope. He is balancing, balancing. It's a tightrope made of razor blades. He braces himself.

The engine vibrates into first, then second. Then third. No braking. He is free. Free and cruising on to the N1. Paul is rigid.

He lets out a long sigh.

The car swings into fifth, then sixth.

What now?

Back, Paul says to himself. He is still shaking. One more time. Can he backtrack?

He takes the next off ramp. The BMW soars up and over the highway, then loops back on to the N1. He heads swiftly towards Midrand. Off ramp, queuing, stop, start and back in a long curving detour to rejoin the road leading out of Midrand. Back to where he started. Back to where it all started. Once again he presses a reckless button and the window slides out of sight.

The sun is brutally hot now, steaming and sultry after the rain. He squints into the silver glare from every puddle and the platinum brilliance of the slick road itself. And out of the viscous sheen it comes. As sudden as light.

The black hand holding a gun and the quiet command, *Maak oop*.

But this time, Paul is ready.

He does not have to think. He cannot think.

He grabs the man's hand and pulls. And as he pulls, he accelerates the car forward in a quick, short jump, and brakes.

The man is not expecting to be greeted, to be gripped.

Many recoil, most freeze. It seems that he has never been gripped.

Paul pulls hard so that the man's head hits the roof of the car, and as that happens with the sudden lurch of the BMW, he smashes the hand with the gun into the steering wheel. But the gun does not drop. Even though the man slips stunned, half in the open window, his hand is locked to the gun. Paul tugs at the loose arm, his hands grip the man's wrist but cannot seem to shake free the hold on the gun. If the man shoots, there goes Paul's leg. He pulls. He screams.

In the protracted pull of that short second he sees himself once again facing his sternest test. The barrel of the gun threatens like the little tube that faced him down. Alone in that cubicle in the doctor's rooms.

Where he, once Skitter van Niekerk, Rifleman van Niekerk, must yield to the demand to test whether or not he shoots blanks, as it is crassly termed. He is now a teacher in the toilet, a bizarre shooting range to be sure. He can be no pacifist now. He must take up his gun, yet again screw his courage to any sticking place he can find and shoot. Outside, Claire waits. Blood has been taken. Now they wait for his semen.

He cannot do it. It is almost as though Korporaal Krause is standing before him, bawling into his face.

Are you okay, love? Claire's voice is soft on the other side of the door.

He makes no sound.

Paul?

Darling, he manages.

But that is all. He is limp and useless. What if it is he? What if he is sterile? What if . . .

What if I slip inside? Claire whispers, and before he can respond, she has pushed open the cubicle door and wedged herself inside.

They size up the situation, and before either of them can think, Claire catches hold of him.

It is not sex. It is a problem to be solved, a riddle to be unravelled. It is a puzzle to be worked at and worried over until a solution is found. It is a conundrum and, yes, he ultimately comes up with a piece of the jigsaw. Claire's tugging hands free him and he spills himself into the threatening tube. Finally. He gasps in agony and fumbles with the tube before shuddering against her. She holds his head to her soft belly and she waits until he no longer weeps. For the moment, he is her giant baby. Tenderly she strokes his hair as he sits like a little boy on the loo. They make no sound as he weeps drily. Then she kisses him on the crown of his head and he stands up and they take the tube to the specialist.

The specialist nods grimly and reaches for the loaded tube.

Paul screams.

The gun does not go off.

Paul barks like a giant ape, as though he can break the man's hold on the gun with his voice.

Thank God! The gun finally wrenches free and flies to the floor on the far side of the car. Then Paul is all action man. The hijacker pulls back and Paul lets him go, at the same time ripping at the handle and kicking open the door.

Suddenly pulled, and now, just as suddenly released, the man falls back into the road stunned and is struck by the car door that flies into his face. The thud is sickening and Paul leaps in its wake. It is over in a blur. The dazed man dragged into the driver's seat, Paul dives into the back seat, rips at the front seat belt and has the man trapped with the .38 right at his head. He is going nowhere. Nowhere but where Paul wants to go.

Take me to her, Paul screams. His voice is an explosion in the car.

Ry! He switches to Afrikaans. Drive! *Soweto toe: nou!* To Soweto: now!

He thinks the man might be unconscious, but he moves. His hands move and he seems to understand. The robots have changed. Green. Green for go. But they do not go. Paul tightens his grip on the seat belt and presses the revolver hard into the man's head.

Aikona! the man shouts as his neck bends to one side. He cannot see properly.

Paul tries to relax but his bladder squeezes uncontrollably and he feels again the warmth spread towards his thighs.

The man's head is bent to one side and he clutches at the gear lever with his left hand.

Paul feels as though he is still shouting, but he makes no sound. Simultaneously, he fights back the gun. Shoot, it seems to be screaming. Shoot. Kill. With a life of its own it screams for death. Paul is suspended in horror. The door slams and for a moment he believes that he has shot the man. But it was the man's right hand slamming the door. Then there is no time for thought as the BMW shrieks and slithers in a blather of tyres. Paul's head whips to one side as the hijacker kills the gears. Paul's door slams by itself, jolted closed. Within seconds they are travelling at shuddering speed. There is a sudden bumping, dragging at the back of the BMW. The man's deep voice curses, and the car rights itself. Paul watches stupidly as his black elbow jerks, changing the gear lever.

Paul cannot stop the gun from pressing into the man's head. Like a dog on a straining leash, it is desperate to hunt. It seems to drag at his finger, which curls around its trigger.

The BMW brakes so suddenly and violently that Paul's head smashes into the passenger headrest. He is disoriented for a dangerous second, then the car lunges forward, tyres squealing again.

Nie so vinnig nie! Stadig! Slow down! Paul bellows. But the man seems not to hear him. The BMW pulls into a parabola of speed as the road loops to join the freeway.

From the corner of his eye, Paul sees the flicker of the

highway lamp posts become a blur. They are in the fast lane.

Stadig – of ek skiet! Slower – or I'll shoot! Paul warns the man. Whatever the man is thinking inside his dark shiny skin and tightly curled head, he does not respond. The car hurtles along, dodging slower vehicles. Fine, Paul thinks, the quicker the better.

You will take me to your boss, he tells the man. *Jou leier. Induna.* He tries three languages for boss or leader.

The hijacker nods.

And Paul is suddenly elated.

He has a hijacked hijacker by the short and curlies. He holds a gun that is making this man do his desperate bidding. He is getting closer and closer to Chantal by the second. He is no pacifist now.

Paul adjusts his position, tightening his grip on the seat belt, which half strangles the hijacker and which serves as a guy rope to anchor him against the tug and swerve of the car. He suspects that the man has already tried to catch him off balance – hence the reckless speed. But now Paul wedges himself against the side of the front passenger seat. He is secure.

The car surges forward. It was a good buy.

Like a baby rocked in its cradle, Paul is rigidly lulled as the BMW swerves in and out of traffic, weaving its way faster and faster. Amazingly, the man cautiously lifts his left hand, revealing no threat, and begins to fiddle with the radio, and the sound of Highveld Stereo floods the car. It's Phil Collins.

Just beneath the barrel of the gun, the man mutters in his own language, in counterpoint to the lyrics: you can't hurry love, no you'll just have to wait. He is not getting into the rhythm. Paul wonders how many times a day this man hijacks cars. He wonders if it is the same man who hijacked him and Chantal. It is impossible to tell. His mother cooks listening to Highveld Stereo and Phil Collins. His mother and her immaculate kitchen and Phil Collins pervade the car. Paul thinks that he might be going mad. *Bossies*. He has heard about the older brothers of friends going *bossies* in the army, back in the bad days when there were tours of duty in Angola or the townships for every white South African male. Stress-induced panic attacks and personality disorders from shooting terrorists. He heard about some SWAPO or ANC militants getting tied to the front of Ratels, the rhinoceros-like armoured carriers, and being driven through thorn bushes until all that was left was a tattered, shredded smear of a body, unrecognisable. And the disembodied shrieks that lived on in the memory. Enough to drive anyone *bossies*. Now it is just Phil Collins. Paul cannot imagine anything more chilling. The gun is still poking the hijacker in the head.

Shakespeare's Sister takes over from Phil Collins and the man does not seem to care for their dark, wailing lyrics. He fiddles with the tuning and finds an African station. It is an animated talk show, it seems. A man's voice monologues with almost comic enthusiasm in one of the eleven official languages of the land. Paul knows only two of them, English and Afrikaans, with barely the rudiments of greetings and salutations in isiZulu and isiXhosa. He wonders if this man filling the driver's seat with his dark bulk is a Zulu or a Xhosa, or a Sotho, or a Shangaan-Tsonga or a Venda or a Matabele immigrant from Zimbabwe, or one of the famed criminals from Nigeria who are taking over parts of

Johannesburg with their drug wars. Maybe this is all about drugs; his mind jars at the thought of child-trafficking or the ghostly white slave trade. And the image of *muti* shops with their dusty, desiccated body parts yaps like a hyena on the edges of conscious thought.

His pulsing brain, the throb of thinking, becomes a siren. It takes a few seconds to realise that there is a siren.

Chaaa! The man swears. Paul sees his eyes roll up at the rear-view mirror, but all that he sees is Paul. They look at each other. Eyeball to eyeball. The man swears again and looks ahead. The car begins to go even faster.

Paul curses inwardly. Bloody police. Not there when you need them, there when you don't. Where will the hijacker go now? Not straight to Chantal. Not to any hidey-hole that will lead him to his daughter. The car skids and straightens. The engine bellows.

They could both be killed. The thought rises like bile. And if the car doesn't kill them, Claire will.

The BMW skids left, then right. Bizarrely, he can hear Claire's voice. Terrific amount of good that will do, if they both die in a smashed car. His life and the hijacker's life tangled together in death, their twisted limbs indistinguishable from each other in a mire of blood and bone. *Bossies.* Maybe that is why Paul suddenly shouts. A sudden ejaculation of sound.

Stop, the yell shoots from his throat.

The car careers in a long slalom that drags Paul heavily against the passenger seat. The speed and resultant G forces press him into the metal hull. The hijacker gives no sign of having heard. Maybe Paul made no sound. His throat is dry and constricted. He can barely breathe, let alone shout. Stop! he cries again. The siren howls behind them.

The BMW motors on aggressively.

Paul cannot stop it.

The gun pushes harder and harder against the man's head. Paul's finger is clamped against the trigger. The sharp trigger pulls into his finger. He can't seem to stop it. He must stop it. He tries not to close his eyes with a wild grimace.

His finger, the trigger, the gun.

The car jerks to one side. His hand waves free.

The trigger, the gun.

In the close confines of the BMW, the explosion is eardrum-bursting. The window beside the driver shatters. The hijacker's shout is whipped out by the sudden gust of air that bangs against the car. The howl of the sirens, now there are several sirens, collides with the BMW and the steering wheel rips to one side. Has Paul hit the man? Has the bullet torn through his cheeks and smashed the window on the other side? Was that blood – blood and shards of silver glass – that sprayed out into the Joburg air? In the last instant of consciousness before the second explosion, Paul looks up into the shocked eyes of the hijacker. Is it the same man?

The car seems to leap into the air and then there is just jolting noise – a sense of shearing speed and rending metal and blackness. He does not even have time to shout Chantal into the blackness.

Paul. Paul, Claire's voice whispers.

Paul.

Pull through. You must pull through.

Paul.

He feels very small.

Paul is lucky to be alive.

His operations have been a success, it seems. His leg is pinned back together, his face stitched, his concussion monitored. His ribs will have to heal by themselves and his cracked teeth will need to be crowned. Nothing internal has been ruptured, just badly bruised. There will be blood in his urine for days.

Paul is lucky. He is truly blessed, as his sister would say.

He does not feel very blessed.

It is Thursday. Another day in the Joburg General. The accident and emergency department has had another busy night in this, the murder capital of the world. Stabbings, shootings, people pangaed – mutilated by machetes and even by axes – and battered by hammers. Is nothing sacred? Is no kitchen implement or gardening tool or do-it-yourself knick-knack safe from the human anatomy? Must they be thrust and flung and slowly inserted into men and women and children? And the cars and buses. Bulldozing into each other. No one is safe from this metal chaos courtesy of overstuffed taxis and fake drivers' licences and the macho appeal of the floored accelerator. And booze and bravado and the pathetic attempt to make a living in a coffin on wheels. Paul is incredibly lucky. Maybe he is blessed. He could weep.

What was he thinking?

Claire holds his hand, a part of him that is free from pain. The rest of him feels like a giant tooth that aches and aches. A great mound rises from the bed over his leg. His chest is strapped and it hurts to breathe. His mouth is numb and his eyes puffy slits. Claire looks very, very cool. If she were a pool he feels that he would sink into her powder-blue top and cream skirt. Compared with his battered body, her perfect hair is a vision.

He tries to sit up but she restrains him and the drip trickles numbing, cold morphine into his veins.

What was he thinking?

What on earth was he thinking?

The hijacker is dead. Killed outright. Disembowelled by the steering column and brained by the dashboard. He would have bled to death anyway. Fortunately, they did not hit another car. Just took out a set of robots and a telephone pole. The car is a write-off. Just another spectacular mangle of South African modern art. The doll has been returned to Nolene's sister. It was perfectly unscathed. It sat primly in the back of the car in the pristine baby seat with all its safety straps. So the plastic doll with its stupid lifelike face is safe and sound.

Paul missed the visit of Nolene and Thandi, who called to see him at lunchtime. His parents are coming in the evening after the traffic dies down. Claire sits and watches him.

So she knows.

When Paul next opens his eyes his parents are there. They have brought him his favourite Peppermint Crisps, half a dozen of the silver-foiled chocolates. He feels sick. They touch him carefully, their broken son, and he gargles sounds at them as they slide past his slitted eyes. Then a night nurse removes the drip and shows him where the call button is artfully hidden. He nods vaguely and listens to the squeak of shoes along the sterile-smelling floors. Someone is wailing in the distance and it is three a.m. The clock on the wall opposite ticks too loudly, something he has hated since his earliest childhood. Sleep abandons him and the neon lights fizz in the new day two hours later. It is breakfast time. He must eat something now, so that he can swallow the cup of pills and get his system going.

He does as he is told.

Later, Claire finds him pulled half-upright and sobbing into his chest as his hands clutch at his aching sides.

What was he thinking? And now no hijacker to lead him to Chantal. The link forever missing. He mumbles to Claire, who tells him to take it easy.

She talks so that he does not. She describes in clear detail how helpful the NGO folk have been. She tells him about the posters that have gone up in Alexandra and Soweto and Joburg central. Even as far afield as the East and West Rand, various schools that are affiliated to the Jabulani Ladder have put up the posters. Claire the boss drove all the way to Brakpan and Springs to make sure that they went up there. Chantal's face now stares down at several thousand people. Someone must have seen her. Someone must know where she is. It can only be a matter of time. Paul's sister has organised a prayer rota with all her church friends. Even now, there is someone praying for Chantal's safe return. That will go on through the night. Kind strangers beseeching gentle Jesus to suffer their little child to come back to them.

Rising out of his subsiding painkillers and Claire's soothing tones comes the ache of Go Naidoo. Like a dark dervish, his image whirls across Paul's chest and scatters Claire's voice. Paul knows that he must get up. The time for gentle Jesus is not yet upon him.

Paul. Claire's voice is sharp.

He tries to smile at her, but his lips feel as though they might crack.

I think you've done enough. Claire leans forward and lays a restraining hand on his arm. Quite enough.

It is the addition of the quiet quite that stings him. She sounds like his mother, scolding him. As though he has somehow been naughty. As though it was a naughty thing to do to crash a car and kill a hijacker.

Paul lies back for a bit, letting his ribs simmer down. Thinking through the pain is tricky. He must have dropped off yet again. When he opens his eyes, Claire has morphed and split into Detectives Smit and de Jager, one either side of him. The smith and the hunter. Shoeing and shooting. His broken teeth ache as he tries to smile.

They look sternly at him.

Mr van Niekerk, de Jager says.

Yes, Paul of No Church, he wants to reply. His mind feels loose, oddly detached. It must be the drugs or the shock, strangely delayed. He feels the overwhelming need to weep or to laugh, he cannot decide.

You are *blerrie* lucky, Smit's voice rasps his eardrums. His great square jaw looks as though it might support a smile. But no. They almost shake their heads, schoolmasters giving up on a disappointing student. Paul does not know where to look. He stares straight ahead. Guilty.

I just don't know. De Jager's head does move fractionally from side to side.

You are a lucky, lucky man, Smit repeats soberly.

Through his cracked teeth Paul wants to say that he sure as hell does not feel at all bloody lucky.

Blessed.

Again that word. Why would de Jager invoke a Jesus?

You see, de Jager says, by way of explanation, you survived a bad, bad crash. The hijacker didn't. But, here is the really lucky bit: you didn't have a weapon with you.

No, Smit agrees seriously.

You didn't pull out that weapon you didn't have in the car.

No, Smit agrees again.

De Jager's voice becomes almost aggressive. You didn't aim a weapon at the hijacker whilst he was driving and distract him. No, you didn't pull the trigger of the gun you didn't have. You didn't shoot the hijacker through the ear, so that most of his brains blew out after the bullet.

Blew right out through the smashed window, into Houghton Avenue. Smit is rather precise. That didn't happen. You see, a .38 weapon is a very big calibre. Makes a *helluva* mess. But that did not happen.

No, agrees de Jager. The hijacker did not die on the spot; he was actually killed by the steering column which *blerrie* chopped him in half almost and then he bashed his head on the dashboard. What little brains were left were all over the dashboard. We saw them. But you didn't do that.

You see, if you didn't do that we can't press criminal charges and we can't not return the gun you didn't use to your wife. She has confirmed that it is your gun.

Ja, you are the victim.

Not the killer.

There was no cold blood.

Just shock and self-defence.

A desperate man.

A defenceless man.

But *blerrie* lucky.

Blessed.

Paul stares straight ahead. These are grown-up men. He is the child. Playing silly games. He swallows with difficulty.

Thank you, he says, barely audible. Thank you, more loudly.

The detectives do not suddenly grin and all is all right.

It happens, Smit acknowledges grimly.

It happens in the new South Africa with our most liberal constitution in the world, says de Jager. And especially in cases concerning white men with guns and dead black men.

You wouldn't stand a chance, says Smit. They'd *vreet* you alive, man.

But, says de Jager, and here is the point. That is why we came all this way for this *indaba*. If you have any clue, *enige, enige* idea about what happened to your daughter, you must let us know.

The men lean forward, pressing in on him.

Smit's voice is low, polite and soft as he swears. *Moenie fok met ons nie*, he lapses into his native, more expressive Afrikaans. Do not fuck with us. Help us, do not fuck us. You got that?

There is a long pause. Paul has the presence of mind to look each of them in the eye, like a man, and to nod. He hopes that they see his pain. Their eyes are hard and calculating, but he hopes that they can measure his pain. See what it has cost him.

Ja, he says through broken teeth. *Ja*.

They weigh that word. For a while they are silent, staring at him, then glancing at each other.

They get up to go. De Jager's hand pats Paul's arm with some reassurance. Paul lies rigid.

Strangely it is the thought that he has let down these serious men, that he has made their job all the more difficult that moves him. Not the thought that he has killed a man. Blown someone's brains out. That is almost a dream. A nightmare of confusion, and the gun doing its own thing and beating him to it. Forcing his hand, so to speak. Paul does not feel guilty thinking like that. An ugly anger rises in his chest. If he could do it again, he would. At least he thinks he would. Would he really?

He presses the call button. He needs a pan. He is going to cough up his pills. The spasms tear at his ribs and he retches drily. There is nothing to throw up.

They kick him out later that day.

Claire has to fight through the Friday-afternoon traffic and every jolt hurts. He was trundled out in a wheelchair as crutches proved too painful for his ribs. Claire held those crutches – for later, much later. His foot, snug in its white pupa, is bloated with a great caterpillar of pain. It gnaws at the core of his leg. He has to yield to it; to fight it makes him break out in a spasm of sweat.

Despite the unremitting pain, Paul has to go home. They needed his bed. More serious cases on the way. More mangled bodies. He has his bags full of drugs, a cornucopia of colour to ease his white leg. He will survive.

Claire does not say a word concerning the gun, and Paul remains silent about the visit of the two detectives. Most of the journey is on the quiet side. Claire concentrates furiously as she struggles through the usual mayhem. Hootings and swervings – in front of them, lane-changings at the last second. For all the most liberal constitution in the world, Paul can think of an impressive list of repressive measures for the drivers of South Africa – probably the worst in the world. Claire does well not to swear. She drives with a ferocious intensity, hitting the gear lever hard and making the engine work.

Paul has sweated litres by the time they drive into their Midrand townhouse complex.

All he wants is several glasses of cold water. He refuses to be wheelchaired into the house. He takes the crutches, and swings awkwardly into their home. The sweat drips from him. The clothes that Claire brought to him at the hospital are sodden. He guzzles water straight from the tap, winces because of his teeth, and then turns to face the hollowness of the house. Still no Chantal. All that and still no baby girl.

He collapses on to the couch and Claire helps to raise his bulbous leg, a plaster-of-Paris cast from just below the knee to his toes, which splay out big and square from the white casing.

Claire brings him a poster. She holds it up and Paul struggles to breathe as he beholds his darling daughter.

Chantal smiles at him, her face two feet wide. Paul remembers the photo distinctly. Taken at Christmas. On Christmas morning, as Claire helped Chantal to unwrap her first present. In the photo, Claire's arm hovers behind her daughter like the white wing of a guardian angel. Paul forces himself to admire the clarity of the photo reproduced and enlarged on plastic, with the bold heading: Missing. Have you seen Chantal? And the telephone number, Claire's mobile number.

His daughter has become a billboard. An image and a slogan. He would have made the lettering black not red: too violent, too bloody. He stops that train of thought by letting the pain in his leg drag at his mind. It does not take much to be distracted.

That's great, he manages to smile at Claire as she again lists all the schools and townships in which Chantal now hangs.

The effort of keeping his face contorted in an expression of attentive pleasure brings on a fresh bout of sweating. Claire does not seem to notice as he brushes away a trickle of perspiration from his eyes or stems a rivulet from the side of his face.

The irresistible forces of entropy, so alive in this country at the tip of Africa, have scattered his daughter to the winds. The pale smoke of her fairest hair wafts north, south, east and west. Anywhere. Everywhere. Paul recalls the image of the broken dog beside the highway en route to Alexandra. Its pale fur glowing furiously in the headlights of the car. Chantal. Where is Chantal?

Her nine-month-old face smiles down from impaled posters, lit by the late-afternoon sun. Nine months inside Claire, nine months with them, now how long will she be hanging on street corners? Do people notice? Do people care? A blonde girl, barely more than a newborn baby with little chisel teeth and an aura of innocence. That's all. On a poster she will fade and flap, tear loose and tatter in the heat and the dust and the wind of this godforsaken land. In nine more months even the posters will be gone.

Paul feels again, though it has never left him, that sense of profound dispersal. As though his entrails have been torn from him and thrown to the winds. That Chantal, the child of his loins, a part of himself, has been whipped away, who knows where?

The phone rings. Claire's cell phone.

She answers it before the second trill. Claire van Niekerk. There is a pause.

Lucky, she whispers to Paul.

Lucky. For a moment Paul's insides liquefy, then he realises that once again it is Lucky. Lakshmi – wife of his best friend, Sunny. Sunny who could not help out a friend in need.

The *braai*. Saturday.

As though from a different geological age, another time altogether, he unearths the memory of a *braai* on Saturday at Sunny and Lucky's. Friends, society, a *braai*. To celebrate Sunny's new garden – again. It must be the third time. Sunny the eternal landscaper and Lucky the lovely onlooker from another brand-new state-of-the-art kitchen.

Claire reassures Lucky. Not to worry on their behalf. No, of course not. It will do them a world of good. It really will. Yes, Claire closes her eyes, as though taking the plunge into deep water. Yes, it will take them out of themselves for a bit. She takes a big breath. If they stay at home all the time they will go mad. They *need* to come to the *braai*.

There, it is said.

Paul closes his eyes. He opens them when Claire, still on the phone, taps him on the arm, nodding, her eyebrows raised in query. He looks at her, her blonde bob shimmering along the angle of her jaw.

He nods weakly. They must go to the *braai*. Of course they must. They have to. They know that they have to. He closes his eyes again and wonders why she has not mentioned the gun, and he drifts off to the sound of her lulling voice against a background of tearing metal then the dreadful silence after the crash.

In the early hours of the morning he awakes, perspiring. His leg throbs spectacularly. He reaches out from the couch to drag himself upright and almost spills the large glass of water that Claire has left for him, as well as his pills in a neat ghostly row. He swallows them all at once, strangely proud of his ability to take a fistful in one gulp. The knot of water and drugs thumps into his hollow stomach. He thinks he will get himself a whisky. In a moment. But then he is lost again to a delirium of guns and the man's face, his eyes, precisely that look in his eyes just before the shot went off.

Paul awakes to more medication and a fresh glass of water. And the sound of Claire in the shower. The sun is hot outside; it is late in the morning. He never sleeps in and yet he has just slept late. Claire must have delayed her shower. The sky through the window is a murderous blue. He finishes every last drop of water. His clothes stick to his body and he shivers. He could do with a bath.

Whilst Claire attends to her hair and make-up, putting on her face as she calls the lengthy procedure, with her phone perched right beside her, Paul tackles the bath. It is an inverse mountain. To be scaled – plumbed – only with effort and ingenuity. After a committed campaign of twisting, bending, jerking and easing, he lies back at last in soapy splendour, his leg resting on the cliff's edge. It was Sylvia Plath who said that everything could be put right by a hot bath. Paul muses cynically whether she had only a shower in that cold London flat when she gassed herself, leaving the famous bread and milk for her two children.

He sinks deeper into the bath. He has none. A lot of posters stacked downstairs, but no child. He wonders at the seeming

European luxury of choosing to withdraw from life, turning gently away from its insistent clamours with your head baked, like Plath's, in an oven's kindly gas. In Africa, death rains down on you as you try desperately to keep dancing to life's complicated medley. There is no pulling back. It's a fight, all the way. You have to roll with the punches and hit back. Very masculine. What would Plath have done in his position? Write poems?

For a while he weeps in the bath. His veins and arteries – every tiny capillary – are dilated and slack from the cloying heat of the water. Claire's pink razor is within easy reach. If he wanted to, he could slit his wrists with that gentle Gillette. Gillette: the best a man can get. He stares at the pink razor and laughs through his broken teeth. Empty slogans and tough, masculine Africa. He is still laughing when Claire's phone rings again.

He can tell by the rise and fall of her voice that it is her mother.

The morning drags on.

Claire, fussy, fastidious, punctual Claire, is determined to be late. After dithering around the house, they leave at two p.m. for the *braai* that begins at two p.m. It is a twenty-minute drive to Woodmead, pretty much the same drive that Claire makes every day of her working life. She drives slowly.

They arrive just before 2.30, and Claire is carefully composed as she presses the intercom button. Sunny's cheery voice greets them and the huge gates lurch aside on their creaking tracks. The tree-fringed driveway invites them in and they drive, their tyres popping over the little syringa berries that have already begun to fall.

Lucky and Sunny meet them with hugs and help Paul out of the car. Sunny's eyes search Paul's face, but there is nothing to find. Nothing that says *where the hell were you when I most needed you?* Lucky's talk is bright and brittle, a careful construction around the van Niekerks' pain.

They have no children themselves. Their choice. Their three obscenely white bull terriers lollop and snort in the background, excited by Paul's crutches no doubt.

Sunny jokes that maybe they think they are big sticks to go fetch, but his eyes travel to the back seat of their car, which is devoid of Chantal's car seat. Yes, she is gone.

They guide Paul and Claire through the dark, cool house to the shining, wondrous kitchen. Lucky looks on with a smile as it is Sunny who shows them the self-closing drawers, the eye-level oven, the silent extractor fan, the Italian marble surfaces that glow richly. Sunny talks very quickly, then they are abruptly escorted through the dining room, down a corridor and past a vista of glass to the sliding doors that open to the back garden.

Claire and Paul step out into the fug of *braai* smoke and friends. It is a familiar tableau. The men, beer cans in hand, around the sizzling *braai*, prodding slabs and coils of meat; the women seated at a table, laughing behind sunglasses and warm, lively gestures, their voices in tinkling counterpoint to the guttural rumbling of the men and the searing flesh. For an imperceptible second, there is silence. Even the long half-barrel *braai* seems to hold its smoky breath. Then the cloud passes and all is sunshine again. Sunny goes around the side of the house to fetch the dogs.

Patsy and a new woman descend on them. Lucky offers

them up to hugs and kisses and commiserations. Claire copes admirably. She warmly greets Bev, the new girlfriend of Jacques, and asks if Bev has managed to coax Jacques into a movie theatre yet. It transpires that their first date was at the drag racing in Pretoria. Female laughter. Paul shakes Bev by the hand and wishes her every success with Project Jacques – a tough assignment. He tries to slide past the pain in Patsy's eyes, Patsy with her two sons clinging to her knees: Peter and Philip, afraid of the dogs that have hurled themselves into the back garden. Patsy's heartfelt aside to him, we haven't stopped thinking about you and Chantal, is gently negotiated and Paul breaks free to lurch at the men around the *braai*.

They stand in an almost ludicrously formal pose, beer cans poised, about to toast the summer air or the slain beasts or the fact that Claire and Paul have arrived. Theirs, this quorum of *braaiers*, is a far more awkward position. What do white South African men do when they can do nothing? Something that cannot be tackled or joked about with thick-bellied bravado. No gruff comeback to an affirmative-action campaign. No ironic bemusement at another instance of high-level corruption or the intense and endless ins and outs of whether or not Nick Mallett is going to be able to keep the Springboks' unbeaten run intact. Chantal's abduction . . . this is not sport or politics or business. Except for Sunny, they all have children. Children who should, in the scheme of things, inherit the earth, or at least that part of South Africa to which they might fairly and through hard work lay claim. Children who will at least grow up under their care, tucked up into bed each night behind burglar bars, razor wire and electric gates as security companies wait, poised to sweep to their rescue at the touch of a panic button. There is no panic button for this; no security company can respond to this.

Paul, they say. *Boet. Ou swaar.* They offer their open palms and let their tough hands do the talking. Pierre, father of Peter and Philip, Andries holding on to his two-year-old daughter in embarrassment because he has a daughter and Paul does not, and Jacques, newly freed from his tempestuous marriage, his children with their mother, somewhere, and a brand-new 'uncle'. The men's eyes are not just moist from the smoke, their voices not just gravelly with Lion or Castle or Windhoek lager.

Howzit going? Paul breaks free from Sunny's solicitous proximity and grabs a pair of tongs. He wobbles dangerously, but then is steady, leaning into his angled crutches. No one has to help him. They squint into the sizzle and fume of the *braai* and turn the marinated chicken – always a bugger to get right, as it must be par-cooked, has it been par-cooked? it has – and loop the spirals of *boerewors* into a new position to make way for the chops. Then, when the coals are just right, at their glowing best, will come the steaks: thick, bloody medallions of rib-eye steak.

This is good. Paul's gaze travels the length of the newly landscaped garden and turns to Sunny. Sunny is heading back inside, no doubt to get more drinks. Or to chat to Claire. Paul knows that Sunny has always had a thing for Claire. Paul and Claire joke about it often: Sunny is ruefully honest in his appreciation of Paul's wife. And Lucky teases him mercilessly. He is a fortunate man.

Helluva lot of work, Paul says apropos of the new-look garden, which now sports various levels and a new fish pond fringed by bulrushes and glowing with a series of stainless-steel sculptures. Very shiny, very nouveau. His *braai* buddies contemplate the meat with almost philosophical abstraction. He knows that they are holding back, unsure of the territory, and it is up to him to guide them to safe ground.

Ja, come the careful responses, *ou* Sunny's put in a lot of work. Him and his team of gardeners.

The remains of sheep, cow, pig and poultry whisper to the spurting flames.

Paul needs a joke. He looks up at Jacques. Jacques can always be relied on to have the latest joke. Louise, his ex-wife, claims that Jacques was just a joke. But Jacques looks rather serious now.

Paul clears his throat, ready to appeal for some topical witticism, the refuge of the white South African. If it works for that section of the population, it must include him. His bruised lips almost smile cynically at the pathetic generalisations: laughter along apartheid lines. What's changed in the new South Africa?

Pierre comes to the rescue. He helps Paul move a piece of chicken that is sticking to the grid. If you don't mind me saying so, he says, lowering his voice because of Andries's daughter, you look rather *kak*.

Paul smiles through the Afrikaans *kak*, so much more expressive than shit or shitty or crap. *Kak* – pronounced 'cuck' or 'kahk'.

Kakker than *kak*. What the hell have you been up to? Jacques follows Pierre's lead. Talk about what's in front of them, not what isn't there. Andries lowers his daughter to the ground and tells her to go and play with the boys. She toddles off doubtfully.

Through the careful turning and rotating of meat, Paul tells them. He avoids the personal anguish and slow-burning agony. His account is more matter-of-fact. He also neglects to mention Go Naidoo. As he talks, he feels his stomach burn at the thought of Go Naidoo.

They are a good audience, attentive, asking questions. They shake their heads in disbelief, nod in agreement, mutter soft bloody hells and fuck mes.

Sunny brings out the steak and stays to hear the rest of it. Paul squints through the billows of soft smoke and sees Claire engaged in similar conversation with the women. They attend, drinks forgotten in their hands, now leaning forward or brushing their faces once or twice with a free hand.

Jacques and Pierre enjoy the fact that the hijacker's come-uppance is swift and not left to the police and the hopeless courts. The conversation shifts to taking things into your own hands and guns. The burning feeling in Paul's gut ignites into a sharp pain. He begins to feel faint and lets Andries help him over to the table in the shade where the women chat. Andries's daughter is being cuddled on Jacques' girlfriend's – Bev's? – knee. Andries moves a chair for Paul's leg and helps him to raise it. They realise that Paul has nothing to drink. All this time with nothing to drink, man! Andries brings Paul a Windhoek lager, then pauses, possibly about to ruffle his daughter's hair, before he changes his mind and saunters back to the *braai*.

The cool liquid slips beautifully into his fiery belly. Paul crushes the can and is brought another. He will drown it. He leans back and lets the combination of alcohol, medication and midsummer heat wash over him.

The meat is almost ready and Claire is crying. Through the surge and ebb of his tranquillised breathing he is aware that she is crying and that Patsy and Bev have summoned Lucky. Sunny rushes past with the cooked steaks and glances in horror as his scheduling begins to go awry. Claire is sobbing now, and the burning returns with redoubled intensity in Paul's stomach.

Claire is apologising, shaking her head and apologising through her tears. The women cluster around her, the men are transfixed around the *braai*. Sunny rushes past and speaks in urgent tones to Andries, Pierre and Jacques. They begin moving the meat to the sides of the *braai*.

The women usher Claire inside, to the loo. They are gone for a while. Sunny starts ferrying meat to the kitchen to keep warm in the oven instead of drying out on the *braai*. He fetches another Windhoek for Paul and a fresh round for the other men. That is when Lucky comes outside to summon Paul. Claire is not doing very well. She is asking for Paul. They have to go. They cannot stay.

Paul clatters into the dark house, bracing himself against the tearful scene. Patsy and Bev hand over Claire, who sobs and again apologises through her tears to her friends. It was a bad idea. Too soon, much too soon. She's sorry. Paul nods at the three women and places a hand on his wife's shoulder. She glances up and smiles through sticky smears of mascara. Lucky locates Claire's bag and the car keys. They are led through the house, out the front door to their car.

Of course, Lucky understands. Man, it was so brave of them to try, so soon. Sunny emerges too and gives Claire a hug and pats Paul on the shoulder. Desperate to touch his friend.

Look after her. Sunny looks like he is about to cry as well.

Paul smiles his reassurances, of course, and thank you. They are grateful to have such friends. Then he realises that he will not be able to drive. Claire dabs her eyes and says not to worry. She will drive, don't worry. It will be a good thing.

No. Sunny insists. No. They cannot drive in this state. Of course, he will drive them. This time he will drive them. Home.

Paul balances on his crutches. The *braai*, the rest of Sunny and Lucky's guests?

They're old friends. They'll understand. They are amazed that you came. No problem, man. Come. Sunny brooks no argument. He gets his car keys, and before they know it they are waving goodbye to Lucky, who sees them off, arm raised in silent salutation, her three dogs milling like confused children around her knees. The gates slide open with lurching clanks and they are gone, Lucky waving to the empty driveway and probably wondering when it will be her turn. Surely, as night follows day, her turn must come.

Paul sits in the back, his leg raised up on Sunny's soft leather seat. Sunny and Claire sit in the front of the giant Audi. They do not talk. Paul feels like the child in the back. Mother and father drive in companionable silence. Paul watches the backs of their heads. Claire so fair, Sunny dark and gleaming, although there could be the beginnings of a bald spot. Maybe he is wishing it.

When they draw up to their house, Claire leans across and kisses Sunny. Sorry about your *braai*, she says.

Sunny makes some dismissive reply, a joke. Claire smiles

and they help Paul to get out of the car. He shakes Sunny's hand again.

Look after her, says Sunny with his usual urgency when it comes to Claire.

Of course. Paul finds his voice deep and serious. I shall.

Sunny drives off, the car reversing slowly. They listen to the departing Audi for a while in the still Saturday afternoon. Someone is *braaing* in the complex. They can hear the soft chatter and smell the meat-tinged smoke. More normality. Yet more of the everyday. Countless such scenes enacted across South Africa. Yet they must enter their house alone with their package of pain, still fresh and brutally fragrant. And they cannot dump it in the kitchen or leave it outside or shove it in the rubbish bin. It has become part of themselves. It is who they are, who they are becoming. Paul senses that they will become not the couple that waited forever for a child but the couple that lost a child, and that something has opened up between them, the gap, the fracture left by their beaming Chantal. On one side of the widening chasm he stands; somewhere on the other side is Claire.

For the rest of the day, Claire berates herself. There are a series of SMS exchanges. She apologises profusely to their friends. Their replies are generic and gentle. There is absolutely no need to apologise. The shock, the shock and the horror of it all. Take it easy, doll. They are thinking of them.

Claire withdraws to the bedroom; Paul lies on the couch. There is no rugby to watch, too early in the season. He tries to get into a crappy film on M-Net, but there are too many guns. Just too many guns. He falls asleep in the early evening wondering what on earth they will do on Sunday. And what will they do for the rest of their lives. The pain in his stomach makes him think that he knows what it is like to be pregnant. He cannot imagine what Claire is feeling.

The next morning he finds out.

He wakes up on the couch, his right arm numb. He tries not to move until the pins and needles have come and gone. It is a bad dose. His arm lies like a lump of wood at his side, almost buzzing with the threat of splintering pain. He opens his eyes blearily: the television is still on and opposite him sits Claire. She is not dressed, her hair is a mess. Her feet are curled up beneath her and she just sits, with her head propped up by one arm, watching him.

Paul croaks. His voice is not his own yet, and he cannot reach out to the glass of water on the table between them. That is when he sees the gun and the bullets beside his water. Without counting, he knows that there are nine golden cartridges.

Paul moves and his arm explodes into pain. He almost laughs, it is so sore. Claire does not move. He does not like the way she is looking at him. Is it pity or scorn or distaste or concern?

The gun, he croaks more clearly this time. What's with the gun?

You tell me, says Claire.

Her voice is neutral. But it could be diluted by distaste.

You always said that you didn't do guns and then suddenly you're in a brand-new car, armed with a gun. She pauses, her voice quiet and even. Putting yourself at risk. Claire pauses again. What are you playing at?

It is definitely contempt and disgust. She does not have to

curl her lip. Her flat voice conveys a weariness, an impatience barely controlled. Also anger.

Paul's arm still burns, but he manages to reach and grab the water. He gulps it noisily. Anything rather than talk when this cold Claire confronts him. His good hand feels for the remote control, finds it and clicks off the television.

I have lain awake the entire night wondering, Claire informs him. I thought you might come up and tell me, like some time in the not too distant future.

He lies back and she continues.

But no. Instead you choose to sleep down here with your whisky – she points at the bottle nestled against the side of the couch – and to go off in the night. Twice last week – in my car. I know because I check the odometer every evening when I arrive home and every morning when I leave. She raises a hand. One of my silly habits, I know.

That's very impressive. Paul wishes he could bite back the response, but it's said. Said and done.

Claire shakes her head. So tell me, she says. And maybe without the sarcasm, please.

Paul takes a deep breath. So she wants to accommodate all this in her world. Enclose it like a womb. Fit all of it neatly into her ordered world. To file his horror in some category alongside her own despair. And then what? He feels a rising sense of panic. Then his loving terror for Chantal is somehow neutered? Cabined, cribbed, confined? Carefully labelled in a little tube?

Claire, he says with what he hopes is a bright, optimistic tone, even if his voice will take some time to warm up fully. Claire, what are you hoping to achieve by this?

I asked the question first. She raises her jaw imperceptibly, with clear defiance. What are you trying to do? Her gaze is long and searching, made all the more intense by her wild hair and lack of make-up. Her appearance is almost spectral.

Let's just say that I prefer to take action, you know, direct action. Paul knows that his words are a mistake even as he utters them.

Action? There is a rising inflection in Claire's voice. You call midnight roaming in my car action? You call flirting with hijackers action? It's crazy. Don't you think it's crazy?

Another question. Another shuttlecock to bounce back in this intense game of marital badminton. Paul does not see the point. He lies back and regards her levelly.

So you don't think it's crazy? Claire repeats. Then she takes a new tack. Detective de Jager was very clear on this point when he handed over the gun and the bullets. Help your man to see sense, were his exact words. He was, in fact both of them were, very concerned about you. I am very concerned about you. Your parents are almost beside themselves. If Rachel prays any more she might become Mother Teresa.

Paul watches her.

Look, she heads off in yet another fresh direction. There have been a lot of stressful changes. You finally gave up on teaching – I know you felt bad about that. And the new job, you know, entering the business world. Seeing less of Chantal, and me. Much more pressure all round. Now this. It's all bloody stressful.

Paul knows that she is trying valiantly to quantify it all. But how can you make sense of a gun up your nose and the knowledge that your daughter was taken from right under that very same nose and that you did nothing, nothing to prevent it.

Paul, she says. Paul, say something.

So what should he say? Tell her his wild suspicions concerning Go Naidoo? The coincidence? The wild, wild chance that he should be hijacked twice, that new cars from Go Naidoo of Midrand BMW should be taken within days of each other? That he might be on to something that he cannot share with the overburdened, overstretched police for fear of losing Chantal for ever. That as a man, as a father who betrayed his little girl, he should be the one to bring her back. Bring her home.

Claire is coming closer to him. Her dressing gown is creased and awry. She seems unsteady. She kneels on the carpet beside the couch. She takes one of his large hands in her small white hands. The last of his pins and needles throbs but he resists the urge to pull away. She senses that and grips his hand more tightly. He blinks.

They said that you fired the gun. Claire's voice is quiet, matter-of-fact. That it shattered the driver's window – startled the driver, the hijacker. Caused the accident. You're lucky to be alive. If you were in the front passenger seat you would've died. Paul, you'd be dead and then I would've lost you both. You and Chantal, Paul.

He cannot argue with that. Those are the facts. He fired the gun. The hijacker died. He survived. But why? What careful nuances of motive and reasoning and emotion and human frailty are neglected, obliterated by the sheer facts? What are the facts when shorn of all humanity?

Claire, he says. Do you trust me? Do you love me?

It is her turn to regard him silently.

Of course, she says. But . . .

He lets the 'but' hang in the morning air fragrant with the fumes of his whisky breath and of her unbrushed teeth.

But not when you're like this, Claire qualifies her heart. Puts a price on her love.

Paul reacts instantly. He takes back his hand and pushes himself upright, his leg still leaden on the couch. He reaches past her to the coffee table and grabs the gun and a handful of bullets.

So, he says as the rest of the bullets roll and plop on to the carpet. So when I do this, he snaps the gun open and inserts the four bullets into the waiting chamber, when I'm an action man, like this, he wrenches the gun closed and raises it in his right hand to the ceiling, then you no longer love me.

Claire's eyes are fixed on his face; she ignores the loaded weapon not two feet from her nose.

Put the gun down, she says very softly.

Paul does not move. The gun points steadily at the ceiling, and beyond that, at their bedroom – or is it Chantal's? And beyond that again, rising up to the heavens, a patch of blue sky over this, the southern end of Africa.

I can't, he says. I am a man. I can't.

Man, she says. You are a man.

That's what I said.

They stare at each other from either side of the great chasm. Who will fall first? Are they falling already? Who will knock gently now on the toilet door and offer to help him be a man? Help pull him towards himself, save him from himself? Will he shoot the gun himself?

Claire stands up. You are a man, she says again. Okay, fine. I'm a woman. I'm going to shower.

Paul watches her march away from him. His finger aches at the trigger and the gun trembles. He is a man. Whatever that means. His finger aches at the trigger. Aches and aches. There is something in him that yearns for the clarifying explosion. The release of a certain bullet. Decisive and sure. The trigger responds gently. The firing pin rises. He calmly watches the archway in the wall, where the staircase begins and where her foot left the carpet to ascend out of his way. The gun clicks and he falls back. The gun fires with a quiet click and he slumps, trembling. He is so shaken that he cannot tell where the bullet struck the ceiling or why the explosion was so deafeningly silent. He has shot a gun in his own home. Fired it into the belly of the house, and he is a man.

After a long while he pulls the gun apart and checks the chamber. Four bullets in the chamber, and one gap. A one-in-five chance of shooting silence, of dodging the bullet. He does not know whether to laugh or cry. The ceiling is whole. Is he going mad? He laughs silently, clutching his aching sides. The gun falls to the floor.

Sunny phones later that day and makes a plan with Paul to fetch their car. Paul knows that he would have been keen to come and pick Claire up and take her to his house so that she might drive the car back home, but Paul insists that he will do it. Sunny does not seem to remember Paul's leg, the very reason why he drove them home in the first place.

Hell, man, he says when he arrives and finds Paul waiting outside the front door, with no sign of Claire. Your leg, he points redundantly. You can't drive with that leg.

Paul wiggles his toes. Watch me, he says.

No, Sunny is adamant. If you crashed, I would blame myself. Don't be stupid, man.

You would blame yourself? Paul feels as though he could be really nasty to his good, good friend.

Give me the keys. Paul reaches out a hand, letting a crutch drop to the brick paving. Sunny backs away.

No, man.

Paul hobbles after him.

Don't make me *blerrie* do this. Sunny backs against his car. Not again, man.

Paul keeps coming. Sunny sidles around to the other side of the Audi.

Sunny, Paul shouts as he half-hops, half-swings on the single crutch. He cannot stop himself from leaning against the car. He feels dizzy with the effort. But he cannot stop now. Too much, far too much rides on this. He looks over the car at Sunny.

Sunny's smile is wary. This is crazy, Sunny's lips twitch. You are being crazy again. His voice is anxious.

Just give me the fucking keys, says Paul. I'll show you.

What's the big deal?

Sunny might be relenting.

Paul's voice is deep and sincere. If you have been through what I have been through . . . But he is interrupted before he can lay on thick smears of sentiment.

Claire's voice cuts in behind him. Don't you dare, she says. Anger sharpens the edge of her words. Don't you dare.

The relief on Sunny's face is instantaneous. Claire, he says. Make him stop.

Claire makes a snorting sound behind Paul. He stands his ground, staring at Sunny.

He can come with us, says Claire, referring to her husband in the encumbering, get-out-of-our-way third person. He can come, but there is no way that he is driving your car.

There is the sound of her picking up Paul's fallen crutch. She prods him in the back with it. Almost cheekily. Here, she says.

Paul leaves his scrutiny of Sunny's expression, and turns to Claire.

Thank you, darling, he says.

Her face sets. She hands over the crutch.

Are you going to accompany us?

Paul hears Sunny's keys jangle loose as his hands relax. He turns sharply to find his friend almost grinning. Go and get the fucking car yourself, he says to Sunny. Sunny's face straightens. Paul turns back to Claire.

See you later, she says. Although I might stay for a cup of tea. I didn't really have a chance to chat to Lucky or to Sunny yesterday. You'll be okay?

He looks at her, admiring the swift, neat strokes as she swims through the pool of their turmoil. Up and down she goes, arms flashing rhythmically and the neat turn of her head as she remembers to breathe. Her feet beat the fluent water with purposeful, bubbling thunder. Claire, the swimmer.

Paul nods slowly. He cranks his crutches and swings back indoors. The car slides smoothly away from him. He slams the security door and the front door.

He spends the rest of the afternoon flexing his toes and pressing down on a cushion that he tossed to the floor. Beneath the white crust on his leg, aching colours shoot up and down. He does not know how he is going to survive the following day. He does not grit his teeth or bunch his fists. There is a calm certainty with which he presses his foot down and lifts it, presses it down and lifts it. The sweat that trickles into his mouth is salty.

Claire is gone for a couple of hours.

Then the doors grate open. She is back. She picks up the trampled cushion and looks at him. Did I wake you? she says, plumping the cushion.

He leans forward so that she might return the cushion to its usual place.

I was thinking, he says.

She waits before him. Lucky sent you some *melktert*. Like she always does.

Thanks.

Would you like some now?

Thanks.

She goes to the kitchen and comes back with a plate and a giant wedge of wobbling, cinnamon-dusted *melktert*. Heaven. The culmination of Afrikanerdom. And no one makes *melktert* like Lucky the Indian girl from Lenasia. Paul can never eat a slice of her wondrous *melktert* without savouring the scrumptious irony. Every last crumb.

Thanks, he says again.

You scared Sunny. Claire watches him run a finger around the empty plate. He couldn't stop talking about it in the car. He's never seen you like that in his life. He said not even when he broke your lunchbox playing soccer during break – in Standard Eight.

Paul thinks back through the ages to a distant time when a surge of testosterone – it could only have been hormones – led him to chase after Sunny when his sandwiches had been spilt on to the dusty field. He had never hit Sunny, but he had caught him and had raised his fist. Then he had let him go. The joke had gone sour. They carried on playing soccer. Sunny had bought him a Chelsea bun the next day at the school tuck shop.

Funny thing to remember, he says. He puts the plate on the floor beside him.

The phone rings. It is his parents. He asks Claire to tell them that he is asleep. Shortly after that Nolene calls. Claire conveys the same white lie.

She collapses into the chair opposite him. Then she remembers something. She gets up and fetches a large swatch of paper. *The Sunday Times*. Lucky says we're in here, she murmurs, leafing through the main section.

Paul watches her. His toes flex and relax, flex and relax. She bends over the paper spread on the floor before her chair. Paul gazes at the top of her head. He looks at the thin line of scalp that runs along her centre parting from which her sleek hair cascades. It is a white-blonde veil. Again he finds himself wondering, what goes on inside another's head?

His toes peer rough and square from inside his plaster cast. His will commands them to move or to be still.

Claire shuffles through another succession of pages. She licks her fingers and flicks the broad sheets with casual elegance, not minding that the pages bend. What goes on in her head not two metres away from him is anybody's guess. She may as well be on Venus and he on Mars, as the bestseller has it.

Here it is, I missed it, she says. A small section squashed at the bottom of page five. Child-jackings they're calling it: eleven in three weeks. Couples from Sandton, several visiting Midrand, some from Germiston, some from Bryanston, couples from Vorna Valley, and us, Paul and Claire van Niekerk. She glances up at Paul and his glazed expression.

She continues reading.

Paul thinks back to when they first met. It was in one of the student bars at Wits. They were in a large group of fellow postgrad English students, all taking the Higher Diploma of Education. They had just completed the Shakespeare Project, the dramatisation of their own abridged, adapted play for educational purposes. It had gone well. He had seized the initiative and had written a send-up of *King Lear* set in a kindergarten sandpit. The old bully asked the three girls, his coterie, who loved him the most. The other little boys were jealous, things got out of hand and the loyal Gloucester's eyes were torn out for toffee apples. That's when he met Claire. She was Cordelia to his Tom O'Bedlam who skulked halfway up the jungle gym. She smoked. Not on stage, but in the bar. It excited him. To think that the gentle blonde who faithfully followed the sandpit bully could be so close to him as she dragged at her cigarette and screwed up her eyes and blew smoke over her shoulder. Her soft mouth seemed somehow filthy. Maybe not filthy, more exciting and dangerous. They danced. He shared her cigarette. Her lipstick clung to his lips and then, days later, he tasted her mouth. She was apt to do wild things. She ad-libbed in the assessed performance. He would never have suspected that it would be she who abandoned his script and showed off. When they all had to share the one changing room, she was the first to say what the hell and to slip off her top to expose a lithe body before pulling on her costume, a too-small pink frock with ridiculous bows. Her legs. Her breasts. And her fascination with rugby, a man's game. How she commanded all the stats. And how she leapt fully clothed into the pool after the Joel Stransky drop goal that won the World Cup. It didn't matter that it was winter and the water was bloody cold. Or that her tight white top became instantly transparent. He had to fetch a large towel for her, to dry her and warm her and preserve her decency. She could be wild. Maybe a reaction to all that training, all that swimming. Illicit cigarettes and so on. Now here she is reading the paper calmly while their daughter is alive and in hell. And he burns with her, with their tiny Chantal. He stares at that soft blonde hair and wonders.

Whilst Claire continues to read, he shuffles around the house getting things ready. Pliers and scissors. The roll of brown parcel tape, with the end found and folded, ready to use. Two dustbin bags. In fact, twenty dustbin bags, which he tapes together to form a large plastic blanket. An old sponge and some kitchen cloths. His leg throbs but his hands are steady. To the collection he even adds a new bottle of Klipdrift brandy, a leaving present – not a very appropriate one – from one of his students.

Claire reads and reads.

He pauses for a second. Teacher, educator, to copywriter, businessman. And now. What now? One-legged, broken, a maniac and a murderer? An obsessive? This compulsion. He thinks again of Sylvia Plath as he hides the things in the washing machine beside the downstairs loo, and retires upstairs for a long, deep bath.

The sports section finally exhausted, Claire finds him standing in Chantal's room. He has let his crutches drop to the floor and he leans over her small bed with the rail and attached unit with the teddy bear changing mat. The towel clings pathetically to his waist. He has lost weight. That is exposed on his long frame. His head is bowed and he is lost in thought. He does not hear her. She retires to their bed. She is asleep when he comes into the bedroom and gets some fresh pyjamas. Then he goes downstairs, turns on the television and eventually falls asleep, rasping the air with snores.

The seventh morning without Chantal dawns overcast and dreary. A fine mist has settled over the world. Claire gets ready early – she has an important meeting at Baragwanath Hospital with Claire, her boss. They are looking to open a Jabulani Ladder centre in one of the administration buildings of this, the largest hospital in the world. It is situated on the outskirts of Soweto, an ideal location. Claire is swimming, all right. She has dived right back in. She swims; he splashes. Fuck.

Claire reminds Paul that she will be gone most of the day. Back at five, if I'm lucky, she informs his comatose form. He waves a bleary hand.

Sleep okay? she enquires, pretending not to notice the half-empty whisky bottle. Paul has left it beside the foot of the couch again. Maybe a badge of honour. Possibly a plea for help. Or just being a man.

He sits upright and flexes his leg. She brings her breakfast through and asks if he would like the other half of her grapefruit. He shakes his head, stretches and yawns. Another day off. Though Nolene has promised to e-mail some work. He might now be a little more useful to BB&P. It seems as though his career in advertising is cursed. He remarks on this fact as he seats himself opposite Claire and watches her chew with her usual gusto.

He rubs his stomach.

Coffee? she asks.

He nods.

She takes the scoured remains of her grapefruit back to the kitchen and leaves him counting the droplets of juice on the polished surface of the table. Nine. Ten. Eleven. Twelve. A dirty dozen.

She reappears with her All-Bran and their coffee. They sip in silence, though he can make out the crunch of her chewing. It is a sound that they find unreasonably and mutually annoying. He slurps his coffee as though to make the point. She continues chewing with purpose.

Try not to slurp, she says brightly. She appears before him, standing whilst he sits. Not a word about the anniversary, about Chantal, about last week Monday. The day he got his BMW and lost their daughter. A cheery goodbye and a peck on the forehead. Then she is gone. It's just as well. But he suddenly feels very alone in the quiet house. A few cars drive past: the complex is emptying as they all head off to make a living in the new South Africa. He thinks of Grace and Happy Mabuza next door, the two Zulu spinsters who have been so kind with their daily enquiries and their sorrowful *eishes*. *Eish*, Paul, they say, *Eish*, Claire, to their continuing lack of news. They asked for paper copies of Chantal's poster, and they say that they have made hundreds of A4 copies to distribute at their respective dental and podiatrist practices. So kind.

Paul swills the last of the coffee around his gritty mouth. He scratches his tingling belly. Today is the day. He stares at the empty mug. The rind of brown staining the white porcelain. If the brown swirls were tea leaves, what might he read about today? The tingling in his belly heralds the on-coming chaos, a certain storm. No. He has prepared carefully. It will go according to plan. There have been too many variables this past week. Too much left to chance. Too much bad luck.

He stares at the Rorschach of brooding coffee. Whirls within swirls. He swings into action.

He fetches the largest item, a chair, from the patio outside. He wipes it dry and carries it slowly upstairs. No injuries today! Next, he fetches the goods from their hiding place in the washing machine. He likes the simple irony of that. He lays out the carpet of taped plastic bags. His feet whisper as he swings carefully over the slippery black surface. He double-checks. Yes, all ready.

Then he forces himself to have a slice of toast. Then another one. He cannot be weak. He must not faint, no matter how painful. His hands tremble as he butters the third slice. It is hard work, but he swallows each dry bolus and winces as it bulges past his Adam's apple. He senses its pulsing, peristaltic progress into the depths of himself. Fuel for the day. Food for more than thought. It is odd to think that his actions that day, for better or for worse, will be, in some small part, powered by toast, lightly buttered and accompanied by a thin smear of ominous purple-black youngberry jam.

Next, he follows the ritual of brushing his teeth. Usually, that would end his morning routine. Today, it begins his ablutions. He runs a hot bath and shaves as it slowly fills. Then he hops to Chantal's bedroom and retrieves the pliers and scissors. He positions them carefully on the edge of the bath, gets undressed and hoists himself over the edge. He allows his entire body, plaster cast and all, to sink into the hot water. If it weren't for his belly itching and itching, it would feel good. Hot water floods on to his dry skin encased by the rough cast, which slowly becomes sodden and soft.

He waits.

He washes himself before the white mist from his cast spreads too widely in the water.

He pulls himself upright and reaches for the scissors. It's tough, but it works. No need for the pliers. He cuts a jagged line down the front of the cast from knee to toes. Then he peels it back. And there is his leg. Still a little swollen and very discoloured. Spidery stitches above his ankle in a neat line. He flexes his toes. Not bad. They respond easily. Not too much pain. He should be fine.

He tests his leg and foot carefully as he stands in the bath. He climbs out of the bath. One involuntary wince. It feels like broken glass inside his leg. But he does have more painkillers. He has made sure that today he will have sufficient painkillers.

The steps he takes to their bedroom are small and difficult. Now it is like walking on glass. Glass that shifts and splinters inside his leg, just above his ankle. It's not good.

He tries to take his mind off his leg by concentrating on every fine gesture that it takes to get dressed in a smart suit. Socks first, pulled slowly over the prickly stitches and not too high up his swollen leg. Underpants and trousers eased on. Belt threaded slowly. White shirt, one button at a time, and tucked in methodically. And then pulled loose ever so slightly so that he does not have an ironing-board belly, too prim and fastidious. He concentrates on every loop and fold of his tie, a serious blue tie. Cufflinks, silver to match his watch. And lastly his shoes. Not easy. Left foot fine. Right, he encounters a definite obstacle. Way too tight. He loosens the lace. Still ridiculously tight. He sits panic-stricken on the bed. Then an idea. He locates an old shoe at the bottom of his wardrobe. A shoe with a much lower side. It swallows his foot – just. He leaves the laces loose; it won't fall off. He stands up. Dressed like a teacher. He remembers his last day of teaching – early December, almost two months ago. How much has happened since then. He tugs at his sleeves and runs a finger around the inside of his collar. He has not forgotten that restrictive tightness around his throat.

And then he gets the gun. Claire has returned it to the oven. A gun in the oven. He slides his hand along its now-familiar length. The bullets from the upstairs loo already bulge in his pocket. He slides all five into the waiting chamber. They lie gleaming gold against the matt black. In another age, another lifetime, he might have thought them beautiful. But they are miniature missiles, lead sperm, designed to wing through air into human flesh. He cradles the gun against his chest and wishes that the fire in his belly would die down.

As from a great distance, he sees himself limp with a single crutch to the door. It is shortly after nine o'clock. The rush hour is subsiding. The mist, too, is thinning. The sun lurks, already high in the heavens. It is white and ghostly. He feels as though he is breathing in steamed candy floss. The air is warm and fecund.

He eases himself into the driver's seat and props the crutch beside him. Seat belt on, key into the ignition, the moment of truth.

The engine stutters, his left foot depresses the clutch: that's fine. He shifts the gear lever into reverse, then slowly raises his left foot whilst pressing down with his right. The shards of glassy pain cut into his leg, but the car reverses. He moves his right foot to the brake pedal and presses down with his left. His hands are strangling the steering wheel. He forces himself to relax.

The gun in his belt is digging into his side. He pulls it out and slips it into the cubbyhole. He thinks for a moment and checks that he has some loose change. He does. Fine. He can set off at last.

Hunched over the steering wheel, he sweats his way up to the security gate and waves cheerily to the guard – a new man, it seems. Paul cannot remember seeing him before. The gates grind open, and exactly a week after making that fateful trip, he drives yet again towards Midrand BMW. He even glances helplessly in the rear-view mirror to see if he can catch a glimpse of Chantal's rosy face and bouncing curls. He mutters to himself. Words of bitter encouragement. Words to stop his belly now from freezing with fear.

Halfway there he has to pull over and mop his brow. As much as he concentrates on the road and the steady traffic, his world is centring on his cracked ankle. Sparks of bright pain fizz and pop down his right leg. He keeps breathing. Keeps breathing.

Driving again, he makes his way via a set of ghostly robots. Out of the grey haze, a newspaper vendor wanders sullenly past his window. Paul has to call him back. He buys the *Citizen* and throws it on to the seat beside him. The car accelerates through a throbbing nimbus of pain, and the morning mist seems now to thicken. He has to turn on the windscreen wipers to clear the film of moisture that shrouds his view. He feels as though the highveld morning is hiding him. In some strange way he is comforted, though. As a child, he always liked cloudy weather. It made a welcome change from the merciless heat and searing sky. It was cosy, gentle. Even rain was good – especially at night. The rumbles of thunder as he snuggled up in bed. The sound of rain on the tin roof of the house – before his parents had it tiled over. He would give anything to be that child in that bed. Simple, unalloyed pleasure. Security. Not much sense at all of a turbulent world, just the pitter-patter of raindrops falling from a blanket of clouds.

He pulls into the parking area of Midrand BMW. This is it.

The mist swirls. He sits in the car for a while, though he must not wait too long. Nothing to draw attention to himself. So he retrieves the gun, wraps it in the crisp embrace of the newspaper in order to hold the paper casually but at the same time to have full control of the gun. Go Naidoo, he thinks, I have some news for you. My fine citizen. The only Naidoo who will ever *naai* you.

He emerges from the car into the warm greyness.

Struck by a sudden thought, he pauses as he locks the car door. Go Naidoo had better be in. He should have phoned first. Bloody hell.

He pulls out his phone and calls. The cool voice of the receptionist dispels his worry. Would he like to speak to Mr Naidoo? Paul hangs up.

The smell of new rubber and polished metal crowds his nostrils as he enters the glass and chrome sales building. It is open-plan. Various desks are interspersed amongst gleaming cars that loom in the showroom like sleek metallic beasts, four-wheeled monsters of the modern age.

He threads his way awkwardly behind several cars that sit almost incongruously indoors. It is like some strange zoo. Two receptionists talk brightly into phones: they are smart black ladies. A white manager talks to a husband and wife in the privacy of an office set in the back of the large room. He gestures to them in a proprietorial way. Three other men, salesmen, tap away at computers with calm concentration. Shortly after nine o'clock in the morning, it is a scene of purposeful industry and enterprise. Paul almost believes that all this could double up as a hospital or a bank. It seems more than a place merely to purchase motion, to purchase modern donkeys that feature phenomenal horsepower, ABS brakes and German engineering. And there, brazenly standing at the coffee machine beside the latest coupé and the newspaper table and waiting chairs is Go Naidoo. He has his back to Paul. He is waiting as a black brew coughs and splutters into his half-filled cup. Paul walks as though in a dream towards him. In his mind he already reaches out to grasp Go Naidoo by the shoulders and to spin him around. Paul feels no pain. That dragging ache way down at the extreme end of his body seems to come from a different world. His shoes squeak softly on the polished tiles. No one notices him. No one at all. He may as well be a dark ghost, Banquo come back to BMW. To spoil Go Naidoo's morning coffee.

A fraction of a second before Paul can tap Go Naidoo on the shoulder, the man glances behind him. If he is surprised to see Paul, he does not show it. Not a flicker of anything other than warm salesman's delight breaks over his features the instant he sees through Paul's puffy eyes and swollen face.

Mr van Niekerk. Paul. Go Naidoo abandons his coffee. He grasps Paul's right hand and pumps it up and down. Paul has the unsettling sense that water might suddenly gush in spouts from his mouth, giant splashing spurts as Go Naidoo seems intent on cranking his arm out of its socket. Paul sees the tiny wrinkles, quizzical flickers at the corners of Go Naidoo's eyes. The man is worried. He is overdoing his professional, default enthusiasm. Paul retrieves his hand. The newspaper and gun wait in the other, slack by his side.

I never thought . . . fancy seeing you here, man, this is a nice surprise, fuck me. Go Naidoo's register clatters through quickly shifting gears. Paul tries to steer him with a nod in the direction of his desk.

Can we talk? Paul's voice is firm. Not a tremor, not a sign of tightness. He even tries to smile. A strange rictus, he is sure. More likely to unsettle than reassure.

Go Naidoo's eyes flit towards his colleagues. The office continues with its quiet bustle. Paul hears his intake of breath. Is he going to call out for help? Or fob him off with oily ease?

On second thoughts . . . Paul's voice drags Go Naidoo's eyes back to him, and at last the salesman notices the folded newspaper. As his eyebrows raise themselves in momentary loss of control, Paul lifts the *Citizen* in an obvious gesture designed to reveal, briefly but brazenly, the gun. Go Naidoo is transfixed.

Not a sound, says Paul firmly.

Go Naidoo's cup is finally filled and the coffee machine sighs.

No, Paul's voice is sharp as Go Naidoo glances to his left. A salesman is standing up, though still tethered to his phone. He does not seem to notice them.

In fact, Paul continues, we are going to get into a demo car. No, he says quickly as Go Naidoo begins to expostulate. You have no other appointments. He repeats that slowly. You have no other appointments today. I am your day.

Go Naidoo, Paul can tell, is frantically trying to calculate a range of odds. His salesman's reptile brain is starting to slither.

Paul makes a natural gesture with the paper. I will shoot, he says. I will kill you if you do not do what I say. Got that?

Go Naidoo is all eyes. He stares down at the newspaper.

A demo car, he repeats in a faraway murmur.

Yes, Paul's voice brightens. Excellent.

They stand.

We will go very slowly to get the keys, Paul says. Nice and casual. If anyone asks, you forgot. You forgot that I was coming. Coming especially to see you.

Naidoo's eyes almost take on a begging aspect. Paul wonders if he is going to break down and cry. He cannot have him weeping before him.

Now, he says. Move.

Go Naidoo sleepwalks his way to his desk to collect his jacket.

That is good, very natural. Paul senses Go Naidoo kicking

himself. He should do the unnatural. Every moment should signal that what is happening is out of the ordinary. That he is not simply getting the keys to the usual demo car, thank you. That they will not drive out and be gone for a while, thank you.

Instead, they make their way through a series of unspoken protocols presided over by a large white woman. Go Naidoo talks quickly to her.

Not to worry, of course. *Ja*, there is sufficient petrol. *Ja*, it might be a long drive, much appreciated. Back in a bit, *ja* man. This is Mr van Niekerk. You remember him. Postpone my ten fifteen. *Ja*. Ciao.

Paul almost has to prod Go Naidoo to leave the showroom. He is growing back into his loquacious self. Paul realises that he is probably terrified to leave the building. Terrified that he is being hijacked on this dreary Monday morning. Go Naidoo will want to keep talking.

Let's go, Paul says.

Of course, man. Go Naidoo throws a despairing glance at the lady in charge of the keys and the signing-out book. She probably thinks that he does not want to go. How right she is. Paul's hand aches, he holds the gun so hard.

Can I go to the bog, man? Go Naidoo's manner is wheedling. I think I've had a little accident. I swear.

Paul watches him clutch at his buttocks.

Tough shit, he says. I can't follow you to the toilet.

Ag please, man. Go Naidoo is shaking perceptibly.

Paul hesitates. This will look strange. They need to get to the car. His leg is beginning to crack along a seam of pain from his ankle to his groin.

Don't try anything, Paul says.

I'm not gay. Go Naidoo stares at him levelly.

You're not funny either.

They walk back past the staggered series of desks, each with its trapped occupant. This time, there are a few glances. Both men walk with a stiff gait. Go Naidoo grips the back of one leg. Paul limps noticeably.

They swing through the doors into the toilet. Go Naidoo breaks into a stiff-legged sprint to the cubicle. Paul hears him cursing as the door clatters against its frame, though it does not lock, and Go Naidoo struggles with his belt. There is a moment of silence before Go Naidoo's relief is all too audible. He must have been terrified.

Paul waits. He feels what seems to be sweat break out along the length of his leg. His shirt collar tightens around his throat and he has to lean against the pair of washbasins in the white-tiled room.

The toilet flushes. Paul approaches the door. The lock clicks across.

Go Naidoo is playing games. At any moment someone could enter the toilet.

Don't be fucking stupid, Paul talks to the door. He tries it. It is locked.

Go Naidoo chooses not to answer.

Paul glances at the swing door beside the basins. At any moment.

He drops to his knees and brings his face against the fragrantly sterile tiles. Go Naidoo's patent leather shoes stand side by side at rigid attention. Paul inches closer. He removes the gun from the newspaper and holds it by the short barrel.

Then he sweeps it savagely through the gap under the toilet door and brings the handle of the gun with a loud crack against Go Naidoo's left ankle.

He squawks and leaps in the toilet cubicle, bashing against the locked door. Fuck, he moans. Fuck, man. There is the sound of his hopping on an Italian leather foot.

Open the door, Paul snarls, and stands up. The newspaper lies in a splash of pages at his feet. Paul is starting to shiver. I shall count to three, then shoot. He has to force his voice down. He could scream, scream and blast bullets so easily through the bland surface of the stupid door into the conniving bag of shit that leaps behind it.

One.

Two.

Three.

The door clicks. It opens.

Don't shoot. Go Naidoo's face peers around the door. He looks very unwell.

We are going right now, or I shall happily shoot you. Paul is surprised at the firmness of his voice. His breathing sounds hollow in his head, as though he cannot draw breath even to utter a word.

Go Naidoo emerges glumly. They walk back through the showroom. The world is busy again. They pass unnoticed, a familiar sight. A salesman and a client. A limping Go Naidoo and a limping client with his right hand shoved deep within his jacket pocket, which bulges uncomfortably.

They pass out of the showroom into the sultry morning. The sun is shining now. The last hazy streaks of mist evaporate. It is going to be a stinker.

Go finds the demo car by clicking the key. The car beeps cheerily, winking its indicator lights at them.

Paul glances at the showroom building. You drive, he says.

My ankle, Go Naidoo counters.

Paul brings the gun forward in his jacket pocket.

Go Naidoo shakes his head and opens the car door.

Slowly, says Paul. He moves around to the other side of the car. This is the trickiest part. If Go Naidoo realises that Paul cannot run, that he is about as fast as a very small child, there could be problems. Paul does not take his eyes from Go Naidoo. Paul opens the passenger door. Now get in the car, he says.

As Go Naidoo lowers himself into the car, Paul does the same. They sink into the soft leather simultaneously.

What are you going to do to me? Go Naidoo says. His hands lie limply in his lap and he stares dully ahead.

Paul removes the gun from his jacket pocket.

Go Naidoo's eyes flicker. Why? he says.

Drive, Paul says. And shut up.

Go Naidoo drives. But he cannot shut up.

I got you a good deal, man.

Did you? Paul says. Turn left here. Then keep on for about a kilometre.

Go Naidoo drives very, very slowly. Paul glances behind them. There are no impatient cars behind them. No one is being held up.

Speed up, Paul says. The car surges forward.

Where are we going? Go Naidoo turns to Paul, his eyes rolling a little.

Paul gestures to the road ahead with the gun. Keep driving,

he says. Life's a journey, enjoy the ride. He does not know why he adds that comment. That might suit some smart-arse gangster. He is not a smart-arse gangster. He again wonders who he is and wipes his forehead. He reaches forward and fiddles with the buttons. The air-con kicks in with a gush of cold air. Instant relief.

I am an only child, Go Naidoo informs him. My parents . . .

Paul brings the barrel of the gun to Go Naidoo's temple. It touches the side of his head.

Just drive, Paul says. Keep it at sixty Ks an hour. Turn right when I tell you.

Go Naidoo's eyes blink repeatedly. I have a wife, he says to the scrolling road. A dear wife. A good woman.

Paul lets him ramble on about his dear wife.

And do you have any children? Paul asks, halfway through the catalogue of Jane Naidoo's great virtues.

That shuts him up for a bit.

Paul keeps half an eye on the road. He thinks about his own wife. Whether Claire has arrived safely in Soweto. She said that she would SMS him. Carefully, he checks his phone. He holds it up so that he can read the SMS as well as see Go Naidoo. There is a message. All fine, lol C. Then an afterthought. Take it ez. Paul leans back in the soft leather. Taking it easy. His lips twist. Slow down, his voice cuts through whatever Go Naidoo was starting to say about wanting to have children. You will be turning in over there. Slow down. Turn.

They bump over the familiar ridge and brake outside the complex's impressive gates. The new guard approaches.

Paul confirms his address and name. Go Naidoo does not utter a syllable as the gun digs into his ribs.

The gates crank open. They are in.

Paul makes Go Naidoo wait. Paul gets out first and then he makes Go Naidoo slide out behind him, easing himself out of the passenger door. Paul gives him the keys to the house.

Go Naidoo takes them and looks long and hard at Paul.

You don't have to do this. Go Naidoo's Indian accent wears through his vowels. His voice sounds threadbare with strain.

Shielding the gun from sight, so that no eyes at any window might spy it, Paul waves it silently at Go Naidoo.

Almost sadly, he turns and fiddles with the locks. His shoulders shake. He is crying.

Just open the door, says Paul.

Go Naidoo pauses briefly, seems to pull himself together and unlocks the security gate followed by the door.

They stand inside the house. Paul takes the keys from Go Naidoo. They feel warm and sticky. Sticky with the man's sweat. Paul locks the door. Go Naidoo lets out a little moan.

I have something to show you, says Paul. Move.

They cross the short entrance, past the kitchen and through the open-plan lounge-dining-room to the stairs.

Go Naidoo stops again, one foot on the stair.

I am not going any further, man, he says, until you tell me what you are doing. I mean it, I swear. He speaks through a film of sweat that glistens on his dark face. Why are you putting me through this hell, man?

Paul regards him through the dull ache that seems to have overwhelmed his body.

So this is hell for you? Paul says. He shakes his head at Go Naidoo, Mephistopheles to his Faustus, or is it the other way round?

Yet this is hell nor am I out of it, he quotes softly. He brings the gun level with Go Naidoo's temple. Go Naidoo can see his knuckles whitening as he grips the handle and his fingers tighten on the trigger. So easy. It would be so easy. Go Naidoo slithers to the floor. Paul nudges him with his left foot and pain brightens along his right leg. He almost gasps.

I want to show you something. Paul steels himself and kicks Go Naidoo again.

The man rises and trudges up the stairs.

Left, Paul commands.

Go Naidoo turns left on the landing and they stand in Chantal's room.

Two men.

Two men standing silently looking down at a child's bed with teddy bear frills. Soft morning sunshine streams through the north-facing window. The scent of baby oils and sleepy pillows is discernible. Paul could weep.

Chantal, he murmurs, almost chants. Chantal. This is Chantal's room.

They stand solemnly.

Shanti, says Go Naidoo. I remember. Shanti. Peace.

No more of your Shanti shit. Paul's voice is flat and hard. He stares at the empty cot with its side bars and attached changing table. Then he turns to Go Naidoo. Turns on Go Naidoo.

Sit, Paul says.

Go Naidoo shuffles back from the blunt gun. His feet rustle on the plastic covering. He looks down in surprise and bumps into the chair behind him. Paul shoves him down. He sits.

Tell me, says Paul.

There is a brief pause as Go Naidoo peers down the barrel of the gun.

Tell you what, exactly?

Paul is stung by the defiance of the man. No weeping now. No tears. His jaw juts out.

Paul can play this game too. He smiles. Go Naidoo, he says, Go Naidoo: the only Naidoo who will ever *naai* you.

Never, Go Naidoo corrects him. It's never.

Really?

Go Naidoo stares at him now. In the eyes.

So you didn't *naai* me when you sold me the car and the special child's seat? And you didn't *naai* me when we left Midrand BMW and you called your contact to say that we were heading towards the N1 on ramp, me and my tiny daughter. Did you mention her name? Chantal? That, by the way, *my china*, her name is Chantal and her stupid fucking father is Paul van Niekerk?

Go Naidoo regards him darkly. I have no idea what you are talking about, he says.

Paul wants to laugh. The brazen lie. The effrontery. The arrogance of the man sitting here in Chantal's room. He wants to laugh and he wants to shoot him.

Okay, Paul says. So you had nothing to do with my daughter's abduction, with the theft of the car?

Go Naidoo seems to sneer at him. To sneer without moving a muscle.

Fine, says Paul. Put your hands on the arms of the chair.

Go Naidoo does as he is told.

So I am not going to tie you up. Paul reaches for the waiting packing tape and the scissors. In fact, you are not going to strap your left hand to the arm of the chair.

You're bloody right I'm not.

The shot when Paul fires it is spectacularly loud. In the close confines of the room it is as though all the doors in the world have slammed shut. He opens his eyes. There is a neat hole in the wall behind Go Naidoo. The bullet shot past his left ear. Go Naidoo has taken the packing tape and is deftly strapping his left arm on to the plastic garden chair.

That's more like it, says Paul.

It is as though the world has changed gear. Did he really fire the gun? The stink of gunpowder is dreadful.

Happy? Go Naidoo lets the tape dangle from his trapped arm.

Paul cuts the flat, sticky cord.

Put your free hand on the armrest, he says.

Go Naidoo does not hesitate.

Is this because I'm Indian? His voice chokes. Some crappy curry-muncher that sold you a shit car? Is that it? Where is your car?

Paul hesitates, then continues strapping Go Naidoo's right hand. The tape rasps loudly in the little bedroom. He cuts the tape. He bends with concealed effort and straps Go Naidoo's legs to the legs of the chair. A whiff of incense, some sense of sandalwood spices seems to squeeze from Go Naidoo's trousers.

Paul goes to the bedroom window. Nothing. He shuffles across the room to the other side of the house, which overlooks the road into the complex. More nothing. No response to the gunshot. The windows he closed that morning must have helped to muffle the sound. And everyone's at work. Surely. Surely everyone is peering at computer screens, whispering into phones, driving who knows where, consulting patients, confirming schedules, making money. Although unemployment is officially around forty per cent. He leans against the cold glass of the window. So out there over Midrand and the highveld and all the way across to the Limpopo and the Orange rivers, down past the Drakensberg and through the Karoo to the Cape, four out of ten adults are not stroking keyboards or digging holes or murmuring about markets and shares or steering tons of mobile metal. Not everyone is selling. And somewhere out there is Chantal. Or Chantal's body. In the midst of the bustle and business and the despair.

He turns away from the window.

Go Naidoo has wriggled the chair across the room. His chest is heaving and he sweats. He does not smell too good. Not much sandalwood now. There are scuff and tear marks in the home-made plastic lining of the floor. Paul takes a breath. He can still smell the gunpowder that hangs in the air.

You're messing up my floor, Paul says.

I'm so fucking sorry. Go Naidoo's voice almost cracks. His eyes roll whitely out of his face, which seems even darker. He is one of those black-skinned Indians.

So why? Go Naidoo continues in the same strained way.

Paul sets about taping up the gaps in the plastic covering. The tape twangs off the roll, he sticks it down, he snips it. He repeats the process. Go Naidoo, facing the door, has to yank his head around to see him.

Is this political? Go Naidoo sounds strangled. Is this the white *baas* showing the Indian who's the *baas*?

Paul finishes the repair job.

Is it? Go Naidoo almost shrieks.

No, Go, Paul says. It's personal. Very personal.

Paul watches the man twist and turn, trying to look at him. The sensation that this conjures up in Paul's breast is sickening. The sight is turning his intestines into knots, into hard coils of brutality. He quickly wraps several loops of the tape around Go Naidoo's neck and then makes a repeated link that connects Go Naidoo's neck to the brass door handle of the wardrobe behind him. Go Naidoo will not be able to throw himself forwards in the chair. He is stretched on a bedroom rack comprising a plastic chair, packing tape and a little handle.

Paul feels himself sliding. Anything is possible. And through the anguish is born, with even greater intensity, the image of Chantal. But her face is fading. He is losing her. He panics that this is a sign.

I'm going to ask you once, Paul moves around to stand in front of Go Naidoo. What have you done with my daughter?

There is no slick salesman's response this time. Go Naidoo regards him with . . . with what, Paul is not quite sure. Hatred? Loathing? Fear? Contempt? Each emotion is possible. It's all terrifyingly possible. Paul blinks. In the chaos of this new country, anything is possible.

Nothing? Paul asks. His voice might be sad, tired.

Go Naidoo watches him.

Look, Go Naidoo says finally, his voice slightly hoarse from the packing tape scarf. I sold you a car, man. A fucking BMW. White, 318i, with leather interior. Brand new. And a car seat. With a free tank of petrol. And that is fucking that. He stares defiantly at Paul. It is defiance. He then clears his throat. Makes a deep sound and, though unable to move his head, calmly spits on to the black, shining floor.

The streak of mucus lands with a crinkle of plastic. It lies on the floor in Chantal's room. Go Naidoo has just spat in Chantal's room. Paul feels faint. He is losing his grip.

Paul turns without a word. Then he changes his mind. He moves behind Go Naidoo and grabs the cloth, the tape and the scissors. Then he comes around, back to the doorway towards which Go Naidoo faces. Changing the things to his left hand, he bunches his right fist and hits Go Naidoo as hard as he can in the stomach. The man sees it coming, jerks his head back wildly, exposing more gut than is good, and emits a crying grunt as the wind is knocked out of him.

Paul watches Go Naidoo's head jerk. Go Naidoo tries to slump forward to clasp and nurse the blow, but he cannot. He cannot crumple like a doll. His mouth twists as he tries to draw breath, and that is when Paul shoves in the cloth, rams it home into his gaping mouth and in an instant has ripped the tape around his head, several times across his face and behind his head and back again, tighter and tighter. Go Naidoo's eyes pop with surprise. They actually bulge on mushroomy white stalks as he tries to draw breath. His face darkens; he sucks at the stifling plastic tape, his cheeks collapsing. Then his nostrils thin and flare as he pulls in air in snorting jets.

Paul goes downstairs. His legs are jelly. His guts are concrete. Despite the gag, he can hear Go Naidoo gurning like a stuck pig. He seems to be able to generate sound from the depths of his stomach. Maybe it's a Hindu thing.

Paul returns, as though from shopping. I'm back, he feels

like saying. I'm home, my love. Home with the goodies. Don't you look cosy, all strapped up in your chair. Instead, he says nothing. He makes sure that Go Naidoo's popping eyes watch his every move.

Paul has learnt well. He feels that he knows a thing or two about such matters in the new South Africa. How to strike fear into the heart of a man. How to play tricks on the mind. How to subject warm, innocent flesh to one's cold, aggressive will: how to bend another body on purpose and with pleasure, to hear it cry out no matter how muffled the mouth. Paul feels the exhilaration of power, brute, blunt power, rising ever further in his throat. His hands shake, his stomach is still rock hard. Go Naidoo is beginning to make squealing sounds as Paul switches on the steam iron and brings it now spluttering and hissing towards him.

This is urban legend alive and well in a little girl's bedroom, amidst the teddy bears and the delicate pastel pinks of the walls. This is the horror of South Africa, the heart of darkness, a savage drum, beating rhythmically in a quiet home on a Monday morning whilst people are at work. No need to stop all the clocks, or pack away that drum. Shit happens, and not even the newspapers care. This is not news. This is ancient, almost tribal. It's a tough country. What the Zulus did to conquered peoples and to each other. What the Dutch did to their slaves. What the Boers did to the African tribes. What Dingaan did to Piet Retief. What the British did to the Boers. What Verwoerd did to them all. Monday mornings have come and gone and come back again. This is a country soaked in blood under a baking sun. The iron hisses like the wind on the veld rustling through the grass whilst the piet-my-vrou sings its maddening song and the go-away bird, the grey lourie, cries its repeated warning to the world rimmed by a mad blue sky. The iron gurgles with the grunt of male baboon, a sentry on the lookout for the silent, shape-shifting approach of the hunting leopard. And Go Naidoo heaves at his bonds, a gazelle caught up in his very own sinews and straining every muscle as he tries to outrun the pride that has him surrounded. *Kweh, go-weh* cries the go-away bird, and Paul comes closer.

Go Naidoo's cheeks suck and puff as he tries to scream. Paul's hands shake as he brings down the stinging plate of metal. The kitchen appliance, created to smooth recalcitrant creases, hovers above Go Naidoo's smart trousers. They are not creased at all. They are serene and flat like the sandy roads that run through the Free State. But a dark stain begins to spread from Go Naidoo's groin. He has wet himself, and worse.

Gently, Paul strokes Go Naidoo's leg with the iron and presses the button that releases a sigh of steam. Again comes the pig sound. Paul remembers a safari trip, parked at a water-hole at midday. It was not what they saw that stunned them. It was the sounds. A warthog trotted off through the bushes, and a second later came its shrieking squeals as it was hunted down and killed, some ferocious jaws and sharp fangs biting into it, crushing its back.

Go Naidoo squeals and bucks and thrashes against the packing-tape bonds. Paul runs the hissing iron up and down his leg. More sandalwood wafts warmly into the little bedroom, as well as the rather sour smell of urine. Perfume and piss. He irons away. Up and down the living leg of the pants.

Paul finds himself watching his hand in amazement. The

adrenalin thunders in his head like a highveld storm. He feels as though he is looking out over an Mpumalanga escarpment, from the viewpoint at God's Window, staring out over the Blyde River Canyon. Far away, his hand holds the steaming iron and runs up and down Go Naidoo's leg. The man is in danger of throttling himself. But it cannot be helped. It must happen. Paul wonders how many millions of black maids have ironed how many billions of white shirts in South Africa's past. Blacks preparing whites for the office, the boardroom, the classroom, the night out. Making them look smart and earning a living themselves. Blacks in white homes. Non-whites, *Nie Blankes*, as the famous apartheid signs had it. And here he is. He has a non-white in his white home, and he, the white, is ironing the black. These are straitened times.

Go Naidoo goes rigid, judders and then is still. His head slumps, slightly to one side, held in place by its tether. Paul thinks he has killed him. He removes the iron from the steam-soaked, burst-blister-moist trousers and checks Go Naidoo's pulse. He has just fainted. He is alive. He is still this side of those iron gates of life. Marvellous.

Paul sinks back and sets the iron to one side. The house is silent.

The tears blur his vision, and he has to press his fingers hard against his eyes to stop them. Go Naidoo shudders back to life.

Paul gets up.

Okay, he says. Okay. Now, are you ready to tell me what happened to my daughter?

For a while Go Naidoo's head lolls and he does not seem to comprehend Paul's question.

Paul goes to the bathroom to gulp some water, then wishes that he had not.

Go Naidoo's eyes are dark and snakelike when he returns. The room stinks. The iron pants in little whispers on the floor. The poor thing seems exhausted. Soon, Paul will never be able to touch it again. Wearily, he picks it up. God, it's heavy.

His thumb releases a spurt of steam.

Okay, he says. Is it grudging admiration he feels for Go Naidoo, or the worm of doubt beginning to turn in his belly? He has heard about families being tortured in their homes with irons and other kitchen appliances. Often it's the weeping wife, tortured whilst the trapped husband looks on, the intruders waiting patiently for the code to the safe, or the whereabouts of a weapon. Pets have been microwaved too. Par-cooked Pekinese yappingly rotate whilst their forgetful owners take their time to remember where Granny's jewels are hidden. Children forced to take a sip of bleach, their parents screaming all the while. Often it's for the hell of it. Gangs crapping on the floor, Daddy tied up and gagging on a stool, a fresh turd, a faceful of shit. Old women raped. They say it's done to insult, to pay back. In the African culture, age is respected. So you rape a grey-haired granny. In truth, it's the Rape and Retribution Commission. This is real life. People do not forget and forgive that easily. And a generation of black schoolchildren who rejected the barbed-wire strictures of apartheid education now roam free in this bloody country, brought up on the syllabuses of the street. Savage codes of conduct, the exhilaration of a life where no textbook can touch you.

Go Naidoo moans, but then shakes his head.

Paul holds up the iron. He touches the trigger of the iron. Steam envelops Go Naidoo. It swirls like a halo around his face. Go Naidoo moans again. He nods his head this time. Each nod twangs the packing tape tether.

Are you sure? Paul asks.

Go Naidoo definitely nods.

More in anguish than in hope, Paul begins to unwind the gag. It takes a while to find the end of the packing tape. It's like opening a present. Paul knows that he will never be able to touch Sellotape and the like without feeling sick. The tape pulls free in yelping strips.

Paul has to fish around in Go Naidoo's mouth to extract the gag. It is sodden and hard. Go Naidoo shudders and gasps as it pops out.

Paul watches him as he coughs and splutters. Go Naidoo runs his tongue around his squashed lips. He whispers to himself.

What's that? Paul says sharply. He realises that Go Naidoo is hoarse from making squealing, grunting pig sounds deep in his throat.

Water, says Go Naidoo. Paul can hardly hear him. He gets Go Naidoo a glass of water. He has to hold it to his lips. He has to gently tilt the glass and ease the water into Go Naidoo's body. His water now becomes part of Go Naidoo. It will infuse so many cells, vivify his blood and then be pissed out, possibly in less terrifying circumstances. But for a while, water will become living flesh. Yet his daughter has evaporated. Her body has become air, sustained only deep in their memory.

Where is she? Paul removes the empty glass and leans up against Go Naidoo's mouth.

For too long, Go Naidoo does not speak. His Adam's apple works away as he swallows some last drop of water. Then his eyes meet Paul's before quickly closing. Go Naidoo speaks with his eyes screwed shut. His voice comes in a whisper, as though he is conjuring up razor blades, one at a time.

His words cut into Paul. Each syllable slips in through his right ear, pressed up against Go Naidoo's mouth, and makes a neat incision in his mind.

Yes, there was a plan. A system. Complicated. Go Naidoo was approached. Not at the office. At home. They knew where he lived. They had followed him home. They phoned him at home and told him that they were waiting outside. Did he want to let them in, or should they simply come in? He couldn't set the dog on them because they already had the dog, a youngish Dobermann with its mouth wired shut and a front foot smashed. How had they done that? Wired its mouth closed and dumped it wriggling in the boot of their battered Audi. All that despite security gates and a wall with razor wire. All that whilst Go Naidoo watched television. What could these men not achieve if they set their minds and guns to it? They had set their minds on him. There are things more profitable than mere cars. The cars are good, fine. But there is a growing market for children. White children. Girls, virgins. And boys. Virgins too. Even babies, they don't mind. White children and light children. Coloured children too.

Paul tries to piece together in his head the slit and severed pieces of his cerebral cortex. It seems that his head has been cut to ribbons.

My child, he mouths.

Do you have a child? he asks Go Naidoo.

Go Naidoo's eyes open and fix on the ceiling. I have a wife, he says. And a mother and a retarded sister. They told me what they were going to do to my wife and my mother and my sister. If I didn't help them. Or if I went to the cops.

He stops speaking. His eyes roll to Paul, who stares unseeing at unspeakable images of Go Naidoo's womenfolk, weeping, wailing, gasping.

Would they do that? Would they be capable of such things? They would. Even as the questions frame themselves, he knows that again, in this land, absolutely anything is possible. Never mind America, this is the South African Dream. Except its nightmarish qualities are more apparent, more tangible and more quotidian. Black children squeal and frolic in the dust of countless townships. Servants work in neat white fortresses. An emerging black middle class buys bigger and better cars. There is separate development, apartheid on another insidious scale. Cracked lives. Different realities. And between these cracks, amongst these myriad fissures in a totally fractured society lurk men who can torture and maim for a living. The smell of Go Naidoo is sour in Paul's nostrils. The realisation is hazy, unconscious. Why, he, Paul van Niekerk, is becoming such a man. He is stumbling his way into the South African Dream. Of necessity. As need he must. He is no émigré. He is not welcomed by a Statue of Liberty, clutching her book and her torch. No Emma Lazarus inscription about bringing Liberty her huddled masses yearning to breathe free, whilst her back is turned on the rest of the continent. No, in South Africa a sailor is greeted by Table Mountain, a vast plateau, incongruously domestic, a table, yet flanked by Devil's Peak and Lion's Head. And as the clouds roll in and set the tablecloth, you are offered to feed at the foot of the continent. And stretching back into the kitchen and the infinity beyond lies the rest of Africa, deepest darkest Africa lying on her back, legs spread wide under the blazing sun. Plain for all to see, even inviting, approachable, but utterly unfathomable.

If I tell anyone, they will come to get me. Now, I've told you. Go Naidoo's voice continues to cut into Paul. Now he is weeping. Go Naidoo is weeping at the ceiling. He cannot move his swollen hands to wipe his face. Tears run in glistening rivulets down the side of his face.

There are still sufficient connections in Paul's mind to continue. So it wasn't a coincidence. The second hijacking. Did Go Naidoo call his contact? The red BMW, last Wednesday?

Go Naidoo nods. No choice. If they found out that he had sold but not called . . . He is sure that they pay a vendor on the street corner nearby to keep an eye. On the comings and goings. They said that they would be watching. And not to be a clever Indian. A cheeky *charra*. They are racists, these black gangsters, Go Naidoo's voice chokes.

Where do the cars go? Where is Chantal?

Go Naidoo is silent. He does not know. Soweto, he imagines. He does not know whether he imagined that or whether he heard them let slip about Soweto.

Soweto.

Even more vast than Alexandra. In Paul's mind Soweto races off to tangled, smoky obscurity. South Western Townships. An urban agglomeration sprawling south-west of Johannesburg. The greatest grouping of people in southern Africa, if not the entire continent. Named by a white woman.

Soweto, a name, a concept, conjured up for a competition and first place went to a white housewife. Paul wonders what she won.

Go Naidoo interrupts his disjointed musings.

If there is any sign of the police getting involved, they'll kill her, he says.

Paul looks at him.

Go Naidoo's eyeballs swivel. Take this bloody thing off me, he says.

Paul thinks.

Damned if I do and damned if I don't, he says. Is there any chance that Chantal is alive? He speaks more to himself than to Go Naidoo.

Go Naidoo's response is oddly emphatic.

Of course she is, he says. She is worth money. They won't waste money.

Paul stares uncomprehendingly at Go Naidoo. He catches the tone, the certainty in Go Naidoo's voice. Meaning follows slowly. Words heavy with freight. Three sentences that will haunt him for a long time. She is alive, of course she is. She is worth money. They won't waste money.

11 days

CLAIRE KNOWS NOTHING. CLAIRE SUSPECTS nothing. She has no idea that her husband has turned torturer. She has no clue that the strong white hands that have stirred the two heaped sugars into her syrupy tea are capable of ironing the living leg of a man in the bedroom of their daughter. Will she ever guess that a shot was fired in that room, that a bullet is buried in one of the walls? She does realise very soon that a bullet is missing. But Paul has covered the hole with a white mask of Polyfilla that hardened quickly and took a dab or two of old pink paint. When Claire comes home from her trip to Soweto on that Monday night, the anniversary of their daughter's abduction, she does not go into Chantal's room. She does not smell the sharp scent of fresh paint or spot the slightly brighter patch of pink. She steers clear.

Maybe she wonders why Paul keeps washing his hands, Lady Macbeth-like. Why he cannot eat the spicy Nando's that she brought with her. Extra hot for her, lemon and herb for him. His favourite. Why he has to keep going to the bathroom as she tears into the seared flesh of the chicken. Since he is not eating, strange man, she rips the skin from the aromatic thigh of his portion and marvels at the speed with which he disappears into the downstairs loo. He is very fidgety. He needs to go back to work.

Paul once again marvels at his wife's ability to pack food into her trim body. But then his thoughts run elsewhere.

Chantal is alive, of course she is. She is worth money. They won't waste money. The thought sustains him. The thought tears at his mind. Who has sold her? Who has paid for her? Why have they bought her? To what nefarious purposes could his tiny daughter possibly be put?

His ribs ache, but they are getting better. His leg is not as bad as it was and his face is subsiding. His body will heal itself, but will his daughter ever come back?

Claire can never suspect a thing.

There was no blood spilled in Chantal's room. It took a couple of minutes to rip up the Heath Robinson protective covering and put it in the bin. Or Heathen Robinson, as a friend of his mother's once said, and it has lodged in his comedy cortex. Scissors and tape restored to their assigned places, the gun laid to rest in the oven, the bullets buried amongst the cleaning materials, the spent cartridge chucked in the bin with the rest of the household waste. The chair carried back downstairs by no less than Go Naidoo himself. Into the garden to rest with the remainder of its fellows. The domestic set that surrounds them as they sit at the dining room table is restored. Order prevails. Quiet and calm. No sense of the prisoner-of-war scenario. No echo of the tortured screams that still make Paul break out in a sweat. No lingering scent of seared flesh – just this fucking chicken that Claire has brought home. It looks like part of Go Naidoo's leg, where the dark skin turned yellow with oozing plasma, where it peeled back in dead, pale fronds to reveal startlingly pink flesh streaked with black and red blood. No need for Shylock's speech about do we not bleed. Hath not a Jew eyes and so forth. It is clear that an Indian has pink flesh and abundant bodily fluids. That he feels pain.

Claire chews loudly. Paul makes it to the loo yet again.

Go Naidoo limped as openly as Paul did. He went to the bathroom to clean up, Go Naidoo did. Like a guest. Paul gave him some underpants and a pair of tracksuit trousers. He rejected them both. They had to cut away his right trouser leg. Paul paid him for the trousers. He strapped ice wrapped in a clean dish towel around Go Naidoo's burnt leg. Go Naidoo accepted these ministrations, swearing silently. Then they limped outside. Go Naidoo called in sick from the demo car. He let Paul take him home. Go Naidoo lives not too far away, an older house, in Vorna Valley. They could have been neighbours. Maybe. Go Naidoo told Paul to go. To take the car back to BMW and to confirm that he, Go Naidoo, felt ill.

Paul drove very slowly back to Midrand BMW. He dropped off the car and collected his own.

A difficult drive home and he set to work on the hole in the wall. Patching it up. Covering it up. The bullet buried deep, so deep in her wall.

Paul does not know that Claire counts the bullets every night now. That she returns the gun to its position on the fourth bar of the grid in the oven. That she knows something is happening. It will take a while for that to come out.

Like the stains on the dish towel.

And the fact that the iron does not seem to work properly any more. It left strange streaks on a blouse of hers. Ruined it. It smells. It absolutely stinks. She will have to get another blouse ready for tomorrow. She likes order; this is chaos. Why did he mess with the iron?

Why would I mess with your iron? Paul lies to her.

My iron? she repeats crisply, but lets it go. She bends open a stiff paper clip and begins poking out pieces of Go Naidoo from the steam perforations along the metal panel. The clotted bits ping on to the carpet. Claire wipes the point of the paper clip on a tissue. Her hands are steady as can be; his own begin to shake. He shoves them deep in his pockets whilst he leans on his crutches.

Once she has picked the iron clean like a blonde vulture, she turns on Paul. She points to his leg, unencumbered by its protective cast.

What's the big idea? she demands.

A moment of madness, he says. Can we leave it at that?

Can we? she says. Should we?

Paul shrugs. I would prefer to, he says.

She waits for the iron to heat up. She gives it an experimental prod. Steam hisses into the room like a curse. Paul inhales the revivified aroma of Go Naidoo. The smell of sandalwood and seared flesh, like the ghost of a strange oriental cannibalistic *braai*, smothers him. He wants to grab the spike of the paper clip and dig the sense out of his nostrils.

It seems fine, Claire says. Apropos the iron, not his leg.

Then she turns on his leg. If you don't want to be a cripple for the rest of your days, we need to get that leg seen to.

Paul throws his crutches down and slumps into the embrace of the couch.

Get up, Claire says. Will you get up.

He does not move.

Get up. I said, get up.

The iron coughs. Its steamy throat clears. It seems embarrassed. First Go Naidoo, now this. Paul cannot take his eyes away from the hissing iron.

Won't you turn that damn thing off? he asks Claire.

Get up, Claire says again. Get up.

Paul knows that the burden of the last week is bending their sense of perspective. That they are sinking beneath the weight of it all. The anguish, the uncertainty, the fear of it, like a sharp file, rasping away at the ends of their nerves.

Claire, he says.

Claire! he says even more loudly.

They are set for a humdinger. It takes a while for the ire to rise in Paul's breast. Claire is more of a tiger. Quicker to pounce.

Get up, she says. Be a man.

Be a man? he repeats senselessly.

Yes, be a man. Claire stands over him. You keep saying that you're a fucking man. Do something useful for a change.

Useful? He can only shout that word back at her. Useful?

I have spent the day putting up posters of Chantal, Claire shouts. With Claire. Traipsing a ladder here, there and everywhere. In Soweto, you know. Watching our backs at every turn. Not lying around at home playing with our plaster casts and fucking up our iron. She is shrieking at him, a blonde banshee now. I could do with some help. Be a man.

The same howl. Over and over.

So who are you? Paul shouts back, his voice deep and wild. Who the hell are you? Lady Macbeth? Florence fucking Nightingale? What more must I do? You have no clue, do you hear me, no clue.

Lady Macbeth? Claire says. She laughs, a short bark. This is life, Paul, you know, life. Not fucking literature. And what the hell do you mean by Florence Nightingale? If I'm nursing anyone, it's you. You're like a big baby.

He bites back his mocking comment about the lady of the ladder. He feels his tongue squirming in his mouth.

If you're not chasing hijackers, you're lying around at home messing up the iron. What have you been doing? Apart from cutting off your cast. Don't you want to be able to walk properly? Don't you want to get better? Won't you fucking get up so that we can get you back to the hospital? Get up.

Paul is breathing heavily. He feels as though he has been hit by a truck. But he gets up. Draws himself up to his full height so that he can look down on her, loom over her vibrant fury.

She throws his crutches to him and gets her car keys. She mutters to herself. Cursing silently. The emotional thunderstorm has not abated. It is just circling. It will return, Paul knows. It will come back. He gets into the car. His ribs ache, his foot aches and he is shaking.

They snarl and snipe at each other on the way to the hospital.

Then Paul has to explain himself to a very young doctor, barely out of university. They have to wait in glowering silence. Finally, a new cast drags at his stupid leg. They return home. Paul thanks Claire for taking him. Forced politeness. An attempt at sincere rapprochement. But she has already scurried upstairs, and Paul gets his whisky and props his leg up on the couch. He sighs, pulls out the stopper with his teeth and drinks straight from the bottle. Drinks long and deep from the cool glass neck and feels the fire of the alcohol settle nicely into his knotted belly. He feels the parody, the alcoholic stereotype, settle on to his shoulders like a mantle.

His hands finally cease their shaking. His torturer's hands. He holds them up before him. Scrutinises their long fingers with their blunt tips all the way down to the strange webbing that stretches between finger and hand. He flexes his fingers, bunches his hands into fists. Then extends them. Bunches them. He squeezes out every last atom of sandalwood that still hides in the minuscule whorls of his skin. Blood on his hands. Blood of the hijacker and now plasma and blood. Go Naidoo's vital fluids.

And then there are the screams. The sound of Go Naidoo's strangled screams. Paul bumps his way upstairs to find ear buds, to dig the sounds out of his head. He wakes Claire. He knows he wakes Claire, but she does not appear to find out what is going on.

He stops short of using the entire box of ear buds, gouging at his brain, like little white levers, attempting desperately to change gear. But his disgust will not be shifted, derailed. He must stumble through dream scenes that replay the horror of what happened in Chantal's bedroom and the look in the hijacker's eyes just before he died. The front door explodes with a shocking bang as Claire disappears on her way to work and Paul wakes up.

He knows that he must get back to work. Otherwise he will

go mad. Already his eyes are drawn to the half-empty whisky bottle, not to the kitchen where the cornflakes lurk. And why does he think of them as lurking?

He coughs and splutters and clears his throat. Then he calls the office. Leaves a message asking if they can send Solomon for him. Solomon is used to picking up a host of bizarre objects, props for the creative process, the artful business of conning people on a national scale. Just a few weeks ago it was inflatable swimming pools and a flotilla of plastic sharks. Today it will be him, he trusts. Paul van Niekerk and his plaster cast and a beautiful hangover.

He gets a reply at five past nine. That's fine. Solomon will be along in an hour.

He waits at the appointed time outside the townhouse complex.

The air is warm, yet fresh. The guard stands at the gate silently. They have already exchanged brief pleasantries.

It is a nice day, *hau*, is too much nice, the guard said. His name is Providence Nkosi. It says so on his badge. A great name for a guard, a gatekeeper. Paul responds warmly enough.

Providence Nkosi lets him through the gate. Paul leans beside the road, the metal of his crutches warming in the sunshine. The air is fine. Life-giving. He draws in great lungfuls. A breeze wafts through the bougainvillea of the townhouse complex opposite. The vermilion flowers stir with a rustle. The palms either side of the gate whisper back. The sun shines enough to sear his eyes, and Providence is a reassuring presence on the other side of the gate.

Solomon's giant *bakkie* pulls up at the appointed time. Its side is emblazoned with a red and yellow monogram, the big bold letters BB&P and the brash claim, Hitting Your Target. A black arrow, of marketing desire presumably, nestles straight in the heart of a red and yellow target. Bull's eye. Dead easy. Simply hire BB&P and your business will wing its way into the consciousness of your favoured consumers.

Solomon's cheery voice calls out through the window as it slides down. Paul yanks open the door.

Solomon is full of good cheer. His enthusiasm washes over Paul like an unstoppable tide. He is enjoying his course at UNISA, studying business management at the southern hemisphere's largest distance-learning university. Yes, Paul has seen it, a monolithic ship of concrete and glass sailing proudly on the rocky *koppies* just outside Pretoria. Incongruous but impressive.

Solomon peppers his synopsis of his latest module, Communications, with wry remarks about Paul's leg. Twice he leans over to pat the said leg. Solomon grows serious for a moment, then is back to his grinning ways. That is nothing. He has seen people with pangas in their heads turn up for work. In the townships you stand every chance of your body being punctured by an impressively wide range of ingenious objects, it seems: kitchen knives, of course, and forks, axes, pangas, the spokes of bicycles, sharpened pliers and garden shears. He has even heard of someone being sliced open with a specially sharpened fifty-cent piece. And does Paul know that the person most likely to be hijacked in South Africa is a black man driving a company *bakkie*, i.e. himself? He bets that Paul did not know that. It was in the newspaper. Just last week.

Paul nods and shakes his head, giddy with the thought of knives and axes and pangas and fifty-cent pieces. The sounds of Claire's spluttering iron and the choked distress of Go Naidoo serve as an uncomfortable backdrop. He is thankful that Solomon does not mention irons.

He leans into the wide seat, feeling the throb of the powerful engine and letting the energy of Solomon carry the conversation – monologue – as the cars whir past.

Solomon was almost hijacked twice, in this very *bakkie*. But he put foot. He didn't stop. A bullet passed through the windscreen here. Solomon leans forward and indicates the trajectory of that bullet. It passed out of the window behind him, not two centimetres from his left ear. Solomon laughs.

When it is your time, it is your time. That's why he goes to church on Sundays. That's why he dangles the crucifix from the rear-view mirror. Solomon's muscular arms wave, and he stretches out a firm hand to fondle the swaying Christ who bounces and jerks on a beaded string.

Solomon shows him a St Christopher medallion too, on a chain around his neck, as well as two leather bags strapped to his wrist. *Muti.* Powerful *muti* to ward off attackers.

Does it work?

Have I actually been hijacked? Solomon fires back with a huge grin. Am I still alive? You got to believe, Paul. He likes using Paul's name. You got to believe, Paul. Then he grows serious. So no news, heh? No news of his little girl. He lets go the wheel and unties one of the leather bags from his wrist. Here, he says. For you. It will help you.

Paul receives the little rough leather pouch solemnly. It is heavy.

Don't open it, Solomon's voice is urgent. Don't let the *muti* come out. Don't break the spell. Tie it to your arm, Paul.

Can I put it in my pocket? Paul asks.

Ja, Solomon says, *ja*, maybe you can. But when you tie it to yourself, then it is working much better.

Maybe later, Paul says. But thanks. Thanks, man.

They drive in silence for a while. Paul feels that a piece of Africa has just crept into his pocket. Here on the M1 into Joburg, amidst the traffic and inside the capacious cab of the throbbing *bakkie*, a black piece of Africa sits in his pocket. Lies rough against his thigh; nestles just above his genitals.

Paul remembers his parents talking about *sangomas*, witch doctors, years ago. He must have been about ten. Nail clippings or bits of hair. He thinks it was about some throwaway bits of a body that were taken and given to a *sangoma*, who laid a curse. Nail trimmings buried in part of the *kaya*, the domestic quarters, of someone's live-in maid. And her madness. Not the usual bed on bricks to stop the *tokoloshe* from climbing up to get her in the night. All the maids did that. Paul remembers playing with his neighbours as a child. They had a live-in maid, Emily. She brought Auntie Barbara and Uncle Bruce tea in bed. A tray of tea to wake them up. Paul could not imagine either he or his parents being woken up by a tray of tea respectfully delivered by a maid as they lay in state. What if they snored? What if they had just farted? Did she knock and wait for their reply? Or was the first sound of their day the clink of cup and saucer, the rattle of teaspoons and Emily's soft voice? Did she pour the tea for them? Familiar with their preferences – such an individual thing, tea. A minefield of preferences. What did they say to Emily? A sleepy thank-you, Emily? And did she make any reply? A quiet *yebo*, my *baas*, thank you, my madam? Paul still wonders. A maid as part of your life. And they, as children, snuck into Emily's room, a dark place that smelt strange. He and John, with the two boys, Ryan and Lance. There was her bed perched on a set of bricks. Rising up from the polished concrete floor, safe from the scamperings and deprivations of the little hairy *tokoloshe*. He remembers sounding out the name: taw-gaw-law-shi: the deep, triple-dark vowels pricked by the initial sharp 't' and final spitting 'shi'.

Standing silently in Emily's room, inhaling her soapy, earthy scent and staring at the bed in the gloom, the four little boys had shivered. They knew that they were not supposed to be in there. This was out of bounds. A small piece of apartheid in their own home. The outbuildings were an extension of the double garage, which in turn was linked to the main house. But this might as well have been a foreign country or a piece of the moon. They were *blankes* standing in a *nie blankes* zone: whites in a dark, non-white area. Apartheid cut both ways, it seemed. And why the allure of a Bluebeard's room? A little cell with its home-made defences against the prowlings of a part of Africa they could not fathom: the *tokoloshe*. Little Paul's nightmares were made of other fears. No hairy little critter that was stumped by beds on bricks. No, his horror centred on the lurking and skulking of unknown blacks on the other side of the wall at the bottom of the garden. At that stage they had only a low, three-foot wall and lots of shrubs that separated their home from the broad pavement and road. Paul remembers vividly a dream, a nightmare, about being under attack. What inspired it, he does not know. Maybe it was 1976, the Soweto uprising. Was he aware of the stockpile of food that his parents had hidden in one of the outside rooms, a disused storeroom as they had no live-in maid? Did he sense the white fear that choked the neat little suburbs when he was just nine years old? Cupboards and wardrobes stacked with baked beans and powdered milk. Tins of syrupy fruit and packets of raisins and more tins – of pilchards and corned beef. He must have been too young to remember that, surely. Yet somehow he dreamt of hordes of black men hiding at the bottom of the garden. They were coming. They were coming to get him and his family. He cannot remember how the dream ended. He just recalls lurking men and the terror. Waiting and waiting as the tide of black men gathered, silent creeping figures insidiously bent on getting into the house. Coming for him. He felt his tiny bladder squeeze and his stomach contract.

Thank you, Paul says to Solomon. Thank you very much.

Eish, are you okay? Solomon asks.

Paul laughs.

I need to get back to work, he says.

At BB&P, they could not be more welcoming. He has hardly been working there for any time at all, but they greet him like a long-lost friend. Possibly they are relieved. It was he and not they. It happened to Paul van Niekerk, did you hear? Let me tell you about him. Not me. Stories keep reality at bay. Urban legends give shape and sense to a nasty, sprawling reality. But Paul knows that there is also the jangle of nerves, the tightening of the chest that comes with the thought that it is getting closer. Every hijacking story, every tale of crime also brings the reality another step closer. Maybe it's a psychological thing too. Preparing you for the inevitable. Words summoning future actions into being. It's a double-edged panga.

He knows how they felt when Chantal was born. Suddenly they were not living for themselves. Suddenly they were asking, is this a country for children? Surely the answer was yes in the new South Africa. Surely an affirmative *ja*, man, for the Rainbow Nation. But that rainbow arches over a bruised and bloody mess. Political turmoil, blunt and suppurating truths and terrible reconciliations. And an economic reality, a horrible sore, that is stark and terrifying. Huge unemployment. How can they raise a child in this country on a roller-coaster ride of fear and loathing and hope and squalor and joy and despair and love and death? Claire has mentioned emigration. Their friends have spoken about emigration. A new concept is coined by Barry Ronge, writing in the *Sunday Times*: semigration. Heading off to the Cape. Abandoning Gauteng, *die ou Transvaal, daar waar my Sarie woon, daar onder in die mielies by die groen doringboom, daar woon my Sarie Marais*. The echo of the nostalgic Afrikaans song. Its longing for the *ou* Transvaal, a way of life that is simple and rural. In the maize fields under the green thorn tree, there waits my Sarie Marais. No doubt she is a beautiful Dutch girl, soft corn-coloured hair blowing in a gentle breeze that whispers through the dry, flat blades of the maize, the *mielies*, and calling to her departed lover with the voice of the turtle dove. Bring me back to the *ou* Transvaal, to the soft breasts of Sarie that crest her simple dress. Bring me back to kiss her bare feet that draw patterns in the cool dust in the shade of the *groen doringboom*. People are packing up for the Cape, heading a thousand miles south to winelands and the Karoo desert and Cape Town. Not quite London or Sydney or Perth or Wellington. Semigration. Driven to the brink of the continent. Pushed to the edge, but not over. Not quite into the freezing Atlantic and the cold Benguela current that they have all learnt about in school. Not quite.

Paul accepts the black coffee from Thandi with gratitude. He feels that he might be going mad.

Thanks for the daily SMS, he says to Nolene.

How is the leg? She joins them in their brightly coloured office that is supposed to inspire a blizzard of creative thoughts.

They chat for a while. Johan Badenhorst pops in, as does Eric Patel. Paul struggles guiltily to his feet. He finds it difficult to look Eric in the eye. His sharp brown eyes seem to see into Paul, into his last white appointee for a long time. Eric's teeth gleam as he smiles, as he says that it is good to have Paul back, and well done on bringing home the Durex account, away from those bastards at McCann.

Paul struggles to smile back. He bares his teeth and makes a sound at the back of his throat.

Better luck from now on, Johan Badenhorst slaps him on the back. Paul nods and grimaces as affirmatively as he can. Johan is a small man with long hair and a penchant for linen jackets and boots with a surreptitious heel. He is a little cowboy. Cowboy and Indian. Paul looks away quickly as Johan Badenhorst and Eric Patel march off. Eric Patel is very quiet today. Paul can barely look at him.

Nolene and Thandi bring him up to speed, as they term it. He feels slow at first, then again comes the shot of adrenalin. Maybe it is the caffeine too, but he thrills to the surge of ideas and challenges, conundrums that have nothing to do with the real world. Not really. What does it matter whether they change a lipstick slogan from Get Lippy to something more attuned to the black market, which research has shown favours deeper colours, plums and magentas and a more direct, less playful, less wordy approach? They consider and reject Light Up Your Lips, Use Our Lipstick, Dipstick, and, simply, Kisses. They all smear some on, Paul included. They smile stupidly at each other, their mouths made large by the vibrant colours. They pose and pout, grinning and looking serious, lean back and hunch forward in a parody of casual sophistication and romantic intimacy. Paul and Thandi touch noses and it takes them a while to stop laughing. Paul's sides ache and he has to beg them to stop. He smears the lipstick on the back of his hand, but then they put some more on and leave it on their lips as they go to an early lunch in the small canteen, happy to stand out from the crowd. Happy to show off to fellow creatives and the quieter crew from accounts and sales. They are a team once again. Paul can't stop grinning. Heady stuff. This is why he left teaching. This is much more fun. This is what it is like being a grown-up, having full licence to behave like a child but get paid rather well for doing it.

In the end they decide on Cool Carnival – a play on Coon Carnival, the big New Year's parade in the Cape, a kind of Mardi Gras. Cool Carnival with the slogan *Lekker* on the Lips. Nolene does not mind the hint of a pun on *lekker*: Afrikaans for 'nice' as well as 'sweet' or 'candy'. There is also a hint of licking: to lick. It captures the *tweetalige*, bilingual nature of Coloured society, as well as appealing to contemporary black and white markets. Though nowadays it's all about the expanding black market, what with the new political class and affirmative action, of course.

Nolene goes off to the art department, to chat to Brandon. Thandi leans back in her chair and stares at Paul.

How are you really doing? she asks. Life must be hell.

Paul fingers a particularly red lipstick. He swivels it so that the blushing tip emerges from the gold cylinder. He touches its creamy surface, then turns it closed, quickly.

She's alive, Paul also leans back. He folds his arms over his chest, across his heart. I know she's alive – and that's not just wishful thinking. He pats his chest. It's more than merely a hope or a feeling.

That's good, Thandi says.

She's somewhere in Soweto. Paul does not know why he is telling Thandi. Why he is telling her things he has not told his wife. Is it because she is not his wife?

How can you be so certain?

Paul admires her candour. Would he have the balls to be so direct if the roles were reversed? He doubts it. He has balls enough, balls aplenty, but not those kind of balls.

You know when you know? You just know? Paul feels stupid saying that. Really stupid.

However, Thandi nods.

Yes, she says. She strums the surface of the table with her bitten-off nails. When you came up with that plan with Nolene's sister's kid, when you were going to get the hijacker, I knew what would happen. I could just see it, smashed car, dead hijacker and you. She looks up at Paul. Broken. Bones broken. You know what that would be if it were a rhetorical device? she says.

Paul smiles. More games. More fun and games. He doesn't mind. He doesn't mind at all. The adrenalin surges.

Irony, he says.

Not quite, Thandi plays the stern schoolmistress. Come on.

Paul responds, almost breathlessly. A metaphor, a metaphor for my broken life.

Better, says Thandi. Yes, an objective correlative. As T.S. Eliot has it. An outer expression of an inner, she pauses, reality.

T.S. Eliot, Paul says. He wants to shout, Good old Thomas Stearns Eliot. Fell in love with England, abandoned America. What are you saying? he says. That I'm a confused old man with poetic aspirations, a poetry of what . . . mayhem and confusion? A Hollow Man?

Thandi looks at him. Maybe a Waste Land. J. Alfred Prufrock.

Paul laughs at her. Fuck Prufrock, he says. I'm more Sweeney Todd. You know, a man of action. Dangerous.

No, Thandi says. I know men who are dangerous. You are not dangerous. Desperate, but not dangerous.

Why are we having this conversation? says Paul. From lipstick to psychiatric. What's the deal?

No deal, Thandi says. No big deal at all. I just don't want to see you get hurt even more.

Paul now needs to breathe. He needs to inhale as the air seems to have leaked out of his side where his ribs press broken and bruised.

I'll be okay, he says. Then he repeats himself. I'll be okay, really.

Nolene comes back with more work. Two radio ads, for toothpaste and an insurance company, as well as a bid for a new client. It's Mr Price. A big account. Johan and Eric want a radically different approach that they can bring to the table, they say. Startling new ideas that they can thump down in front of the suits that own and run Mr Price.

Nolene hands Paul the toothpaste. Thandi gets the insurance company and Nolene sets to work on Mr Price. Remember, she says yet again, nothing clever-clever. Witty, yes, intelligent, of course, just not clever-clever. Barry and Eric want sales volumes to soar, not Loerie awards gathering dust in display cabinets.

Paul puts his mind towards breaking through the looking glass of the whitening properties and minty-fresh breath that previous campaigns have promised a yellow-toothed, halitosistic public. How to build the brand? How to strike out in new directions? As he scribbles on a pad, a part of his mind wanders off along the throbbing highways heading south and west out of Johannesburg, towards Soweto. Countless black taxis – the name, no doubt racist, that describes the minibuses crammed with black commuters – driven dangerously by men who mostly have fake licences and threadbare tyres. He thinks of the Putco buses, the busy trains, all heading to the sprawling conurbations, the tangled mass that is Soweto. And amidst that throbbing haystack, somewhere, lies his lost daughter, the slimmest, tiniest, littlest, brightest needle in the shifting husks and chaff and stalks of Soweto. If only he had a magnet large enough. If only he could fly over Soweto and pull Chantal out of the place like a fluffy bunny from a huge dark hat. Paul wonders again how many posters of Chantal are peering down at people who are too busy with their own lives, too busy looking at the pavements and the surging traffic to glance up and see a white smiling face, and notice the tragic incongruity of a tiny girl loitering on street corners, leaning on lamp posts, breathing in the fumes and the fug of rush hour as her skin darkens with the dust and the smog of thousands upon thousands of busy vehicles and her smile disappears.

The rest of his active brain plays with the whitening properties of a slender tube of toothpaste. How to render that on the radio? How to convert the image of a brilliant smile and the scent of fresh teeth to sounds on the airwaves? First-person accounts, breathless people telling similarly astounded people how whiter-than-white their teeth have become? What a joke. Maybe a joke would work? One day an Englishman, an Irishman and van der Merwe went to the dentist . . . Paul shakes his head but his heart is lifting. Yet again he is glad of the distraction: the more intractable and convoluted the problem, the less he can think about Chantal. He beats himself up with irrelevances and tries to pin down the precise fragrance of the toothpaste. Is it pure peppermint, or is there a hint of subtle spearmint and even a peppery aftertaste? He lumbers off to brush his teeth, and then brush them some more, and some more.

In the small staff toilets in front of the mirror the idea strikes. He has been swilling the toothpaste around in his mouth, tasting it, chewing it, almost like wine. Trying to divine its essence. Now he just has to close his eyes to realise it. There it is. The sound of teeth being brushed, amplified a bit. It would have to be rapped. He hears it now. The swish-swish of a toothbrush scrubbing away, intercut with a bass of humorous gargling, a quick spit and an aaaah. Aaaah, fresh breath, clean teeth, scrub, scrub, aaah. Fresh breath, clean teeth, scrub scrub, aaah. Making a hip and happening medley out of simple ablutions. The voice would be African, savvy, cool, streetwise, sophisticated. One of those voices that does not immediately announce, I am white, or I am black. A universal voice that breathes success and cleanliness and pleasure. Just a man and his toothpaste. Maybe the final aaah could be voiced by a similar female. Hint at a back story. Clean teeth equals female pleasure and satisfaction: aaah. Fresh breath, clean teeth, scrub, scrub, aaah.

He returns to his desk with a big white grin. He breathes fumes of happy peppermint and, yes, there is a hint of spearmint too. The thirty-second script springs seamlessly to life. His vision is transferred brightly to the computer screen, a crisp clear Word document almost ready to be printed and brought into A4 existence, for Nolene to grasp in her slim brown hands and to smile and say *voilà*, aaah, you are a genius.

The phone rings somewhere. Creatives should not be disturbed by phones. Remember Samuel Taylor Coleridge and the apocryphal person from Porlock who knocked *Kubla Khan* out of the skies of poetic reverie? God forbid that mere commerce should get in the way of delicate imaginations. That a rat-a-tat-tat on the door or the urgent trilling of a telephone should kill a creative idea in this pleasure dome.

The door opens and one of the secretaries – Gill, Paul thinks – silently hands him a note. Paul nods and puts it to one side. Fresh breath clean teeth, scrub, scrub, and when does the product get mentioned first? He strums the surface of the desk, the note flutters to one side. He is aware that the secretary – is it Gill? – has not gone. She stands there. He looks up at her, then down at the note. He picks it up.

Come home quick.

Three words. Bold, ungrammatical. An imperative. Not

quite a postman and not quite Coleridge. But an urgent inter-
ruption. Creatively held up. But at least the butterfly notion
for the toothpaste is pinned down, securely fixed in an
electronic file.

Thanks, he says. He saves the Word document. What
should he call it? Should he e-mail it to Nolene? Nolene is not
in the room. Thandi is staring out of a window, pencil poised
in mid-air. Fishing for thoughts, ready to spear the slippery
salmon of an idea. It's like hunting. And you must not scare
the fish or the nervous *duiker*. Paul attaches the document and
sends the e-mail. Take that, Nolene, *my skattebol*!

Paul is aware of Gill still behind him. He turns. Gill hands
him another piece of paper. Paul frowns.

Solomon will take you now.

He has forgotten that he cannot drive, that he must be
driven. That a thousand practical realities must dog his heels.
Forget about Kubla Khan and Xanadu.

Thanks, he says. He slips out. Thandi has not moved. All
the while her mind is out of the window, flying free.

Gill hands him over to Solomon. Solomon helps him into
the *bakkie*. They retrace their morning route, back to front,
reversing through space if not time.

Paul cannot help his inner dynamo; he cannot stop it
whirring. He asks Solomon which toothpaste he uses. Solomon
has to think for while.

Aquafresh, he says at last.

Why? Paul asks.

Solomon has to think again.

My wife is buying it, he says.

Why? Paul asks.

Solomon looks at him.

Why does she buy that toothpaste and not any other? Paul asks.

Solomon laughs.

The people at BB&P are always asking me, he says. They are always asking me, Solomon, why you are buying this and why you are buying this. My wife is buying the groceries. I am eating the food and brushing my teeth. My wife is buying the bargains. Things are too much expensive.

Paul smiles. Thanks, Solomon, he says.

Xanadu on discount; paradise at a knock-down price. How much of advertising is just bullshit, just so much *kak*? He laughs softly. Never mind back stories, he should be emphasising freebies, discounts, bargains, special offers and the like. He looks out at the afternoon traffic and sighs spearmint into the cab. So, everyone is driven by simple imperatives.

The off ramp to Midrand comes cruising towards them. Paul is in a limbo of thought. The *bakkie* swoops off the N1. Paul has to blink and refocus as Chantal greets them at the traffic lights.

Solomon turns to him.

Hau, Solomon says.

Jesus, Paul says. Jesus Christ. His heart has just been wrenched from his chest and dragged across the intersection. Someone is nailing it to the traffic lights. Cars, trucks, motorbikes will be driving over the trailing arteries and veins any second. He will suffer a cardiac arrest under the afternoon traffic. Jesus Christ. The poster of Chantal hangs from the robots, the traffic lights, surely illegally. The light above her shows red. Then sudden green.

They arrive home. Solomon has driven quickly. Paul has not appreciated just how speedily Solomon has got him home. They drive through the gates, Paul waving at the guard.

Thanks, Paul says, fiddling with his crutches. Thanks, Solomon.

Solomon drives off. Claire opens the door and the security door.

I kept calling your cell. She steps aside to let him pass into the house.

Paul pulls it out of his pocket. It's dead. Battery gone. He does not remember not charging it. A double negative. Not a positive.

What? Paul says, and then the man in the lounge gets up. He is thin and wiry. He has a beard streaked with silver. He wears *velskoens* and his checked shirt hangs out. Paul wonders if he is looking at an older, much smaller version of himself.

This is Victor Vermaak, Claire says. Her voice is strained. He is from the *Star*.

The *Star*. Joburg's main broadsheet.

Victor shakes his hand. Thank you for seeing me.

Paul glances at Claire. Has she been crying? Is she about to cry? He does not know his wife any more. Chantal on the robots?

The lights in Paul's head jam as Claire utters the words he thought he would never hear.

They . . . have . . . found . . . Claire says. They . . . have . . . found . . .

The blood bangs in Paul's temple. He can barely make out Claire's words. It is as though he already knows what she is trying to say.

They have found your car, Claire says, and Paul has to sit down.

Where is she? he asks. Where is Chantal?

Claire looks at him. Is it pity or disgust? Paul begins to realise that he does not understand what she is saying. He looks at the hairy man and back to Claire. His head is going to burst.

They have found your car, your BMW. Claire repeats herself.

Where is it? Paul feels those caves of ice come crashing down. His universe turns on a tiny personal pronoun. From she to it. Where is it, the car? If they found the car, surely she will be found. She went with it.

Paul looks at Claire and wonders why her voice has changed. It is mellow yet precise, the timbre is oddly resonant. Paul realises that it is the bearded man, Victor, who is talking to him. Claire regards him. She plays with the chain about her neck, fingering it, pulling at it, worrying it. Paul turns from her towards Victor Vermaak.

There was a police raid this morning. Victor slides a small notepad out of his pocket but does not consult it. He anchors a loose strand of hair behind his left ear in a feminine gesture.

There was a police raid this morning, in the early hours, in Soweto. In Orlando West Extension, at a suspected chop shop – where they cannibalise cars for expensive parts or erase serial numbers and suchlike.

Ja, Paul says. His voice is soft, flat. Cars, things, stuff. What about Chantal? But he does not say anything other than *Ja*.

The gang was there, sleeping in a back room. But someone

sounded the alarm. No doubt a lookout. They probably paid some kid to stay up all night keeping a lookout.

Paul feels his hands tighten on the crutches that he still holds, that he leans on as he sits on the edge of his seat.

A shoot-out ensued. Victor Vermaak seems to speak in newspaper paragraphs. A shoot-out in which four gang members died. The fifth man died on the way to hospital, was pronounced DOA at Baragwanath Hospital. There were no police injuries. For once the police emerged unscathed.

Chantal, Paul says. Chantal.

Victor Vermaak shakes his head.

I am sorry, he says.

Paul would like to pick up his crutches and beat the man. Him and his column inches. Within an inch of his life. Why has he come here to tell them about a dead gang, but not their daughter?

You are sorry? Paul repeats.

Paul, says Claire. Paul.

Paul leans further forward. As far as he dares.

Victor fiddles with his pad.

I can help you, Victor Vermaak says.

You . . . ? Paul's query hangs in the air.

Victor stares at him. Your wife has put up a lot of posters, he says. That is good.

Paul keeps staring at him. What is this man from the *Star* trying to say? That he, Paul, has not put up any posters and that is bad?

That is good, Paul repeats.

Yes, continues Victor Vermaak. Chantal is in the public eye – like the Gert van Rooyen girls, you might remember?

Their faces were everywhere, those missing girls. Abducted. And then the leads came. Then the finger of suspicion came to point at Gert van Rooyen. I can help you take that further, offer a public platform.

My car was found in Soweto? Paul asks.

Victor's eyebrows move slightly. That's what I said, he says.

Paul nods. So just how many people in Soweto read the bloody *Star*?

Paul, says Claire. Paul, don't be rude. Victor is trying to help us.

Paul does not think the small bearded man in his *velskoens* and checked shirt looks particularly helpful. He looks like a little weed that has suddenly sprouted in their lounge. He looks like he has insinuated himself in the dirty space that has opened between them.

People in Soweto read the *Sowetan*. So what are you selling? Paul asks the journalist.

Victor Vermaak stares at Paul, his notepad forgotten.

Everyone is selling something, Paul says. Are you peddling our pain?

Paul, Claire's warning fires in the background.

What will it be? Paul asks. A human-interest feature – not in the main newspaper, surely? I know. You will stick us in the Life section, general interest: Paul and Claire van Niekerk living in limbo; their life sans Chantal. What clever headline will you create? What fucking wordplay? What fucking wordplay, you smug little *doos*?

Paul.

Mr van Niekerk.

Both Claire and Victor Vermaak flinch at his outburst. But

he cannot stem the flow. He feels it pour from his rock-hard guts; he marvels at the roar from his throat.

Don't you think we have tried? That we are trying? Do you think we have been sitting here on our fat arses waiting for you to rock up with your smug stupid notepad? Where were you when we wanted you? Where were you when we tried to call the papers? Non-stop, Paul is shouting, we have been at this non-stop. It has taken over our lives. I sleep downstairs now, our marriage is dying: do you want to stick that in your bloody Life section? Paul does not realise that he stands up, that his crutches have fallen with a clatter and lie crossed at his feet. Every waking moment, do you hear that? And it's worse in our dreams. Where do you want to stick that in the *Star*? Paul van Niekerk does not sleep. The man who murdered sleep. The Macbeth of Midrand. The man whose mind is fucking incarnadine.

Claire is pulling him back from Victor Vermaak. Paul's world has narrowed to the desire to punch the nasty little bearded face of Victor Vermaak. What white man in this day and age in South Africa is called Victor? Mandela came back into the world from the Victor Verster prison. How can a white man called Victor live with his name in this country? It's insane.

Claire manages to push Paul against his crutches so that he loses his balance and he sits down. His head spins. He is gasping as though he has just gone ten rounds in the ring. Yet he has not landed a single punch on Victor Vermaak's face.

Paul does not know what infuriates him so. Whether it is Victor Vermaak per se, or what he represents, or the infuriating look of pity that crosses the man's face as he watches Paul.

Paul brushes a hand across his eyes. Just fuck off, he says.

I am sorry, Victor Vermaak says.

Paul hears him slowly rise, still wary. Paul does not move, does not look at him.

There will be others, says Victor Vermaak. You can be sure there will be others. You have entered the public domain. I thought that you might . . .

The cry that Paul lets loose gets rid of Victor Vermaak.

It seems a long time before Claire returns and stands in front of Paul. He does not open his eyes.

That went well, Claire says. That was really helpful. Thanks, love.

She disappears upstairs.

Paul lies back in the seat. He can feel his heart beating in his eyeballs. The blood seems to whistle around his body. He does not trust himself to move. What others? What others could invade his pain? Their pain?

After an age, after a few seconds, he has no idea, the buzzer sounds from the gate. It buzzes several times like an angry insect. Claire has to come down from upstairs to press the intercom button.

It is the two detectives, Smit and de Jager, again. Claire lets them in. They agree to coffee. It is becoming something of a ritual. They sit opposite Paul once more. De Jager's taut body sits where the man from the *Star* had perched, a lithe feline to the ratty little *mossie* that picks on the scraps of others' lives. Claire seats herself on the single chair beside Paul.

We know why you are here. Paul does not see the point of exchanging formalities.

But Smit and de Jager, maybe because they are men of

brutal action, of hunting and tracking, hold fast to the principles of etiquette and decorum.

The weather is very hot, says de Jager.

Paul cannot believe his ears. He finds himself glancing at the two men and Claire as they exchange observations pertaining to barometric highs and lows. They seem to be impersonating Graham Hart on the weather report.

You have come to tell us that they are all dead, Paul says.

They look at him through the wisps of steam that play about the mugs they hold to their lips. Smit sips noisily. Paul detects Claire's intake of breath.

Every last one of them, Paul says. Killed. *Sommer mors dood*, he switches to ironic Afrikaans. Simply, utterly dead.

Ja, de Jager and Smit say. They look at Paul and at Claire. They seem genuinely sorrowful.

A terrible business, says Smit, his voice making the phrase seem old-fashioned. His accent rolls the 'r's and flattens the 'e' of terrible to make it turrabull. Ut eez uh turrabull buhsniss.

Ja, says de Jager.

Oh yes, says Paul. Not a single one left to question about our daughter's existence. Not a clue. The trail goes cold.

The two men look at each other.

Who told you this? De Jager's voice is neutral.

Claire describes Victor Vermaak's visit. The detectives nod.

Blerrie reporters. Smit puts down his coffee mug with a clunk on the low table that stretches between him and the van Niekerks.

And he wasn't even there, says de Jager. We were.

You were? Claire leans forward.

Of course, de Jager looks at her.

Turrabull, says Smit again.

They go on.

Information from ordinary people. Then staking out several suspected chop shops, you know the places?

Claire nods.

Ja, where stolen cars are 'processed' before being driven off to Botswana and Lesotho and Mozambique and other places that they *blerrie* use as launching pads to the rest of the world. Of course, quite a few of the cars remain here, local, and are just stolen to order. Hey man, I'd like a metallic sapphire-blue Audi Quattro or a red VW Microbus, that kind of thing. And off go the hijackers with their shopping list and it's *sommer* bad luck to anyone who drives along in a metallic sapphire-blue Audi Quattro or a red VW Microbus.

Smit keeps talking.

He tells of the perverted delights of fate and chance that strike like lightning out of a clear summer sky. They, the crack police unit, tried to strike with the same finality, and it became just that, too final.

The gang were not surprised. They must have been warned, maybe with only seconds to spare. But such moments matter. Such moments ring in eternity. The biblical turn of phrase underlines the gravitas and weight of their work.

They describe step by step what happened. They chart the territory carefully, taking the van Niekerks deeper and deeper into that world where everything is possible because criminal ingenuity can make it so. The will of shadowy and desperate men gives birth to every possibility: they have seen it time and time again. *Alles is moontlik*. Everything is possible.

One place had a tripwire linked to hand grenades. Hand

grenades! In a sprawling suburb they come across the relics of war. Others have booby-trapped doors, hidden chambers, hostages – women kept as sex slaves and serving as a living barrier to protect their furtive captors from their own entrapment. But often they are careless. These unfathomable people living in the twilight of society can make mistakes. Often it is thanks to drink and drugs. A ballooning sense of their own importance and power, inflated and floating high on cocktails of *dagga* and Mandrax and brandy and coke – cocaine and Coca-Cola. It takes all sorts.

The gang that they knew had taken Chantal was not high on drugs. They were on edge. They were professional and ready. They had factored in all such eventualities. So even though it was five o'clock in the morning, when usually these criminals are not quite waiting with their best foot forward, the team from the police were the ones that got the surprise. They had the place surrounded. They were trying to open the lock on the back door, break in like burglars themselves, when a shot burst through the door at point-blank range hitting a colleague full in the chest – right in his bulletproof vest, *dank die Here*. Thank God. He is a tall man, again thank God. Three inches shorter and he would have been spraying blood out of his neck. There are no bulletproof collars or scarves. He would have died in seconds.

So they hit Plan B. If there was any resistance, they had to go in strong. It was big guns, show them who's boss. Fight fire with fire, *my magtig*. And they blitzed them. Smoke grenades and tear gas in the soft morning light, and automatic gunfire. No rubber bullets. Those were live rounds. The only things missing were bazookas and anti-tank missiles. Disorientate them. Overwhelm them. Take them out. Shooting first at the legs, but as they returned fire, they had to go for the kill. For twelve minutes the gun battle rattled on, like popcorn in a pan. And just as the final few pops surprise you when you think everything is quiet, they got one last man who was hiding in the ceiling with a set of grenades. This gang was serious, man. They were the real deal. But no Chantal. The neighbours knew nothing. Nothing except of course that there were a lot of cars that kept coming and going from the compound at the back, but otherwise this was a busy neighbourhood and concrete walls make good neighbours, as do averted eyes and hurried footsteps past the place. Head bowed or face turned fixedly in the opposite direction. They made brilliant neighbours.

But no sight nor sound of Chantal. No white toddlers or babies. No sight nor sound in the day or the night. Just men laughing and occasionally there were angry voices. Swearing and fights. And just once a gunshot, but that could have come from anywhere on the street. The sound of a gunshot is nothing new, it happens all the time. On so many township streets. Shots and screams.

Before, it used to be the white security forces patrolling in their Samels and Ratels. Mighty metal beasts that once policed the borders of the apartheid system. *Ja*, there was less crime then. But not quite the good old days. No, not by a long shot. Now it's their own people with all the guns and that is a problem. *My magtig*, it is too much of a problem. And that has spread to the white areas. The white neighbourhoods now also know what it is to live in fear and terror. That is progress. That is true democracy South African style. Universal suffrage. Universal suffering.

Now some blacks live in white areas. Rarely is it the other way around. And many whites are jumping into the sea, sailing off to white areas further afield. Australia, England, New Zealand, Canada. All popular destinations. Far away from the fear, the fear that gets under your skin, becomes part of you, gnaws away at your insides.

So there is no sign of Chantal. The trail has gone cold.

The posters of their tiny daughter beam down and tremble in the wind or hang limp in the heat. They fray and curl at the edges. Many tilt askew. Chantal's face starts to bleach in the sun. Paler and paler, she begins to fade. The posters rustle gently and the traffic roars past. Will that call ever come?

1 month

H OW MUCH MIGHT CHANGE IN a month? A full cycle of the moon. Another ebb and flow of the menstrual tide so wondrously tied to that celestial body. A twelfth of a year. Midsummer becomes late summer but the days are still hot. February marches on. How little might change in a month.

Paul tilts his head back to drain the last drops of his Windhoek lager. The stars above him swoon and he pauses, mid-swallow. Beyond the base of the can, the African sky is all black velvet and close. The Southern Cross almost caresses his cheek. The beer can falls away with his arm and he remains standing, head tilted to the heavens.

He has come to the far side of the swimming pool, closer to what seems to be an orchard of thorn trees. Further away, beyond sloping lawns, the party thumps on. Music pulses from the thatched house, Johan Badenhorst's holiday home near Hartbeespoort Dam. It is Johan's fiftieth. The entire office is there, as well as Johan's extensive family and a wide range of his friends and business associates. Even the stuffy crew from The Jupiter Drawing Room and Ogilvy & Mather have deigned to celebrate amongst the champagne and the whispering and the summer stars.

Paul wonders what lies beyond the thorn trees. Thick elephant grass rises up and plays host to a billion crickets. Paul senses that a few steps to his left would take him away from the foaming music, all bouncing bodies and bubbles and froth, and if he wanted to he could be instantly lost in the African bush, his senses saturated with the screaming crickets. Through a wall of sound, he could slip into the dew and the dark, and inhale the husky wonder of the warm night air.

He recalls the camping trips as a child. His father, possibly hankering after some ancestral experience, a compulsion to return to the veld, drags the children off to a farm about an hour's drive from Benoni. They leave the main road and bounce along a dirt track amongst the rocky *koppies*. Hey presto. Within sixty minutes, the small matter of some 3,600 seconds, they have left home and are deep in the African bush. They play amongst the weathered rocks and chew stalks of thick veld grass. They find the perfect white bones of a hundred small rodents, dreaming in the black earth. It is a graveyard of mice and who-knows-what beneath a rocky ledge close to the crest of a *koppie*. An eagle owl's feeding spot, their father tells them. That night they hear the owl through the billowing walls of their flimsy tent. Their father is outside, lying beside the red embers of the campfire, sipping brandy and Coke and thinking about his paternal ancestors trekking across the Vaal River, cutting tracks across the virgin savannah and having to fight for the right to inhabit this wild land. Paul knows that his father has brought his gun with him. That it lies snug beneath his pillow, within easy reach. Not much has changed in Africa. Not much will ever change. It is the selfsame gun that years later he would use on Go Naidoo – and more besides. His childish games of cowboys and Indians with John and Rachel would become the life-and-death affair with a different Indian. Paul takes a futile sip from the empty can and tries to forget Go Naidoo. He has heard nothing more from Go Naidoo. Except at night, in his fretful sleep.

Someone splashes into the huge swimming pool on Paul's right. He looks down, his neck stiff from stargazing. The ripples in the pool surge towards him, the creamy gauze of the Milky Way rides the crest of the waves and shudders into black currents. There is a shout and someone switches on the pool lights. From the knees up, Paul is bathed in blue light. Another cry from a cocktail dress comes as a giggling woman is nudged into the water. The blue light waves crazily. Paul feels giddy just standing there. He takes a step back, content to return to the quiet bush and the zithering crickets. He almost stands on Thandi's toes. He turns as she says, Hey.

Whilst his skin glows a pallid blue, the weird light polishes Thandi's blackness to a burnished ebony. If anything, it makes her almost purple, the colour of royalty. She seems carved out of the night itself.

How did . . . ? he begins to ask. His voice trails off as more splashes and squeals tear through the soft darkness. The heavy bass thumps in counterpoint in the distance.

What a night, says Thandi. Her ambiguous laughter is rich and low. She sips her champagne with a smile and the empty can in Paul's hand slowly crinkles with metallic squeaks as he crushes it. When it has buckled as far as it will go, he does not know what to do with it.

Ja, agrees Paul. I don't know if I can get used to all this bloody bonhomie.

Thandi nods. She knows about the recent meetings. Paul told her himself.

Paul can't abide being in trouble. It brings back his schooldays like a sudden cut to the bone. Teachers, male teachers, Afrikaans and aggressive. Even though they were in an English school, there were many Afrikaans men. Often teaching subjects like Physical Training and Physics. Manly subjects. Very few men taught Afrikaans, though, the compulsory second language: terse, guttural, the lingua franca of apartheid. And although Paul had an Afrikaans surname and an Afrikaans father, he was English, with a mother who swam against the prevailing currents and strove for a clearer, more anglicised pronunciation, which her friends tolerated despite its perceived pretentiousness.

His name, when bellowed out by such a teacher, had a pair of vowels to crush. Paul was compressed to Pol or pronounced the Afrikaans way, Pole. But mostly it was just van Niekerk. Fun Knee-kehrrk. Nothing could have been less fun. Paul of the No-church, if you translated his name literally. Small of the No-church. Those Afrikaans teachers did not spare many souls. Dignity as well as 'educo', the Latin origin, to draw out what intelligence was already there, were not much acknowledged. It was all pour in, shove knowledge into these empty vessels and ensure that they made no noise. Shove in facts, ram home truths. And if a tendril of independent thought sprouted, lop it off. He recalls bending at the front of the class, waiting for the swish of the cane, all because he had persistently – cheekily! – tried to suggest another way of completing a formula for the motion of an object. When a car of 2,000 kg mass travels at the speed of 90 km/h along a frictionless road and so on. The wait for the cane to whisper its message of bright pain to his buttocks was worse than the agony when it came. He recalls thinking that at least his head was not shoved beneath the ledge of the blackboard as school legend – and in some cases practice – had it. That, in certain instances, you received the burning poker to the backside and, when you whipped up to clutch yourself as all schoolboys must, you then bashed the back of your head against the board. A double whammy. No doubt very much to the class's delight. It was always very funny when it happened to someone else. The connoisseurs commenting in the toilets afterwards at break that Dupi – du Plessis, Mr Frik du Plessis – had excelled himself that time with the three whips of the cane com-memorated by a single red weal. Dupi had managed, God knows with what beautiful skill, to land the cane in precisely the same spot despite the jerking subject and the careful delay between each stroke to maximise the pain and the humiliation. Low whistles, grave appreciation and the emphatic consensus that *ja*, Dupi must really hate your guts. He really, like really has it in for you, man.

And so it was that Paul sat before the directors of BB&P, all three of them. The black directors, the two strange names, were nowhere to be seen. They never were.

Paul sat quietly whilst Eric Patel made the absent directors' apologies. And although Paul was not standing bent over, waiting for the swish of the cane, it certainly felt like it.

It was an awkward meeting. Paul appreciated that it could not be easy bringing to task a man who three weeks ago had

227

lost his child, who had almost colluded in her disappearance, and whose marriage was in free fall.

Johan, the trim little cowboy, spoke first. Eric Patel and Karel Brown nodded sagely and seemed to accept that Johan spoke for them too. Maybe they had put him up to it, since it was he who had had the biggest part in hiring Paul, in taking a chance on a man with a good literature degree from Wits University, but no practical experience in the industry. It was Johan who had said that there was no substitute for intelligence and the desire to succeed. Why, he had those same qualities – and look where they had taken him. Paul remembered looking down from his greater height and wondering just where Johan believed himself to be. He was fabulously wealthy, yes, and his third wife was younger than Paul by several years and astound-ingly buxom and blonde, but it was also widely suspected that Johan did not just play golf. He was into coke in a big way; his nostrils always looked tender and he resembled nothing so much as a gunslinger with his finger on a shaky trigger. He was keen to shoot – and to shoot his mouth off.

That is exactly what he did with Paul. Look, with no disrespect, he had begun. But we are a business. You get it, a business.

Paul got it. A business. And what business was it of his if Johan's eyes were out on stalks, like overinflated mushrooms, that he was obviously coked out of his skull.

Johan had spoken in short bursts, like the pneumatic burr of machine-gun fire. Punctuality, important. Going the extra mile, essential. Walking the walk as well as talking the talk. He did not see much walking. And Paul, it seemed, had also gone quiet. Yes, Johan sympathised about the personal circumstances earlier that year, that 1997 was a bit of an *annus horribilis* for Paul, but for God's sake he must snap out of it. Johan drew breath, and then Paul felt the little cowboy come bashing through the swing doors of the BB&P saloon for the next phase of the show-down.

Loss is a strange thing, Johan had conceded, but for fuck's sake, man, fill the hole in your life with something other than this weird compulsion. You know, disappearing here and there. Taking it out on the staff. Paul's temper was hotly referenced as well. And his productivity. Johan paused, no doubt to make some contorted reference to a literary or artistic figure that might tangentially be relevant to the scene. Maybe, Don't cut off your ear to spite your face. Or, Don't do a Hemingway on BB&P. Or, You're not Franz Kafka, are you? Paul knew that Johan felt the need to reference some culture because he did not have a good literature degree from Wits or anywhere else. That although Johan might have made his millions in advertising, he still felt somewhat lacking on the BA, BA (Hons.) and MA fronts. That was when Nolene had appeared on her high horse. She whirled in, scattering decorum. Why had she not been consulted? On whose say-so was this meeting called? Why had she not been informed? Surely in a professional organisation like BB&P there were procedures, due process, legal requirements? Where was HR? She was Paul's line manager, for God's sake.

Paul sat bemused. His long frame reclined between the pop-eyed Johan Badenhorst and the force of nature, Nolene. The stand-off worked in Paul's favour. The grounds for dismissal yielded to the advancing might of Nolene, so skilled in the arts of politicking and persuasion. Those grounds became the little promontory of an official warning that jutted out into the future. Johan, Eric and Karel had been trapped in no-man's-land, and they knew it.

The best of a bad situation, Nolene had said afterwards, smiling and shaking her head. Then she had become serious. You are a great asset to the team, she resorted to cliché to make her point, but then had reached out and touched Paul on the arm. Look, she had said, keeping her hand on his arm. This is a dog-eat-dog world. Do some barking. Snarling. Dig up some bones. You know, mark your territory. And do it fast or they'll unleash other Rottweilers against you – and I won't be able to step in to help. I've seen it too many times.

Paul had nodded and for the last two weeks had thrown his empty heart and soul into the job. He stayed late; he arrived early. One week, for three consecutive days, he slept under his desk, using cushions from the reception couches. Ideas fizzed from his overheated brain: he lived and breathed slogans, fresh angles, unique selling points. He juggled marketing statistics and clients' special pleading. He came up with multiple strategies. He offered his accounts a range of options; he made them happy. He asked them to convey their oily satisfaction to Johan Badenhorst. For a brief spell he was the blue-eyed boy, the star pupil who took his lessons seriously, was attentive in class and worked his backside off. Almost hourly, another shiny apple arrived on Johan Badenhorst's desk.

Nolene and Thandi told him to slow down. But he was running.

If Claire could spend every waking moment either at work or at the gym, then he could do the same. Except for him it was work and Johan: no gym. He grinned weakly as he shaved yet again at the tiny washbasin in the BB&P toilets.

He scraped away at the persistent stubble, doing his best not to feel Chantal's warm body as she hugged his leg, crawling up to him then leaning against him that morning not so long ago. After the December holidays together, she had become *pa-vas*, attached to Dad. That had made a welcome change from her earlier obstinacy as far as her father was concerned. Paul had looked forward to the time when Chantal might perch on the loo beside him and chat away whilst he shaved. It would be their time together. Father and daughter, starting the day together. He kept shaving long after the foam had been cut away. His cheeks were as raw as his heart for the rest of the day.

Now Thandi is warm and close. He runs his hand down the side of his thigh, where his leg tingles. They make their way to the far side of the pool, to a pair of loungers. Paul finally relinquishes the beer can beside the lounger. Half a dozen more revellers have splashed into the shimmering water and their bodies ripple in the azure light. The music has gone quiet for a moment and the crickets shriek in the darkness, a high-pitched throb that if he isn't careful might seem to be the onset of a pulsating migraine. Paul has never before heard such a crescendo. He remarks on this fact to Thandi.

Thandi seems to be preoccupied. She sips her champagne, leaning back, watching the sky. There, she says finally. And there. Two shooting stars. You wait and wait for one, and then suddenly there are two.

Paul leans back. But he tilts his head to watch Thandi. The blue light from the pool makes her skin ever richer and darker.

Purple velvet. Her hair is ruched up. Her lips are full, the line of her chin and cheek is firm and strong. Yes, she does seem to have been fashioned out of the night itself. The splashes and laughter and neighbouring chaos make it easier for Paul to reach out his hand and to place it on hers.

Thandi does not move. She does not withdraw her hand, but she does not move it to hold his.

During the four years I spent in England, she says, I never once saw a shooting star. Look, she says, look for one more. I want to see one more to make it lucky number three.

Her skin is warm beneath Paul's hand. His large hand encloses hers completely. He begins to shiver. Thandi stares up at the black sky.

It has been a long time, Paul starts to say, but Thandi shakes her head.

Shut up, she says.

Paul lies back in turmoil. His eyes take in the African sky. The blue-rinsed splashes and squeals have gone quiet. People seem to be kissing in the pool and someone switches off the brilliant light. The water laps hungrily around the sides of the giant pool. There are romantic swishes and swirling, and low voices, but Paul keeps his eyes on the sky, letting the soft light of a million billion stars rain down upon him. In counterpoint to the warm urgency of the supple skin beneath his hand, he can feel the caress of heavenly light so many millions of years old against his cheek. He lies there in strange limbo. The warm here and now, the cold and ancient past, he feels caught between the two. The crickets throb and throb. He thinks, if possible, they are getting louder and louder. The earth tilts as he watches one star come tearing free from its place and drift sideways from right to left. He watches it with bemusement, then realises that it is a satellite. Its course is quick and certain, a perfect line across the heavens, threading its way amongst the powder-burst of stars. He watches it until its trail is lost in the branches of the thorn trees. His neck is turned now and, refocusing, Thandi fills his gaze.

My wife, he says softly.

I said shut up, Thandi repeats. She keeps looking at the sky.

I must speak. Paul is transfixed. He feels like the satellite, sliding inexorably across the African sky, seeming to find its way without trying. Just falling beautifully. Feeling its way across the face of the heavens.

I love my wife, Paul says. The declarative quietness of the statement is drowned by the maddening crickets. He takes a deep breath. They could tear one's sanity to shrieking shreds.

But it's difficult, he says. Our marriage is . . . difficult. When Chantal was taken . . .

It is the first time he has named Chantal to anyone. Before, he has hidden behind the elision, the circumlocution of my daughter, our child, my little girl. Now, Chantal is named to the night sky. But her soft syllables are instantly lost in the piercing wail of a million hidden insects that rub their legs together in a desperate plea for a mate. Chantal is spoken, evoked through the gentle sound of her father's voice, and immediately drowned. Paul feels that keenly. He rubs his temple with the hand that reached out to Thandi.

That rouses her. Thandi turns on her side, her third shooting star abandoned. She looks at Paul for a long time.

We could go into the grass, she says.

Paul looks at her in surprise. Her white top and tight white trousers glow in the darkness.

We could easily go into the grass, Thandi says. Her hand reaches out for Paul. He jumps at her touch. Thandi leans forward. You and me, in the grass, lying or standing.

Paul lies still, Thandi's hand on his arm.

It would be the easiest thing. Thandi's voice is very soft, almost inaudible. She seems to look at him tenderly. Or is it pity? In the darkness he cannot be sure.

You are attractive. Thandi pauses briefly. And I like white men. I've known quite a few white men. She turns away from him as on the far side, a couple emerge from the pool. Their voices are murmurs, auditory blurs in the night, and they go dripping back towards the house, their feet slapping wetly on the bricks of the broad path. The woman giggles.

But, Thandi continues, her hand rubbing his shoulder, I would be wondering about your daughter. I would be thinking about you thinking, or trying not to think, about your little girl. I would feel your pain, not your love.

Paul cannot find the words to clear his throat.

And maybe it was different in England, Thandi continues. I don't know. But here, here in South Africa, it would still be the white man taking the black woman into the bush. Wouldn't it?

Paul makes a sound in his throat, but Thandi's hand restrains him. I would feel like a black woman. I don't ever want to feel like a black woman. Not here. Not now.

You are a warm, intelligent, wonderful woman, Paul says to the black sky. His words hang in the humid air that pulsates with the night chorus.

This is South Africa, Thandi murmurs. And there is another reason.

Another reason?

Nolene, Thandi says simply.

Nolene? Paul can only repeat.

Thandi laughs. Her hand pats Paul's shoulder one last time. You haven't noticed? You haven't wondered why Nolene . . . ? Her voice trails off into a low chuckle and she turns away.

Paul pulls himself upright in the lounger and looks at Thandi. She is lying provocatively on her back, her legs spread wide along the lounger. He feels as though he could move across and lie on top of her without a moment's hesitation. He feels his resolve harden. She is right here. So is he. The night is dark and the sound of madness thrills in his ears. Her body curves fully and sensuously. Surely. Swiftly. Do or die.

Paul swings his leg with its plaster casing over the edge of the lounger. He leans towards Thandi.

Nolene, Thandi repeats. Nolene . . . She pauses. Nolene fancies you.

Nolene, Paul says to Thandi's white form. Thandi turns towards him. Her breasts shift against her tight white top.

Why do you think she stormed into that disciplinary meeting? Thandi says. Why do you think, after knowing you for such a short time, she was prepared to help you find, Thandi pauses, find Chantal? She would have risked her bloody life for you.

Nolene, Paul repeats. He thinks of her trim, precise person. Her efficient manner. He does not think of her, he has not thought of her, as having soft romantic feelings. He likes her. He likes her a lot. He respects her, her hard work, her thorough professionalism. But he can't laugh and joke with her quite like he can with Thandi.

Are you sure?

Thandi stands up. She reaches out a hand. Come with me, she says. I'll show you.

For a moment Paul resists the pull on his arm. He lets the tension stretch along their arms joined at the hand. He could simply ease Thandi towards him. Pull her down on to his lap. She looks at him and shakes her head.

They are just another couple who leave the pool and head back to the music that has started up again. Paul is both saddened and relieved that they are abandoning the craziness of the crickets. He swings on his crutches beside Thandi. She moves with easy grace, her high heels carried in her hand. Like two moths they flutter into the throbbing lights and heavy bass of the party.

The ultraviolet lights again thrust Thandi into lurid focus. Her white clothing glows painfully, whilst her face and arms fade. She looks around the gyrating bodies in the vast veranda and lounge. No Nolene. Thandi leaves Paul.

He swings across to the bar area, set to one side. Eric Patel is propped up against it. Living up to his uncharitable nicknames. The Babbelas Baas. The Rum 'n' Coke Coolie. He turns to Paul but looks through him, unseeing. Piss Artist Patel. Paul leans against the counter, glad to leave his crutches trailing from his arms. A Windhoek lager appears before him, but he asks for a Scotch.

There are a surprising number of people dancing. Mostly women, and a lot of youngsters. Teenagers all the way through to grannies. It's Macarena time. Paul pulls at the whisky as the dancers jump and flap to the irritating and insistent rhythm. The Bayside Boys should be shot. Eric Patel rests his head against the counter. Paul waits to see if he is going to fall asleep standing up. Eric Patel is famous for such feats of drunken narcolepsy. He has written off two cars and, office legend would have you believe, spent the night going up and down in a lift in the Sandton Sun. And he supposedly had to be carried off a flight to Gatwick after having missed the one to Heathrow.

The Macarena stops. Eric lifts his head and gestures for another drink. He notices Paul, tries to wave cheerily but ends up scowling instead. Without his asking, the barman refills Paul's glass. Cheers, says Paul as Kylie Minogue plunges into the Locomotion. The entertainment areas become a tangled mass of weaving human trains. Everyone is hanging on to someone else. Paul and Eric catch each other's glance and down their drinks. The liquid keeps coming. In the middle of it all, Johan Badenhorst is clicking his heels and waving an imaginary lasso around his head.

It seems to loop and catch Eric Patel on his right shoulder as he tilts towards Paul and is toppled in slow motion. In a graceful clatter of crutches and limbs and whisky glass, Paul finds himself on the floor with Eric Patel on top of him. The man is limp and warm. And fast asleep. No one has seen them go to ground. For a while, Paul struggles, but his plaster cast is well and truly trapped by the felled man, who seems to weigh a ton. From far away a slow number is playing, Chris de Burgh. Paul can feel the wooden floor thumping slowly beneath him. Eric Patel lies across his chest and legs. Paul finds himself laughing weakly. It's all true. Every word about Eric Patel. He

237

does weigh a ton, and Paul yields to the whisky and the wooden floor and the Lady in Red.

It is Nolene's face that swims into focus to the strains of Dolly Parton. She seems to be laughing at his predicament, then there is a call of concern. His one free hand tries to scratch his face, but it slips from his cheek. Then the smell hits him. Eric Patel has been sick all over him. The sour stench of his drunken vomit burns Paul's nostrils and skin. No wonder he needs to scratch himself. With one hand to her face, Nolene uses her other hand to tug at Paul, to try to free him. Paul's limbs are leaden and far away. Eric Patel lolls loosely. Nolene struggles to free Paul from his limp weight. Eventually she uses both hands and a crutch to lever the catatonic man to one side. He flops over, sick trailing from his mouth. There are no serviettes at the bar. Nolene has to help Paul to the toilets. He moves like a somnambulist. He and Nolene tumble into the nearest bathroom.

Paul leans against the basin and rips at his shirt. The sodden garment tears free in his hands and he throws it to the floor.

Ugh, he says. Man, ugh. A slick yellow streak shines down the side of his face. It's in his hair. His right eye burns too. Nolene runs the hot water and grabs the hand towel.

Quick, she says.

Paul washes cold water over his face. The water warms quickly and liberates the stink.

Ugh, he says again.

The water comes warm and fast. Nolene pushes the towel under the stream and then helps Paul to rinse his hair and wipe down the side of his head and neck.

There, she says, offering him the towel. You finish off. She presses the towel to his chest.

Paul swivels on his good foot to face her. He sees her pale face, her green eyes. The tight line of her lips. Her dress fits her neatly. Her figure is trim, slightly boyish, but her lips are a startling red. The towel is held to his chest. The shock of the cold water followed by the rush of the warm has woken him fully, though the sudden movements have sent the blood draining from his head. He feels a little dizzy, but at least he is free from the stench of Eric Patel.

His hand holds the towel to his chest. Her hand is still enclosed in the towel.

Thank you, Paul says.

Her hand stays trapped.

I seem to be making a habit of saying thank you. He smiles as the bathroom leans to one side. He reaches for the basin beside him with his free hand. The crutch clatters to the tiled floor. Nolene has not said a word.

Paul breathes in deeply. Thandi, an image of Thandi and the echo of what she said swims before him. He leans against the basin and watches his hand without the towel reach over to Nolene. His large hand touches her face, cups her cheek in the palm of his hand. The washbasin keeps him upright and the water gushes and steams behind him.

He watches Nolene tilt her head to lean into his hand. She closes her eyes and seems to sigh. Like a kitten, he thinks, just like a kitten she nestles against his hand. He has forgotten what to do next. Claire would be advancing at this stage. She would be taking charge. He would never have to undress Claire. She would be slipping off her top and even her bra with surprising purpose. Paul never stopped being amazed at the transformation in his beautiful wife. Neat and chic to panting and urgent within seconds. He couldn't invent her. If she featured in a television commercial for the ideal romantic partner, people would laugh. If he pitched her to anyone at BB&P they would shake their heads and pour scorn on the proposal. A projection of pure male fantasy, they would snort and deride him. What happened to Second Wave Feminism? And Paul would enjoy the last laugh as Claire's thighs heaved busily above him and her breasts rippled and swayed in an urgent rhythm.

Nolene is timid. Paul has to draw her towards him. She makes no sound as she is enfolded in his arms against his chest. The towel slips in a rumple around his feet.

Her coarse hair is ticklish beneath his chin. Paul tilts his head to look at her, but she does not move. She simply snuggles into his chest, her arms held up between her body and his. The floor shifts to one side and again he has to lean back heavily against the washbasin.

Nolene's strong perfume replaces the smell of Eric Patel. Paul holds her close. Slowly, he moves a hand up, to stroke her back. Nolene stiffens under his touch.

No, she says.

Paul's hand locks around her.

They stand there for a long time. Nolene nestled against his chest, Paul leaning back in drunken gratitude for her gentle kindnesses. The hot water tap runs quietly behind them until the bathroom door is flung open and a teenage girl bursts into the steam. At first she does not make them out through the clouds of vapour. Then her voice comes nasal and brash. *Ag,* do you mind? she says and points to the toilet.

Nolene leads Paul slowly back to the dance floor. There,

amidst the swirling lights and popular rhythms, they hold on to each other. Paul's damp shirt slowly dries in the gentle warmth of Nolene's body. Thank you, he tries to say thank you, but Nolene puts a finger to his lips and simply holds on to him so that he does not collapse.

And he does not fall again.

It is past three in the morning when Thandi drops him off outside the townhouse complex. Paul waves goodbye and nods to the guard who lets him in. They do not exchange a single word.

The townhouses loom on either side as Paul slips home. The crutches clip against the interlocking bricks of the drive. The air is still. There is no moon. Apart from the faint swish of cars on the highway, all is quiet. Paul pauses at the security door of his home. His hands tremble.

For a moment, he thinks that he has lost the keys. He finds them in the pockets of the borrowed tracksuit top.

Inside, the house is dark and warm and watchful. Paul locks up and then stands for a long while in the entrance. His breathing slowly settles. He can detect the lingering tendrils of Claire's supper in the air. Pork chops. Apple sauce. He slides into the lounge and into his easy chair. He wonders if Claire is awake. He gets up and finds the whisky bottle. It is nearly empty. He drains it in a few quick swigs.

When he next opens his eyes, Claire is standing before him. Paul almost drops the bottle in surprise. The heavy curtains shield any light from the streets. He can only just make her out, like a ghost. She does not wear her dressing gown. She has emerged straight from her bed; her nightie is short and filmy in the dark.

You're late, she says.

It coincides with his Sorry I'm late.

Perfectly synchronised: accusation and apology.

They are silent for a second. Neutralised.

What is that smell? Claire's voice is tight and her arm falls to her side.

Paul realises only now that she is holding the gun.

Jesus, he says, pointing.

I thought you might be an intruder. Her voice is toneless. Have you been sick? Her voice sharpens. She steps closer. God, what is that smell?

Paul stands up. It got a bit wild, he says. Put down the gun.

Claire remains steadfast before him.

I wish you had come, Paul says. His voice rises as he repeats, I wish . . .

Claire holds her ground, uncomfortably close. Don't let's go there again, she says. I went to the Meeting.

She pauses. You smell.

How was it? Paul feels as though he is talking to the darkness itself.

Claire does not answer him.

Paul knows how it went. The first Meeting was excruciating. He had known that it would be. Too many emotions. Too many emotional people. Sunny had offered to drive them. Claire had accepted on their behalf. The three of them arrived at the church hall in Observatory, a suburb of Johannesburg. The hall was obviously used as a nursery school during the week and reverted to a more ecclesiastical function only on Sundays. It was a bit of a nothing kind of building.

There were too many people there. Too many people

bringing fresh hampers of terrible grief. It was an indoor picnic of despair.

Paul and Claire and Sunny must have been amongst the last to arrive, even though they were ten minutes early.

The church chairs had been set out in a big inclusive circle, pushing the nursery school desks and tiny chairs to the outer edges of the hall. They were a few chairs short; there was a problem with the keys and the storeroom. The latecomers had ended up squatting on children's chairs to one side of the circle. Paul's plaster cast stuck out awkwardly. He wondered if he might be better off on the floor. Sunny smiled his commiserations. Claire looked fixedly ahead.

A large woman got up. Welcome to the Meeting, she said. If they didn't mind, she was going to start proceedings with a prayer. Then she prayed aloud, her sentences coming in sincere but breathless bursts.

Paul looked across the room. Maybe forty people there. Mostly white, though a few Indians and three black couples sat like little islands stranded in the pale pink ocean. They all had their eyes closed and one or two couples' mouths moved in their own silent supplications. A bearded man, mostly fierce bristle and jutting *boep*, was also looking around. Their eyes met. Paul raised his eyebrows in friendly query, possibly with a hint of self-mockery. The man promptly closed his eyes. Paul was left to his private survey of a cross-section of the recent victims of violent crime.

Amen, said the large woman.

Amen, came the loud response. Amen, said Claire and Sunny on either side of Paul.

I am Jean, said the large woman.

A few people said, Hello, Jean.

Too American, thought Paul. This is way too American.

Jean was speaking. She was telling them about her ordeal. That was three years ago, her rape. And her husband's shooting. And her son's death as he tried to stop his father's death and then his mother's rape. And now it was just Jean. She was all the immediate family she had left, apart from a set of senile parents-in-law and a sister-in-law in Perth. She had made it her mission to get people to talk about what had happened to them, because it was only by talking about what had happened to her that she had been able to move on.

Move on? Paul cast a quick eye at Sunny. He was rooted to his chair, an odd expression on his face. Claire's jaw was tightly clenched.

Move on? Paul repeated to himself. How did she move on from that treadmill of horror. No way.

But the rest of the crowd seemed visibly moved. Paul felt the dangerous circle that pitted them all, face to face, tête-à-tête, eyeball to eyeball, begin to constrict. The man with the beard kept staring at him.

Jean walked up and down, around and around inside that circle of trust. It was well-known psychological and psycho-therapeutic practice to articulate one's experience of terrible trials and tribulations. She was living proof that to go on living, you had to talk your way out of the hole in your life. And you had to stop blaming others. It was all down to you. Would anyone like to speak? No one would be forced to say anything, but surely the point of them all coming that night was to talk? They were welcome to speak in English or Afrikaans, and if anyone wanted to talk in any other language they were more than welcome to do just that. Like a politically correct ring-master in an old frock, Jean then turned around a full three hundred and sixty degrees. Who would like to speak?

Paul felt that old urge. Back at school. He hated that inner compulsion to obey, to do the right thing, to contribute to the lesson. He felt his voice stirring in his throat and he raised a hand to cough, to squeeze his Adam's apple to prevent any sound emerging. Sunny nudged him in the ribs. Paul knew it was no joke. Sunny truly believed that Paul needed to say something. He wanted Paul to say something.

Fortunately, a woman was already crying. In precise Afrikaans, she told them that the charred remains of her husband had been found at the side of the R22 near the Gillooly's Interchange. It had been made to look like a botched hijacking but had turned out to be a white-collar crime. Her Gerhard had recently taken out all his pension money to invest. It seemed that the investment company had some crooks who were prepared to stop at nothing. It was all under investigation and subject to a trial. What could she tell her children of twelve and ten, her Izak and Frieda? They had no father and they had no money. Everything that was going to be reinvested was stolen. Paul stared at the charred Gerhard's sobbing wife. She was prepared to cry before them, her voice soft and strained, almost husky as mucus streamed from her nose and down her chin. Other people in the audience were quietly crying.

There was a surge in sudden narratives. A man whose wife had been battered senseless by the gardener and left for dead when he robbed the house. The man's wife was now perm-anently brain-damaged. A mother of three had had all her children trapped in the car when she was hijacked in the Pick n Pay car park. They had made off with her shopping and her children. The children had been found discarded and dead at a building site. Chucked out like rubbish, rubbish, *vuilgoed*, the woman shrieked and collapsed. Jean helped lift her back into her husband's arms, but Paul was becoming restless. Too much, too much to bear. How could such grief be articulated? How could it help? Another's mother raped at seventy-eight. Someone else's father set alight with petrol, and then they couldn't put it out. And they had laughed and had kicked him as his father died and he had struggled because he was tied up and could do nothing to stop it. And now he could not sleep.

Animals, Paul heard Sunny mutter to Claire. We live with animals. What human could do such a thing to another human? Petrol, knives, guns – you wouldn't treat a dog like that. Claire was red-eyed. Paul had to get out.

The Indian man stood up. He had a clothing shop, he told them, a family business. A gang came in waving lots of guns, took the takings in the till. But as they left, having got what they wanted, one of the gang turned back and fired a single shot. It struck his son in the throat and he bled to death within minutes. Nothing they could do to help him. His eldest son gargled to death on his own blood in the shop and they could do nothing to help him. They had given the gang the money. Why did they shoot? Why?

Outside, Paul gasped for breath. He had begun to feel as though he was being swallowed by that circle. Slowly chewed so that the truth could be spat out. That he, too, was a torturer. That he too had shot and killed and maimed. And for what? What had he gained? What had he lost?

For two hours he had leant on the railings, then sat on the hall steps. There was no way that he could go back in there to confront himself. How could he talk about being the victim of violent crime when he was technically a violent criminal? How could he parade before these traumatised folk as a slapstick hypocrite, a sincere charlatan?

He wondered what Claire was saying. Of course she would speak. She would stand up and express herself in neat sentences, conveying her anguish precisely. She would cry, yes. Her tears would be quiet tears, warm and salty, and would stream down her soft cheeks in two mascara rivulets. It would have to be Sunny and the rest of the crowd that listened and commiserated. That clapped her bravery and maybe reached out hands to touch and to pat her.

Sunny was the first to emerge.

He threw himself down beside Paul.

That is some woman you married, *bru*, he said. He shoved a cigarette into his mouth, lit it and inhaled.

Paul watched the tip of the cigarette glow red and eat its way into the rest of the slender white stem, leaving a sausage of ash behind it. Sunny flicked it into the warm night air.

They sat for a long time.

If you hadn't married her, I am sure I would have, Sunny confided.

Paul thought of Lucky, the three dogs and the beautiful home that had never quite been finished being built.

I know, said Paul. I know.

Sunny turned to him.

Really? Sunny said. He seemed surprised. Even agitated. He blew some smoke rings for a while.

Lots of truth happening in there, Sunny said to Paul, his words following the last smoke ring. I don't know how the reconciliation works, but fuck me, there is a shitload of truth in there. He stubbed the cigarette on the step and lit another.

Halfway through the third cigarette, Sunny again turned to Paul.

There are things, Sunny said, and stopped.

Paul turned to him, inviting confidence.

Sunny shook his head. I don't know how this works, he said.

And into their companionable silence came Claire. Behind her the quiet crowd heading home to hug their pain. Maybe it would be less of a load now. Maybe they would be able to fit their arms around it slightly better now.

Paul and Sunny stood up, with Claire beside them, to let all the people pass. Last out was Jean. Before she locked up, she came over to Paul. Paul blushed. The lost sheep. Jean the ringmaster shepherd was coming out to round up the one lost sheep.

Don't leave it too long, she said, glancing at Claire. She is such a brave one, this wife of yours. Don't leave it too long.

Thanks, Sunny said. Thanks, Jean.

Paul had nodded, glad that his friend had at least said something and that he would not have to offer any handy platitude. They left Jean locking the empty hall. Claire did not say a word in the car.

Sunny scuttled off in his car.

By mistake, they had ended up brushing their teeth together in the bathroom, before going their separate ways. Claire had paused at the top of the landing as Paul clanked downstairs. As he dropped off on the couch, his leg propped to one side, he was sure that he could hear her muffled crying. He fell asleep to the hoarse sound of the steam iron as it blew broiling kisses over the living leg of Go Naidoo.

In the darkness, his wife's voice is a jet of steam.

You smell, Claire repeats herself.

She leans over the chair. Her arms stretch out on either side of him and she leans forward. Paul is aware of the gun in her left hand, now just beside his right elbow. He is aware of her warm presence, her aroma of soap and cleanliness, as well as the vague sense that her nightie hangs forward to expose two full breasts, pendulous and close to his throat. He hears her snuffling inhalations.

My God, she is sniffing him out.

Claire, he says, but she overrides him.

Alcohol, she says. And puke. You stink of piss and puke. And sex. You've had sex. I can smell it on you.

Claire, he repeats. I . . .

But she refuses to let him speak.

Do not start telling me lies, she says, still pinning him down with her soft proximity. Do not open your fucking mouth and start telling me fucking lies with that fucking voice of yours. All your fucking. Lies.

Her voice rises on the final word. It becomes a cry: lies.

He sits, stunned.

That's right, Claire lowers her voice, regains some control. You just sit there. Don't say a word.

Paul does not know how to protest. His fucking voice? Now his fucking silence? Should he speak or shut up shop? What does this frantic woman with her beautiful breasts and forgotten gun want from him?

It's all about you. Claire screws up her face. You feel bad so you go out, you take out your frustrations left, right and centre and then when it doesn't work out, you sit here and sulk or you fuck off to work and office parties. You . . . how you can manage to be so bitter and twisted is beyond me. I mean, it's not even as if . . . Claire's voice trails off.

He does not know how to respond. His anger is roused, but it is undercut by a huge dragging weight of hopelessness. He could say nothing in the Meeting. Nothing to help her, help them, help himself. Nothing at all. Maybe she is right? Maybe it is all about him? His guilt, his anguish.

You . . . she hisses and again the steam iron comes to mind and he sits, at a complete loss. Her revulsion washes over him and it seeps into every orifice. It invades him. He feels the disgust, the nausea rise like a tide, pouring in from her, yet also welling up from deep within. A surge of suppressed bile. The dead dog on the way to Alexandra, the look in the hijacker's eyes before he pulled the trigger, Go Naidoo's screams and the gunshot in Chantal's bedroom, the sound of Thandi's laughter and Nolene's gentle silence, the shearing metal of the car crash, the voices of de Jager and Smit, the crunch of Claire's chewing and the happy, carefree gurgle of Chantal playing in the bath. Always the happy, carefree gurgle of their beautiful daughter.

His famous voice is silenced.

You . . . Claire hisses.

1 year

HE DOES NOT THINK OF it as a penance.

And there is no conscious thought that he is a St Paul searching for his Damascus, that there has been or will be some sublime Damascene moment. There is not much feeling at all. Soweto is not Damascus.

He lives in Soweto. He knew that he could not hover in the limbo of Midrand, stuck in the midst of all that. Claire was right; he was fucked up.

More accurately, he squats in Soweto. To squat is to inhabit Kliptown, one of the camps – in politically correct terms, an informal settlement – for souls existing on the margins of society, whatever that means.

He does not feel that he exists on the margins of society. He is surrounded by society. He is buried by society. The small shack – or informal dwelling, though it is most decidedly a shack – is part of a heaving mass of society. There are no security gates, no guards, no burglar alarms, not much to steal. Maybe for the first time in his life, he is part of society.

Society is certainly part of him. The first thing that struck him was the noise. It was non-stop. It was right under his nose.

Corrugated iron and plastic sheeting do not make for effective separate development. And never mind that his shack, a dilapidated affair even by squatter camp standards, was initially stuck on the fringes of the camp, set fractionally apart from the host of other shacks. It was soon overtaken, swamped. Part of the knotted tangle of it all. It was always noisy. It is always noisy. Voices, dogs, music, pots and pans, clanking buckets, children laughing, children crying, sneezes, arguments, radio chat shows, more music. Everyone here listens to music. It is always noisy.

And it is always changing. No sooner had he pulled his shack together – he could not think of his 'building' the shack; it was rather pulled and scraped and eked into existence – than he was surrounded by other shacks and lean-tos. No sooner had he claimed his dusty patch of Soweto West than he was swallowed up by the tide of humanity and liberating chaos.

Not that his life is chaotic now.

But it had started in a drunken stupor.

He had just driven away. His second-hand Toyota Corolla, paid for by the insurance payout on the BMW, found its way to Soweto South. There were still some posters of Chantal hanging about. He took one down and propped it up on the back seat of the car. Chantal was dusty and faded and ghostly white. Then he had driven deep into the bowels of Soweto. Just to be with her; he was surely driving towards her somewhere in Soweto and now, already, she was back in his car. No more BMWs for him. And just a poster for a daughter.

The rest of the money from the insurance he kept, and the severance pay from BB&P. Not that they had paid him very much at all, but he hadn't really wanted to fight for it. The fight had left him. Nolene had let him go. To be honest, he just wanted to drive away. Drive deep into Soweto.

His cell phone contract expired.

He had written a long letter to Claire. He had left it waiting for her on the dining room table, pinned down on the soft yellow wood by a fresh grapefruit. He wondered if she ate the fruit whilst reading the letter. Page after page of his ramblings, his own thoughts, as well as quoting from J. M. Coetzee's *In the Heart of the Country*, the beautiful lines about straining to catch the pale smoke of each other's signals. He was leaving her for a while to catch the pale smoke of Chantal. Maybe to find the living flame? He had to keep hoping. Or maybe simply to breathe in her ashes, the remnants of her pale fire that had burnt and wafted her ashes over the heaving anonymous mass of the South Western Townships. Soweto. Somewhere her dust would have settled where he could trace a finger in her ashes and then smear it on his forehead. Like a Hindu. The pain of Chantal. Now shanti. Now peace.

As he drove deeper and deeper into the heart of Africa, he wondered if Claire had squirted grapefruit juice over his letter. Whether the ink had run, or not? Did she read the letter dry-eyed, and with a waxing sense of relief? Was it a load off her mind? Could she now finally spring-clean the house, purge it of his presence? Paul the six-foot-four gibbet, the slouching, drinking, awkward memorial to their pain.

He made a few hurried goodbyes. Told his parents, brother and sister that he was taking some time out. Would be gone for a while. Made it sound like a business trip. His business, none of theirs. He interrupted his mother's rising inflections and her questions. He had to do this. Each time he hung up, he felt sick with relief. Yes, he had to do this.

He avoided the gentrified suburbs of Soweto, the famous Vilakazi Street with the Nobel prize-winners, the tall walls that could have been any South African suburb. No, he drove on. Through thronging queues of taxis, past streaming pedestrians and loud buses. On and on. It didn't matter where. He did not look out for Chantal. It was good just to be where she had been, and possibly was. It helped that he was half drunk. He doubted that he could have packed his bags and left quickly if he wasn't *'n klein bietjie babbelas* – just a tiny bit tipsy. Besides, he had her poster in the car. Yes, he was drunk.

Claire had gone to the gym and he had gone for ever. For the second time he had hacked off his plaster cast and left it jammed in the bin. He did not bother to sweep up the powdered remnants. He left the mould of his leg, standing stiffly in the bin. An objectionable correlative in plaster of Paris.

The streets in this part of Soweto petered out. They gave way to dirt strips studded with dips and *dongas*. This was more like it, more African. The little Corolla lurched and shuddered. People got out of his way. No one waved like they used to when Paul and his family had gone on holiday as children. When the so-called little *piccanins* at the side of the road in rural Natal had stopped and waved to the white *basies*. A friend at school, he remembered, had had the privilege of travelling on holiday by train. He and his older brother, the friend told Paul, had used their father's cigarette lighter to heat a pile of ten-cent coins. Then, when they passed hordes of black children who waved and ran a little way with the train, they had thrown them money, as some people tended to do, it seemed. They had laughed at the greedy hands suddenly flinging down the searing coins. That would teach the little buggers.

Few faces turned to Paul. The pedestrians merely gave up the track to the white car and waited briefly for the dust to settle, before walking on.

Suddenly he was in shackland. He passed a suburb of very small but neat houses, which then tripped into a tangle of lean-tos and single-room huts. Here there were people, lots of people. Here, people did look up at the approach of a car. But the look seemed to be blank, accepting, uninquisitive. They had seen it all.

He drove for half a kilometre, then seemed to reach the outskirts of the camp. Shacks gave way to stretch of veldgrass and dust. In the distance were the walls of another small neighbourhood with street lights and houses. This was no-man's-land. Perfect.

It was mid-afternoon when he parked the car. He slid the seat back and stretched out his legs as best he was able. His leg was fine without its protective casing. It felt a little painful and tender, his calf had withered to a shred of muscle, but he had been able to drive for over an hour and a half. Now, having parked, he leaned back, his hands behind his head. The spare tufts of veldgrass shimmered in the heat and the soft breeze. Amongst the tangle of things in the back of the car, Chantal's whitened face looked on. The car grew warm in the slanting sunshine. Paul opened the window a fraction. The doors remained locked. Then he unlocked those too, and opened the windows slightly further. He was here. With the lowest of the low. He was squatting in his car. Whatever happened, happened. He leaned back and waited. He was happy to wait.

That first night passed and gave way to the first day. He was not attacked and killed. None of the squatters came near him. No police car approached.

In the early hours of the morning, when the air was black and cold, he had to step out to urinate. Despite it being early April, not quite heading towards autumn, his breath came in cold tendrils of steam and he urinated some way off from the car with a shivering stream of relief. He was surprised by the noise and stench that came from the camp. Smoky fires burned, dogs barked. Someone seemed to be singing. He shook out the last trembling drop and stepped back to the car.

Only when he sat down once more did he realise that he had stepped in several piles of viscous crap – human no doubt – and that he had probably parked on the edge of an open-air toilet.

He levered his feet out of the car and wiped his shoes on small tufts of grass. But the smell remained part of the car and he had to keep the windows closed. It was too cold. His first day dawned to the scent of shit. He watched dark figures stream past the car into the vacant patch to urinate. Others emptied buckets and trundled back. No one took the slightest bit of notice of him.

Later that morning, Paul drove a little further round the camp, away from the acre of excrement. He found a patch on the end of a row of shacks and parked there. No one came to move him, no one bothered him.

He ate half a packet of Eet Sum Mor biscuits and washed them down with whisky. Then he simply sat in the driver's seat and did nothing. He felt no need to switch on the radio. No compulsion to get out and explore. He did not even notice the children who came and spied on him throughout the day or the men that looked around the sides of the corrugated iron shacks and speculated with quiet voices. Several dogs limped past and marked the Corolla's wheels as their own and scuffed earth and dust in his direction. But he stayed quietly in the car, a hermetically sealed hermit, content to be alone with his luggage and his poster.

The second day came. He thought that he might move on again, maybe deeper into the camp. But when he turned on the engine, put the car into first gear, and eased the accelerator pedal forward, nothing happened. He repeated the process. The engine coughed in the cold morning air and then roared, but he stayed put.

When Paul climbed out to check what was wrong, he stepped back in amazement. Then he started laughing. Dry, hacking, choking laughter.

Somehow, he could not guess how, during the night, they had propped up the car on bricks and chunks of cement, and had taken his wheels. All four of them. The brake casings had disappeared too. There was his car, floating on bricks, like the bed of the neighbour's maid, raised up to a careful height that kept it safe from the lascivious depravations of the *tokoloshe*. And all the while he had slept peacefully courtesy of Johnnie Walker.

He got up and put his hand on the car. He pushed it gently, and it rocked very slightly under his hands. But it was stable. It was going nowhere. He was stuck. His car floated above a patch of squatter-camp dirt, and he was tied to it. He was going nowhere, and it was right. He laughed again. He could not have done a better job himself of ensuring that he remained buried in this new life. He did not think of himself as a persecuted Jew tied to his cross, strangely proud of his crown of thorns. No. He was simply Paul van Niekerk, small and of no church, and he had come here so that he could forget and so that he could die, just as his daughter had surely died. His chariot of fire would not ascend into the heavens. Its wheels would try to whir. But like little round paraplegic stumps, they would slowly rust and become part of the earth that bore its weight. He was going nowhere.

The surrounding walls of tin and wooden planks were quiet. The camp seemed quietest just before dawn. And lifting his voice to accompany the lone dog that barked somewhere far off, Paul laughed again.

The following morning he was further amazed. The petrol cap was levered open and the delicious scent of fresh petrol filtered into the car. He knew as he turned the key in the ignition that they had siphoned off his petrol. But there was not even a responsive click from the car. With trembling hands, hands shaking with wonder, he unclipped the catch, got out and slid open the metal bonnet of the car to reveal more soil and dirt. His second-hand Corolla was gutted. They had taken the engine, the battery, the water pump and windscreen wash, everything. And they had silently closed the bonnet. Again he laughed. Had they wanted to kill him for his car, or kill him just for the hell of it, they could have done it. He would not be waking up at all. And yet each morning, here was the wonder of it, he was waking up, albeit to less and less of his car. What would the third morning bring? Would he find himself lying on the pillars of bricks, naked and minus the fillings in his teeth, the car having vanished completely?

Then he checked the boot of the Toyota and found that his supplies were untouched. Maybe they thought that there would not be anything valuable in there? Maybe . . . He had no idea what to think. But he took out the bags of dried fruit, the long-life milk and the Provitas, rusks and other biscuits, and the pilchards and tins of tuna. He stacked those on the floor of the car and covered them with a blanket. All the while he knew that it was a futile enterprise. That if they wanted the food and if they wanted to kill him for the food, they would do it. The food was probably better off hidden in the boot with the car keys in his pocket. He would surely wake up if they snaked their hands into his trouser pockets?

There came a fine drizzle, and again he spent the day in the car. He watched the droplets collect on the windscreen. They huddled into larger and larger drops and then ran together into streams and rivulets. Then the process happened again. Outside, the world was misty and quiet.

He finished the bottle of Johnnie Walker. Instead of tossing it out into the grey mist and rain, he got out of the car and placed it neatly on the bonnet. Like a strange crest. No leaping jaguar or silver angel or even the tri-spoked wheel of a Mercedes Benz. No, it was just a whisky bottle and an offering to the gods of the camp, a gift for the hands that came in the night and helped themselves to things. Like the tooth fairy. Though these Toyota fairies were something else.

Paul sang songs in the wet night, snatches of all sorts of songs, from the dark refrains of the Depeche Mode of his youth to 'The Teddy Bears' Picnic'. He sang as he watched the bottle, glowing in the moonlight that broke through the shredding clouds. He sang and sang to keep himself awake, but in the morning the bottle was gone and he had no idea when it had disappeared or who had taken it.

He smacked a hand on the bonnet so that it boomed in the fresh morning air and promptly nearly died of fright when a dog and a child broke cover from beside his feet and ran yelping off amongst the shacks.

Carefully he bent to peer beneath the car. In the small dry patch created by the Corolla, just beneath where the engine had once been, was some rough sacking. He slid a shaking hand on to it. It was still warm where the child and animal had lain, no doubt sleeping and snug together right beneath him. Paul stood up quickly and walked to the alleyway between the nearest shacks. The child and the mongrel had vanished. All was quiet. He returned to the car. He leant against it for a long while.

Then he bent down and placed his hand on the dirty hessian and kept it there until he could no longer feel the ghostly warmth of that tiny body.

Almost weeping, he took out a box of Lemon Creams, his other favourite, and placed it beneath the car in the folds of the sacking. He added a packet of mixed raisins and nuts. Then he got back in the car and dozed off his late night.

At around midday, he peered again under the car, but the biscuits and the dried fruit were still there. The sun shone hot and fierce. The air steamed with fresh moisture and a bustle of noisy life came from the shacks.

Paul drank some long-life milk. With the carton still in his hand, he locked the car door manually and limped along the line of the outer shacks. He stopped and returned to the car. Bending in, he scooped up the poster of Chantal. He emptied some tins from a plastic bag and placed the poster inside the bag. It just fitted. He locked the car again. Then, swinging the bag from a single finger, he set off for a second time, limping in a line that ran obliquely along the sprawling fringes of the squatter camp. Chantal was safe beside him. The milk he clutched in his left hand.

Voices everywhere. There were voices everywhere. Conversational, commanding, laughing, calling. There was singing as well as wailing, and someone crying. He walked the ragged fringes of the squatter camp almost on tiptoe, trying to peer in to the tangled knot of humanity.

He could discern life within the outer shacks. He passed a woman scrubbing clothes in a huge zinc bath, chanting quietly as she scrubbed and scrubbed. Children's faces peered through haphazard doorways as he passed. They seemed wary. He could not blame them. He must look rather ominous. His must have been the only white face for miles around, so he assumed, dishevelled, a dark fungus of beard about his cheeks, and there was his unsteady gait and his great height. And then there was also the mysterious plastic bag that swung gently beside his right leg as he limped along, staring, staring. Three men sat smoking, squatting on their heels in a manner that could not be comfortable. They watched him as he trundled past.

One man raised his tattered cigarette and called something to him. The other men stared as Paul stopped. The man who spoke stood up. He uttered some rapid sounds at Paul. He sounded angry. He pointed a finger and waved it at Paul, then at the open field with its hot khaki grass. Then came the words, the only words he understood. *Hamba* – go – and *voetsek* – scram, piss off. And Paul saw the bottle in the middle of the group of men and he hurried on. The ragged black man shouted after him. Paul kept going until he could hear their laughter no more.

To avoid them, and to get back to the car, Paul took a risk. He plunged down an alleyway between the shacks. The dark earth was slick from the rain, slimy and slippery. Several times he had to lean suddenly against shacks for support, and a few creaked or shuddered dangerously. Twice voices within shouted out and he moved on quickly. He bore left down a different path, past yet more terrible lean-tos. Some had small garden areas, little wastelands of frayed weeds and dull earth. And the stink was the same wherever he turned. He had to discard the milk carton very quickly, and hold his free hand to his nose, or use that same hand waving and windmilling to keep his balance. He began to feel breathless. The plastic bag with Chantal inside flapped and rustled at his thigh. It caught on a wire spoke from a makeshift fence and snagged loudly. But Paul hurried on, surprising more chatting folk, more squealing children.

He bore left again, certain that that would bring him out of the maze at a point beyond the shouting man. But it did not. Dirty alleyway yielded to dirty alleyway. The sour stink of excrement caught in his throat. He began to feel as though his mouth and oesophagus were furred with the stuff. His stomach heaved. He did not relish the prospect of having to stop and throw up the milk he had just drunk. He could feel it turning sour in his gut. He began to panic. How much longer, how much more labyrinthine could this place become? And then he knew he was being followed. Without turning around, he plunged on, the plastic bag flapping against his leg.

He slipped and an ochre strip of mud sheared down his leg. He managed to keep the bag with Chantal's poster inside free from the cloying earth. His leg throbbed. His breath came in gasps. He realised that he had not exercised much over the past month. He was sweating. There were low voices. Whoever was following had stopped. They were waiting.

Paul scrambled to his feet. *Hamba wena*, he thought he heard. *Hamba wena*. Go, you. The curt command. Go. You had better be gone.

He went. He broke from the cover of the shacks after another two minutes of panic. He had overshot the mark. The car was now a hundred metres to his left. He stopped. Was it shaking? Was he shaking?

He arrived back breathless. Home sweet home. He could not manage a sardonic smile.

The car was there. It was whole. Not a smashed window, not a wrenched or buckled door. He knelt to peer beneath the bonnet. The Lemon Creams and raisins were still there.

He got up and leant against the car. Then he lay back in the hot afternoon sun, his back stinging from the hot metal. The ugly smear on his leg slowly dried like blood, leaving a long scar on his jeans.

Why did he feel so bad? Why did his free hand slam down against the car, smacking it hard?

He stood up and opened the car door. He peered inside. Yes, all was still there. To his amazement, every tin and carton. Even the money folded into the car manual and service record in the glove compartment.

He collapsed into the driver's seat and leant his head against the steering wheel. He laughed weakly. That was it. He knew why he felt so ill at ease.

If he were honest, he had expected the car to be gone. Based on the events of the past few nights, he must have known, assumed in his heart of hearts, that when he left the car an hour ago, abandoned it in the broad daylight to the tender mercies of the squatter camp, he would return to a ransacked vehicle. In fact, if he was honest, he had expected the entire car magically to have vanished.

Yet here it was. Unviolated. Whole. At least what was left of it.

He knew that he wanted it to be gone. He knew that he would have been relieved had its windows been smashed and the doors wrenched open. If there had been nothing left but the clothes that he wore and the poster of his daughter that he carried, he would have been perversely relieved.

At last he could admit to himself that he had indeed come here to die. He sought obliteration. He longed for release. He wanted the ache to be gone. The car was an extension of himself. This white, second-hand car with its haphazard burden of household stuff. Things to sustain him, he who did not want to be sustained. He who had reduced his daughter to a mere poster, broken his wife, killed a man and, lest he forget, tortured a living man with a stinging iron. He deserved to die.

That night he slept with the car doors unlocked. He had drunk not a drop. Inside his jacket, which was zipped up against the cold night air, was the poster of Chantal. If a bullet came, his blood would anoint her image. If he was bludgeoned to death, she would remain close to his heart before his clothes were ripped from his inert body, before he was left to lie in the veld, alone and at last at peace, prostrated in front of the shacks and the trembling stalks of veld grass. He waited. Even in his delirium, he breathed calmly, knowing that the inevitable must come. That as night follows day, they would come and it would be over.

But he does not die.

He is not killed in the night.

No shadowy hands ease open the doors or slip a knife into his chest. No gun taps at his window promising oblivion. Often, he glances to his right, but there is nothing. No one. His body remains bizarrely intact and complete. No skin is broken, not a hair on his head is harmed. No matter how often he weeps in the night, he does not bleed.

Dawn comes with the smoke and the smell of fire. Burnt orange smudges the line of the horizon. Still he waits.

He sits out the day. Surely it must come. It will come. But, like the gutted car stranded on odd lumps of concrete and brick, nothing moves.

As the sun rises higher he winds down the window. The heat becomes stifling. Feeling short of breath – a little dizzy even – he sits. He registers thirst, but he does not drink. He is not hungry. His torpor is overwhelming.

He feels careless of his body. He feels oddly disassociated from himself. He simply desires the weight of his flesh to drop from the world.

He faces out into the blinding sun, his back to the squatter camp, waiting.

The sky cools through shades of blue to soft lemon, before the rind of the day hardens into black night.

Still he does not drink.

He cannot think.

If only he had brought the gun. If only the car had wheels – and an engine. He could have shot himself. He could have driven at full speed into a concrete pillar or a brick wall. The readiness is not all. He needs a gun. Or a mobile car. He is held up, stalled inside his own body.

Some time later, squealing sounds pull his eyes into the rear-view mirror. Just beyond the ragged fringe of shacks, two men hold down a writhing creature. It could be a small goat or a dog. It bucks and kicks. It is a goat. One man slices open its throat and they hold it as its tiny voice dies in a gush of blood. He sees that the men catch the dark stream in a tin bowl. They proceed to carry the goat closer to the car. They lift it with a thud on the flat shelf of the boot. It makes a nice ledge. He watches them skin the goat and quarter it. Right behind him. The pieces are dropped into two plastic bags. With a sharp rustle, the sodden, dripping flesh is packaged.

Then they are gone. They emerged to slaughter and carve up a goat. Now they retire into the world of the shacks to consume it no doubt.

Before Paul can stop himself, he has clambered out of the car and stands before the bloodied boot. The smears are black and thick in the night. But that is all. Everything is gone. No glowing coils of intestines or anything else on the ground.

He reaches into the car. He takes out a bag of tinned food.

Chantal is still wrapped up close against his chest.

Paul leaves the car door open and walks towards the shacks. He follows the line taken by the two men.

They have not gone far. Their fire is already burning in a tangled space amongst several taller shacks. There are voices. Laughter. The fire crackles beneath a small grid. He stumbles on the scene. His is a white face materialising out of the flickering shadows and the orange light of the fire, a small dawning at their feet. The group looks up from where they squat. The two men. Three women and four children and a baby. The goat is already sizzling on the fire.

The baby is feeding from its mother's ripe breast. The children gawp at him open-mouthed. One small ragged child picks its nose. The men rise slowly, both holding sharp bloody knives.

Here, Paul croaks. His voice has not worked in a while.

Here, he tries again and holds out the plastic bag of food. No one moves. Then the child finds something in its nose and transfers it to its mouth. Paul holds out the bag.

The woman closest to him stands up and takes the bag.

Baas, she says, dipping her head. *Dankie, baas*. Thank you, boss, thank you, master.

The rest of the group continue to stare.

Paul turns and leaves as abruptly as he arrived. As though he has fallen from the orbit of the glowing fire.

He shakes his head. Exhausted, smelly, unshaven, a derelict, broken man, he is still the white master in this world. *Dankie, baas*, he mutters to himself and returns unseeing to the car.

Its door is still open, like the single wing of a white dove.

This time, the food is gone.

The car is bare.

He reaches over to the glove compartment.

Yes, the money has disappeared as well.

He leans back in the soft seat. He sighs, and then he chuckles.

At last.

Now he has been reduced to nothing. At long last he has followed Chantal. His kinship with her is finally established. From everything, they have both embraced nothing. She is here, in Soweto. So is he. She has no one to call her own. Neither does he. If Chantal is dead, it is only a matter of time before he, her father, by a series of profound declensions, will follow her. And like her, he must wait to be plucked from a car. He must offer himself up to Africa. Paul Owen van Niekerk, like his child Chantal Claire van Niekerk, must yield to an unstoppable force. Oh yes. It must come and it will come. Of that he has no doubt.

His hands grip his thighs. After a long while, the blanket of a thousand sounds from the squatter camp spreads thin and dark over him. His mouth is cracked and dry. He raises one hand and places his thumb in his mouth. It tastes of dust and sweat. He sucks it, like the baby he has just seen. The saliva flows and sleep comes.

It is a mongrel sleep, though. It darts and scurries. It is tentative and fearful. He cannot get rid of it and neither can he hunt it down.

He awakes in the morning exhausted and unsure whether or not he has in fact slept.

He feels stained by the blood of the goat. For an unaccountable reason, he feels as though his body is smeared with the fat and dark stench of the goat that coughed up such thick fumes the previous night. The smoke that comes from the camp is fragrant with stolen wood, and ruptured flesh. The air tastes of burnt blood, and it cannot all come from that little goat.

His thumb is soft and white. It is a newborn thumb that he presents to the world.

He spends another day hunched in the car, becoming steadily more delirious with thirst. He sucks his thumb. Surely not even Chantal, if she is still alive, sucks her thumb?

Later that day, he tries to resist the panicky urge to check under the car bonnet to see if they have indeed taken the windscreen wash. The compulsion to drink water is rising. But he knows, as he lifts the bonnet, that there is nothing. Only the hessian sack, the Lemon Creams and the peanuts and raisins remain. They do not want his gifts.

He sinks back into the car.

He wishes now that he had parked facing the squatter camp. But even as this thought dawns, he is aware during the day of people hammering and pulling things. He spends an hour peering in the rear-view mirror. The world reflected in a silver sliver reveals the tumbling sprawl of the camp. More shacks spill into life. New arrivals drag sheets of corrugated iron. There are odd planks. Where do they get them? What shop around here sells construction kits for shacks? He bares his teeth at the mirror and sinks into remembrance of the tree house that he and John and the neighbours tried to build. It was a disastrous affair. Rickety planks, bent nails, bruised thumbs. But when it was finished, when they had run out of planks purloined from an old door, they felt like kings. Until John fell off and broke his crown. Then their arboreal kingdom had had to be dismantled in a parental coup d'état. John sported four stitches in his head, and a black eye.

He wonders, as the sun sets on another day, if he lives long enough, whether the shacks will rush past and engulf him, like the flow of an unstoppable tide. He knows the answer and sinks into fevered sleep. His thumb finds its way into his mouth.

He awakes shivering. The sun is already up. Before long, he has removed most of his clothes. He feels hot, though the dashboard is freezing cold. He needs to get out of the car.

He stands beside it stretching, but then he is forced to lean heavily against the car as his head spins. The sun stings his bare shoulders and the top of his head. He can smell his own armpits. He urinates where he stands, pointing away from the camp, which has crept that much closer. The sounds of the day echo in his head and he finds himself laughing as the dark urine sends a stinging, tearing sensation through his loins. He looks down and sees that he has passed one drop of water. He could piss himself laughing. He laughs and laughs.

He has to lean with his buttocks against the car as his chuckles subside. The metal burns through his underpants. He gets back in the car, panting like a dog.

He barks. Then he laughs.

He wakes up to find that he has bitten his thumb. Blood seeps into his mouth and he has swallowed it greedily. His throat feels clotted with the salty fluid. Maybe if he tears his thumb off and really chews it?

The pain is bad. He grips the steering wheel instead and watches the drops of black wetness drip on to his lap. He is spotting. He is having his first period. His white underpants blossom with rust-coloured spots. *C'est la vie.*

He mumbles the phrase to himself. *C'est la vie.* Say la vee.

Sailor V. Say luvvee. Sail a V. Sale a fee. *C'est la vie.* Then it is dark and he cannot find his thumb.

The shivering and twitching of his body in the night cannot be stopped. He knows before he can fumble blindly for them that his clothes, cast aside so merrily in the morning, have found a new home. He tries to open the window; he can't. He tries to open the door, but can't. He leans his head against the dusty window and looks into the darkness. His clothes are not beside the car where, singing, he cast them.

He shivers and shivers and cannot tell whether it is night or day.

The cold is loud and black. He hugs himself greedily, his arms searching for his back, wrapped around his chest. He is certain that the car rocks with his dark shivering. He is a baby in a cradle. Moses. Holy Moses supposes. That way madness lies. Release comes as a tingling oblivion. He sleeps the sleep of the dead.

In the night and the flickering day, the shacks lift up their skirts and scuttle past. They stop. They dance and sway. When he awakes he knows that they have overtaken the car. Without signalling, they have cockroached past. Shack attack. With the tides of metal and brick, plastic and wood and stone, they have flotsamed and jetsamed past. Yes, the world is awash with refuse.

He tries to open the puffy slits that are his eyes. He cannot. He tries to raise a hand to do the job manually, but he cannot find his face. He has lost his face. He sighs. It saddens him deeply to have no face. How may he ever face up to anything? Maybe it is just as well. There are faeces, though. He has misplaced his face but his free hand seems lodged in warm, soft faeces. He feels the gloom. He smells it. He knows it. Emily's room with her tin bath and her bed on bricks. The *tokoloshe*. Well, the *tokoloshe* has come for him. Got him. The smell of dust and Lifebuoy soap. Soft and creamy, and not of this white world. He is buried in the smell of Africa. The darkness sings to him. No Sarie Marais. No. No Afrikaner longing for the beautiful white girl who embodies freedom and peace and hearth and home. No war songs. No Anglo-Boer War songs. The warm darkness sings with thick lips. Ripe with tenderness comes the *tula*, the *tula wena*, the *tula tu tula baba tula sana*. Hush, you must hush my little one. He is rocked. A teat squirts warm fluid into his mouth, which he somehow swallows. He drinks in the voice. He imbibes the soft sound. He nestles into the rough blanket and sleeps and sleeps. A baby's voice cries. For a while he thinks that it is his very own voice. That he is back in his first home, fresh from the Glynnwood Nursing Home in Benoni. Benoni – Jewish, Son of my Sorrow. He opens his mouth and the mewling sound keeps coming. But it continues when he closes his mouth. He does not mind. Mouth open or closed, he rocks to the sound of the child.

He knows that the shacks have overtaken his car. He lies in the middle of the squatter camp, engulfed. The baby's crying is drowned by voices and movement and scuffling business.

He knows also that he is inside one of the shacks. As the shivering subsides and his eyes begin to see vague blurs, he becomes aware of the shack. From the parameters of smell that he has already established, there is added the more certain dimensions of sound, and now sight. The tin roof creaks above him. Light streams in dusty shafts from the corners, and there is a tiny hole in the centre. Profound warmth radiates from the roof in the day. The blanket disappears. Cold creeps down in the night. The blanket returns. He is not sure about the walls. He knows only the flap of tarpaulin that serves as door. When it hangs closed, the place is womblike. When it flaps aside, his eyes hurt and stream tears.

As for the voices, he knows that he shares the room with a baby in a cardboard box and that there is another child who gets in the way. That there is a woman about all the time. She sings and at night she lies beside him with the other child. That some nights a man lies on top of her and she stops singing, and instead breathes heavily across his face. Paul whimpers but they carry on. The baby and the child sleep soundly.

The sensations keep crowding in. That is the infernal bargain with the material world. His body is a bridge across that divide. The link between the 'him' and the 'them'. He cannot walk the plank into sweet blue oblivion. Instead, out of the ocean of sensation the chaotic world comes crawling aboard.

As warmth streams down from the corrugated ceiling, he hears the tinkle of water and feels the soft scrape of a sponge on his skin. He could open his eyes, he really could. But he lies back as she bathes him. His oily white skin, his sticky nooks and crannies are carefully cleaned. There's the rub. The rub of the sponge. The overwhelming scent of Lifebuoy soap. The splash of warm water as the sponge is rinsed and a rough cloth tingles along his anointed body. He is moved to a profound sadness when she stops. Even the skin behind his ears is spruce and tingling. She was extra careful when she cleaned his face and washed his hair. His sprouting beard caught on the sponge, but the bristles were already quite long. This huge hairy baby of hers who lies along the full length of the shack, who requires two blankets to cover him, and whose frame is now fitted with a giant shirt and trousers that are too tight.

When she is done, he utters his first word. It is *yebo*. Yes. Then he says *ngiyabonga*. Thank you.

She does not reply. She feeds her own child in the opposite corner. The baby sucks greedily at her chest. The tears well hotly in Paul's eyes. He curls into a ball and turns to the metal side of the shack.

Later, when she feeds the baby another time, she talks to him.

Her name is Agnes. Her baby is Precious and the little boy, her sister's child, is Sipiwe. It seems that she is no more than a child herself. The man who visits in the night is Alfred. He comes more often now. He does not like it, this sharing of the shack with a long white man. When he dragged the white man in two weeks ago, he did not think he would live for so long. Although he is a rough man, this Alfred, although he must have his sex and she is pregnant again and still cannot go back to school to finish Standard Three, he is deep down a good man. Otherwise she would run away. Maybe back to Kwa-Zulu. Maybe to Egoli, Johannesburg, with her baby and her impossible nephew. No, she has not much money. Things are hard, too much difficult. It is Alfred who brings the food. He finds the things to sell for the *mielie* meal to make the *pap*, though the *nyama*, the meat, is rare – maybe once a week if they are lucky.

She talks whilst the baby feeds, her pink-soled feet stuck out before her, almost touching him. He lies and looks at her.

274

If he had any money, she could have it. Also, his car – what is left of it.

That is gone, she tells him. They, the other squatters, have taken the doors and the seats, everything. Nothing is left. If he goes there, he will not find it. Here everything goes and becomes something different. Becomes part of a shack. Furniture. A roof. Or it is sold for vegetables and if it is very good, meat. Live animals are too much expensive, so is the meat from the market. Does he like meat?

He likes meat.

But why is a white man, a *baas*, who could eat meat all the time, why is he here?

I am here, he says. He becomes quiet again and does not talk for a while.

He is here. That is enough.

She lets him be. Her giant baby.

But that night there is a problem.

Alfred is there. He heaves astride Agnes. She lets out a crying sound and Paul turns from the side of the shack. He turns his head in the semi-darkness. His eyes meet Alfred's. Alfred is busy on Agnes but he is looking at Paul. And in the puny light of the single candle, his gleaming eyes lock on to Paul's.

Paul forces his eyes closed, as though he has rolled over in his sleep and he has not seen this naked man glistening with sweat and Agnes's tears.

But he cannot soften the grimace on his face, and Alfred's words, his loud words during the last frenzied thrusts, are directed at him. Paul knows that. The words are unintelligible, but the tone is unmistakable. There is a thumping sound in the background too, a dull, repetitive accompaniment. The night is long.

In the morning, Alfred is gone.

Agnes asks him if he has no family.

Paul does not reply.

Instead he gets up and manages to sweep the tiny area around the shack with a bundle of twigs and grass, Agnes's home-made broom.

Light-headed and exhausted, he sleeps after that. His dreams are threaded through with Chantal and Claire, Claire and Chantal. He knows that no matter how far he has gone, how deep he has sunk, what depths he might yet plumb, they are more the very essence of himself than he is. It is as though his skin is worn through and there, at last, they move. He awakes, a dry husk of a man who cannot weep but who tries to scratch free of himself.

Fighting back the panic, he plays with the baby whilst Agnes goes out to get more *mielie* meal.

It is the fattest, cheeriest little boy. Precious. Interesting name for a boy.

If he is very careful, Paul is able simply to play with Precious. Precious is not Chantal. There is no mystical healing process. He has divested himself of his past. He is pruned. He is now by name and by nature a van Niekerk. Utterly of no church. There is Paul and there is Precious and that is that. But when he sleeps, it is the dreams that keep him awake.

He plays with Precious.

Agnes returns. Because Paul is so tall, he is able to help fix down the corrugated panels that make up the roof. They have worked loose; the thumping in the night was not just Alfred. The wind lifts and drops, lifts and drops the roof.

Why did Alfred help me? he asks her when she is feeding Precious.

She does not hesitate. Alfred is the kindest man she knows, she tells him. He is too much kind. Often he gets cross because he is too much kind.

Paul does not try to unpick the ambiguities.

He tries to be as useful as he can to Agnes.

He learns how to cook the *pap* over a small fire. He makes trips to the common toilets to take Precious's gifts of shitty newspaper, which they use to wipe out his nappies. He even learns to scrub the frayed cloth nappies in the tin bath and rinse them. His most helpful job is to fetch water, to wait in the snaking queue, there is always a queue, and to lug the slopping buckets back to their shack. He is impervious to the stares and the talk. He does not understand it. They look at him and his bare feet, his tight trousers and his loose shirt. His wild beard he knows provokes comment, as does his dull-white skin. And they are all women or children, crowding around the single tap that gushes and gushes. But he does his woman's work and he knows that Agnes tells Alfred that he is useful, now that Precious is sick again and clings to his mother with a fearsome desperation.

Paul is the object of some pride to Sipiwe. Sipiwe is at the age where he ventures forth amongst the shacks to his friends. Now, he brings home a steady succession of grinning faces, boys and girls, to look at Paul. Sipiwe's very own long white man with the big beard. Whilst Paul is squatting over the fire, stirring the *pap*, the thick porridge, so that it does not burn through the thin metal of the pot, they crowd around him. Sipiwe asks him in Zulu the question he already knows is coming. Can they touch his hair? Can they touch his beard?

Yebo, he says and they all laugh. Then in a solemn procession, strictly ordered according to the rank of Sipiwe's friendship, they put their hands on his hair and stroke his beard. *Hau!* They draw back amazed and laugh. They rejoin the queue for another touch of his strange hair.

The *pap* cooks slowly and Paul has his hair stroked by a score of hands. It is their gentle touch, their gasps and whispers, that draws from his scalp the sudden impulse.

Phone, Paul suddenly says to his admiring urchins. Please. Is there a cell phone? It seems madness to ask, but he must. They could just laugh. Several do. They wriggle and kick the dust in a spirited dance and take up the chant of cell, cell, cell and then, after a squirming interlude, the smallest boy pushes through the crowd. They part with some surprise; their respect is tangible. For the little mite bears a large, old phone. He carries it like a gift of gold to the white man with the softest hair.

Hau! The gasp is taken up by all. *Hau.* That someone so small, one of them, should have in his hands a phone that is usually the preserve of the adults, and not all adults at that.

Paul looks at the phone in his hand with some surprise. He said phone, and lo, there came a phone . . . But does it work? It won't work. It does.

The little boy nods. He gestures to Paul and laughs and puts his hand to his ear.

Yes? Paul asks. *Yebo?* And the little boy laughs and laughs.

Paul prods the slab of the phone. Gingerly, as though it

were a foreign creature. But then his fingers know what to do, and before he can understand what is happening the phone is dialling, and then it is Sunny's voice, leaping to life from the buried past. It is as though a brontosaurus has burst through the sides of the shacks.

Who? Sunny's voice is sharp. He does not recognise the number or the voice.

It's Paul, Paul croaks as the children cheer.

Paul! They roll about laughing, Paul!

The line goes dead and Paul feels as though he is falling back, falling back to roll in the dust with the tangle of squatter-camp children. But then the phone rings. From Paul's fist there comes the twentieth-century trill of a cell phone. The children stop for a moment and watch him. Sipiwe glows with pride. Paul, his white man with the soft hair and now the cell phone.

Paul croaks his friend's name. Sunny. Sunny Raine.

So it is you! The exclamation tickles Paul's ear as Sunny swears with surprise.

Chantal, Paul coughs up the two syllables of her name. He may have shunned his old life, but he cannot shun the language, the *taal*, of his beloved daughter.

There is a terrible pause. The connection twangs and thumps into a *donga* of blurred sound. Paul thinks that he has lost Sunny, that they have lost Chantal, that there must be the confirmation of her inevitable demise. How much weight can a voice bear?

Sunny's voice surfaces again with its heavy load. He is mid-sentence and sounding strained.

. . . afraid and that's pretty much that . . .

What? Paul shouts into the phone. What did you say?

Sunny's voice comes thick and solid now. I'm afraid there's no news, he says. Not a fucking thing. That's about that. But then maybe no news is good news, hey?

Paul stares through the dust, through the cooking pot, the smoking fire and the rollicking children. He stares through his feet. No news. Good news. Still no news.

You there? Sunny's concern now climbs into Paul's ear. His old life is suddenly leaping aboard.

Yebo, says Paul. Yes.

There is a momentary silence. Perhaps neither trusts himself to speak.

But then Paul coughs up a single syllable. Claire?

Sunny does not answer straight away. Paul thinks that the line has died, but there is no sound to announce that, no sudden burr or electronic growl.

Sunny's voice, when it comes, is thick with feeling.

Man, he says, man.

What? Paul asks. What?

I don't know, says Sunny.

Paul waits, the phone slammed against his ear, hot and hard.

The last time we visited, two days ago, we found her in the pool . . .

The pool? Paul repeats stupidly. What?

The line shudders and throbs again and it sounds as though Sunny is speaking underwater himself. The line reconnects just as Sunny says . . . called for help.

Pool, help, what? What happened? Paul is instantly back home at his wife's side. Midrand leaps into view as Soweto fades. What has happened to Claire?

The line clears. Paul trusts that the battery will last on this fat old phone.

Sunny's voice comes again.

We found her in the pool, he says. Paul can hear that his tone is strained, oddly formal. As though he is telling something intimate to a third party who, strictly speaking, should not be told. This is privileged information; this is personal. Sunny's doubt seeps through his words.

Your wife was swimming, Sunny says. At six o'clock at night, your wife was in the pool doing lengths. Underwater. We knew she was home, we had phoned earlier. But she didn't answer the door. So we panicked. We called the guard. He got the set of spare keys and opened the house and then Lucky and I found her. We went right through the house but we had to go outside to find her and she did not hear us call. She had no idea we were looking for her. She was underwater, swimming up and down in your little pool, pushing off from one side and swimming straight to the other side. Lucky could not believe it. It was getting dark, man, and there was Claire under the freezing fucking water and not coming up to breathe. We waited for a fucking minute not knowing how long she had been doing that and then I jumped in the pool. Lucky shouted jump in so I did. My watch is not waterproof, by the way, but I got Claire. We fished her out. You never saw anything like it. I swear she would have drowned if we hadn't gone looking for her. She was fucking blue in the face and coughing and spitting up pool water like she had swallowed litres of the fucking stuff. Lucky put her in the recovery position, but for a good while it did not look like she was going to recover.

Sunny's voice lowers. It was like being at a car crash, he

says. You know, when you get out and you see them and you know that the poor bastards are not going to make it. Well, I tell you true, that was the feeling I had as your wife, he pauses momentarily, as your wife was lying there coughing up her guts, man.

How is she now? Paul's voice is small.

There was no way of getting hold of you, Sunny says pointedly, and then Claire said she was okay. I was ready to call the ambulance, man, it was that fucking bad. Then we carried her inside and Lucky sat with her on the couch and I got her a towel and some Milo with lots of fucking sugar. And she was okay. Except she kept trying to get up, actually fighting against Lucky, and saying it was six o'clock and time for, you know, her bath. Chantal's bath. She fought like a bloody demon, man. Shouting all sorts of stuff and crying . . . It wasn't nice.

Paul is stung. The sound of his daughter's name stings his ear and almost sends him reeling. The shock of six o'clock. The flood of memories, excoriating, searing memories that he has sought to escape. They come flooding to the surface, great rupturing images and sounds, and now they are chaotically tangled with the thoughts of Claire's pathetic attempts to swim away from it all.

He stands far away on a different shore.

Where the hell are you? comes Sunny's voice. Where the hell . . . ?

Soweto, says Paul simply. He feels as though the word has washed up from the pool of his mouth, as though he too has nearly drowned. So wet. Oh, so wet. Soweto. Kliptown in Soweto. Now the secure sense of a shore, of the pebbles invoked by Kliptown. *Klip* – Afrikaans for stone.

Does he gasp? Does he surface now to lie gasping at the side of the pool? His mind is a swirl.

We are worried about Claire, Sunny's voice rattles urgently, we think . . .

The line dies and Paul stares with horror at the *pap*: it must be burnt for sure. But Sipiwe has been stirring it.

Paul feels the little hand pull the hot phone from his ear. He feels as though part of his brain is pulling loose. But he manages to look up and say thank you. *Dankie. Ngiyabonga.*

Many of the children have gone, driven home by their growling bellies, but a fair few remain. Their hands still stroke his hair, which he suddenly feels. They have been laying on their hands throughout his conversation with Sunny.

Paul shakes himself and stands up. The children leap back with laughter. Paul shudders and shakes himself again. He is waking up from a bad dream, another bad dream. He is surfacing from the dark depths that he thought he had forever forsaken. He shakes himself and the children laugh and scream. He sighs. He takes a deep breath.

Now that the *pap* is ready, Paul sends them away with a slow-motion Boris Karloff impression. That is the best bit, it seems, better than soft hair: Frankenstein's monster amongst the shacks. They run, screaming with mirth, whilst Paul roars into his beard and his arms and legs crank spasmodically after them. The neighbours laugh. Paul breaks out into a sweat.

Alfred appears from around the side of a shack. He is early. He brings no food, no meat.

Paul dishes up for them all, his hands slowly becoming more steady. He ladles out little bowls of glutinous *pap*, which they eat with their fingers in the traditional way. Every last smear is wiped up and swallowed. There is not enough. They are all hungry. Sipiwe cries that he wants more. Paul offers to cook some more, but Agnes says no. That *pap* must last them as long as possible. If Sipiwe is still hungry, he must learn not to run around so much. Many of the squatter children adapt and sit still, hugging their knees, conserving their energy. Paul has seen their hungry eyes, their hollow cheeks. They will cavort like kids, and then suddenly retire, exhausted, to squat. Yes, they are the children of the squatter camp.

Whilst Paul and Sipiwe are doing the washing-up, scraping the bowls and the pot with the red sand, Alfred talks to Agnes. It is the most Paul has heard him say. He does not have to wait for Agnes to do the translation. He knows what Alfred is saying.

Paul must go. They cannot keep this big man in their tiny home. He eats very little but it is too much. Alfred did not expect him to live this long. He does not know why he brought back this white man when others were taking his car to pieces. Agnes does not say much. She is a child herself and cannot interfere with these two men. And Precious is ill, still, and demands too much of her time. Can Paul stay until Precious is well again?

Alfred considers this. He does not reply. He will think about it. But the food will run out soon if he does not get money for more. And then they will starve and Precious will die. Has Agnes noticed that Sipiwe is not looking too healthy?

Agnes conveys this to Paul that night. Alfred has gone. There is peace and quiet. Sipiwe sleeps alongside Paul's legs like a faithful dog. Agnes holds Precious, who mewls quietly and persistently. They have got used to his wail and his shitty smell, even though he is spotlessly clean.

I will find work, says Paul. His deep voice fills the shack, and Agnes laughs.

Work is to be looked for, but not to be found. It is not like someone has dropped a twenty-rand paper money that you can just pick up. No one has work. That is why they squat. And the people who have work look down on the people who squat and who have no work. They hate the people who squat because they might take their work and then they will have to squat. It is not good, at all, this squatting and this no work. It is hard. Four years ago everyone voted ANC for their jobs, jobs, jobs. All the time they said three times, jobs, jobs, jobs. And houses, and water, and electricity. But there is nothing. Agnes's mother voted before she died. But there was no job for her. She died. Agnes is still too much young to vote. It is too much hard.

Too much hard, Paul agrees. But there must be something. For too many reasons Paul feels that he must find some work. His hands still shake unmistakably.

But he marvels now that his car was not ransacked much sooner, that he was not ripped to shreds the second he arrived on the fringes of this world. He of the tinned food and the ready money, an ambassador from the world of white plenty. He was a have. Now he is a have-not.

He will do it for them, as well as for him. Find work. Just work. Not a career path, no development plan. Just exchange the labour of his body for money that will buy food that will sustain all their bodies for another day. Then he will work some more and they will live a little longer. Day to day. Day by day. Like Alfred, he will be a man.

Yebo, says Agnes, rocking Precious. That is all she can do it seems, rock poor Precious and be rocked by Alfred. Sipiwe snores against his legs.

After a night of terrible dreams, Paul is gone before first light. The air is even colder now in the mornings. Rather fresh, as his mother used to say. As he picks his way across the camp in the semi-dark, he thinks of his mother, but then she disappears beneath the sensations of his chilly bare feet. He is glad of the cold and the chaos that keeps him from thinking. There is a small market on the far side of the squatter camp. Hawkers come in to sell to the squatters who somehow manage to find another rand here or there. There is bartering that goes on too. Not everything has been earned in the traditional way. A clock radio, a car radio, some cardigans might be exchanged for food and other essentials, no questions asked. Just what is the going rate in bread and meat for such goods?

Paul wanders along the line of vendors setting up their stalls in the sunrise. He asks if he can help. The answer, along the entire line, is no. They look at him with sharp suspicion, this huge white man with the beard and strange clothes and bare feet. He can have that *vrot* banana if he goes away.

Paul takes it and goes away. It is better than it looks; he eats the whole thing. The hooting taxis come and go, delivering more vendors, some with large bags. There is laughter and loud conversation. They all know each other.

From nothing, the market springs up. By the time the sun has warmed the sky, and the day begins to bake, there are pyramids of tomatoes, knobbly piles of potatoes, *mielies* in their fresh green sheaths, still with their jaunty tufts of hair at the pointed end. There are tins of things too, and then an array of dead creatures, and some live ones. Chickens making throttling sounds in wire cages. Dead chickens lie limp on the planks, their eyes closed and dreaming, still fully feathered. There are joints and knuckles and offal by the gleaming thump and coil. Paul stops by a vendor on the end of the row. He stands mutely behind a basket of chickens' feet. A vivid yellow tangle of padded skin and hooked claws. Legs severed somewhere above the shank. Feet waiting, but going nowhere. This is the fourth man with chicken feet that he has seen. The others are situated in the heart of the meat market. He stands between a woman with toothpaste and what seems to be medicines, and another with old shoes. Trade is not brisk.

Paul takes another turn around the market, which is getting busier. The banana repeats on him and he walks about making little burps. As he strolls past, they say no job. He has asked once, they do not want to be bothered again. Paul watches them then returns to the fringes, to the man with the chicken feet.

The thin little man watches his approach. He looks hopeful. Paul stops before him.

Are these good chicken feet? Paul asks.

The man shrugs his narrow shoulders.

Paul repeats the question in Afrikaans.

The man looks at him.

The woman next door calls out to Paul.

He is not wanting to talk, she shouts in English. He is not wanting people to be knowing he is coming from Zimbabwe. Illegal immigrant. *Makwerekwere*.

The thin man ignores her, and shuffles his feet.

He is not belonging here, the woman shouts. He is making trouble.

Paul moves back to the meat counters.

How much? he asks the vendors, pointing to the chicken legs.

One rand for two, the man tells him.

Any size? Paul asks.

The man nods.

Paul checks the price with the other chicken men. It's the same.

He wanders back to the fringes of the market. People are emerging from the shacks. Taxis come and go off to the one side. They churn up a fine dust and spill their sharp hooting sounds into the morning air.

I can help you sell these, Paul points to the feet. The thin man from Zimbabwe shrugs his shoulders. Probably he has been hired to stand there to dispense the feet in the hot yellow sun. One rand for two, but you get the third one free? Paul nods at the man. The man looks blankly at him.

One rand for two, the man repeats.

Yes, says Paul. But the third foot, number three, is free.

The man stares at him.

How many feet did you sell yesterday? Paul asks.

Ten rand, the man says.

Let us sell the lot today, Paul says.

The man grins and shakes his head. He says something, maybe in Shona. Paul suspects that he doubts this white man's sanity. The challenge rises in Paul's chest. I will help, says Paul. The third foot free – special price.

The man thinks and thinks. Then he repeats the phrase. Special price, he says.

Paul takes three feet. He arranges them in his hands and

pauses for a moment. He takes a breath and then struts along the line of vendors, amongst the throngs, crowing loudly.

It's not quite cock-a-doodle-do. He makes a more authentic chicken sound in his throat and barrel chest. But it is his jerking movements, his lurching and the thrusting forward of his head to emulate a strutting chicken with madness in its beady eyes that gets the crowd going. Cock-a-doodle-doo, Paul yells, the sound grating loudly from his throat so that he almost coughs.

People stare. Then they laugh. A six-foot-four bearded white man who thinks he is a chicken.

Special price, Paul yells, pointing with all three feet at the startled man from Zimbabwe. Two for one rand and you get the third foot free. Special price. Special price.

More people laugh. The man is not mad. He looks mad. A crowd gathers. Paul crows. Paul struts. He repeats his special price. He stops and faces the crowd. They take a step back. Paul fixes a mad chicken eye on a fat woman. He kicks back on one foot, like a scratching chicken. He points the feet at her. Special price, he shouts, and he takes her by the arm towards the man from Zimbabwe.

Hau, she says covering her mouth with her hand. *Hau*.

Paul presents her to the man, who looks as though he might run away.

This is the moment. This is the instant when sales pitch might translate into action, when motivation becomes money.

Special price, Paul bellows, and the woman takes two rand from about her person.

Two rand, she says, two rand for six.

Paul crows. *Yebo*, he screams. Oh, *yebo*.

The man from Zimbabwe shakes his head, but hands over six feet for two rand. The woman takes the used plastic bag and waddles off. Paul follows her with his chicken strut. The crowd laughs and Paul peels off to attack another buyer, a man this time. He raises his hand and shakes his head as he grins. But the next man and the next both buy.

Within two hours only a handful of chicken feet remain and Paul has to sit down. His leg aches and he feels light-headed. The man from Zimbabwe watches him. The vendors down the line watch Paul and pass comment, shaking their heads and laughing – except for the men with their own chicken feet.

Another man arrives. He fires some isiXhosa clicks at the vendor. The man from Zimbabwe empties his pockets and nods at Paul. The new man sees Paul for the first time. He watches him as he speaks rapid-fire at the thin man. The little vendor nods. The new man, maybe the owner, grabs a plastic bag and shuffles a hand around in the box. Then he is gone.

The man from Zimbabwe walks over to Paul.

He says this for you. He hands the packet to Paul. There are the last five feet.

The next day? he asks Paul. Tuesday?

Paul stares at the feet.

Tuesday, he says. He feels the need to stand up and shake the man by the hand. They do the African handshake, a protracted affair, and the man from Zimbabwe looks startled.

Tuesday, is all he can say, and Paul leaves.

He limps with the bag swinging at his side and his head spinning.

Agnes tells him to boil the feet. To boil them for a long time otherwise they are tough.

He and Sipiwe make the fire and fetch more water. He tells Sipiwe the story. Sipiwe does not understand a word Paul says, but he laughs at the cockle-a-doodle-doo and the re-enactment of his chicken parade. Sipiwe shows him how, if you dig your nail into the top of the chicken leg and draw it upwards, you can make the feet extend and relax. Sipiwe tries each foot and it is Paul's turn to laugh. The yellow legs twitch to life. Paul continues to laugh. The luxury of playing with his food.

They sit in the shack picking on the yellow legs. Sipiwe tells Agnes about Paul playing at being a chicken. She shakes her head. *Hau*, she says, *hau* Paul.

They leave two of the feet for Albert. The lion's share. The feet, swollen from the cooking, and paler now, lie in wait for Albert in the emptied, covered pot in a corner of the shack.

Albert comes in late. Sipiwe is already asleep, like a dog at Paul's feet. They share the flat mattress, which is hitched up against the side of the shack during the day, useful as a kind of insulation against the hot metal side where the sun strikes.

No *shisanyama*, says Albert, no *braai*, no meat. He hands over half a loaf of bread to Agnes. Just *bunnychow*. Bread, no curry also.

Agnes breaks off a hunk for herself, then hands the bread to Paul. Albert stares at him. Paul gets up and passes Albert the pot. Paul removes the cover.

Albert eats the chicken feet in silence, apart from the smacking of his lips and the licking of his fingers. Paul eats some of the bread, then hands it over to Albert. Albert tears off a wedge and uses it to wipe out the inside of the pot. He chews the rest, leaning back against the side of the shack.

When he is finished, he remains sitting there. His power-ful hands and arms rest on his knees, dangle over the edges of his knees.

You are the Chicken Man, he says to Paul. I heard it. They tell me in the taxi. The white man, your white man you found, he is the Chicken Man.

Albert's eyes hold Paul fast. His mouth does not smile, but Paul can tell that there is wry amusement hiding behind his lips.

I was coming to tell you, you must go. I was coming today to say to you, go. But they are telling me that you are the Chicken Man. You help to sell chicken feet. Now we eat the chicken feet. You bring home chicken feet tomorrow, you stay even when there is no space. You are our Chicken Man.

It is the most words by far that Paul has ever heard Albert utter.

Yebo, Paul says. *Ngiyabonga*. Thank you.

Paul goes outside with the facecloth and the small bucket of water. As he stands in the darkness, the voices and music of the shacks washes over him. He removes his clothes. The air is chilly already, despite the smoke and *kwaito* beats and the throbbing sense of a thousand lives pressed into this cramped, sweaty space. Paul scrubs under his arms and between his legs. He rinses the cloth, wringing out the sour water. Then he rubs down his entire body before pulling on his smelly clothes. Voices call and murmur in and around the dull tin shacks. Paul listens carefully to the pulsating tones, to the laughter and the loudness. He cannot consciously think of Chantal or Claire. He does not think of his parents, or of

John and Rachel. He listens as hard as he can, his heart yearning, reaching out. And he finds himself stretching out his neck and beginning to sway; his one leg kicks back as though scratching in the dust. He finds himself moving in an almost-dance, a chicken trance. His lips curl and he whispers a soft crowing sound to himself. He is the Chicken Man. Paul van Niekerk can be poured away with the smelly water. He just needs to bring home a few feet each day for them to eat. He can do that. He is the Chicken Man.

He strolls through the shacks, trekking with bare feet to the tap. His head jerks in rhythm. He knows the way, even in the dark. Candlelight, and the soft slatted light of car-battery-operated light bulbs, gleams through slits in the more established shacks. More music spills, more tangled conversations. Some people cook inside on gas stoves fed by bulging blue canisters. There are many fires too. Many coal stoves that puff out warm smoke into the cold air. Paul sidles past, inhaling a hundred hundred meals. He tries not to crow.

And so begins the reign of the Chicken Man.

But he is almost dethroned the next day. Out of the blue they come.

Through the thronging taxis, the milling crowds, the old car comes with a hunched and nervous Indian woman at the wheel. It is only because they drive right past the Kliptown market and the fact that it is a car, not a minibus taxi, that Paul even notices Lucky crouched at the wheel of the car.

And with reciprocal surprise, she spots the only white face for miles, the Chicken Man taking a brief break from being an overgrown chicken.

Paul lurches forward; Lucky beckons madly from within her

cocoon of metal and glass. Paul asks the Zimbabwean to watch the table. He crosses the road.

Lucky winds down her window a fraction, and Paul looms over her like a vendor. But he has nothing to sell.

Howzit? comes Lucky's voice through the nervous slit, and Paul bends closer and sees Sunny in the passenger seat, leaning back as far as it will go, basically keeping his white body out of sight beside his Indian wife. His pale face is taut.

Lucky, Paul says. Sunny.

Sunny sits up and glances wildly around.

Paul sees the Kliptown scene through his friend's bulging eyes: chaos, noise, blacks, a serious piece of fucking Africa, man. Jesus Christ. And then Lucky's voice slots through the crack and catches in his beard.

Can we stop? Are we safe?

Paul looms like a beggar, a hijacker, at their window. Anything is possible, as his very presence seems to be proving. Just living makes it so.

Hop in! shouts Sunny. For fuck's sake, get in the car. He looks around wildly as though anticipating an instant horde of armed assailants.

His voice comes squashed and trapped. Like someone talking inside a tin, or using one of those children's walkie-talkies – the cans connected by a length of string. Paul feels the tenuous string tugging at him from his anxious friends. Only connect, they seem to be calling. Come on. Get in the fucking car.

Paul tries not to smile. He is the Chicken Man, after all. Maybe he should crow. Maybe he should do his dance. What would Sunny manage to say to that?

But he gets into the car, the ancient blue car that he knows his friends must have bought or borrowed for the express purpose of coming into Soweto. Nothing worth stealing. But they do not know Kliptown. They do not know squatter camps. They do not know just how much the have-nots do not have.

Drive, shouts Sunny. But Paul says no. Paul, in the back seat, puts a reassuring hand on the shoulders of his friends. His strange humour gives rise to angry gratitude: they have come all this way. They have left their universe and come on this mission to outer space. For such is this monstrous satellite, Soweto. South west of, and to hell and gone. That is their view, no doubt.

Lucky leaves the engine running and they whip around awkwardly to face Paul.

Man, says Sunny, taking in the full-frontal view of the Chicken Man. Man. He cannot even manage an expletive.

Paul. Lucky cuts to the chase, or maybe she tries to reassure herself that it is Paul beneath the beard and the rags and the dark tan and the stink.

Paul wants to crow. He does not. He does not think that that would go down well, and he just pats his friends on their side-on shoulders. It is a cramped car.

Paul, says Lucky. It's Claire.

Paul takes back his hands. He does not know where to put them now. He has only holes in his tight trousers, no pockets. His hands lie awkwardly in his greasy lap.

How is she? he asks.

How long has it been? He has little sense of days and dates. There are old newspapers, yes, and his beard, like the rings of trees, gives some clue, as do the colder mornings, longer nights and shorter days.

No sign of Chantal, says Lucky, while Sunny gawps, and we are losing Claire.

Shit, Paul says. It is a soft shit. He has not found himself, and now Claire is lost. What happened to the lanes for swimming, the routine, the swift and certain strokes? If anyone was going to survive, it was Claire. Why, he has barely latched on to the lifeline of the Chicken Man.

Claire is on medication, says Lucky, whilst Sunny stares and stares.

Paul tries to look at them both. To return the sympathetic eyes of Lucky and to face up to the hard staring of Sunny. He feels Lucky's compassion; he senses the affront he presents to Sunny's white man's sensibilities, such as they are.

You would not recognise her, Sunny blurts out.

Paul looks at him.

Lucky raises a hand and manages to touch Paul.

It's not good, she says softly. Sunny told you about the pool.

Paul nods, even though it is not a question. They will keep coming back to the pool, he knows that.

Lucky carries on. We couldn't stop her, she says. Claire was going to get back in that pool.

I held her down, Sunny speaks suddenly again. I had to hold her down. Hard.

I swear she wanted to drown herself. Lucky searches Paul's eyes. She plunges on.

She tried to fight off Sunny, it was terrible. Shouting terrible things, you know, about you and what happened to Chantal, and her father as well. Her father and mother, not nice at all.

She scratched Sunny – Sunny turns his face for Paul to see the long, thin scab down the side of his face, along his ear – and would have hurt herself, really hurt herself if we hadn't wrapped her up in her towel and taken her to hospital. It was horrible. I have never seen someone break down. Claire broke down.

Sunny clenches a fist and his face twists. Lucky tries to carry on. So they sedated her. She went under. She screamed like mad, like they were trying to kill her, and then she went quietly. Lucky's voice shakes. It's like she got her wish and she is under. It is like looking at someone drowned at the bottom of a pool – except she is on a dry white bed.

Her mother is with her, Sunny offers pointedly. She has got her mother with her, and us. He whips his head around as a large group of people walk past. Taxis hoot and roar. It is very loud outside. The car's engine coughs and fidgets nervously.

We wanted you to know, Lucky's voice is very soft. Sunny tried to call that cell number but it never worked again. And he remembered you saying Kliptown.

We bought this old *skedonk*, says Sunny, almost harsh, almost proud of his prudent ingenuity. We came to get you.

Paul's hands leap involuntarily. The wings of a startled chicken, they flutter in the confines of the old car, scattering his confusion like feathers. They have come to get him. Like a child's game. Nine, ten, eleven, twelve: coming to get you! He tugs at his beard. He smells the offal on his hands and feels the grease. He rubs his head and squirms in his seat. His old friends right before him. His old life right in front of him. Claire silent and comatose in the background, and Chantal's face bleaching to oblivion on a thousand sad posters. One step forward, two steps back. Just when he felt he had taken two steps forward they come hijacking him with this. Claire, Chantal, always Chantal. But also Agnes and Sipiwe and Precious and Alfred.

And the hootings from outside fill his mouth with the dust that swirls, and his throat is already rough from repeated crowing and his bare feet are squirming because he is the Chicken Man. They have come to find Paul and before them crouches the giant Chicken Man. And their car seats and their unspoken accusations are thrust up between them and they are strapped in by their seat belts and by their first-world fear that perpetually flickers. Another group of men shouts past the car, overwhelms the car, and the seats and their eyes and the noise from outside and his thundering heart all say, no, not yet and the whole of Soweto seems to say no, not here.

Not yet, not here, and he bursts from the car in his rags and his beard, his words of farewell hollow in his head. Just as Claire lies still and abandoned, he must move and not be loved.

He must fall from the car and go running back to the table of offal, of bright claws, and he must strut his desperate stuff and crow his heart out, for he is the Chicken Man. He must stay here where Chantal was last known to be, just as Lucky and Sunny must drive off in a blurt of anxious tyres. Not yet, not here. If only they can forgive him, as he has already forgiven them. And he leaps and crows with mad tears streaming from his eyes.

And so, in exchange for a few yellow feet each day, Paul promotes the wares of the thin, nervous vendor. He crows long and hard and struts with diligent desperation. It is not long before the other sellers of offal also cut their prices, offering three for two. But it is Paul who has captured the attention of the thronging buyers. He is the Chicken Man. They bring their children to see the white man with the big beard doing his Chicken Man dance. Two of the vendors try to get him to advertise their wares, but Paul sticks with the man from Zimbabwe. He soon becomes the only purveyor of chicken feet, as well as necks and intestines. The feet-and-neck combination is known in the local slang as Walkie Talkies. Paul crows while the other vendors change their wares. They mutter and move further away, before fighting to reclaim their spot closer to where the action is.

Alfred accepts the daily offerings of feet, and now necks and spiced offal, with lordly detachment. But he is impressed when the Chicken Man begins bringing home some money in addition to the usual bits and pieces. Business is going so well, that the Chicken Man is now paid for his strutting services. Alfred takes the money. He buys special *muti* for Precious, who continues to ail, and Sipiwe gets a football. Several weeks later, Agnes finally is given a gas stove. It is another while before Albert comes back with new clothes for both himself and Paul. Paul cannot bring himself to put on the shoes. It is the new underwear, the crisp clean underpants, that brings him close to tears.

But he wears his old clothes each day. They have become his uniform. The caramel-coloured trousers and mustard-yellow shirt. The belt made of old rope. His feet are hard and tough, almost as tough and scaled as the chicken feet he sells. It is only in the evenings that he wears his new tracksuit to sleep in, or on Sundays that he puts on his new clothes. The shoes remain gleaming and new. Albert asks if he is saving them for his wedding day. Paul laughs into his beard, his big bushy beard, but when Albert arrives in the shack with a new cell phone, Paul asks if he might make a call.

There is someone in hospital whom, at last, he must call.

He does not get Claire's number right at the first few attempts. Albert shakes his head and tells him he has one last go. Paul stands outside the shack and punches in the numbers, in a slightly different order. The phone rings. Again it amazes him that even over the squatter camp there is network coverage. *Yebo. Yebo gogo.*

When Claire's voice answers with her clipped Yes, hello, Paul almost hangs up. It could be a first date. His mouth is dry. She knows it is he.

Claire, he says, his voice rasping like a chicken's.

There is a rigid silence. Paul turns against the corrugated metal of the shack wall. The heat from the dying sun glows against his face. He leans his head against the warm waves of metal. His toes dig in the soft dirt. The silence drags on.

Claire, he says again. His voice is his own this time.

Claire's voice comes close in his ear. I wondered if you would call, she says.

Yes, he says.

So you're alive and kicking, Claire says. Just like Lucky and Sunny said.

Yes, he says.

There is a long pause.

So I can let the police know to stop looking?

Yes, Paul says. I didn't know they were looking.

Well, not very hard, Claire says. They hardly had the resources to look for Chantal . . .

Chantal, Paul says. He cannot stop her name. Yet again he

has buried her name deep in his guts, but it vomits out in an instant. The soft hiss of the first syllable, the clipped then elongated triphthong of the second.

Chantal, repeats Claire. You haven't found her? Lucky and Sunny said that you had not found her.

Paul is silent against the bitterness. At least she is up and about and on the phone.

Because that's what I've told everyone. You left home, effectively vanished off the face of the earth, looking for . . . your beloved daughter. Lucky and Sunny seemed to think so too. That you are looking for something. Not just running away from everything.

Paul does not know what to say. Was he looking for Chantal? Is he trying to lose Chantal?

Claire's voice has caused his intestines to clutch and contract as though a chicken foot is flexing inside him.

Claire lets the silence drag on.

You are out of hospital? Paul says.

Claire does not reply.

I am glad, honestly I am, that you are out of hospital. Paul tries to keep his voice from rasping.

Paul, she says.

Just the single word. Paul.

Then there is a long pause. The line swishes. They could both be very deep underwater.

I need you, she says suddenly. I am selling the house. I need you to come in and sign. It's in both our names, if you remember.

I remember, he says. Yes, I do remember.

She ignores his sarcasm, which is not sarcasm.

Life goes on, she says. You know life has to go on. We can't all run away. We have to be strong.

He swallows the slings and arrows. The barbs stick in his throat.

Of course, he manages to say. Each to his own.

Claire greets his riposte with silence. Paul can sense her jaw tightening, her nostrils flaring.

Fuck you, she whispers down the phone.

He stands for a long while, holding the phone to his ear. Neither speaks. Neither hangs up.

From their home in Midrand to the shacks of Soweto, there stretches a straight line of silence. They are linked by a bitter loop, an arc of air, chilling radio waves.

Paul waits. Does neither want to be the one to hang up on their relationship?

The line goes dead.

I remember, Paul says to the dumb slab of a phone.

He lets the warmth from the corrugated iron pulse through his forehead.

He hands the phone back to Alfred.

Thanks, he says.

Alfred checks the credit on the phone, then slips it into his pocket. Paul has the strange feeling that, with the phone, Claire has just been packed away, clipped closed, switched off.

When should they meet? When should he 'come in', as Claire put it?

So she is selling the house. She is selling Chantal's room with the teddy bear border and the bullet buried in one pink wall.

Paul takes Sipiwe to the dusty patch beyond the shacks. They kick his football about, close to where he first parked the

Corolla when he arrived. Shacks have indeed taken over that space. Sipiwe chases after the football loyally, a small dog.

When should he go? Should he shave? Should the Chicken Man shave off his trademark beard?

He realises that he is going to have to call her again.

He waits until the next day. At work, he asks Stephen, the man from Zimbabwe, if he might use his phone.

Stephen is happy to hand over his phone, his flashy phone.

Again, Paul cannot get the number right.

Then finally Claire answers. She is in the car. Travelling to Witbank, racing in the opposite direction to him.

Thursday? Can he make Thursday? she says.

He works during the day. He will need time to get to her. Can he aim for six o'clock?

He is working in Soweto? Her voice registers no surprise. Not even mock interest. But that is the point. Her point. With him, anything is possible, it appears. Six o'clock, after his work, that will be just fine. She is sure that the estate agent will be more than happy to witness the deed.

Where will you live? Paul asks. But she has already hung up.

Part of Paul would like to arrive barefoot and stinking in his old clothes and rope belt. Maybe dare Claire to recoil from him. Dare her to wrinkle up her nose in unfeigned disgust.

He will not shave. But that night he washes his hair. The shampoo takes too much water to rinse out properly. He has to fetch more. And he will have to wear his new shoes for the first time.

As he gets dressed the next day, he feels like a charlatan. Chicken Man goes formal, he pictures imaginary headlines.

The smart shirt and trousers, possibly a little louder than he is used to, are a good fit. You can see that he has lost weight. That beneath the effusion and excess of his facial hair, as well as his flowing locks, he seems to have withered somewhat and shrunk. He realises that he has no socks. And that his feet seem to have spread, widened and spread from having been freed from shoes for so long. The shoes are too tight. He takes them off and explains to Agnes and the watching Precious that he will put them on when the time comes. Agnes wishes him good luck.

Hamba kahle, she says. Go well.

Salani kahle, he says to them both. Stay well.

There are good sales that day. They have started to sell cooked food too. Stephen does the frying of the offal so that Paul might keep his good clothes clean. Stephen tells Paul which taxi signals to use, his index finger pointing straight up, to get to Jozi – Joburg. From there he'll have to make his own way to Midrand.

Paul is the first in the taxi. He is obliged to sit in the back. The taxi will only leave once it is full. And there is a very loose definition of full, as Paul well knows, for the average Hi Ace taxi. Most of the taxis are coming back from Jozi. Throwing people back into the camp. The wait to make the reverse trip at this time of the day is longer.

Fourteen people finally cram in. Paul still keeps his shoes on his lap, his toes curling on the rubber mat beneath him. He listens to the loud voices around him. People chat and laugh. Some include him. Chicken Man, they say, how was business today? You are looking sharp, Chicken Man, sharp sharp. And Paul answers in a mixture of English, Afrikaans and Zulu – the *tsotsitaal* of the township.

The journey to Jozi is a jostling, swaying, shuddering experience. The passengers seem compelled to laugh and chat as a defence, a distraction against certain death. Their driver does turn down his thumping music, but twice they all lurch forward as he hits the brakes, and they press against the left as he veers towards the right.

They emerge, shaken and relieved. Paul feels as though he should be celebrating the fact that he is alive. As though he should do something momentous, make a difference, invent a cure for AIDS, put on his new shoes.

Instead he wanders barefoot, his shoes dangling from his hand, asking for a taxi to Midrand. It does not take long to find one. Again, once the fee is paid, there is the wait for the remainder of the taxi seats to fill up. Paul sits near the front, and soon they pull away.

Joburg recedes into the swaying distance. They fly along the M1. After the squatter camp, everything seems so neat and ordered. Trimmed. Maybe even truncated? The taxi delivers them outside the Boulders shopping mall. It is a half an hour's walk home.

Home, Paul thinks as he walks swiftly, his shoes still dangling from their laces, the laces he has knotted together and looped around his neck. It is only when he arrives at the townhouse complex in the darkness of the evening that he squeezes his feet into the shoes. He ties them loosely but they are tight and hard.

There is a new guard at the gate. He does not know Paul. He will not open the gates. Paul has to buzz Claire, and only then, on her say-so, do the gates crank open.

Paul shuffles inside. The gates shudder closed with their usual clang.

Paul walks the uncomfortable steps to his own front door.

There is a long wait after he presses the buzzer. Why? He has just spoken to Claire via the intercom. Paul looks at the Honda Ballade, and at the black BMW beside it. And there is another black car, an Audi, also squeezed in behind the two cars.

Quite a gathering. Quite a formidable alliance of gleaming metal and German engineering. Japanese in the case of the Honda.

Hello, Paul. Claire's voice is neutral. Carefully clipped and shaved of any frills of emotion. Her gaze holds him steadfastly. She does not raise a quizzical eyebrow. He stands before her, in the gloom of the gathering darkness. The light spills on to his face, which is thin, rising up out of the bushy tangle of his beard. So he has a beard. And his face is tanned, ruddy and brown. He stands there, in his natty clothes, new and oddly jaunty, his feet at uncertain angles.

Come in, Claire says, unlocking the security gate.

Thank you, Paul says, and enters.

He knew that Sunny and Lucky would be there again. Moral support. There are handshakes and hugs. But behind the warmth are the anxious eyes. So once again this is Paul. What happened to him? What happened to the old Paul?

The estate agent is a small man with a big handshake. Paul tries not to grin as his right hand is returned to him, crushed and limp. He flexes it experimentally.

The agent pushes ahead. That's a great beard, man. A very Paul Kruger kind of beard. Must cut down on the shaving time, hey? Give you more time in the sack.

Shack, Paul says without thinking.

But the agent has moved on, sidestepping the non sequitur and breezing over to the dining room table.

Here they are, the agent says. The documents are introduced with a flourish. They wait splashed out on the yellow-wood table. There is a black pen.

Paul moves through the pain in his feet. The man's voice washes over him. It's all about onward chains, approved loans, guarantees and checks and balances. In front of Paul lies a set of A4 route maps out of his marriage, out of his old life. As he turns each neatly stapled page, each one yielding ineluctably to the next, he is leafing on in time. He will flick through his house, turn over another page, sign away his marriage. He should feel sad. Instead, his shoes are squashing his feet, and his beard feels soft and silky beneath his hand. Will the agent never shut up?

Just once Paul looks up at Claire.

He ignores the proffered pen. The little shovel that is going to dig the heart out of their marriage, going to undermine the foundations of their old life.

Claire's eyes cannot hold his stare. They slide from his face down to the creamy white pages with their mindless legalese and bureaucratic syntactical contortions.

Paul sighs. He does feel a deep sadness. But he now accepts the pen. His feet ache and his heart aches and the pen is smooth and small in his huge hand. He looks at his own nails, surprised at how clean but how long they are.

Paul, Sunny says. He stands beside Paul, between Paul and Claire. That's all he says. Lucky has shushed him.

Paul bends over the pages and signs beside the Xs marked here, here and here. And he has to initial there, there and there. It is easy. Claire has already done the deed, repeatedly. He marries his neat, precise hand to her loose scrawl. Again, the inherent contradiction. He would have thought that her writing would be controlled and chiselled. Not wild. Was she angry when she signed? Is he sad as he signs? Or just resigned? He pauses at the last X. The final crossroad. Time to kiss Midrand goodbye. X marks the spot, but this is no love letter. He feels as though Claire is daring him to sign. He glances up, aware of the dramatic pause he creates.

Sunny shifts uncomfortably.

Claire looks down at the document.

The estate agent cracks some witticism about screwing his courage to the sticking place. Paul thinks that there might well be other things he can do with his courage.

The pen scratches in the silence and it is done. As simple as that. Their future together, all their plans, their little family home, gone. Rent asunder. Torn in two.

The estate agent takes the pen from Paul. It slides out of his grasp and is offered to Sunny. Sunny signs as witness, here on this day, this Thursday, April the second 1997, in Midrand. Four days before Chantal's first birthday.

His business concluded, the estate agent wastes no time in packing up and clearing out. The money will be through soonish. They have made a tidy penny. The property market is about to hit skid row with the bond rate climbing to above twenty per cent. Good timing, man. It's been a good investment, but time to call it a day.

Paul waits for the man to go, to go as soon as he has finished counting out their lives and telling them what they are worth.

But then he wishes that the estate agent had not gone. The

little man had lent a sense of formal proceedings. Now it is this. Two couples, old friends. Husbands and wives.

Chantal is gone, Paul might as well be announcing. Fleance is fled. Here am I. Incongruously bearded and attired. My outfitter is Alfred. He is a shack dweller. I am a shack dweller. I now live in Soweto. I have gone native. I am Chicken Man. I have run away – chicken. Yellow-bellied. I eat offal. Yellow feet. Cold feet. Sore feet.

Won't you sit down? Lucky says from her position on the couch.

Paul's lips stop moving and he tugs at his beard. This is dreadful.

Thanks, he says, but does not move.

You will get half the money, obviously, Claire says.

He is glad that it is obvious to her.

He waves aside the thought that soon – soonish – he will have to open up a new account, because his wallet with his cards was taken when the money was stolen. He does not want to think of such details. They overwhelm him. They fill him with such a weight of sadness and despair.

Now, he needs to be on the move. There is no way that he can sit down. He stands, still.

Then with a wry smile, he asks the question. Does anyone have twenty rand he can borrow?

He remembers the look on Sunny's face as he hands Paul five twenty-rand notes, quickly peeled from his pocket.

Just twenty, Paul says. But Sunny will not take back any money.

I have some, Lucky says. But Paul crashes from his home before his best friends and his wife can hand out any more money.

He takes off his shoes in the taxi.

He hunkers down against the cold glass and watches the lights of the highway flit past in dreamlike succession.

Soweto rises to greet him, to swallow him.

His feet leave a neat imprint in the red dust of the dark street. He makes his way towards the shacks. His shoes dangle from his neck. Sipiwe will cling to his legs and laugh like a puppy. Agnes will be feeding Precious, who will snuffle and cry. Alfred will be playing on his new phone, and will grunt when he reappears. A million voices, muffled and amplified through the metal of the shacks, will rise up to drown him. Music from a hundred thousand tape decks and CD players and radios will thump with a heartbeat in the darkness, and the smell of smoke and *mielie* meal will overwhelm him. He knows these things. There are many things he does not know, but he knows these things.

11 years

EVERY YEAR, ON THE ANNIVERSARY of his daughter's abduction, he drives to Midrand, to the spot where it all happened. For him, it is a pilgrimage, an annual haj. And there, held up at the side of the road, right beside the very spot, he sits in his car. He has long since stopped worrying about locked car doors and closed windows. He winds down the windows and switches off the engine. Then he sits back and watches the digital clock begin to flick up the minutes to 2:02.

At 2:00 he closes his eyes for a minute.

Over the years, the traffic has got busier and busier, if that is possible.

He sits in silence.

The cars crawl past. The cars, the *bakkies*, the minibuses and trucks and vans and big buses.

Invariably, the sky is an unremitting blue. Suggestive of hope and possibility, every good thing clear and tangible under the sun.

Invariably, he weeps.

The heat from the dashboard sings in the car and the steering wheel can become too hot to handle. The cars purr past, windows winking in the searing light. No one takes a blind bit of notice of him. The traffic growls, and through his quiet tears he inhales the petrol fumes and the diesel exhaust. A gentle breeze might blow through the open windows.

He opens his eyes. At 2:02 he stiffens. He sits rigid for that minute. Then he glances to his right, remembering the gun. He feels his fear and the hair come tearing from his scalp. He remembers the rubbed-raw feeling between his thighs, where he wet himself, and he looks over his shoulder to the back seat, to a ghostly Chantal, who still sits and slumbers in his mind's eye, her little fist still attached to her half-gnawed Farley's rusk.

He relives those fearful seconds.

It never gets easier.

He relives those final seconds, when he still had a daughter.

It will never get any easier.

Some vendors approach the car. He simply shakes his head, not allowing himself to talk. He does not go to church; this is his memorial service. This is his Easter and Christmas, his Passover, his Hanukkah, his Ramadan and Eid and Diwali. He sits in silent communion with the past, with his daughter's ghost. He knows that she is dead. She must be dead. If he can feel her haunting presence surely she must be dead.

At last, he will begin to move again.

The eyes that glance at him in the rear-view mirror are older now. The crinkled crow's feet and the streaks of salty grey in his hair denote the fearful passage of time. Though for him it seems that it is forever 2:02 in the afternoon and the sun is terribly hot.

He starts the engine, checks, indicates and rejoins the

traffic. He is jolted back into reality, whatever that means. And he drives along the precise same route, as he heads back along the N1 to the M1 before looping around Joburg and flying back home to Soweto.

At this point, as he leaves Egoli behind him, and the road snakes away to Soweto, he will think back to Sipiwe and Precious and Agnes. And Alfred, always Alfred, who brought him to his one-room home, a Sowetan Samaritan.

Both children died of AIDS, within months of each other. Precious was always ill; Sipiwe was a little more stout. But they did not last. And Agnes, barely more than a child herself, followed them. The anti-retroviral drugs, their one true hope, never came. The doctors at Baragwanath Hospital, the largest in the world, were even angrier than Paul. Try beetroot, they said bitterly, try the African potato and garlic. He returned to the shack, the Chicken Man bearing only the doctors' desperate sarcasm and some vitamin supplements. Nothing else.

Paul went back when Sipiwe took ill, and was repeatedly ill, and again and again as Agnes faded away. And again and again the doctors were forced to offer him quack remedies and more vitamins. Do you know, this is not right, this is genocide, said the one doctor, ironically a Dr Zuma himself. His voice shook. As he took off his gloves and looked hopelessly at Paul with Sipiwe, or Paul with Agnes. They are making us stand by, our hands tied up with 'Africanist' remedies whilst your Sipiwe dies, whilst your Agnes dies. It is nothing less than genocide. I may as well be an Eichmann in Bavaria, not a Zuma in Baragwanath. This he said with whispered rage to Paul, almost spitting in Paul's ear on his second visit with Agnes. On his third visit, Dr Zuma was no longer there; redeployed, someone muttered, before they listed the options of beetroot, the African potato and garlic, as well as handing out the familiar plastic bottle of vitamin supplements.

Alfred lived longer. He was Paul's first employee.

When Paul set up his small advertising agency with the money from the sale of the Midrand house, Alfred came with him. They moved from the camp, from the shack they shared with Agnes's stove and the sad display of the dead children's toys and Sipiwe's beloved football. That Paul took with them. The football and the poster of Chantal. The rest of the things they gave away to their neighbours. When Paul visited some weeks later, a family from Zimbabwe had moved in, all nine of them. They returned his cheery greeting. They seemed happy.

Paul and Alfred did not go far. In Soweto, poverty and wealth exist cheek by jowl. So when the Chicken Man flew the coop, he did not fly far. Just a few hundred metres, maybe half a kilometre to the more established side of Kliptown with the characteristic little box houses, four rooms in a simple square, and fronted by a tiny garden.

Then Alfred's coughing started and the perpetual flu, and soon, after much beetroot, bitter African potatoes and garlic cooked by Paul, as well as the standard doses of vitamins, Alfred was dead and Paul moved again.

A slightly bigger house this time, with a room for his one-man art department and another for reception and meetings. Paul lived in the back of the house, though he spent most of his time working.

The Chicken Man Agency was a growing success. Initially he wanted to call his baby Umkhonto we Umbono, the Spear of the Notion, but that had seemed too clever-clever. He remembered Nolene's advice. He thought about Nolene and Thandi. He had heard that they had both been poached by other agencies as the affirmative-action pressure mounted. He missed them.

And so he stuck with the Chicken Man Agency. There was no problem running a business from a residential district. Five doors down was Sophie Mahlangu's hairdressing and hair products emporium, and a taxi driver, Vincent Sibanyoni, lived next door with his wife who sold African remedies. There was a constant stream of people to her, as well as to the hairdresser's, and so, through word of both hairdresser's and traditional healer's mouths, they came to the famous Chicken Man and his advertising agency. They smiled at his sign, and respectfully asked about the little girl in the poster that was attached to it. Paul had made a copy of the original poster, changing only the contact number. One poster for outside, to be replaced when it was too faded; the original hung above his bed.

The Chicken Man's successes were very local at first. His first three clients were his immediate neighbour, the taxi driver, and Sophie's Superior Styling within five doors.

Vincent's profits doubled after Paul had arranged for his taxi to be spray-painted with the logo Safe. Steady. Slow. Vincent did his best to live up to this marketing, and joked with Paul that the slower he drove, using less fuel, the faster the passengers streamed to his taxi. He was trying to convince his boss that Safe. Steady. Slow. was the new fast way to make profits, but the going was tough. Maybe another month of record profits would convince the taxi tycoon?

Vincent was paid a small commission to distribute flyers for Sophie's Superior Styling, and to sing her praises. He did just that, and Sophie's business shot through the roof. So much so that she had to move house. Paul, and especially Alfred, had been sad to see her go. But she, too, spread the word and the Chicken Man business grew.

With AIDS and related diseases affecting so many, and with the government health-care paralysis, there was no shortage of clients for Mrs Sibanyoni. Apparently she was quite high up in the THO, the Traditional Healers Organisation, obviously a South African counterpoint to the World Health Organisation. Vincent, a thoroughly modern man, often joked with Paul over the rickety fence on Sundays when they tended their lawns. That wife of mine, he would pretend to moan, just WHO does she think she is?

Paul would laugh bitterly, though he and Alfred were possibly her best customers as Alfred's health declined and no anti-retroviral drugs were forthcoming, not even on the black market.

The going was never easy, though. After Alfred's death, Paul nearly chucked it all in.

In his mind's eye he recalls sitting home alone, trying to make sense of a pile of invoices. Alfred had been a genius with the calculator on his cell phone, a natural accountant, but now he too is gone.

Then there is a knock on the door. Paul gets up slowly. Before he can open the door, it jerks aside and three men step into the Chicken Man Agency. They do not look as though they have come to avail themselves of his services. They look mean. They look as though they mean business, other business.

Sanibonani, the greeting dies on Paul's lips. He marvels at his resolve never to lock his front door. To refuse to live behind bars. For a year now, in the run-up to the millennium and despite all sorts of Y2K and crime uncertainties, his decision has been vindicated. Until now. What might the men want? He banks any cash at the end of every day and the float is measly.

From the midst of the men, a child, a small child of about seven years, stumbles forward. For a moment, Paul thinks it is Sipiwe. The child stops, and turns back to the men.

They stand looking at Paul.

Can I help you? Paul's voice is pretty even, though his legs feel loose and a long way down. He remembers the last time he was held up at gunpoint, almost two years ago, on the way to his wife in his new BMW. Up until now, savage Soweto has been safe. His home has never been invaded before. However, in South Africa, in Soweto, there is a first time for everything, he supposes.

The men point at the little boy.

Five hundred, one of them says, his voice thick and dark.

At first Paul does not understand.

The child looks confused. It wants to run back to the men, but they push it at Paul. The little boy runs back at them and one of the men grabs him.

Five hundred rand, the speaker repeats himself, and nods at the man holding the boy.

The large man squeezes the boy's face, forcing open his mouth.

Good teeth, the speaker says.

The large man forces out the boy's arms.

Strong, says the speaker.

The large man turns the boy around, pulls down his trousers and bends him over, exposing two little buttocks. The child growls and struggles.

Paul stares.

Clean, the man says. No AIDS. Five hundred.

Paul swallows the realisation with difficulty. They have come to sell him the child. For five hundred rand he could purchase the tiny boy and do anything he might like to him. These men have come to sell him a human being, a child. Paul's own child has been stolen and these men have brought him another, at a price. Just five hundred rand.

He finds his voice at last.

No, he says. No. This boy – his family?

Street child, the speaker says. We find him. We feed him. The man grins. We make him strong. Five hundred.

The large man pushes the boy so that he stumbles backwards towards Paul, and falls on his bottom. The boy does not bellow with anger. He simply gets up and pulls up his ragged shorts.

He faces the men. Both he and Paul face the three men.

Then something seems to snap. A torrent of tearful abuse streams from the child. Weeping, the young boy shouts through his tears at the men. The tall man steps forward, his arm raised. The child backs away screaming and stumbles into Paul's legs.

Tshaya wena, the tall man spits at the boy. I'll hit you.

The child snarls something back and the tall man lunges forward.

Okay, Paul shouts. He steps over the child to confront the tall man. They square up, the child safely behind Paul.

The leader grins.

He is naughty, that one, he says. Four hundred. Last chance.

Okay, Paul's voice says. Okay. But then you must get out of my house.

Paul moves to one side. Slowly.

The child stands up. It rubs its face furiously and stands glowering at the tall man.

Leave him alone, Paul says.

The tall man grins. Sharp, sharp, he says.

Paul moves slowly to his bedroom. The tin cashbox hides under the telephone directories. He finds R370, in notes and coins. He knows that the men will take it. Are lives worth so little?

The leader accepts the wad of money and handful of coins.

It's R370, Paul says.

The leader makes a show of thinking. He flicks through the notes again, his lips pouting.

He fires a comment at his friends. He does not realise that Paul understands essentially what he says.

This white man is lying.

The words are soft. The threat they carry is hard. Paul feels a surge in his chest. It is not fear. It is a sense of anticipation. At last. Is this the reason why he has left his door unlocked all this time?

The child starts bellowing with tears and Paul's blood runs cold. He knows that now he cannot die. He cannot embrace a bullet or a blunt blade, open his heart and chest to oblivion.

There is another child.

Okay, Paul says, take the cell phone.

He turns to the small table against the wall. There, never

moved since he relocated after Alfred's death, lies his phone. As Alfred would have left it. It was the latest model, Paul knows that. Now, of course, it is almost two years old.

The leader thinks for a while.

Then he speaks. Sharp, he says, and Paul hands him the phone.

They actually shut the door quietly behind themselves.

They have gone.

The child stops its angry monologue and looks at Paul.

Food, the boy says.

Paul is surprised that a street child knows any English.

He stares at the child. Wiry hair, dirty. Thin. Is he five or seven? Impossible to tell. His manner suggests fifteen.

What is your name? Paul says.

The child gestures to its mouth.

Paul repeats the question in isiZulu, then in the *tsotsitaal* of the township.

The child stares at him. Stompie, says the child.

Paul leans against the table. Of course. Stompie. Cigarette butt. Small. But there was a Stompie, a Stompie Seipei. Winnie Madikizela-Mandela. Her bodyguards – the horrifying murder of a young boy, Stompie Seipei. Now here stands a Stompie.

Food, says Stompie, pointing to his mouth, and his voice is angry.

Food, says Paul in *tsotsitaal*. Come with me.

And the boy follows him. Like man and dog. The boy Stompie follows him into the tiny kitchen and into his life.

It is not easy. It was never going to be easy.

Of course, the child cannot stay. There is no way that this Stompie can stay with him.

He gives the child food and watches him tear the bread with his teeth. He sees the prompt peanut butter and honey sandwiches – quick, nourishing protein and healthy sugar – disappear in a flurry of bites and smacking lips. Stompie holds a wedge in each hand and shoves the food into his mouth. Paul watches him across the quickly cleared dining room table. Paul makes more sandwiches, another four slices of thick wholemeal bread – peanut butter and honey, with golden discs of sliced banana added. Stompie eats with desperate, all-consuming concentration. Finally, he relinquishes his embrace of the large plate and leans back and looks up at Paul.

Stompie's gaze – so frank and fearless – turns to the dining room. He appraises the space and looks back to his host. You are a very rich man, he declares in *tsotsitaal*. *Ja*, you are like a king.

Stompie's eyes wander from the tiny couch to the wood-effect shelving, the piles of trade magazines, the lurid curtains given to Paul by Sophie five doors down. The huge rug, from Vincent next door, that covers most of the concrete floor. There is a radio and a small television and lots of books in ambitious heaps. So Stompie reckons that this is what it must be like to live as a king.

I am Paul, they call me Chicken Man, Paul tries to say, but his voice is stuck somewhere in his chest, somewhere in the distant past. In the end, he rouses his voice. Not a king, just Paul, just Chicken Man. He reaches out a hand, to shake Stompie by the hand.

Are you going to *fok* me? Stompie asks.

Paul shakes his head. Eventually he can speak.

I will never do that, he says. But I am going to bath you and wash your hair and tomorrow we shall get you new clothes. And we shall return you to your family.

Sharp, says Stompie. Only one time I have new clothes. I like new clothes without a collar.

Stompie says nothing about his family. It will take a while for him to talk about his having not a single stitch of family.

Stompie allows himself to be taken to the bathroom. Paul runs the bathwater. He makes it much deeper than usual.

The child stands peering over the edge of the bath.

I have never seen so much water, he says. Even in the *dongas* when it rains there is not so much water. This water is not brown. My water is always brown. Even from the tap in the street, it is brown.

Hop in, says Paul. I have a feeling that it will be brown before long, don't you worry.

He hands Stompie the soap and his own sponge, as large as a loaf in Stompie's hands.

Wait, says Paul, hair first. He takes back the soap and sponge and reaches for the peach and almond shampoo. Wait till you smell this, he tells Stompie. It smells good enough to eat.

Paul wets his hair and begins to rub dollop after dollop of shampoo into Stompie's filthy hair. Stompie does not try to eat the shampoo. Instead he spits and complains.

Paul feels the small scalp and the frothing loops of wiry hair. He is running his hands through the six o'clock bath times of many, many months ago, and as he feels Stompie's hair, he recalls Sipiwe's hands and the hands of all Sipiwe's friends running through his own strange hair.

Then Paul lets Stompie wash himself. Paul watches him and thinks that a comb will not be enough. A brush, a strong brush, and even a barber's set might be required for Stompie's tangle of hair.

Could he bring scissors close to Stompie's head? Will Stompie trust him to tackle his hair?

Does he ever trust Stompie?

It takes years.

There are no relatives.

That first night, at some time in the small hours, Paul remembers suddenly waking. His eyes flickered open and there, with his nose almost touching Paul's, was Stompie. Just staring at him. Eyes wide and white, face breathlessly hidden in the dark. And before Paul could speak, the child had disappeared back to his bed on the mattress in the living room. Paul followed him, but he was soundly snoring. Paul waited for a very long time while Stompie slept with his fists bunched under his little chin.

That happened for a long time. Every night, at some time in the darkest hours, Paul would gasp awake to Stompie's urgent stare, then Stompie would disappear to sleep without stirring. Was he checking whether Paul was still alive?

Paul got used to the nightly disturbance. It carried on for years. As Stompie grew taller, he crouched down over Paul. Paul would awake and then Stompie would grin and go back to sleep in his own bed. The child did not want to be held. He did not want to speak. He would claim not to remember any such thing in the morning. I like living like a king, he would say, and look at Paul as though he, Stompie, were a benevolent despot himself.

There were more than just the nightly disturbances, the wild eyes and little fists in the dark.

There was the running-away from school. The teachers' concerns that you can take a child from the street but can you take the street from the child? Paul fought them on that. Nothing is impossible, he would tell the principal as soon as he had found Stompie after another brief AWOL spell in the middle of the day. He always went back to the same places, did Stompie. Back to the road on which his granny had lived before she died. He had sat with her for a long time when she was dead, Stompie told him, when he was older and Paul could understand. Understand some of Stompie's yesterdays. He had lain with his granny in her small bed. After much coughing, she was very quiet. Too much quiet. And her eyes were looking at the ceiling, but she did not move. He kept waking up to see if she had moved, but she had not moved at all. He made her tea, black and sweet, but she did not wake up. He sang to her, her church songs, but she did not join in. And she became very hard as he lay with his head against her, his arm trying to keep her warm. She got cold, though, and the smell came. But he could not leave her. The neighbour found him. Starving and silent. And then he had left because they had taken his granny and she was the only person for him because too long ago when he was very small his mother had gone away to Vereeniging with his sister in a taxi and they had died in a crash. He remembered not wanting to sing at the funeral and that that was the only time he had worn a suit. The collar of his new shirt was not nice and his shoes hurt his toes. He did not like it when they put the large box with his mother inside in the ground, and the small box with his sister inside also in the ground. He was left on top of the ground, with no one but his granny. He did not like to run on top of the ground, because even though it was far away, the cemetery, his mother and his sister were under the ground and he did not want to hurt them. He threw away his shoes and he did not run, even when his friends played football in the street. He became Stompie, the boy who walked. Until he ran away. But that was not proper running. He simply left the house of his granny just after they took her out, also in a box, because he did not want to see her being put in the ground. Everyone he knew best was going underground and leaving him in the air. He was breathing the air whilst they were underground. Glue-sniffing helped. The other street children gave him little packets and the tubes of glue and showed him how to breathe quickly, very quickly like a dog that has been chased with stones, and then the buzzing came in your head and you felt like you were sinking under the ground and that was nice because you went to sleep and did not worry about not running on top of the ground. You also did not feel hungry or even cold. But when you woke up you did feel sick and you coughed and the burning in your throat was not nice. But then you stole some things and the bigger boys got you more glue from the shop.

Once, Paul found a large tube of glue under Stompie's bed. It was hidden in one corner. Stompie's bed was beside his own larger bed at that stage – an attempt to stop the *nagapie* routine, as they called it – jokily comparing Stompie and his large eyes to those of a nocturnal lemur-like creature of the bushveld. Paul gave Stompie a small amount of pocket money, mostly for domestic chores, and sometimes a modest payment for delivering flyers. He must have used the money to buy glue.

When did he sniff it? But searching further, Paul found the chicken that Stompie had made out of wooden ice-cream sticks, the secretly stored remnants of Magnum moments with King Paul over many months. He had made an ingenious chicken about one foot high and mid-crow. A week later, on Paul's birthday, it was presented to Paul and he unwrapped it. He never needed to check under Stompie's bed after that. The chicken went straight on to a shelf by the front door, where it silently greeted the dawn of their new life together. Maybe they could put the past behind them?

Stompie did not know how long he had lived as a street child.

One morning over cornflakes, he told Paul how the street children had heard about men who came to get you, so they could take you away. They heard about men putting things into you, that they liked sticking things into street children because the street children were naughty. They were bad, and these men came and you were *fokked* because you were a street child. Stompie had almost been *fokked* once. But he had kicked the man between the legs. The man had thought that Stompie was asleep with the glue, but he wasn't because he had heard that the men were coming that night. It was a Saturday night when the men came most times to under the bridge where they stayed. Stompie had no glue that night and he was just sleeping so he woke up quick and then he kicked the man bad. Stompie did not have to run away. He walked into the field and hid in the veld grass. But another time when he had had glue the three men came for the street children and they got him and they scrubbed him hard with a cloth and hot water and they took him to Paul's house. That is what he remembers.

That is when he can talk openly to Paul and he does not need the glue because he can sleep now in the same house as Paul and he knows that Paul is the Chicken Man and the Chicken Man does not hurt or *fok* street children. But Stompie does like to see his friends. He does not mind that Paul comes too and that they take food to the street children. Especially the ones with AIDS, for most of them are AIDS orphans. Stompie is very pleased if they give food to the ones who cough and cough and whom Paul takes to the hospital and to the orphanage even though there are bad things that happen at that orphanage. Some of the street children have run away after being at that orphanage. Stompie grows and his friends move off to other places. Some are dead, but the others go to other places that he does not know of.

Paul often finds Stompie arrested by a window or trapped behind the garden fence. While he is playing about the house and in the small garden it seems as though an echo of his past life is heard and he stands up to confront a certain shaft of light or the sound of three boys his age scuffling a football past the front gate. Paul leaves his work, maybe asks a client to wait a moment, and his warm hand comes to rest on Stompie's shoulder. Stompie's lips cease their worried murmuring and he looks up and says, Chicken Man, with a big smile.

Stompie would tell him that he hoped that his friends would find Chicken Men like he had found a Chicken Man and that Jonas and Thabang and Tshepo and Tsholofelo and Raymond would then not cough so much any more and have to sniff the glue all the time. And *ja*, he misses his friends, but he does not mind so much because he lives with Paul at the Chicken Man Agency and he does some work for Paul for pocket money and that is good. And Paul is a good man who does not try to *fok* him. He has a funny beard and his voice is nice.

They get M-Net and watch soccer matches together. Orlando Pirates. Everyone is crazy about Orlando Pirates or Kaizer Chiefs or Moroka Swallows. But they support Orlando Pirates and they even go to watch some of the games. Paul buys Stompie his own *vuvuzela* and he learns to make the wild sound as though it was a kudu horn and he was a tribal warrior. Paul tells him stories at bedtime about the Zulu warriors, their strength and cunning. About Shaka, one of the great Zulu generals, and about Napoleon, who was not a Zulu but who was a very good general, like a Shaka for France, a country that has summer when it is winter in South Africa.

And Napoleon could make himself go to sleep straight away, this is a true story. Even when there was fighting or the night before a big battle. That makes Stompie happy. He does not have to lie awake thinking about things. He does not have to wonder as he does every night what it must be like to sleep under the ground with the weight of the world on your body, with the feet and the tyres of the taxis and buses on top of your head and your chest and your toes. He does not have to think of the thumping sound that his granny made in the box as they lifted it to get it through the doorway and out of the house for ever. He can think of Napoleon telling himself to go to sleep and so he can simply go to sleep. It seems to work and he feels like Napoleon, the little general from France, which is far away on the other side of the world where they eat snails and chocolate rolls called pain au chocolat and the national symbol is a chicken.

He is also pleased that he now lives in a place where the

door can be locked. There is a door, a heavy door, and it locks. He watches Paul lock it every night, now, and the key is put in a special place. Not left in the lock where it might be wiggled free in the night on to a sheet of newspaper and drawn back under the door by the *tsotsis*, or the bad men who *fok* small boys or sell them.

And Paul watches Stompie carefully. Watching with terror when he catches a cold and starts coughing, lest he never stop coughing. For how many are dying with common colds, or colds that become tuberculosis? Paul attends the funerals of well-known clients at least once a month, sometimes more. And when the anti-retroviral drugs finally, finally become available, the situation does not improve. It is already far too advanced.

So Paul watches fearfully over this growing street child who has become his child. It takes forever to adopt him officially, legally. Paul has to hire a black lawyer and pay through the nose, so that Gideon Ncgobo, BA LLB, can grease the palms of the right officials, otherwise there is no way, Gideon explains, that a white man might legally appropriate a black child. It would smack of the country's colonial past; it would be redolent of imperialism and Afrikaner paternalism – you're a van Niekerk, let us not forget that, Gideon Ncgobo peers over the top of his designer spectacles – such behaviour so repugnant now in a progressive South Africa. Paul listens to the lectures and pays Gideon Ncgobo handsomely so that he might bribe the appropriate officials in this, the new and progressive South Africa. It works. The right papers are signed by the right people for the right price. It is terrifyingly simple. Stompie is his.

Stompie grows up. He learns to stay at school. He no longer minds the jokes about Stompie who lives with the Chicken Man who helps people to sell things. Jokes about Stompie who is small and black, and the Chicken Man who is big and white.

Paul checks with Stompie before they have to buy a house again. This time, the new house is even bigger, but they stay in the old house. The new house, not too far from the old house, becomes the new Chicken Man Agency because business is booming, as they say, which means that things are going well.

Stompie helps Paul to move all the office equipment out to the new house. They hire a *bakkie* and do the job over a long weekend. Stompie is becoming a man. Paul notices the rippling muscles along his forearms, almost more sinewy and stronger than Paul's arms. The broad shoulders, the deep voice. Where does the time go? Paul lets Stompie attach the poster of Chantal to the new sign – now the Chicken Men Agency. Stompie is delighted. They leave the old sign at their home, with the other poster attached. Forever an appendix to Paul's existence.

And there comes the night when Paul wakes up and there is no staring Stompie. He gets up hurriedly and finds his adopted son asleep. It happens – or does not happen – the next night, and the next. No longer does Stompie need to check up on Paul to see if he is still breathing, just like when he watched over his dead grandmother to see if she had started breathing again.

Paul now has to learn to sleep through the night. It takes longer than he might have dreamed possible. No wide eyes. No *nagapie*. Too often he is the one to get up now to check on Stompie.

Another election comes and goes. An ANC majority but no longer exceeding two thirds. Another World Cup soccer tournament – in Germany, though South Africa is to host the 2010 games. Another World Cup rugby tournament. The Springboks are world champions again in 2007 and the country is happy. Another year passes. More power cuts, over a thousand a year in the greater Johannesburg area, and they buy some battery-powered lights.

That helps when Stompie is studying for his mock matric examinations. Paul tries not to interfere with his adopted son's progress, but there is so much at stake. It is his future. Does he realise the significance of these examinations? If he works hard for his final examinations, they will close the Chicken Men Agency for the whole of December, and go on holiday. Where does Stompie want to go on holiday?

The answer is France, to the land of Napoleon and the Chicken Men and Women. And when the mock results come through and Stompie has done well, Paul buys tickets even though it will be the middle of winter there and they will be leaving the height of the South African summer. But at the moment, it is not even the end of May.

Then there is bad news. There is trouble in the townships all around them.

It is to do with jobs – lack of jobs. Unemployment is still worse than the official figure of forty per cent. The Chicken Men Agency struggles along, managing to do okay. But things are tough further down the economic pecking order. And then they really start attacking immigrants. The poor folk from Mozambique and Zimbabwe and the Congo and Nigeria and Somalia. They are the ones who bear the brunt of people's fears and frustrations. You do not want to talk with a *makwerekwere* accent on the trains or in the townships. Many of the squatters, looked down on for being the lowest of the low, are immigrants. People who have come to feed on the scraps when there are no scraps. And they must go away. They must go home, that is the refrain that Paul hears from his customers. Johannes, who has joined his new young art department, believes this strongly. They must take their hunger and their thieving hands back to Mozambique, back to Zimbabwe. Get back on the other side of the Limpopo River, preferably in a crocodile's belly. They hear stories about the flight south of yet more immigrants, desperate enough to brave electric fences on the border and leviathans in the muddy river to escape from Mugabe's thugs and to get to South Africa. They hear first-hand about new arrivals in the squatter camps. How the tension is building, how there is going to be trouble. Big trouble.

And so it comes. The cruellest month of May, early-autumn strife and savage violence. Paul hears about it from clients. He also sees it with his own eyes.

A woman, an immigrant, trying to get home after hanging around a nearby market. She tried to steal some tomatoes, it seems. She is caught red-handed and the crowd discovers that she is from Zimbabwe. She is pushed and shoved. Paul calls out, but there are too many. She falls. Someone kicks her. Kicks her hard in the head, and she is down and cannot get up. Paul and Stompie push people aside and shout but there are too many all of a sudden and they are angry. They are kicking against their hunger and their fear. Every kick is trying to kick away the hunger and the fear from them and their children.

The woman is silent, an inert bag of ruptured skin and limp flesh. The sound of feet thumping into her unprotected body and the shouting of the mob leaves Paul and Stompie feeling sick. They call the police, but the police never come. The woman's body lies there. Then someone drops a rock on her head. Paul has to drag Stompie and his anger back home; they don't want trouble.

But it is happening more and more. People beaten up. People attacked on trains, thrown from trains. People electrocuted as they climb screaming on to the roofs of moving carriages. And then it ignites. After a few fires and flares, the powder keg explodes. Paul thinks there will be civil war. The army returns to the townships. Large machines patrol the streets and there are rubber bullets and tear gas. Military might but no Mbeki. They hear about massacres and butchering.

Paul is relieved, profoundly relieved that he is well-known in the community. The Chicken Men Agency has entered into folklore, it seems. He, one of the Chicken Men, is hailed wherever he goes. And so is Stompie. *Heyta*, they call, *heyta! Howzit Bra*, Chicken Man? He is no immigrant; he is one of them. A man from Mozambique comes knocking at his door one evening. He batters at their door. Paul thinks it is Stompie, who is out with his friends, but it is a desperate stranger.

Paul, after a lengthy discussion in the kitchen, leaves a note for Stompie and drives the stranger to Joburg Station. He gives him R200 to help him on his way. The man cannot go home; he must go to one of the smaller townships, away from the heat and the hatred of Soweto and Alexandra. Paul sends him off, feeling sick. He will die. Paul knows that he is sending the man to his death.

Paul arrives home. It is late. He parks the car outside the fence, and the Chicken Men sign with its downward-pointing three-toed chicken foot forming the M of Men, and there too is the ghostly appendage of Chantal's poster.

The light is on in the house. Stompie is back.

Paul opens the door and steps inside.

Stompie is standing beside the small couch. Beside him, with her back to the door, sits a small black woman. Paul steps into the room. More trouble? More help? How much longer can this go on?

Stompie seems to brace himself. The small woman with a *doek*, simple and black, very old-fashioned, whips her head around and stands up too. But in a stern voice Stompie tells her to sit down. Paul moves around to say a cautious hello. The old woman lowers herself on to the couch and drops her head.

Stompie nods at Paul and gestures to the woman's feet. Paul looks. There, seated on the floor, dressed in old clothes, is a grey child. It is a girl. Her hair is long and stringy. She is grimy, dressed in a tracksuit and *takkies*, but he can see that her hair is blonde and that her jaw has a particular line, and she looks up at her father and Paul sees that it is Chantal.

In his house, in his refuge. In this very place, here she is. Chantal.

She looks down at the floor. Her hair falls forward over her face and her little head is bowed.

Chantal, his voice tries to say her name, but cannot.

Stompie looks at him and at the strange woman. Then Stompie speaks again with a grown-up voice that is belied by his spreading grin.

This *gogo*, this granny, she has something to tell you, Stompie says.

This *gogo*, she has brought you this girl, Stompie says. You will know this girl. Her name, the girl's name is Soneni.

Chantal, Paul speaks at last. Chantal. Chantal.

Chantal does not look up. She sends out a hand to hold the black woman's leg. She seems to be biting the thumb of her other hand.

Is it Chantal?

Paul does not move.

Stompie speaks sharply to the old woman, who seems terrified. Like Chantal, she does not look up. Her hands are pulling at her old black dress.

The woman speaks. At least her mouth moves, but Paul cannot make out a word she is saying. He shakes his head like an ox, stunned.

Stompie? Paul says.

It will be a few hours before the full story emerges. Before Paul learns just how busy Stompie and his little gang have been that day. Before Stompie tells him about the rumours that have been growing amongst the street children that there is a witch in the neighbourhood. That there have been sightings of a grey ghost child in a house where there is no child. Where there has never been a child. That there is a nasty woman who lives by herself, who is *makwerekwere*, and who has made a child out of a broomstick and some long veldgrass. That the witch brought a broomstick to life with long hair and made it shout. No one has gone near the house because there is bad *muti*, very bad *muti* by that house. But Stompie has gone right up to the house when the witch was out. He and some of the boys watched the house and when the witch left it late that afternoon, then Stompie crept up to the house. He did not die. He did not feel sick or start coughing or feel burning up his *poephol*. He knocked on the door to let the ghost know that he was there, to keep things nice and friendly, but there was no reply. Stompie had to knock again and some of his friends ran away. There was too much fear, too much *muti* in that place. They could feel it. They knew the ghost child was in there but it did not come to the door or make a sound.

So Stompie looked in the one side window and there, hiding in a big cardboard box like a dog under the table, was a face. It was a wild grey face, just like a ghost except that Stompie could see it was crying. It was not full of fright, but full of fear. He could tell. He, Stompie, who lived amongst fear and fright for much of his life. He has not forgotten what it was like under that bridge and the men who came in the night to *fok* the street children no matter how much they cried and shouted to them to stop.

So Stompie waved through the window to the ghost child and knocked on the window, but the ghost child was too much afraid. She just hid under the table, which was silly because he could see her in her box and he could see her big eyes.

Then this woman, this Mrs Mda, came running out of the house next door to shout at Stompie. To shout, hey, what are you doing by my neighbour's window. *Voetsek! Hamba wena!* Go away! But Stompie already was beginning to hope as he had secretly hoped when he first heard his friends talking in whispers about the grey child ghost in that neighbourhood. Stompie was not going to be chased away by some old *gogo* dressed in black because someone had died. He shouted back at this woman, shouted who is this child, this girl who is grey, who is hiding in this house where there should be no grey child?

The *gogo* told him she would call her big son to beat him, but Stompie shouted that he would call the white man who once had a white baby and that he would also call the *polisie*. That made the *gogo* stop shouting.

She came over to Stompie and the rest of Stompie's friends, those friends who had not yet run away, and who had also come out of hiding. The *gogo* asked about this white man and Stompie told her about the Chicken Men Agency and that he was one of those Chicken Men. He was in business with Paul van Niekerk and this Paul van Niekerk had a baby called Chantal stolen from him too many years ago, when this Chantal was just a baby. Had the *gogo* seen the poster by the Chicken Men Agency sign as well as by their house – on the other side of the neighbourhood?

No, the *gogo*, Mrs Mda, had not seen the signs. What was on those signs?

A baby, Stompie told her. A small white baby with a smile and a soft white arm behind her and a telephone number that they had cut off the poster.

The *gogo* had agreed that this was too much bad, *eish*, that it was very bad. And how long ago was this? Mrs Mda asked, and Stompie had told her all about Paul the nice white man and what had happened to this nice white man.

Eish, eish, Mrs Mda had said, making her fingers pull at her hands and shaking her head. And then she had said that they must go away because the bad woman was coming back. That there would be trouble for them, and for her, Mrs Mda, as well as for the child who was Soneni and not a ghost or a Chantal. That the bad woman did not stop people talking about the ghost child because it meant that people would leave her alone and they would be afraid to come to her door. Then they would not hear Soneni crying or shouting. And Mrs Mda was too much frightened of the bad woman. And Mrs Mda's old husband had died last year and the bad woman said that if Mrs Mda did not want to lose her children and her grand-children also, then she must keep her silence. Mrs Mda was keeping her silence. She did not want her family to die.

But Stompie would not keep his silence. He had this feeling, and his friends had this feeling about the child. A child should not live in a box under a table, and a child should not be grey. They should be black or they should be white, not grey. It was not good. And Stompie and his friends knew what it was like to live under a bridge, and now here was this child living under a table. Did this bad woman have a man or other men who *fokked* children?

Eish, it was very bad.

They decided that they were going to do what Paul did for Stompie. They were going to take this grey child to Paul, the Chicken Man, and Mrs Mda was coming with them to tell the Chicken Man what had happened.

Mrs Mda tried to run into her house, but she was very slow. Stompie's friends caught her easily whilst Stompie smashed the window with a brick and cleared the glass so that he could climb in and save this grey child. That's what he did. The child kicked and screamed like she was sniffing glue and having a bad dream but Stompie and his friends picked her up. She had a bad smell in her clothing but they carried her all the way to Paul's house in the dark like a grey present. It took half an hour. The grey girl fought them, but then was very still like a big baby. They hoped it was Paul's baby. And Paul was not there, but Mrs Mda stayed and that made the grey child stay quiet. As long as she is sitting there with Mrs Mda, the *gogo* she knows, then all is quiet and here she is in Paul's house.

Paul shakes his head, stunned. He stands, even though the room is skew, and Stompie repeats what the old woman is saying.

A long time ago, this girl was a baby, she could not walk yet. She was taken from a car. This woman, the one they call the *makwerekwere* witch, was the sister of the hijacker. She, the old woman, lived next door, in the Orlando West Extension. Her name, her own name, is Dorcas Mda. She doesn't want trouble.

Paul sits down suddenly. He cannot stand it. He cannot take his eyes from Chantal.

He wants to reach out, with his life in the palm of his hand. He wants to show her how his world has been reshaped, changed forever by a gun at the window and the squeal of tyres all those years ago. It is ancient history in many ways, though it could be yesterday. In many ways it is but a heartbeat away. He feels his chest heaving; he is breathing hard. Still Chantal does not look up again at her father.

He needs to hear her, to hold her. He gets up and moves forward. The ancient woman bends down and puts her hands under Chantal's arms. She half lifts Chantal towards him. Chantal now stands, still looking at his feet.

He reaches out a hand.

After all this time, he touches her.

tle face, just under her chin, and tilts

that he can look into her eyes.

erious, maybe like his?

s eyes.

ing. He cannot stop the shudders that rack his body and the tears that course into his beard. He is weeping, but he cannot yet enfold her in his arms. She glances across at the woman, uncertain.

Then Chantal speaks.

I want to go home, she says to the woman. Her voice. Paul is amazed at her voice. It comes softly and fluently. Chantal speaks *tsotsitaal*, the pidgin isiZulu and bastardised Afrikaans of the township. Paul glances at Stompie. He breaks the spell.

She wants to go home, Stompie confirms.

Chantal, her name, his voice, wrenches from his heart. My daughter, my child, you *are* home.

He tries to keep his voice soft and gentle. He tries not to speak too loudly. He tries not to grab her and hold her, this quiet grey child who looks respectfully at his feet. He stands before her. How can she know what her absence has caused him to become? How can she realise that the void that was created was filled with such pain? Now that she stands before him, a complete stranger with Claire's jawline and hair, he hears again, ever louder, the sound of the gunshot and shearing metal. He hears the hiss of steam and Go Naidoo's screams. Claire's voice and sharp silence, too, resound within him. How can he tell her, this child that seems to speak only *tsotsitaal*?

He can speak passable isiZulu, but how can he articulate all that? He cannot.

He speaks simply in isiZulu.

Soneni, he fits his tongue around her new name, though the name Chantal will chant in the *taal*, in the language of his heart. Soneni.

She looks up.

Soneni.

Yebo. Her reply is barely audible.

Soneni, I am your father. You are my daughter. You were taken from me a long time ago. A bad man took you, from me and your mother. Your mother, her name is Claire. She was sad, she was very sad that you were gone.

Chantal glances at the woman. The woman nods, to affirm Paul's words.

And Paul can speak no more. He cannot say how Claire has gone to live in Cape Town. That Claire, Chantal's mother, has remarried, and by the last reckoning, the last Facebook exchange, has had a third son. That Claire, too, left him. Shacked up with an orthodontist, a van Biljon. Fumble John, in Paul's mind. With small neat hands and a nasty propensity to sire sons. To beget a string of boys out of Claire, Paul's wife. That at present she is Claire Fumble John, with a posse of white-haired boys: Bertus (Albertus), Koos (Jakobus) and now Drikkie (Hendrik), all Afrikaner consonants and vowels, names several sizes too large for the little lads. Paul has seen the pictures. The frolicking on Blouberg Strand with Table Mountain in the background. The bronzed skin; the gleaming Aryan hair. They frighten him, this loud, healthy tribe. And he tries to forget the pictures of Fumble John and Claire, arm in arm, laughing into the camera whilst the Cape Doctor, the wind that arrives fresh on the African continent, tousles their hair. Their words, their laughter, are scattered out of the picture frame by the wind. Echoes are blown up the escarpment and reach him, a thousand miles away, distorted and indistinct and mad.

The woman is speaking. Stompie helps out, even though Paul knows his township isiZulu.

Soneni's – Chantal's – mother, the hijacker's sister, is dying of AIDS. And now there is violence and they are looking for immigrants. The woman they call the witch is terrified that they will come for Soneni, that she is belonging to Zimbabweans. Even though they speak a kind of *tsotsitaal* at home, they will know that they are from Zimbabwe. And the fact that Soneni has been kept hidden all these years, the fact that she is hiding indoors for so long, if they come searching they will be thinking that she is a witch with this white child, this grey child, spirited away, secreted away all these years. But she does not care, this bad woman. If she is a witch it is maybe better than just a *makwerekwere*.

The plump old woman shakes her head. It is very sad, she says.

Paul and Stompie listen. They look from the old woman to Chantal and back again.

Paul can hardly breathe. So close. So near, yet so far. To think that Chantal was barely three kilometres away, that she might have eaten his chicken feet or heard his Chicken Men Agency adverts on the radio. To think of her trapped, spending her days incarcerated.

The woman, this Mrs Mda, keeps talking. When the young woman's brother did not return, when they heard that he had been killed in a car crash, there was big trouble. Then the police came. They found no other children, and not even this one. They did almost find Soneni and her new mother. They were a few houses away, silent. Soneni did not cry out, even when the policemen with no uniforms, the special police, came down the road looking and knocking for gang members. She stayed bundled up on her new mother's back in a thick blanket, completely covered by a hat and shawl. And she never made a sound and they left. They never looked that far down the road.

Paul sits on the couch. Chantal, he cannot yet bring himself to think of her as Soneni, sits beside him, but not too close just yet. The bitterness, the anger burns again inside Paul. All for the sake of a BMW. A white BMW that was ordered from a hijacking syndicate. And a child. A thousand-rand bonus for a child, not too young, that might come with the car. What a bargain. And that young child, a baby, bought to be used once. For the horrific belief is that sex with a virgin will purge one of AIDS. And a young child, a mere baby, naturally is a virgin and so more than qualifies. The mad reasons run through his head. The reasons why this happened.

And so he, Paul van Niekerk, killed the brother of that woman. The bitter woman who became Chantal's surrogate mother. And the rest of the gang died so that Chantal might live. Thank the stars. Paul feels light-headed. And now he owes her return to the threat of more violence. The *toy-toying* mobs. The chanting in the streets of Alex and Soweto. The necklacings again. Not since apartheid have the townships been so volatile.

Paul presses his hand to his eyes, and rubs them. President Mbeki is on his umpteenth overseas trip and here, right under his fastidious nose, South Africa is rank with fear. Supposedly it is just a criminal element. That is the political angle. But it is the very heart and soul of a beloved country racked by unemployment and poverty and prejudice. Where is the government? Why does it not govern? Paul feels his heart aching. Yet out of this general pain comes such specific joy.

And he owes the return of Chantal to a teenage black boy. To his adopted son. To Stompie.

Paul looks at Stompie, perched on the edge of his seat. He catches Paul's eye.

A police siren sounds in the distance and drones past.

Mrs Mda starts, but then keeps sitting. She shakes her head. It is very sad, she says again. She touches Chantal on the shoulder, then looks at Paul.

Sheila, the one who is looking after this child, the *makwerekwere* who is my friend, I told her too many times, you can't keep this child. But she did. It was a big secret. Sheila, she was very cross, that one. She says that this child helped to kill her brother, that this child is bringing bad luck to her brother. She calls her Soneni – meaning what wrong thing has been done. So she keeps this girl locked up in the house. She does not play in the garden; she stays inside. For too many years. The police don't come back. They came that one time and killed many people. Then they did not come back any more.

Mrs Mda looks down at Chantal, and shakes her head.

I bring her some toys from my grandchildren, some old toys, and clothes. She has no toys. She plays with spoons and things from the kitchen, in the old clothes that are too much big for her. *Eish*, the old woman sighs. *Eish*.

Every year I bring her clothes from my grandchildren.

Sheila says that she is naughty this one, the old woman nods at Chantal. Sheila tells her to clean the house when she is getting older and bigger. But Soneni shouts at her. Sometimes I am hearing it from next door. Shouting, very loud, then crying. Sheila is not a kind woman. She is seeing Soneni, and she is seeing her brother dead. All the time. But she does not want to forget. All the time.

Sheila is using the money her brother was keeping hidden in the house. This Sheila, she is helping me too. When two of my children are getting the TB, and they are very sick, Sheila is helping me. When those children die and I am looking after my grandchildren, three boys, I am asking Sheila to give me this child too. But she is always saying no. And she is saying that if I tell anyone, there is big trouble for me and my grandchildren.

Mrs Mda reaches into her dress to find a handkerchief. She blows her nose.

She looks sorrowfully at Paul. It has been a long speech.

She must go. She says she must go.

She is sorry. She is glad that Soneni is back with her father. And all the time he was nearby. *Eish*.

She is sorry that her friend, her neighbour, is dying, and she is losing this child. But she does not think her friend cares any more. She is too much sick. Now Soneni is back with her father. And her mother will be very much happy.

Her mother will be very much happy.

Chantal stands up when the woman leaves. Old Mrs Mda hugs her, holds her tightly and whispers to her. Chantal does not try to run after her. She stands very formally in her baggy tracksuit, in her ancient *takkies*, and watches the woman leave.

Paul closes the door and turns to look again on his life, on the rest of his life.

Chantal runs to the door. She raises her fists, as though to beat the door. But then she just stands there, fists poised, immobile. Paul and Stompie stare at her.

Chantal looks at the door for a long time.

After an even longer time, Chantal baths, and he leaves a large T-shirt for her to wear as pyjamas. She sleeps in his bed. Stompie shakes Paul by the hand and grins before going to bed himself.

Paul can find no words to say to Stompie.

Stompie says that he is happy. He says that now he has a sister, and she has blonde hair and he can teach her some football moves.

There is a power cut, another bloody power cut, and Paul does not have Claire's number. He cannot remember when last he tried to phone her, and she has never tried to phone him. It is only via Facebook and through friends that he keeps some track of his ex-wife. That he keeps count of the ridiculous number of sons and their strange names. With the power off, there is no Facebook. He does not start up the generator for fear of disturbing Chantal.

What will Claire make of Chantal's return? Where will their past lives graft back on to the future? Do they have a future?

Paul lies on the couch in the dark. He cannot banish the vision of Chantal standing before him in his shirt, with her small knees and soft fair hair. He cannot forget the tingle of her scalp under his fingertips as he washed her filthy hair. He can still feel her hard little head against his fingers. The hard fact of her skull. And her lively wriggling and shouting (so alive!) as he tried to brush out her knotted hair with his little comb, then with Stompie's brush. It took a wonderful hour. He lies in the dark with the ache of not yet being able to take her in his arms and press her to his chest. In his mind's eye, she comes out of the bathroom and stands formally in front of him. Watchful. Polite. He tucks her gingerly into bed and stands for a long time on the other side of the door. Chantal tosses and turns. She mutters to herself in *tsotsitaal*. She opens the door and asks for *amanzi*, water. Paul fetches her a glass and again tucks her little body back into bed. He can't fail to notice her tiny budding breasts, already pressing against his T-shirt, and he stands for an hour on the other side of the door, silently mourning her vanished childhood.

It is eleven years, four months since he has seen her. So much time has trickled through his fingers. So many todays have become yesterdays. So much of her life has been lost to him and to Claire. She is a complete stranger.

Again, as has become habit, he locks the doors of the house. Then he takes the cushions off the couch and lies down against the door to the bedroom. He does not sleep at all.

He thought that you relive your life with such clarity only the moment before you die.

Now there is so much to live for.

He phones a series of friends in the morning. It is early and both children have not stirred. Wondrously, Chantal is still in his bed. She sleeps peacefully.

He gets Claire's cell number from Lucky.

It rings.

Claire answers quickly.

Don't hang up, Paul says. It is I.

He kicks himself, but he cannot avoid the English teacher's habit. It is I. The verb 'to be' always takes the nominative.

God, Claire says. Why so bloody early? You gave me a fright. I thought . . .

Chantal, Paul says. Chantal came back. Late last night. Chantal.

There is a long silence on the other end.

Chantal, Paul says.

Still Claire does not speak.

Paul lets the silence drag on. He couldn't keep the excitement and the hope from his voice. He had meant to sound much more matter-of-fact. Chantal is back. There. Stop all those damn clocks. Wind them back. It is no longer May 2008. It is 28 January 1997. We live in Midrand, we are married and we are together and we have a daughter named Chantal who is a little pork chop full of wrinkles and joy. Her bath is run and her nappy is waiting for her. Her bedroom is soft and pink, like a womb, and waiting for her to snuggle down and sleep. Claire can sing to her, her favourite lullaby, you are my sunshine, my only sunshine, and the world can carry on as before. Whatever mayhem might happen beyond the gates of their secure complex, it matters not, for they are together and they have Chantal, their bundle of joy.

Oh shit, says Claire before she bursts into tears. Sobbing and sobbing. She can speak no more and Paul has to hang up in the midst of her tears. He would have stayed on the line, but her sobbing makes him unable to speak and he has to hang up.

Later, days later, they arrange to meet.

Chantal, Soneni, is paraded before her aunt Rachel and her

granny and grandpa. Rachel weeps too. She and her friends have never stopped praying for her lost niece, and for poor Paul and even for Claire.

Paul's parents are stunned. They try to hug their grand-daughter, who turns away and speaks to her father in a black language. Paul knows that their tears are tears of relief and love – and consternation too. A son who has gone native. Lives with the blacks. Has a black son and now their only granddaughter in South Africa might as well be a Zulu or a Xhosa. What is she saying so loudly? Is it Zulu?

They drive to Monument Park, to Claire's mother too. She is grateful to Paul, but she is a spectacularly bitter woman. They have hijacked the country, she says. Gautrains and world cups, but no basic services. Twice they haven't collected her rubbish. And have you heard about this joke called Jacob Zuma? He could be our next president. Can you beat that? And are you also going to bugger off to the Cape? she asks Paul. Paul is glad that that duty passes without Chantal having one of her shouting fits. Chantal just looked bored, then worried. Stompie's help and quiet words are invaluable.

Paul has lost touch with many of his friends and they quickly run out of people to see and to show. Surely the more people they show, the more real Chantal's return will seem? He phones his brother in Australia.

Paul does not have the number for Claire's father.

Sunny and Lucky have also moved to the Cape, about an hour away from Claire, and he phones them. He will bring Chantal to see them in Paarl once they have taken her to see her mother.

He is shocked by the news from Sunny that Claire and the Fumble John clan are thinking about emigrating.

Sunny is surprised that Claire has not said a word to Paul about it. Paul admits that he has done most of the talking and that Claire has not really had the chance to say much. But then he realises that he has spoken so much because Claire has said so little.

Their plans are made. Before they find a school for Chantal, they are going to drive down to Cape Town. It is too expensive to fly, and Claire cannot leave her boys. On that point she is very clear. Not with Drikkie cutting his teeth. They must be the ones to come to her.

Fine, Paul says. No problem. They wanted to get away after Stompie's prelim exams and things are really hotting up in the townships. So it is fine. They agree the day and the time.

Tinus is very sensitive about you, and the whole Chantal thing has set him back a bit, Claire says.

Paul bites his tongue.

Claire suggests that she meet them on neutral territory. Because they live out in Simon's Town, they could meet either at the Boulders penguin sanctuary or at Cape Point. Both places are close by; both are excellent tourist attractions.

Paul bites his tongue again. Then he says again that he does not mind.

He is swallowing barbs – for old times' sake.

Cape Point then. It's beautiful, says Claire.

And Paul dares to hope.

From Joburg, they are to drive to the tip of Africa, to the Cape Point nature reserve, and there Chantal will be reunited with her mother. They shall be a small family once again with

Stompie and three wild boys with dangerous hair. Paul wonders what Martinus, Claire's husband, will do. Will he stand in the background and wring his neat little orthodontist's hands? Will he offer to correct Stompie's top teeth, which protrude because of a rather enthusiastic underbite?

Chantal is remarkably accepting. They are going to Cape Town, to the Mother City, with Table Mountain, Green Market Square, the old fort and the Victoria and Albert waterfront and Clifton and Camps Bay and the Just Nuisance memorial in Simon's Town. They are going to buy her new clothes to meet her mother. They are going to drive a thousand miles to the other end of the country. She nods. She seems so calm.

But then there are tears and the shouting. She kicks the door, even though it is not locked. Paul does his best to comfort her but has to call on Mrs Mda to come back again. Chantal weeps at the sight of her and runs and clings to her. The old woman is kind. She will come back in the morning.

Chantal cries at night. She misses Sheila and Mrs Mda and she prefers to be called Soneni, not Chantal.

Suddenly, she is terrified about leaving the house.

She holds on to Mrs Mda, and will not let her go. She wants Sheila, her mother, but Sheila is dead. She cannot go to Cape Town.

Paul speaks urgently to Mrs Mda. He will pay her for her time and the trip. Will she come to Cape Town with them? To help Chantal – Soneni?

Mrs Mda agrees. It gets her out of Soweto for a while, until things have calmed down. Does Paul know that they are necklacing people again? Three people have died that week with burning tyres around their necks, screaming into the circle of flames? *Hau*, it is like P. W. Botha and apartheid all over again.

Generally, Chantal prefers to stay inside, although she does like Paul's car. She likes to fiddle with the radio buttons and her favourite station, her old companion, the sounds with which she grew up on Metro FM.

Stompie helps to look after Chantal when they take her shopping for new clothes at the Maponya Mall. Chantal is fearful: so many, too many people in the world. She clings to Paul's hand. He could not be happier.

Stompie watches her play in the car whilst Paul packs.

At supper, Stompie glances at Paul as Chantal eats her *pap* and *wors* in the African way. She scoops up the thick maize porridge with her fingers and smacks her lips. She has cooked this meal for them; she is used to many kitchen chores and she is calmest when cooking. Stompie's food stays perched on his fork as he stares at Chantal. *Jislaaik*, Stompie says, that's different. Paul does not pursue the irony.

Paul remembers teaching Stompie how to use a knife and fork. That was a struggle. Now he wonders what all the fuss was about. Paul puts aside his knife and fork and dips his fingers into his *pap*. Chantal has cooked it after all.

Paul and Stompie and Chantal and Mrs Mda drive to Cape Town with Metro FM DJs talking at them loudly in the car. And there is music, African music. Chantal listens carefully, whilst peering out of the window. Her eyes drink in every passing hill, valley, farm and town. A smile sometimes plays about her lips. Often, she has no expression on her small face.

Paul has to concentrate on keeping his eyes on the road, on

not staring at his beautiful daughter in her brand-new clothes.

Stompie and Chantal sit in the back. The busy road twists and turns. And still Paul's eyes keep straying to the rear-view mirror to look at Chantal peering out the window as Bloemfontein and the Orange Free State, now just the Free State, pass by.

Just under two hundred kilometres later, they stop over at chalets at the Hendrik Verwoerd Dam. Now it is called the Gariep Dam, the name of the architect of apartheid long since wiped clear from the landscape. Paul smiles as he drives through the site. He wonders what H. F. Verwoerd would have made of the cargo of his little car.

They picnic under the bare willow trees and watch the water ripple on the huge dam. No one says very much and Chantal barely eats at all.

In the cold and dark of the early hours, they set off again.

They make good going. They are glad of the air-conditioning as they cross the Karoo. The interminably straight road cuts through the dry and desolate scrubland. Small dusty bushes and dry sand. That is all. Occasionally the road bends around a rocky outcrop. Paul drives steadily whilst his passengers doze. The car hums along, sliding towards a mirage that forever retreats. A hazy, shimmering world of silver fantasy, but when they get there it is as dry and as dull as the landscape through which they have just passed. Paul points this out, but the others barely open their eyes. Chantal is curled up in a ball, as far as her seat belt will allow, and she looks sleepily at her father.

Paul has to grip the steering wheel tightly and he tries not to sing.

Finally, towards the end of the second day, they get to the fairest Cape. Desert yields to dry land, and then to green. The winelands finally hove to: Worcester, Paarl, Stellenbosch. Stompie asks why people make nice grape juice into wine. How does that work? And they discuss the vagaries of the human palate as they drive through rich brown land, furrowed as well as vined with the hunched figures of the plants, which are resting in endless rows, leafless and whiskered with ancient bark.

It is a bright clear day. The sunset is lovely and quick. They find their small hotel on the outskirts of Cape Town with no problem. Stompie is great with the map, even though he tells Paul that it is high time they got a satnav if they are going to do much travelling.

One trip at a time, Paul responds, and helps Chantal with her new pink suitcase.

He barely sleeps that night. He patrols the corridor outside Chantal and Mrs Mda's room. Stompie tells him that he is mad, but Paul ignores him. Paul remains in the corridor. He wakes up in the morning, his neck stiff from leaning against the door frame even though he had moved his pillow and duvet to set up a makeshift bed. Two couples, on the same floor, had to step over him when they left very early.

The day is sunny, no winter rain. The Cape can be foul at this time of year, but the weather seems to be playing along. Chantal can wear her new dress and jersey. Both are deliciously tender pink. Paul asks if he can brush her hair and Chantal nods.

Paul has dressed carefully too. Smart chinos and a matching jersey. He brushes and brushes Chantal's hair. Then he leaves the spun gold loose, to frame her beautiful face with the firm jaw.

Claire, when they meet, will be looking at herself. She will see, held up before her, a younger version of herself. It is amazing. Paul cannot stop looking at Chantal. He has to swallow hard at his toast to get it past the lump in his throat. He does not notice the bitterness of the marmalade that the others complain about or the saltiness of the bacon.

He is already halfway up the climb to the Cape Point lookout. There, Claire will be waiting. There he will finally return to her mother the daughter he lost. Their child. The beautiful blend of his love and hers. Their Chantal.

They pack their bags. The boot of the car is full.

Stompie carries his new camera carefully. It has its own special bag and he makes sure that the battery is fully charged before they set off. They are meeting at eleven a.m.

Stompie calls out highway junctions and confirms road names. They are making good time, on the right track.

The coastal road runs past the quaint little towns of St James, Kalk Bay and round towards Fish Hoek. Stompie snaps away with his camera at the big blue bay. He exclaims at the size of the waves that surge into False Bay. They drive through Simon's Town and pass Boulders. To their right the mountainside is steep, to their left the bay swoops in an arc of aching blue, spiked with silver sunlight. Further out is the deep ocean and Seal Island. Paul points out that right there before them is the world's largest concentration of Great White Sharks. He remembers family holidays along this stretch of coast, back in the ancient past, when he and John and Rachel would swim and clutch each other on the legs as though they were sharks, and he was always chilled to the core to read about attacks right here, off the very beaches where they had swum as children. Always this beauty and horror.

They slow down to let a small troop of baboons cross the road. Chantal is amazed. So are Stompie and Mrs Mda. The children have never seen these humanoid creatures; Mrs Mda does not remember them being so big. Stompie goes wild with his camera, even when the large male with the swaggering bum has led them off into the scrub. Again Paul thinks back to the picnic they had here, years ago. He must have been Stompie's age. The huge male baboon, after their bread rolls, barking savagely. The car pulls away, and before long they have turned off left and are driving through the nature reserve that anticipates Cape Point.

There are not many cars in the car park. They are early; it is well before eleven. Paul glances around. Which car would be Claire's? She has not had far to travel. Is she early too, or will she be uncharacteristically late? He wonders again why they could not simply have met at her home. Maybe he is relieved that they have not met in a beautiful house overlooking the bay where the Great Whites swim free in such world-beating concentrations. Yes, better out here in the open. Here where the wind is always wild and strong is certainly a better place. Not cramped and surrounded by the awkward accoutrements of Claire's other life, her new existence. He still thinks of it as her new existence even though she has been married to Martinus Fumble John for two years longer than she was to him, Paul van Niekerk. Paul would not have been able to offer up Chantal in front of a grinning array of little Fumble Johns, whether in the flesh or in photographs. The Facebook images still unnerve him.

He locks the car and walks with Mrs Mda. He has to take her arm, soft with thin, old skin that he can feel through her ancient coat. Ahead of them Chantal walks with her head bent and Stompie fiddles with his camera. Paul has already asked him to capture the moment. The split second when Claire is reunited with Chantal. He would like his own photographs of that particular moment. His life has been lived with the impossibility of it for so long now. Now it is real. He does not know whether he will weep, or simply stop breathing. He feels light-headed and has to slow his breathing, consciously tell himself to breathe slowly, breathe slowly.

They fold their arms in front of themselves as the wind becomes more fierce. The climb up to the lookout is steep, very steep. As they ascend, they rise into the teeth of the wind that always seems to blow here. Chantal slows down and walks closer to her father and Mrs Mda. Stompie shouts into the wind. Orlando Pirates! he bellows and his voice is whipped away. They laugh into the buffeting air, and Chantal slips a chilly hand into Paul's warm grasp. For a moment he stops walking, but then remembers to put one foot in front of the other, one step at a time. The wind beats at his face and his eyes would have been moist anyway. He does not let go her hand as he blows his nose.

There before them, way below them, is the point where the Indian and the Atlantic Oceans meet. Out in the blue, the vast blue before them, is a panorama of heaving water. Their vantage point is spectacular. They must be over two hundred metres up. Below them and to each side are wild cliffs. A spray of cormorants and gulls, a bursting array of screaming, shrieking birds wheels and rises in the wind. Their cries come calling up from the cliff sides below. The scent of their guano gives an acidic, bracing edge to the wind.

Stompie and Chantal and Mrs Mda stand stunned. Even Stompie's camera is forgotten. Paul gives them a few minutes and then nudges Stompie. Don't forget, he says to the grinning boy.

Chantal leans out, as far as she can. Paul's heart races, but the rocky retaining walls are strong. Besides, the wind pushes back at them, blows them back from the edge. Mrs Mda exclaims to Chantal as another surge of gulls shrieks up before them, their wings bent back to release the wind. Why are they not torn from the skies? How do they manage to land safely in their cliff-side nests so far below? Paul closes his eyes, listening to Chantal's voice exclaiming in *tsotsitaal*. He feels the sun warm on his cheeks, despite the big wind. His breathing calms and he feels that he could soar with the birds.

It is ten to eleven. Still a while to go.

They stroll around a corner to get a better view of the nests on the sides of the cliff. The waves crash way down below. The wind is salty to the taste. Paul licks his lips and there, standing with her back to the view, waiting against the backdrop of two mighty oceans, is Claire.

She starts, throwing a guilty cigarette to the wind. For a second, smoke is torn in streaming ribbons from her nostrils. For a second, she is on fire.

Her hair is in a sensible ponytail, although the wind pulls and torments her fringe. She removes her dark glasses and steps forward from the wall. Then she stops. She comes no further. There she stands.

Paul reaches down beside him and finds Chantal. Mrs Mda hangs back. Stompie and his camera are nowhere to be seen.

They stand there, only the sky and sea moving.

Paul steps forward with Chantal. They go right up to Claire. She has not moved. She does not move.

Claire, Paul says.

Claire looks at Chantal. Chantal looks at her mother's feet, respectfully. Then her eyes move up her mother's legs to her face. They stand there, looking at each other.

This is your mother, Paul says suddenly. He repeats the words, louder this time. He seems to be shouting into the wind, this is your mother.

Claire says something. She bends down and says something to Chantal. Chantal looks again at the ground. Then she glances up at her father, and turns to see where Mrs Mda is standing. Chantal calls something to Mrs Mda. The old woman shuffles forward.

Claire looks up at Paul. So she speaks Zulu, Claire announces. It is Zulu?

Paul nods. It might as well be.

Mrs Mda puts a hand on Chantal's shoulder. She says she is happy, says Mrs Mda.

Chantal, Claire says, her voice very loud, calling her daughter though she stands right before her. Chantal!

Paul does not point out that she is Soneni. Chantal, the name they hatched in Midrand, has been tossed to the winds, and here before them stands Soneni. Chantal has died and is reborn. Here, here before them is the township reincarnation of their tiny child. What has she been through? What have they been through? What will they go through?

Stompie appears and starts taking photos.

Claire holds up one hand. No, she says. It is an awkward tableau. They are bunched before Claire. Paul and Chantal and Mrs Mda, with Stompie to one side, holding on to his camera guiltily. The wind blows and blows.

Paul wonders if Martinus Fumble John is close by, waiting around a corner. Or is he at home with all the boys?

Claire lowers her small bag. Then she stretches out her two hands to Chantal. Paul cannot hold back his tears as she enfolds Chantal, as she presses Chantal to her chest and hugs and hugs her. Claire is crying too. She is crooning to the wind. My baby, my baby, but very possibly it is the moaning of the wind and she makes no sound at all. Claire weeps over Chantal's head whilst Chantal leans against her, stiff like a little board. Finally, Claire lets her go. Chantal takes a step backwards, and reaches out to hold Mrs Mda's hand. Paul will not forget the expression on Claire's face.

Paul asks Chantal in *tsotsitaal*, are you okay?

Chantal nods. I am well, she replies. Her voice is clear in the wind. I am well. This madam has a pretty face, Chantal adds thoughtfully. She holds tightly on to Mrs Mda.

Can we take a photo? Paul checks with Claire.

Claire nods.

Oddly, formally, they stand beside Claire. Behind them, the sun burns out of an infinity of blue. They put Claire beside Chantal. Mrs Mda is in the photo too, as Chantal will not let her go. Paul stands beside Claire with Chantal nestled on the other side of her. He thinks of raising his arm, of putting it around Claire's shoulder, but he does not. He does not think that Claire would like that.

The photo is taken by an efficient Stompie. Like a tourist, he kneels to get a better angle, then he clambers on to the ledge opposite for a different perspective. Then he is finished.

Still they stand there.

We must talk, says Claire. She says the words louder than perhaps she intended, as the wind drops for a second.

Yes, Paul says.

Mrs Mda and Chantal move around to view the cliff side. Stompie turns his camera on the waves below.

Paul and Claire move back to one side.

She speaks no English? Claire says.

Very little. But we've made a start, Paul says.

Claire shakes her head, and raises a neat hand to her temple. She slides her sunglasses back to the top of her head.

You're looking well, says Paul. Your hair is longer now; you look well. He does not say that she looks older, more thread-bare, less perfect.

Yes, says Claire, unconvinced.

There is a long pause. Stompie wheels to snap a gull that hovers above them. With a flick of its wings, the gull veers away towards the oceans.

This won't work, says Claire. She fiddles with her new wedding ring, Fumble John's ring.

Claire, says Paul.

No, let me speak. You must let me speak. She glances at Stompie, who moves off in search of more gulls.

Paul waits. He feels that he has been waiting for most of his life. That he has been waiting for a decade. Now Chantal is here.

Tinus and I, Claire says, then she stops.

Paul glances to his left. Chantal and Mrs Mda have gone around the corner, but they can't be far.

He looks back at Claire.

Tinus and I, we have decided. Claire pauses. Then her voice tries to come clearly and steadily.

We are leaving, she says. At the end of the year. England. Tinus is selling the practice. He has a job lined up in Hampshire. We leave after Christmas.

Paul looks at her mouth, her neat red lips. They stop moving.

Claire smoothes back a strand of hair that flickers across her face. She pulls it behind her ear, but in a second it has flown free again.

That's a surprise, Paul says. Although Sunny did say.

We have been considering it for a long time, says Claire. Ever since Bertus was born. We didn't want what happened to Chantal . . .

The rest of her sentence, the rest of their lives, is stolen by the wind and sprayed over the fynbos and proteas that grow in such profusion.

But she's back, Paul says loudly. It was my fault, and she's back.

Claire looks at him. He knows the look. Knows it and remembers it well. The cool eyes are underlined by the firm set of her jaw. The look that declares, get on with it, do what you must, but I have made up my mind. But is that the past? Is there now a new note? Coming out of those clear eyes, is there a sense of pity?

She needs a mother, Paul says. Don't you realise, a mother.

After all she's been through. I was thinking about moving the agency, opening a branch in Cape Town so we could be closer to you.

Claire half turns to the sea. When she looks at Paul again, her face is pitifully hard.

We are going, she says.

Veraaier. The Afrikaans word escapes his lips. He does not know why he suddenly speaks it. The obscene 'f' sound rips open the deep rolling 'r' then unleashes the cry, the 'aaier'. Like a wave crashing ashore, the word breaks in the turbulent air. *Veraaier*. Traitor.

Claire turns back from the view, from the edge of the continent.

What? she says. What did you say?

Paul looks at her, amazed. The word is said.

You have the nerve to call me a traitor? Claire throws the question at his face. You have the nerve. She looks ready to summon a list of his traitorous past. His leaving. His driving off that night into Alexandra without saying a word. The bullet, yes the bullet, in the wall of Chantal's room. Did he think she never noticed, had never accounted for that missing bullet? The wasted money on the second hijacked car. His scant regard for his own life, never mind the fact that she was his wife drowning in a sea of despair. He had broken her iron and her heart. And then he had gone native and slummed it in Soweto. Simply tried to vanish off the face of the earth. Now he appears again after eleven years with Chantal, breaking into her life with their savage past. Who is the traitor? Who is the real traitor?

You cannot leave, Paul says. He plays his trump again. The single card. His only card. Chantal.

No, Claire says. She almost puts her hands up to her ears.

It is Paul's turn to invoke the oceans. To turn to the expanse of blue, so big and so remote.

Claire, he says, but you're her mother. Her mother. He brings his gaze from the horizon to her. As her father, and as her mother . . .

Claire looks at him. She glares at him as the wind whips her hair all over her face. Her ponytail waves madly.

Thanks, she says. Thanks for pointing that out. Then she says something more. Her voice is barely audible. Her lips move and her words stream forth in the wind.

Paul has to lean forward.

What? he says. What? What has Claire said? Has she said something about love, or is it hate?

Claire looks at him. Then she shouts up at him like a gull. Her voice detaches itself from the wind and slaps his face.

He does not understand the words. He is hit by the sound.

Then she stops, her fists bunched. Fuck, she says, and turns away to the sea and the sky. She mutters something again.

What did you say? Paul says. He grabs her shoulders and turns her to him. He may be hurting her. He holds her roughly. She stands firm in his grasp.

What did you say? he repeats.

Claire stares at him. Nothing, she says.

Don't, Paul says.

I wasn't going to . . . Claire's voice is almost hard and strange.

Although he grips her, he feels as though he is held up by her body, that she is the support on which he leans. That support tears away and he starts to fall. He shakes her, a drowning man, drowning in the surfeit of air that eddies and billows all about. Strange currents that ebb and flow, shrieking with the gulls and their guano, fresh from the sea yet stale and sour. The perfect moment of their reunion is passing. It is growing threadbare in the wind, becoming almost ragged with his impossible expectations.

No, she says.

Yes, he shouts. He actually lifts her. He has picked her up so that she is pressed against him, her face within kissing distance of his contorted lips.

She appraises him again with those cool eyes. She sees the madness, the desperation. She gauges his anguish, weighs up the risk. Paul moves a fraction closer to the retaining wall. Her feet barely trail on the ground. She speaks.

Okay, she says. Okay. But put me down.

His lips twist, soundless, but the hiss comes from her mouth.

I should hate you, she says. I should hate you. Like I hate this country. I do hate. I hate what it has done to Chantal, to me, to us . . . I hate . . . I love Chantal, her voice catches in her throat, but I almost hate her too . . .

Her voice shocks itself. Her face is angry and bitter, but is she angry and bitter with herself? She might hate him, she can hate a country, but how can you hate a child? Can she hate Chantal?

Look at me, she weeps. Look at what all this has done to me. And her bleeding, bitten fingers shake and curl into impotent fists.

He puts her down. He cannot breathe. He cannot face her if he cannot breathe. Maslow's hierarchy of needs, so beloved of advertisers. He needs to draw breath. All this godforsaken wind and he cannot breathe.

Claire is stunned by her own admission. But then she fidgets for another cigarette. She cannot open the little packet so she hurls it to the ground.

Still, Paul cannot breathe. He sinks to his knees to join the cigarettes. He has never had an asthma attack. This must be an asthma attack. He will black out any second. Maybe it is a heart attack. His chest, his lungs. The lameness that extends down his arms. The crushing weight of the blue sky as though it were a mile of heavenly water pressing down on him.

Claire does not move. She might have put an arm on his shoulder but he is sure that she does not move. It is horrible, hateful, she sobs. But it is true.

Then he gasps drily. Air retches into his throat. The African sky pumps wind into his lungs and he chokes and gasps.

He gets to his feet. Like an old man.

Claire regards him.

They stand there.

I am sorry, Claire says. And tears are streaming down her cheeks. Her bravado has worn thin; it could not last much longer. The carapace about her pain has cracked. Her hands shake in the wind. She seems to be shaken by the wind. I am sorry, Claire says. I am sorry.

He looks at her.

He is sorry too. He says so. Quietly. Far too quietly. I am sorry too.

He reaches out his hand. So there is no chance?

Claire shakes her head. How can she? Her place is with her new family. Her three little boys. She is weeping now. And they must leave. Does Paul not see? Her place now must be with her family. She has no choice. What this new life has cost her. What he and Chantal have cost her. Sleep, sanity, psychiatrists, now this. She is really sorry. She cannot. Not now. Not after all this time. They are leaving.

But there is one more thing. One more terrible thing.

Paul knows.

Does he know?

Claire reaches out one more time to touch him. Paul, she says.

Yes, he says.

I have to . . . Claire tries to speak. I have to ask you . . .

Paul nods. It is the moment he has been waiting for ever since that gun tapped against the glass and that car made off with their baby girl. It has been a lifetime in the making, in the recovering.

And the big wind buffets Claire's little words. Tears her sad words to shreds.

After all we have been through, after everything . . .

You are her mother, Paul speaks into the wind. She is part of you.

No, she is part of you, Claire says. After all you have done. Chantal is part of you, Paul. That will not change. But, Claire stops. She speaks again. I can leave you, but can I leave her?

Claire continues. Her voice sighs in the wind. She is sorry. Her heart is broken. It was broken long ago. She must break his heart too. Break his heart again.

Paul stands before her. A tall man, but so small. He cannot speak. He must not speak. He knew it. He knew that he was returning Chantal, Soneni, to her mother. What had been taken from them, is now returned. He takes her hand in his.

Claire smiles through her tears and for one last time squeezes his hand.

Her skin against his skin.

Paul grabs her other hand. They look at each other. Who is drowning? Who is drowning now? Who has been drowning all along?

And it is Claire's turn to gulp the silence. Her hands struggle but he is pulling her up from such depths. She is coming to him. Surely now she has finally let go of that weight, that heavy hatred? Surely Claire is coming to him? Claire the swimmer is finally free?

It is said. It is done. With streaming eyes and an ineffable sigh, Claire surfaces. Her face twists and she coughs. Again, it is the sharp bark of a deer. Chantal, her mother barks. Chantal.

Paul struggles for breath. Wait, he manages to say.

He turns and stumbles. Around a rocky corner and another, there is Mrs Mda and her faithful child. Paul wades through the thick-streaming air and clutches Chantal. Not a moment to lose. And before Claire can sink once more from sight, he returns again to his wife the daughter he lost.

He waves a hand as Claire tries to speak. He cannot trust her to speak.

Here, he says. Here she is. Your daughter. Our daughter.

Chantal is their daughter. Yes, they are forever bound by their daughter.

He shudders and seems to fall back as Claire clasps Chantal to her. They are together, mother and daughter. For this moment, now, they are all together.

But he knows that it cannot last.

Claire looks at him. She sees him. Still, he does not understand.

Yes, in the mess of their lives there has been so much taking, and breaking, and losing. There are goodbyes and more severings to come. More cords to be cut. And it seems strange, almost perverse, in the instant of Paul's greatest giving, his final yielding and returning, it is now finally she who will offer up Chantal. Yes, the pale smoke of Chantal has long since dispersed. Here is his Soneni. Here is his South Africa.

And even though her daughter's blonde head fits snugly beneath her chin, Claire can shake her own head and say clearly, No, Paul.

For a second, the sky stops and the air is true. Claire's meaning crowns, and Chantal is born again. Soneni. His daughter. And Paul finally understands as that other cord is cut and she is his.

I shall wait in the car, he manages to shout as an almighty gust of wind threatens to set his bursting heart free. Claire and Soneni, in each other's arms, look up and reach out to him.

He can breathe now. He can continue to breathe for the rest of his life.

He can breathe through the everlasting regret and hope of that day. He can recall with the sharpest clarity the exact sensation of the gusting wind and the precise salty-sour taste of the air that refilled his lungs and the touch of their hands and Claire's eyes.

He can go on to remember how he turned and, with Mrs Mda and Stompie, went to wait in the car. And so Paul's little party made its way down the slope without Soneni or Claire.

He can see how they might have appeared. A husband and a

wife, with their daughter and her black friend, maybe the son of their ancient maid, a certain Mrs Mda. And then Claire held back with her daughter, riding the wind and the big horizon, with her darling daughter and with a heart filled with such hatred and such love.

And Paul left them to go and sit, once again, in a car. And his lungs filled with air and his heart beat with terrible joy. Behind him, on the top of the slope, with her mother, was the daughter he would never have to abandon.

He can think back for ever afterwards, think about himself standing halfway down the slope, held up momentarily as he watched his little tribe walking back towards the African continent, which stretched before them. Stompie bearing his camera bag whilst Mrs Mda hobbled along behind him. In his mind's eye, he turned to see Claire standing with head erect, fiercely clutching Soneni and looking just like her daughter. She did not wave, but neither did she light another cigarette nor turn away to look out to sea, towards a future that was overseas. No, mother and child just stood there.

And in his memory, he stood there too. He was held up in the wind.

And whilst he stood there, having turned away, the rest of Africa lay before him, from Cape Point all the way to Cairo.

There he was, on this tip of the continent: was it the end or the beginning? Was it time yet, was it here?

And as he stood there, he can always recall how Soneni would come skipping with her mother, come skipping into a vast land that was deep and dusty and hot. The wind called to them with a thousand voices. The earth throbbed under the harsh sky. He offered them up to a continent whose capacity to surprise and shock is matched only by its impossible ability to engender both hope and despair.

And as he leant forward to yield to the slope, to sail with the wind at his back, still he was held up by the sheer weight, the impossible thought of the entire continent. He could not move.

Here was no fresh green breast of a new-found land. Here was little succour to be found and less romance. No, here was an ancient giant, rugged and mighty. Mother Africa with her pounding heart, big and prehistoric and beautiful and terrible.

And so it must have seemed to the nomadic tribesmen and to the original farmers beneath the brilliant heavens sprayed with gouts of the Milky Way and blistered by stars. And so it must have seemed to the first Dutch sailors borne up by the wind into the arms of that incredible bay. Before them, the flat-topped mountain decked with billowing clouds, and beyond that the vast mass of Africa.

And yes, they sailed on, yielding to the wild currents and to the savage winds, pushed and pulled closer and closer towards an unfathomable future, simultaneously enchanted and repelled, blessed and cursed.

And so we beat on, living drums with our tightly drawn skin of many, many hues. And we are beaten on, and beaten up, and beaten down. But also, thank those starry heavens, we hold on. We hold on too, and sometimes we are lifted, raised, held up.

Acknowledgements

I am very grateful to:

Lesley, Mom, Dad, Paul and Glenda Radmann, Andrew Murray, Belinda Thompson and Tess St Clair-Ford for their careful reading of early drafts – and to Betty-Mom for her reading and meticulous annotations.

Nanna, who would always 'read me', and my school teachers: Mrs van Rensburg, Jill Wilson, Bryan Lotter and Sandra Gouws.

Catherine Thompson, Chris Green, David Kirkham, David Cooper, Alison Keay and my fellow OCR and Pre-U examiners for whom literary analysis and discussion is a way of life. And Peter Doughty, the nonpareil, whose profound appraisal of the final pages of *The Great Gatsby* cut me to the quick.

My lively students at Benoni High School, St John's College Johannesburg, Supedi, St Maur's School and Lord Wandsworth College from whom I have learnt and continue to learn so much.

R.W. Johnson for his magisterial *South Africa's Brave New World*.

Annabel Merullo and Tim Binding at PFD for their generous and rigorous discussion of the first draft.

The very efficient and friendly Emily Griffin at Headline, and Jane Selley, copy-editor extraordinaire, whose complete grasp of Polyfilla, punctuation and Afrikaans spelling put the teacher in me to shame.

Martin Fletcher, my astute editor at Headline, for his faith in *Held Up*, penetrating insights and brilliantly guiding, often restraining, hand.

Andrew Murray, sui generis and ultimately generous, for always making me think more deeply – and laugh more loudly.

Lesley, my wife, for adjusting her sleep patterns and for her constant support and love.

My wonderful agent, 'Ah, Juliet' Mushens, for her total enthusiasm, love of diving into the slush pile, resolute belief and energetic championing. For her insistence that there was more to the character Claire than initially met my eye. And for every email swiftly sent that gave me hope. It was Juliet who first held up *Held Up*. The book is not just Martin's and mine, it is yours.